THE
DEEPEST
LAKE

THE
DEEPEST
LAKE

ANDROMEDA
ROMANO-LAX

Published by
Soho Press, Inc.
227 W 17th Street
New York, NY 10011

Library of Congress Cataloging-in-Publication Data

Names: Romano-Lax, Andromeda, author.
Title: The deepest lake / Andromeda Romano-Lax.
Description: New York, NY : Soho Crime, 2024.
Identifiers: LCCN 2023038300

ISBN 978-1-64129-560-4
eISBN 978-1-64129-561-1

Subjects: LCGFT: Thrillers (Fiction) | Novels.
Classification: LCC PS3618.O59 D44 2024
DDC 813/.6--dc23/eng/20230829
LC record available at https://lccn.loc.gov/2023038300

Interior design by Janine Agro

Printed in the United States of America

10 9 8 7 6 5 4 3 2 1

For all the Scarletts

You own everything that happened to you. Tell your stories. If people wanted you to write warmly about them, they should have behaved better. —ANNE LAMOTT

THE
DEEPEST
LAKE

PROLOGUE

THAT NIGHT

I should be terrified stepping into the rowboat, but for the first adrenaline-spiked moment, I'm not. Not when I'm told to hurry up, not when my first questions go unanswered. Not when I lift a leg over the middle seat and feel the wooden boat list to one side until I drop into a squat, just in time to preserve my balance.

For a moment my lifelong fear of water is replaced with something more primal. I'm following orders both external and internal—the barking voice behind me, the quieter voice within.

The volcano ahead is a gray silhouette against a navy sky. The lake is black. *Don't think about it. Don't look down.* But every glimmer and splash draws my attention. How many mimosas did we finish off, followed by how many shots, over how many hours?

As the boat glides away from the dock, I try not to think about how fathomless the lake is: an ancient dark hole in a bowl of mountains. I don't want to be here. That's a selfish thought, and I shouldn't be thinking it, but I can't help it.

All week I've managed to keep a safe distance. No daytime swimming. No nighttime skinny dipping. As few water taxis as possible, and then only reluctantly, my stomach flipping when the spray dampened my face.

But now I've violated my own rule. And it's not because of a dare. It's not so that someday I'll have a good story to tell, or to write. It's only because everything happened so fast. There wasn't time to make excuses or find others to help. No time, even, to get a life jacket or flashlights. There was only enough time to jump in the boat and hope we weren't already too late.

Whether someone lives or dies is up to us. That's what I believe for the first ten minutes as we move through the water, searching and silent. This task should allow us to patch up our differences, finally. Bring us together. That's what I try to believe, still, as our trajectory incrementally shifts, until we are heading out into the very center of the lake.

"You're taking us out too far," I say.

No reply.

I'm shivering. Alarm bells are beginning to ring in my brain. But I have to face the truth.

There is no shared goal.

There is no "we."

Herringbone clouds slip across the pale face of the moon. One more angry dig of the oars and then we are stopped in a pupil-black slick of still water.

"I want to go back," I say, but it's too late.

PART
I

1

ROSE

————————————

————

Rose didn't count on this. The view itself has stolen her breath. Before she thought, *a lake is a lake is a lake.* But she was wrong. This is where it happened, and this is why she had to see it firsthand: because you can't count on others to look past the pretty surfaces of things.

"Gorgeous!" says one of the other women, exiting the shuttle bus just behind her. "Don't you think?"

Rose doesn't answer. Her hand has crept to her chest, massaging the tense spot below her collarbone where the ache sits, a hard knot of grief and regret. You can dislike a place even without seeing it. But you can truly despise it only when it's in front of you, glittering quietly, making a mockery of what you know and even more, what you don't.

One by one, they all exit the small bus and gather at the bottom of the sloping, sunbaked concrete ramp, alongside a half-rotted wooden dock, united in their confusion about the geography, not sure what will happen next. They've been told they're taking a water taxi to their cabins.

"But why couldn't the bus have taken us there?" someone asks.

"We must be staying on an island," another woman guesses.

"Not an island," explains the twenty-something guide, Ana Sofía, gesturing for all twelve women to come closer. "Villages ring the lake. San Felipe is only a few miles from here, but the road doesn't go all the way around. It's easier to hop from village to village by boat or sometimes by tuk-tuk. Anyway, it's more magical, yes?"

That will be the answer for every inconvenience, Rose thinks. Bad roads, limited internet service and three-wheeled minitaxis are magical. Boat trips and seasickness are magical. Rustic cabins that aren't conveniently located by the famous writer's house: more magic. And to figure it all out they will have to stick together, this small group of women, and that, too, will create its own kind of spell. Already, the outside world has begun to drop away, the bonding has started, though Rose remains at the fringes, willing the others to forget about her so she can orient herself to this place and this moment, in her own way.

Near the waterline, an old man is rinsing silver fish the size and shape of salad plates, dragging each one back and forth in the murky water, then dropping them into a white utility bucket. The fishy smell wafts toward Rose. She pulls the brim of her straw sun hat lower, waiting for her stomach to settle from that last hour of hairpin curves.

Across from the boat launch rise two volcanoes, the larger one wreathed in clouds. In front of Rose, Lake Atitlán, the deepest lake in Central America, is calm at this hour. Blue-black silk.

Rose imagines the feeling of that silk, stuffed down her throat. She envisions trying to pull it out, hand over hand, like one of those magicians' scarves. She feels herself clawing for air, legs thrashing in the black water as the lake's glittering surface recedes.

The moon was two days past full when her daughter disappeared.

The lake was perfectly calm.

The weather was mild.

It doesn't matter anymore, Rose's ex-husband Matt said after the official six-week-long search ended, when Rose was still reading about cases like their daughter's—horrible stories of backpackers who wandered off the beaten track and were never seen again. Few of the experts they'd hired wanted to say it, but she and Matt could read between the lines. No one seemed to think Jules was still alive. No expert who understood the specifics of her "last seen" location, in deep water far from shore, thought her body would be found.

A week after their last text message from Jules, it had been decided that Rose would stay back in Illinois. Making the most of his military background and comfort dealing with consuls and police, Matt flew to Guatemala and hired private helicopters for an overland search. With the cooperation of local authorities, he formed a separate team to drag Lake Atitlán the old-fashioned way, using lines and hooks. The first odd thing they pulled up, aside from beer bottles and soda cans, was a pair of white gloves. Rose remembers puzzling over the photo, snapped and texted by Matt moments before the police bagged the gloves as evidence. They weren't gardening gloves, and they weren't winter gloves, and they weren't for golf or cycling, much as Matt wanted them to be, because sport gloves were something Jules might have owned.

The question paled in significance when Rose's phone dinged an hour later. A few hundred feet down the lakeshore, a more important item was found: Jules's shirt, a pin-striped button-down Roxy cover-up. In response to Matt's question,

Rose texted back with shaking hands: *Yes. I'm sure.* She was in the bathroom throwing up when he replied with his typical reticence. *I thought so too.*

That same day, a Canadian retiree made his way to the police substation in San Felipe and filled out the report that Rose would reread every day for a month. The man, one of many North Americans who owned second homes on the shore of Lake Atitlán, had returned to his house one late afternoon in time to see a girl matching Jules's description swimming dangerously far offshore. He saw her once, treading water, backlit by the sun, which was just minutes away from dipping below the far mountains. He went inside for several minutes, to find a pair of binoculars. When he came back out, there was no girl. He forgot about it until he heard the helicopters and saw search boats amassing, a full week later.

While the boats continued to prowl every inch of Atitlán's lakeshore, Rose read more about drowning than her therapist would have advised. She learned that gases caused by decomposition force corpses to balloon, allowing them to rise to the surface within days. But if a body sinks to a place that is deep and cold enough, time stops. The body barely decays. The corpse may never surface at all.

Still, the shirt, found not far from the location reported by the Canadian, had given them hope. While Rose remained behind in Evanston, monitoring social media accounts and reading emails and DMs from anyone who might have interacted with Jules during her trip, Matt ramped up the lake-based search. His team turned to scuba and sonar imaging from a motorboat steered by a couple who'd made an art of finding bodies in lakes and reservoirs all across North America. But never deeper than about 170 meters.

Lake Atitlán is 340 meters—deeper than Lake Michigan,

back home. A lake that deep can swallow any number of secrets.

Hills searched, lake dragged, town walked end to end by Matt and a private detective, that left one stone unturned, in Rose's view. Only the local police succeeded in talking to Eva Marshall. Even though Jules claimed to have started working a job for the famous author and writing teacher just before Jules's disappearance, Eva refused to schedule a visit or even a phone call with Rose or Matt. The only email to which Eva bothered to reply, and then only briefly, referred them back to the official police statement she'd already given. Then: nothing. Rose's next four emails to Eva went unanswered. The message was clear: stop emailing. But what mother would?

Finally, an admin assistant named Trish replied, informing Rose that Eva was busy running her memoir workshops and wouldn't be replying personally.

The workshops.

Before she'd even floated the idea to Matt, Rose was already signed up, using the maiden name she hadn't used in twenty-five years, McKenna, on the application form for the upcoming Lake Atitlán session. She already knew, from googling herself first, that a search of her common name turned up hundreds of women's images—none of them hers—plus several rose varieties. Someone idly searching wouldn't make a connection with Jules.

Rose has no ambitions whatsoever as a memoirist, not even the tiniest desire to be published. She's not a good storyteller and she's an even worse liar. But you do what you must after you've already tried everything else.

Rose has stopped massaging the tight spot below her collarbone. She lets her hand rest there, feeling her heart's sped-up staccato, trying to will herself into a state of serenity. The closest she can achieve is a tense, purposeful dread.

Near the bottom of the concrete ramp, a cute little girl with ink-black hair approaches the women travelers and tries to sell them woven bracelets by tying them directly to their wrists, accepting payment after the fact. Even the guide gives in and buys one, allowing the precious little fingers to secure the knot. The little girl's dark eyes flit toward Rose, but she seems to know better than to approach.

At the end of the ramp, Ana Sofía hands out bottles of water, warning the group about the mile-high altitude and the potential for dehydration. When the guide holds a bottle high in the air, shaking it in Rose's direction, Rose nods without hurrying over. She needs one more moment to take it all in.

Out on the lake now, a small white dot motors toward the women and their pile of luggage, churning the silky waters into froth. Ana Sofía calls Rose and a few other stragglers closer, but before Rose can comply, her seatmate from the bus—a British woman named Pippa—approaches. She puts an arm around Rose's shoulder. The women are so touchy, as if they're all friends, already.

"You've been quiet. Savoring every moment, are we?"

"Oh—yes."

"Smart girl. Treat every day as if it could be your last."

"I do," Rose says.

Stepping off the San Felipe docks, the women move slowly despite Ana Sofía's attempt to rouse them with cheer. "Someone else will get the bags. You're almost there, I promise. We'll gather in the reception area first. It's just up this little path and then into a garden."

Past a stony beach is a low wall around some sort of compound, with several trees and lots of vines and big-leafed tropical plants.

A woman behind Rose says, "I hope they hand out those fragrant little washcloths. I've been sweating all day."

When Rose turns, Isobel smiles at her. She's a heavyset woman with olive skin, big dimples and jaw-length black hair with a purplish sheen. At the first group dinner in Antigua, Isobel helped steer the group in their drink selections and told everyone about the memoir she's writing, chronicling her family's fourth-generation Mexican-German-American vineyard in Sonoma. Rose enjoyed the ten-page sample she read on the plane, one of a half dozen manuscripts forwarded to them for advance study.

"Whoa, here they come," Isobel says, as their group is encircled by a group of pre-adolescent boys. They reach for the legs of Rose's white capri pants, calling out *Zoos, Zoos* and *Cassava!*

Rose doesn't understand why they associate her boat's arrival with zoo animals. And she doesn't know whether cassava is grown in Guatemala.

"Hola," she says to them. "Hola, hola," keeping a firm grip on her purse and her laptop bag.

The biggest and boldest of the boys, eyes half-hidden under messy black bangs, jabs a finger at her tote bag. "Zoos?"

"Lo siento," Rose says. *I'm sorry.*

"Cassava? Zoos?"

Rose stops and looks at him squarely. "Cómo te llamas?"

"Diego," he says, hand out, palm up.

She reaches into the side pocket of her laptop bag for a bright orange pencil with a sports car eraser, one of a dozen she brought for moments like these. He takes it without any change of expression, slides it into his back jeans pocket, then jabs at the tote bag again. "Zoos?"

Ana Sofía herds the group of visiting women through the garrulous children, up the beach and through a gate. "He thinks you have shoes. Eva collects and distributes hundreds of pairs. If you *did* bring clothing donations, just remember to bring them tonight, when we gather for the party at Casa Eva."

Casa Eva. Cass-eva. Cassava.

The clothing donation notes were in the thirty pages of instructions all the participants received, a torrent of emails that arrived within three hours of Rose submitting her short writing sample, the lame partial essay about several years of estrangement from her sister, which—god only knew why—evidently passed muster. The emails never came directly from Eva, though they always contained her best wishes and firmly worded advice.

Bring sufficient quetzales in small denominations, for tips.

Bring US dollars as well, for Guatemala City and Antigua but not for San Felipe.

Don't wear skimpy clothes.

Don't wear jeans (they don't dry quickly enough).

Consider leaving your makeup at home; we are an all-women group; try something new and go natural!

This is a big adventure but it will be wonderful and you're going to have a life-changing experience and most important, you're all going to be okay. The countdown is almost over!

Rose remembers Jules's first text about the new job. *I just got the most amazing opportunity with the most amazing person.*

With a peculiar sense of apprehension, Rose sees it more clearly now. This is what Jules was doing, holding the hands of some dozen or more skittish visitors. First by email, later in person.

Tell me! What are you doing?

Everything. You didn't ask who the person is!

What's everything?

I'm a troubleshooter.

Meaning?

A Girl Friday. But every day. Whatever is needed I do.
You really don't get days off?
It's only twelve days. Writing workshop plus four days
before and a couple after. Mom! You still haven't asked!
Who is it?
Eva Marshall. The author!
Getting paid?
Jules evaded the question. *It's a learning opportunity.*
Does that mean only tips?
Most of the women who come are loaded. I'll take you to
dinner in a few weeks when I'm back. Promise.

A few more weeks. Before coming to Lake Atitlán and somehow meeting Eva, Jules had been talking about coming home any day. She'd already been in Guatemala over a month; Panama, Nicaragua and Costa Rica, for six weeks before that. She'd gotten her travel fix, she told Rose and Matt in a rare video call.

Rose and Jules didn't argue often, but they did argue about Jules's postcollege plans. Last year, she'd been rejected by two creative writing programs, a huge blow to her dream of becoming an author. Rose thought she should keep trying and get a Master's, in hopes of teaching later. Jules said there were no teaching jobs anyway. Taking on so much debt was risky. Plus, a degree didn't make you a writer. But then, Rose had tried asking Jules without success, what did?

Jules completed several new grad school applications just before leaving for Guatemala. She seemed to be bouncing back from rejection. But that was before the week at Eva's. Then something changed.

Fewer texts, no photos and a different tone. She seemed to be questioning everything, feeling both worthless and hopeless. *How can I be a writer? I've never had any interesting experiences. I've never done anything. I have nothing to say.*

A few minutes later: *I'm pathetic.*

Two texts, buried amidst hundreds of others, that Rose noticed only later, in those frantic first days after Jules was last seen.

2

ROSE

E ven as they make their way into the simple hotel compound, Rose can still feel the lake behind her, always closer
than she'd like. She tries to put it out of her mind, focusing
for the moment on sussing out which of these women would
have posed a challenge for a young, inexperienced woman
like Jules, working as a "Girl Friday" or personal assistant.

There are two women in their early twenties and one over
seventy. Nearly everyone else is Rose's age: forties and fifties.
Lots of linen and cotton, crisp white blouses, chunky statement
necklaces, flashy silver earrings, a few suspiciously smooth
foreheads, many large-brimmed sun hats. Well-dressed. Mostly
fit. With a few exceptions, almost entirely white.

Rose tries to figure out who is crazy rich. Who is merely
comfortable. Who has spent her last cent hoping to untangle a
knotted-up storyline or get an agent referral, something Jules
often talked about, along with terms that meant little to Rose,
like "slush pile" and "blurbs."

At the open-air reception area, they gather amidst their
mounds of luggage. Three hotel employees bring out pitchers
of something red that looks like sangria but turns out to be
hibiscus tea.

"Is that alcohol?"

"Unfortunately not."

"I'll pass."

On the boat, they learned that their guide, Ana Sofía, is a recent college graduate from Mexico City—not Guatemala, but at least her Spanish is perfect. Now she hops from cluster to cluster, stepping over bags, approaching each new participant with a strained smile.

Rose steps closer and with the most sympathetic voice she can muster, says, "I hope they're at least paying you well for this?"

Ana Sofía says only, "Not exactly."

So she, too, is probably working for tips.

"Are you a writer?" Rose asks.

"No." Ana Sofía doesn't bother to look up, too busy focusing on the damp sheet of paper in her hands. Her smooth black ballerina bun has begun to escape its pins. Rose feels bad for distracting this young woman who is busy doing the sort of thing her daughter would have done—a thought that makes Rose both uncomfortable and determined to keep talking to her.

"Have you been doing this job long?"

"Two weeks. Eva only has full staff when the workshop is running," Ana Sofía says, distracted, moving her finger down a list of names. "This is all wrong. Pippa can't do the stairs, so we'll have to switch her with someone. Diane, you wanted a private room, but the bathroom is broken, so I think you would be happier in a double."

Other women huddle closer to hear what Ana Sofía has to say. One of them, an older woman with gray-blond hair done up in an elegant twist, says, "Will you be staying at Casa Eva with us, honey?"

"No," Ana Sofía says, focused on her sheet. "I am the town *enlace*. How do you say? Contact."

"Liaison, yes," the old woman purrs. "But whenever I've come, Eva has a nice girl helping—"

Rose asks, "Were you here for the last session?"

"No." The woman frowns, shaking off Rose's interruption. "Ana, I need to ask someone about my massage, and last year, they gave me a special chair in the classroom. I can't sit on the hard ones."

Ana Sofía shakes her head. "I don't know. You'll have to ask Eva, later, or maybe Barbara."

Rose butts in again, stepping closer to Ana Sofía. "If you're in town, do you stay in the cabins with us?"

The assistant looks up, visibly annoyed. "I have a friend who lives here. I stay with her. Now please. I have to solve this."

Rose backs away, making a mental note. A Girl Friday works in town. Other helpers work at the house. Also: Ana Sofía is not a memoirist wannabe, which makes her situation slightly different from Jules's.

They've always known where Jules stayed during her first nights in San Felipe: a local hostel. But then there was a week-long gap until she was last seen, swimming away from shore. If she was working for Eva in town, Jules must have transferred to another small hotel or some informal town lodging. Rose has a list of all the places their bilingual investigator checked. He could have missed something.

Rose hopes the frustration isn't written on her face. She can't even nail down the simplest things, like where her daughter slept once she started working for Eva, but Matt and the PI didn't do any better. She doesn't know if she is asking too many questions, but at least the other needy women give her some cover.

Rose notices that Isobel has moved to the shady back of the garden, where she's chatting with a tall, fine-boned woman with spiky platinum hair. The woman's linen pants and matching vest are somehow unwrinkled. Her red lipstick is still fresh.

Rose would prefer to find a corner where she can take out her e-reader and finish the Eva Marshall memoir she started reading on the plane, a book with such a heart-wrenching premise that she didn't hear her zone being called for boarding at her second gate, in Houston. But meeting her fellow workshop participants is research, too. She rouses herself to appear more social.

"This is Lindsay," Isobel says as Rose approaches. "She arrived too late for the Antigua dinner." Isobel introduces them with eyebrows raised, as if she expects Rose to attach a story to the name, but she can't just yet.

Lindsay is striking: half-corporate, half-rebel, if it's really possible to be both. An Emma Thompson lookalike. She has good hair. Isobel, with her black-purple sheen, has *fun* hair. Rose's shoulder-length brown lob is okay, at best.

"Sorry I missed the dinner. I've still got jet lag," Lindsay says.

Isobel winks. "I thought you said it was a hangover."

"That's how long you can keep a secret? Two minutes?"

Isobel laughs and glances back to Rose again. "Now, *Lindsay* on the other hand . . ."

Rose is trying to decode the comment. Then she gets it. Lindsay's essay was the one about bluffing and conning people. It was probably the best among the half dozen manuscripts forwarded to them.

"You wrote the piece about being a card sharp," Rose says. "Or is it card shark?"

"Depends on whether you're in England or America. But cards aren't my specialty. It was just an easier thing to write about in a fluffy, short essay."

Rose doesn't think it was so fluffy. In a few pages, Lindsay told the story of a mistake she'd made, having dinner and sleeping with an unfamiliar man she needed to beat in a poker tournament the next day. She managed to keep up her false pretense of being a poker novice, but learning about his pending divorce and financial problems added friction to the con. That was the word Lindsay used. Not guilt. Just *friction*.

"I wanted to read more. You're a good writer," Rose says. "Is that the wrong thing to say?"

She has no idea how to talk about the pages people submitted. Back home, she doesn't even belong to a book club.

"I don't think anyone minds being called a good writer," Lindsay says, pushing her sunglasses on top of her head. Long lashes, plenty of sparkly olive-hued eyeshadow: she isn't concerned about Eva's no-makeup suggestion.

Rose wonders if they will have to worry about Lindsay. Surely, you can't trust someone who steals for a living.

"Actually," Rose adds, "I was surprised by how little Eva asked us to hand in. How could she judge if people were, you know . . . serious about writing?"

Isobel leans closer to them, whispering. "Fewer than half the women turned in manuscripts. Ana Sofía told me. Several women just sent emails about what they wanted to write, or nothing at all."

Now Rose understands. It isn't actually a selective workshop, like the website claimed. Maybe it's more like summer camp.

"Anyway," Rose says to Lindsay, "it's hard to tell any story in two thousand words. But both of yours grabbed me from the first paragraph."

"Thank you," Lindsay says.

Isobel smiles. "You're not going to tell us whether our submissions were any good."

"No." Lindsay's face is bright, relaxed. Her posture is impeccable.

Isobel says, "You don't want to lie to us, do you?"

"No, I don't."

"But you're sort of a professional liar."

"Yes. But I'm on vacation."

Rose finds herself staring at them both, wishing she could borrow a touch of Lindsay's self-assurance, a little of Isobel's color and shine. They must find her plain. Jules once criticized her mother for dressing like a kitchen cabinet. *Mom, do you even own a sweater that isn't white, gray, black or brown?* She told herself to buy some more colorful shirts. To schedule a shopping trip with Jules.

And then, Rose ran out of time. Clients wanted their remodels finished well before Memorial Day. Weeks flew by. Jules left on her trip. Too late.

"Is the altitude bothering you?" Isobel asks, gesturing to a rusty garden bench at the back of the shady garden. "Do you need to sit? Let me get you something to drink."

Rose doesn't want to sit. She's breathing heavily, almost sighing on the exhales, as if she can't get enough oxygen. From the corner of her eye, she sees a young woman leaning against the pile of luggage in the center of the open-air reception patio. Dark blond hair, an eyebrow ring and admirably muscular quads, visible beneath a sporty, wraparound skirt. Rose thinks: *Jules.*

The hallucination lasts no more than a second. She's had these flashes countless times—in Chicago, at the airport in Houston, now here. She knows there are parents of missing children who imagine their children will show up one day, but that isn't Rose's issue. She believes Jules died in the lake. She doesn't think her daughter is wandering the world as an amnesiac or ran off to join a cult or was ambushed by aliens or drug traffickers—the sorts of "helpful" suggestions that popped up on social media and in the *Chicago Tribune* comments section, waning within mere days, as public attention migrated to fresher tragedies.

Maybe it was the nightmares that convinced Rose, because they felt like a vivid glimpse into Jules's final moments. They started the day Matt called home from San Felipe with the authorities' conclusion of Jules's likely fate. Ever since, Rose has woken up at least once each night, gasping. The nightmares are telling her: Jules is gone. The universe has given her a piece of the truth—just not all of it. So, when will the sightings and the nightmares stop?

It will stop when you properly grieve.

Matt told her that. As did her sister, via long distance phone call.

Jules wasn't a runaway, she was a young woman at the end of a pleasant trip, ready to come home. Someone saw her in the lake. The last time she texted, she was drinking and maybe dabbling beyond that. She wasn't a good swimmer. What more is there to know?

A lot, Rose thought. Everything important. Why and how. Her daughter's last hours. Why she was swimming when she hated to swim. Whether she was depressed and suffering, or just unlucky.

Her therapist came closest to understanding, "You need a narrative. That's how humans are. We are story-making creatures—some of us more than others. Your husband needs facts—maybe just one fact. That Jules drowned. You need a story."

Yes, she does. But Rose is afraid of stories, too.

There's something about being here in person, with the lake's smell of fish and boat gasoline still in her nostrils and the sound of Spanish in her ears, that makes her feel uncomfortably far from home—and dangerously close to admitting Matt was right to question her trip. Rose might be doing something worse than wasting time. She might have come all the way to Guatemala only to prove she didn't know her daughter as well as she thought, meaning she was a bad mother: unobservant, clueless, insufficiently caring. That's an even more terrifying prospect than discovering nothing.

Isobel comes back with a plastic cup of agua de jamaica for Rose.

"Ana Sofía is still trying to sort out the room assignments," Isobel says. "And who are all these women? I thought we had ten or twelve people. But there's like twenty women waiting for their room keys."

"Eva's alumni groupies," Lindsay answers, nodding toward another group of women, talking and laughing in their own circle. "Most of them don't mix with us, except at tonight's opening party and on the field trip, midweek. Some of them return to Casa Eva every chance they get. At breakfast in Antigua, I talked to one woman who has been coming for seven years."

Regulars.

"Did you catch her name?" Rose asks.

"No, but she has a memoir that's almost finished. That's why she keeps coming back."

"Do you remember what it was about?"

"Incest? Death of a spouse? Recovery from a rare disease? Maybe all three. That would be the winning ticket."

"You're terrible," Isobel says to Lindsay.

"Do you think she comes for every session?" Rose asks.

"I doubt it." Lindsay cocks her head. "I think there's some soft rule against coming twice in a row—or is it three times in a row? I guess there have to be *some* limits on regulars or they'd outnumber the new writers. Why?"

Rose pivots. "I've just always been curious how much work it takes to finish a memoir."

"More than a writer can ever bear to think at first," Isobel says. "It's like childbirth. If you knew what it was really like, you might just skip it. Or so I've heard! Am I the only childless-by-choice woman here?" Lindsay lifts a pointer finger. Rose looks down at her leg and gives it a slap, then proceeds to scratch furiously. No one seems to notice she's evaded the question.

Isobel nudges a duffel with her toe. "By the way, I've got good wine in there."

"Your vineyard's?" Rose asks.

"No, I loaded up in Guatemala City. They tell you not to stop anywhere in zone thirteen but I knew pickings would be slim in San Felipe. The minute we get into those cabins, I'm opening a bottle—and please, please join me."

Rose ventures her next question carefully, not wanting to alert anyone that she'd dare criticize any aspect of the workshop. "Can you believe we haven't met Eva yet? I thought she would come to Antigua, or at least meet our boat."

"I'm not surprised," Lindsay says. "She's smart enough to stay out of the fray until we're all settled and somewhat happy. Timing matters. And territory. We go to her, she doesn't come to us."

Rose reconsiders her description of Lindsay. *Emma Thompson with a touch of David Bowie.* It's the white pants and vest, the sharp cheekbones and the prominent collarbones and the stance, but it's more than that. A certain *fuck-y'all* look, Jules would have called it.

"Wow," said Isobel. "Here's our human behavior expert."

"You'll see at tonight's party. I predict a grand entrance."

Rose asks delicately, "You think Eva Marshall's being phony in some way?"

"Not at all," Lindsay says. "She's a performer. I wouldn't have paid to meet her if she wasn't. We all come wanting the magic, and she'll help us feel it. You can't have an experience like this without a strong leader."

"Amen," Isobel says. "I've been working on my manuscript forever. If I learn just one new thing that helps me finish it, this week will be worth it."

Lindsay looks at her watch. She steps away and returns a moment later, shaking a key on a long wooden dowel. "C'mon, roomies."

"We're in the same cabin?" Isobel squeals.

"We are now."

Isobel grabs her duffel. "You're the best. Come on, Rose."

"Me, too?"

She's lucked into one of the cool crowds without knowing how it happened, but she's grateful.

Mom, when's the last time you met any women your age?

What are you talking about? You make it sound like dating.

Not dating, just friends.

I've got work friends.

You're self-employed.

I have an office manager. Colleagues and clients.

Fun ones? People you can really talk to?

I've got you, Jules. I've always got you.

3

ROSE

_____

_____

____

The cabin is rustic and dark, the only visible decorations a few handwoven striped blankets on the main floor's twin beds. A simple round table and four chairs occupy the center of the room. A ladder leads to a low-ceilinged second floor and two more twin beds.

Isobel asks, "You're sure you don't mind taking the loft? You don't have a lake view."

"I don't want a view," Rose says a little too sharply, thinking again of the water they motor-boated across—how shaky she feels just thinking about its lightless depths. "Thanks, really. It's quiet up there. I'll sleep better."

After hauling her bags up the ladder, Rose stands in the loft, glad the window is covered by a sheer curtain. Taking her cue from Lindsay, who already started unpacking downstairs, Rose opens her suitcase.

From upstairs, she hears the cabin's front door opening. Two new women enter, chatting excitedly. Lindsay and Isobel claimed they wanted rest, but it sounds like cabin nap time won't be happening anytime soon.

Rose pulls out a long skirt, draping it over a wood chair next to the bed. The T-shirts she considers putting into a small dresser, but when she pulls open the drawer, she smells something off—a bit mousey.

Rose thinks about Matt and Ulyana staying in a budget cabin like this. No way. Matt's a big-name-brand-resort kind of guy, always intent on using his travel points. When Rose started planning this trip, Matt suggested she put it off and wait for the one-year anniversary, when they could all go together. He thought he was being nice, willing to plan a trip with his ex-wife. He didn't realize he was undermining Rose, proving how little he understood about her need to go now—and not only to mourn.

Whenever they disagreed about whether a search should continue, Matt pointed to the good work that the local police had done and would keep doing, supposedly.

It's not like they closed the investigation.

When the first active phase of searching had wrapped up, Matt returned to Illinois to tie up some work details. He intended to return to Guatemala within the week, to meet again with police and press for ideas about a phase two. But then Police Chief Molina called, telling him there was no need. His men had made two critical discoveries.

First, they'd arrested a local small-time drug dealer who confessed to supplying a girl Jules's age and general description with a locally popular party drug. The police, desperate for a win, sent "Paco" to the capital, where they promised Matt he would rot in jail.

Second, they'd caught a German backpacker shoplifting in a larger village across the lake from San Felipe. Inside his bag was a paperback belonging to Jules, with her name and endless personal annotations. Luka claimed he'd gone for a dawn volcano hike with Jules and a van load of fellow travelers, but barely knew her beyond that. She'd given him the book to lighten her own load.

The group volcano hike checked out. The date of the hike matched up with the date the party drug was sold to a girl who looked like Jules. The "last-known sighting" of Jules, swimming on the lake, occurred later that afternoon, just around sunset. *Check, check, check.*

In response to which, Rose, even now, standing near the cabin loft window, catching the glimmer of light on the lake through the gauze curtain, thinks *No, no, no.*

Rose doesn't believe that her daughter was the person who bought the strangely unspecific "party drug."

Rose also has a hard time believing Jules would have ever given away her favorite book, the Eva Marshall memoir she'd been rereading since high school.

Matt told her to let the local professionals do the work. *It's diminishing returns from this point. There's nothing more we can do. It's time to grieve.*

But it isn't time, yet, for Rose.

She should have come to Guatemala, herself, those very first days after Jules's texts stopped. She shouldn't have let Matt lean on his military background so heavily, prioritizing tech over old-fashioned communication. The aggressive approach might have scared away someone who knew *something.*

They should have shouted less. Demanded less. Talked less—and listened more. But isn't that what a mother thinks whenever she looks back on her parenting?

So, she has regrets, she thinks, shaking out a pair of pants with a satisfying snap. Everyone does. But not about finally coming here, now.

Rose has slowed her unpacking, realizing there isn't a place to put most of her clothes. Pushing a nightgown back into a side pocket of her suitcase, she hears a telltale crinkle and pulls out a tissue-wrapped package, sighing.

It's the last-minute gift that Ulyana gave her when she

dropped Rose at the airport. The twins were both kicking and flailing in their car seats, but Ulyana took it all in stride. With O'Hare traffic behind her and spilled Cheerios at her feet, Ulyana reached over the gear shift and pressed a small, soft package into Rose's hand. *You mentioned you wrecked your favorite sports bra in the dryer. Those first weeks after my mom died, just getting dressed each day was hard, but little comforts helped.*

Rose knew it was Ulyana's version of a peace offering, meant to offset Matt's bossy handling of nearly everything over the last few months. It wasn't fair that women felt they had to patch over the emotional rough spots men created, but even so, Rose was grateful to her ex's new wife. She imagined the text she'd send Jules: *You won't believe the thoughtful gift your stepmom just gave me . . .*

Rose kept forgetting. Every time she had to remember, the shock returned, barely diminished. Jules was gone.

Gone. Still holding the bra, Rose sits down at the foot of the twin bed. The center of the thin mattress squeaks and sags. There's one pillow, very small, in an oversized case. At least the accommodations were included, as are breakfasts at the "hotel" and lunches at the writer's house—but $5,900 for a week?

The truth is, that's a lot of money after the hundreds of thousands of dollars she and Matt spent together on the search effort—not that she has any future weddings or grandchildren to plan for now. To make things worse, she isn't scheduling new remodels for the time being, despite her office manager's warnings that long-term clients are deserting them. But Rose can't think about design work. Kitchens are gathering spaces, for families. Rose doesn't have one now. She'll keep receiving occasional holiday invitations from Matt and Ulyana, and from her sister, Christine, but really she's just the pitiful outsider looking in.

"Hey, Rose!" Lindsay calls up the ladder, only the platinum spikes of her hair visible through the opening in the loft floor. "You coming down for some wine?"

Rose rubs the tip of her nose and clears her throat. "No, thanks. I can wait for the big party."

"Suit yourself."

Downstairs, the group laughs without her. She hears them quizzing Lindsay about her grifter life. She explains, as she did to Rose and Isobel before, that her submitted essay isn't representative of her normal jobs.

"Then what do you do most of the time, if not beat men at poker?" a girlish voice asks.

"I give them what they want."

Someone whispers, "Sex?"

"With the big jobs, they never even meet me. I'm the new online girlfriend who suddenly has a car accident, or a son in rehab, or a dog that needs to go to the vet. They just keep paying and paying, getting deeper until they're too embarrassed to face facts. Sometimes we break up without them even knowing they were conned."

Rose is glad to listen from afar and not respond. What would she say? *How can you trick people like that? How can you lie about things that are so serious?*

But Rose is planning to lie, here in Guatemala, to everyone she meets.

"Well, if they're that dumb," Isobel says from below.

"On the other hand," Lindsay says, "at least they know what they want. Even if what they want is a fantasy. I promise you: many of them feel like they've gotten a good deal."

Everyone laughs again, a sound that makes Rose feel even more alone, and suddenly cold.

Fully dressed, she pulls back the thin blanket and gets into the sagging bed, e-reader in her hand, intending to finish the second of the two Eva Marshall memoirs. Jules begged her to read both books—the first that Eva had published when she was only nineteen and the second, Eva's runaway bestseller, published five years ago, after a string of modestly successful novels. Rose read the first one, *Last Gasp*, a month ago, when her focus cleared up enough to read anything longer than an email. It wasn't until this week that she started the second one.

From online summaries, she already knows that *In a Delicate State* ends sadly, with the death of a child. Her allegiances were torn. She couldn't read about other people's tragedies for more than a few pages without spiraling into her own dark and paralyzing thoughts. At the same time, she wanted to know everything about Eva that might tell her something about Jules, or at least why Eva was Jules's favorite author.

As it happened, *In a Delicate State* engaged her so quickly it wasn't a hard read at all—not the happy early chapters, anyway, when Eva Marshall makes the bold decision to have a baby in her early fifties, against the advice of family and doctors.

Reading the first half of the book yesterday, in airports and on the plane, Rose lived through all of Eva's difficult midlife reproductive questions. She's never admitted it to anyone, scarcely even to herself, but once Matt remarried and became a father again, Rose realized she regretted that her mothering years ended when they did. She would have given an arm to have another baby. Even now, when she spots famous women in the tabloids, having babies, even twins, at fifty years old, she thinks, *Why not me?*

Rose knows why: she's a normal person. Not a Hollywood actress with a millionaire husband or a bestselling memoirist or even just a privileged woman with great health insurance and admirably thick skin.

The sad part of *In a Delicate State* will come at the end.

Rose hasn't gotten there, yet. She swipes to the next page, reading slowly, knowing this is part of the process: connecting with a book beloved by Jules and facing the universality of grief. By the last page, she might even feel a special kinship with Eva, once she fully understands what the author has suffered and survived—possibly even why she won't answer a grieving mother's emails.

Downstairs, the voices continue. One of the younger women shrieks with laughter, about what, Rose has no idea. She can't read here. She needs to get out of this cabin.

Rose packs the e-reader into her purse and descends the ladder. Four faces look up, including the young, fit blonde from the reception area who reminded Rose so much of Jules, and an equally slim, ebony-haired girl who could easily be a model. In a workshop of mostly older, wealthy women, they're the young ones: tan, taut and brimming with energy. They don't realize how beautiful they are, how fortunate. She shouldn't start resenting young women just for being alive, but she can't help it.

"Scarlett and Noelani are here," Isobel calls out as Rose reaches the bottom ladder rung. "Come join us."

Rose seizes the first excuse that comes to her. "I have to find the ATM in town. I couldn't get the one in Antigua to work. I want cash on hand, before we all gather for the party."

"I'll loan you some quetzales."

"Thank you, but I really just need to do this."

"You're from Chicago," Scarlett says to Rose, stepping toward her. "I *love* Chicago. I stopped there on my bike trip—"

"You read Scarlett's chapter, right?" Isobel interrupts. "From her travel memoir? She biked across America on ten dollars a day. This girl is amazing."

So was Jules, Rose thinks. She could have biked across

the country. She could have climbed peaks in all fifty states. She could have written a memoir, or a novel, or screenplays. She could have done anything, if she'd just had more time.

"I have to go," Rose says again, aware that her voice is trembling and that she is coming across like a killjoy or something worse. This is all too much. Too soon. She's out the door before anyone else can beg her to stay.

Rose opens the garden gate separating the hotel compound from a high-walled lane, off-limits to most cars, and heads along the paved route toward the center of town, uphill and away from the shore. This isn't a vacation. She can't sit around drinking expensive wine. She needs to start searching, but she doesn't know where to begin.

When she passes her first corner produce stand, she pauses, thinking of the ten Instagram photos Jules posted over her entire trip. One was a close-up of limes, papayas and some kind of squash—chayote, Matt guessed. The photo could have come from anywhere in Central America. Still, Rose will never stop mentally indexing the photos, trying to match backgrounds, objects and geographical features she is now seeing. It's a strange way to expend energy, considering they already know every city and village Jules visited. But Rose wants to know her daughter's trip in a deeper way. To feel like she is standing, at least sometimes, in places where her daughter stood, looking at things her daughter saw.

To the left and right of the cobble-paved lane are curio shops and a few restaurants, including a pizzeria with a sign that says "good Wi-Fi here" in English. Rose remembers Jules's excuses for the scarcity of her calls and texts, especially toward the end of her time in San Felipe. She claimed that the Wi-Fi was okay at the hostel and at a few places in the village, but unreliable elsewhere. In the words of Eva's voluminous instruction sheets: *If smartphone addiction is a problem for you, get ready for a wonderful detox!*

Alleys branch off at irregular intervals, a maze Rose can't map out just yet. The main lane is mostly in shadow. Some side lanes are so narrow that with her arms outstretched, her fingertips can almost brush both walls. The claustrophobic charm reminds her of Venice—one of those places that could seem either romantic or sinister, depending on how lost you feel.

It doesn't seem sinister today. She doesn't notice any aggressive hawkers or leering men. Instead, she passes only quiet, seemingly friendly people. A man selling textiles doesn't look up, even when she pauses to run a finger along a brightly colored tablecloth. Three children ahead are tap-kicking a soccer ball, gently and carefully, but when she needs to pass, the oldest boy tugs his younger sister close to the wall, out of her way.

Uphill another few hundred feet, two short women in embroidered shirts, wide cotton belts and modest long skirts stand against the alley wall with their shopping bags. One of them is rebraiding the long rope of gleaming black hair over her shoulder.

"Buenos días," Rose says.

"Buenos días," the woman replies, lifting her eyes to Rose.

Rose feels she should say something more, so she ventures, "Bonito aquí." *It's pretty here.*

The woman cups her hand over her mouth, covering a silent laugh. Then she drops her hand, dips her head and says, "Muy bonito. Bienvenida."

These women seem so kind. They are sharing their village, the limited span of lakeshore, these precious narrow alleys.

Mom, it's different here. The people are really friendly. Stop reading the travel warnings!

If anything, on first impression, it's the other tourists who give Rose pause.

Passing a jewelry and bead shop, she catches a whiff of marijuana. At a small restaurant just next door, Rose sees a young white couple lingering at a table near the arched doorway. They're Jules's age, in full bohemian rags: dreadlocks, nose and eyebrow piercings, baggy Aladdin-style pants. The man's outfit is topped with a roughly woven sweater, the same design sold in Mexico and Guatemala since the 1970s. Rose owned one of those, a lifetime ago. The woman is only half-dressed, wearing a tiny crocheted bra, the shape of her nipples visible even from this distance. Below the bra: a taut, bare belly. The girl stands, bare foot propped high on the chair, doing an ostentatious sideways ballerina-style stretch, one bangle-covered arm over her head.

Rose can't help staring. Surely the locals don't make a practice of dressing so immodestly. Surely they don't prop their dirty bare feet just anywhere.

The tourists, who seem to have less spatial intelligence than the locals, are the ones who block the alleyways. They stand in spread-out throngs, puzzling over signs advertising locally made chocolate, weaving co-ops and Mayan medicine tours. They're oblivious to the locals, like a child with a starched white shirt, blue pants and a tiny backpack, trying to dart around their legs.

But Rose knows that she's noticing more because she's alone. If she were in a large group, she'd be distracted as well—taking up too much space, chatting too loudly, high on the adrenaline buzz of being in a new place.

Going solo has its advantages. Her daughter had tried to tell her that, but she wouldn't listen.

I'm not alone all that much, Mom. I always meet people in hostels. I find friends. But when I want to move on, I can.

And I like to be alone. That's when locals talk to me. That's when I start to feel part of a place.

Rose replied with anxious questions about the civil war, which Jules said happened a long time ago. The midnineties didn't feel long ago to Rose. They sparred about crime rates. Rose refused to drop it. It wasn't true what everyone said about the capital being the only dangerous place. The countryside was dangerous, too.

Not Lake Atitlán. Mom, this is why I travel. You can read about a place and you can go to a place and the two are completely different things. Please let's not fight about this.

Rose gets to the top of the alley, a T-intersection on the main road, where all the colorful three-wheeled tuk-tuk taxis line up. She pauses, out of breath and overwhelmed. This larger road's swirling dust makes her eyes sting.

Guatemala is just different. Mom, I can't explain.

The drivers give her a moment of peace before one of them calls out in good English, "Señora, are you trying to go somewhere? Do you need a ride?"

She must look dazed. She is lost, more lost than she's ever been in her life. Rose has had dark days: depression in her early twenties, divorce not much later, the loss of her own mother to cancer. None of it came close to this. Nothing prepared her for the singularly devastating experience of losing a child.

Jules, I'm so sorry.

Her vision blurs. She has to turn away, pretend to be studying the glass window of a small corner grocery, puzzling over the display of Coke products and a chalkboard boasting the currency exchange rate.

She doesn't want to keep apologizing. She's here, isn't she? But this is a new apology and a new realization, one she couldn't have had back in Illinois.

Jules, you had every right to travel alone. You had every

right to go out in the world, to see new places and talk to people and be yourself. You were absolutely right. Every place can be dangerous. And every place can be kind. We can't just stay home, being afraid.

And yet, how she wished Jules *were* home. She'd trade every beautiful view in the world, every exotic experience and every stupid fucking postcard for just one more hour with her daughter, cooking dinner, talking and laughing as they brush past each other, the steam rising from the pasta pot, the salmon darkening under the broiler, pausing only long enough to change the music on Jules's phone, resuming their dancing and laughing, refusing to rush. Her daughter, smart and funny and compassionate, the best friend she could ever have, even though you weren't supposed to put that much pressure on a child. Jules has her own friends; *had* her own friends. Just one hour. One or two glasses of wine, together. Give her another hug and don't rush it. Smooth her hair one more time, feel the softness of her arms and her chest against yours. Laugh when you are still hugging, while the steam billows and the kitchen timer rings.

Rose wipes her nose on her bare forearm, but one discreet swipe isn't enough. She was supposed to be doing something—looking for clues, making notes, *noticing*. Instead, she is back to wishing she could turn back time, a delusion more easily fostered from the comfort of her own home. The tuk-tuk drivers are all staring at her. The only way she can stop crying is to be angry at someone. The image of that dreadlock-wearing woman with the crocheted bikini top comes to mind. *Didn't anyone teach you to have respect for the places and people you visit?* Her daughter had respect. Always. Her daughter didn't stay up all night, running half-naked along the stone-covered beach, making the married women nervous, sleeping with the local men.

At least, Rose doesn't think so.

4

JULES

"You are so, so nice to meet with me on such short notice," I say, clasping my hands together to keep them from shaking.

"You met Mauricio at the pizzeria in town?" Eva asks over her shoulder as we climb the stairs to the second story of her house, an adobe-walled building with huge windows overlooking Lake Atitlán.

I'm glad she can't see my stressed and sweaty face as I fumble for an answer. "Yeah, just a chance meeting. We didn't talk long. He said you're always looking for staff."

In less than a minute, I've told three lies.

First, it wasn't chance. Mauricio walked by my table and saw I was reading my old copy of Eva's first memoir, *Last Gasp*. He's never read it, but he recognized the cover, of course.

Second, we talked all afternoon, ending up on the beach, where we finished off a six-pack of Coronas, chatting the whole time in Spanish.

Third, Mauricio didn't say Eva was looking for staff, only that the "lady workshoppers" were on the way and everything was getting crazy. When I pressed for details, he got skittish. He wanted to see me again, in town, but he didn't want to lure me to Eva's semihidden lair—my words, not his. I have to assume it was for my own benefit—*you're on vacation, why would you want to work?*—but I don't need anyone, even a gorgeous twenty-year-old guy with café au lait skin, hazel eyes and dark wavy hair, telling me whether or not I need a job. The answer is: I do.

"We're almost there," Eva says, gauzy fern-green pants fluttering as she strides through the living room and toward a large bedroom, a corner of which is occupied with a desk, printer and banker's boxes. "Not the best layout. Pardon the mess. We'll use the balcony."

I swallow hard, eyes so dry that every time I blink it feels like I'm clicking the shutter of an old-fashioned camera, taking in the huge framed photo of Eva posing in an adoring crowd of twenty dark-skinned children, all dressed in matching T-shirts, like it's a charity event. Red dirt. Acacia trees. Africa, probably.

Another click as I try to capture the décor: narrow kilim rugs from the Middle East, underfoot. Guatemalan tapestries on the wall and folk art on low tables.

A final click as I pass a framed photo of Eva standing in a one-piece bathing suit at the end of a weathered dock. I saw that one a year ago, in the *New York Times* Travel Section.

Eva calls out to some invisible helper: "Iced coffee, please, out to the balcony!"

I hope she isn't calling Mauricio. He'd be appalled to see I'm here, carrying my backpack, having checked out of the hostel one night early. I'll settle things with him, later. The truth is that I've fooled around with three guys—sorry, four—on my Central American tour. But I've only met one famous author, and she happens to be my favorite writer of all time. A girl has to have priorities.

"I emailed you my resume," I tell Eva, following her

through a combination bedroom-office, then back out into the open sunlight, through French doors. On the balcony, she moves yellow legal pads and piles of paper-clipped printouts, clearing space on a white stone bench. Aside from the clutter and a few wilted plants that have seen better days, it's gorgeous up here: Red and turquoise throw pillows, everywhere. A small table with an inlaid mosaic in sunset colors.

"I didn't get the email," Eva says in a low, throaty voice. "Ever since Simone left me high and dry, I haven't been able to manage the inbox."

She gestures to the stone bench. I sit. She doesn't. "You said you're a yoga instructor?"

"Among other things," I say, ready to rattle off my resume: Planned Parenthood internship, various short-term secretarial gigs, tutoring.

Eva glances toward the doorway where a teenage Guatemalan girl has appeared, wearing a traditional long skirt and woven faja sash. A tucked-in T-shirt reads "GUCCI."

"Gaby. This is . . ."

"Jules," I offer.

In fluid, accented English, Gaby says, "Hans wants to know if you're still going to eat the yogurt or if he should put it away."

"Never mind the yogurt," Eva says.

I pull my backpack onto my lap sideways, talking over it. "I saw on your website that you have a new workshop session starting in four days, which is awesome—"

"Gaby," Eva says, just as the teenager is turning to leave, "you're off the hook."

Gaby's mellow smile fades into a confused pucker. "You don't want the coffees now?"

"No. I don't need you to teach yoga to the women who are coming. We might have a real teacher."

"Oh," I say, realizing what I've done, and only by mistake. "You were going to be the new yoga instructor?"

Gaby's shoulders droop.

"Now, now," Eva reprimands her, "there's plenty to do in the kitchen. We've got to prep meals for thirty people, and Mercedes hasn't been feeling well lately." Eva turns to me, explaining, "Mercedes came to us when no one else would hire her. Epilepsy and a developmental delay of some kind."

"But you promised," Gaby says, pouting.

"I've actually never taught adults, only kids," I clarify. "And you don't have kids here, right? So, Gaby's probably the better choice."

Eva doesn't seem overly offended by my transparent fib— or does she believe it? I wrack my brain for another way to pitch my higher-level skills, already second-guessing my attempt at altruism. *Maybe I shouldn't have turned down the yoga job so soon? Maybe Gaby would have been happier in the kitchen?*

Eva turns to Gaby. "Go get the coffee. Just one, with ice. Please."

Just one coffee. Interview over.

"It's too bad," Eva says, still standing. "I mean, you were the perfect package: available right now, admin skills, plus yoga. But you don't do adult yoga."

I glance past the balcony's edge, down to the lawn, where sometime later this week, on a fresh and misty morning no doubt, a dozen yoga mats will unroll in silent preparation for a glorious sunrise—and I won't see it.

What I love about writing, as versus life, is the endless chance to revise. There must be some way to start over, but I'm blanking. Gaby has a job. Even Mercedes has a job, thanks to Eva's kindness. I'm Eva Marshall's biggest fan, at a critical juncture in my life—and I wrecked my chance. I feel like I'm watching a drawbridge go up, staring at some fantastic castle, and I've gotten myself stuck on the wrong side of the moat. It's a melodramatic thought, but I'm sure I'll come up with something even more operatic tonight, back in town, moaning into a margarita glass the size of a goldfish bowl about how close I came to my dream job and how quickly I botched it.

Frazzled, I reach into my backpack and slide out Eva's first memoir, the one I was rereading at the pizzeria. "Would you sign it, before I go?"

Eva rearranges her lips into a thin-lipped smile of benign indulgence, taking the book in hand. She flips it open—not to the first page, but to the middle—and extends her arm, seeking the right distance to correct the focus. (No reading glasses. My mom won't wear them yet, either.)

Ten seconds pass. Her smile relaxes and broadens.

I lean forward and see what *she's* seeing: my underlining and margin comments. The smiley faces are the marks I left when I was only fifteen. The more thoughtful scribbles and private codes are from early college. *Oh my god*. How can I explain? I've been making notes in this book's margins for seven years.

Is this the time to tell Eva Marshall that I first read *Last Gasp* when I was a sophomore in high school? Should I admit that, after losing my virginity to a guy I didn't like in the bathroom of a Subway sandwich shop that reeked of ham, I went home and cried and didn't feel better until I'd reread the scene in which *she* lost her virginity on a London park bench to a man who smelled like glue?

"I get 'exposition' and 'flashback,'" she says. "But what's 'A'?"

"Awesome," I say, tongue thick in my mouth. There's nothing worse than letting someone see directly into your brain and discovering there isn't much there, but I have no choice.

"You write in your books. That's good. You can't believe how many of the women I teach think they're not supposed to."

At a loss for words, I grin vacantly.

Eva grabs a pen from the little table. "So, you're a writer," she says, signing the title page with a quick slash. She closes and hands the book back to me.

"I want to be."

Four words that can't begin to contain the dreams I've built up so dangerously large I'm terrified of being crushed by them.

"Which you didn't tell me when you first asked for a job."

I take a deep breath. It didn't occur to me that Eva Marshall would want to know about my small ideas and overheated ambitions. Even the word "writer" makes me uncomfortable. I haven't earned it yet.

"Interesting," she says. "Sometimes what we hide is more important than what we tell."

I want to think that she's right—that I might have depths, hidden even to me, and strengths that could be nurtured by the right person in the right situation. Never mind that I *feel* like an impostor. Everyone feels that way. Right?

Eva leans against the waist-high adobe wall that encloses her second-story patio, an aerie high up in the trees, and gestures to the stacks of paper-clipped pages which must be the work of the women writers on their way to Guatemala soon. "You've gotta see these manuscripts. There's practically no point in reading the first pages. They never admit what the real story is. They hold on to it. You have to wrestle it away from them."

"I believe that. All my creative writing workshops at Northwestern were the same way."

Eva doesn't look impressed. She never went to college. She may even have a grudge against formal writing instruction.

"But I didn't really learn much there—not about writing," I

say, improvising. "Travel and life have taught me more." They haven't. But I'm here. I'm willing. I've shown up.

Eva seems to be thinking. Over her shoulder, two hummingbirds dart behind a bush and dance into view again: flash of purple, shimmer of green. *Stay focused. Don't mess this up.*

"Julie?"

"Actually, *Juliet* on my passport, but I've always gone by Jules."

Eva narrows her eyes again, like she's tasting my name in order to decide whether she likes it. Behind her the lake sparkles. I can't stop glancing from Eva's face, framed by her tousled blond bob, to the shimmering blue water, to the cloud-topped volcanoes. It's more than a view. It's a combination of things I never even knew I wanted, because I've never seen them all in one place: natural beauty, timeless inspiration and the signs of Eva's success, everywhere. This place represents enchantment, but it's an *earned* enchantment. Eva deserves this, I know from following her life story a little too closely. I want to be the kind of person who deserves it, too.

"Let's start over," Eva says, big green eyes fixed on me. "I don't need just admin help, I need help dealing with everyday hospitality issues once the women get here. Stuff happens when people who are used to being comfortable leave their safe bubbles. And I desperately need social media, too. You do that?"

Maybe it's time for a little truth at this point. "I could learn."

"Let's have you learn right now."

"Okay," I say, letting the backpack slide down to the floor. I scooch my rear to the hard edge of the stone bench.

"Take out your phone. Make me a video. Tell me what you liked about one of my books."

"Do I aim the camera at . . . you?"

"Not for this one. Focus on the book cover or the scenery. Just make it casual, and one minute or less. Something I can put on our feeds, which got way too quiet this week, thanks to Simone going AWOL. Can you do that—and sort out all the email, too?"

I turn twenty-three at the end of this week. Maybe this birthday will be special after all. A fragrant white blossom falls from a tree over our heads, into my lap.

"Absolutely."

5

ROSE

———————————————

———————————

———

Vision still blurry with tears, Rose huddles near the window of a small shop, pretending to be fascinated as she studies the jars of salsas and traditional wooden cocoa whisks. Really, she's waiting for her eyes to dry and her sinuses to clear.

She skims the sun-bleached flyers stuck to the inside of the glass, facing the street: a meditation workshop from last spring; a reggaeton concert in Antigua, in June.

Matt promised that the entire village had been plastered with flyers of Jules, but she sees no signs of them now.

In the photo they picked of their daughter, Jules was wearing a tank top, cargo shorts and white tennis shoes. Her dark blond hair was in two braids, and she was crouching and cuddling a stumpy-legged dog. This was in Panama, at the dog shelter where Jules volunteered for several days. It was the best, most recent and neutral close-up they had. She didn't take a lot of close-up selfies. When she did, she hammed it up, made fish lips or crossed her eyes while striking a yoga warrior pose.

When you're the parent of a missing child, sitting at home, sifting through photos, you realize how difficult it is to pick the right one. No crossed eyes or jubilant high kicks. No beer bottles, either. (*No sir, she doesn't drink too much, she doesn't party, not any more than any other person her age.*)

The clothing in the photo must be typical, and not in any way suggestive.

Is your daughter reckless?

She's active. She's healthy. She does sports. She travels.

The scruffy dog in the photo made Jules look like the type of person who volunteered, which she was. It made her look like a good and generous person. Which she was.

Did you get along? Any serious disagreements?

The police, consul and private investigator all asked stupid questions and they all seemed equally incurious about the answers. They didn't want to know about Jules's life and the normal sorts of arguments they had—that any family has. Like Jules's admission to Rose, a week before flying to Panama, that she wanted to get her own apartment after the trip. Which made no sense financially. Jules had three parents—two bedrooms available, in two perfectly comfortable houses. If she wanted to go to grad school, if she wanted to be a writer, as she claimed . . .

If I want to be a writer? Jules asked at that final dinner before her trip—a dinner that was supposed to be celebratory. *If?*

Rose thinks about all the thought they put into those flyers, the social media posts, the hiring of so-called experts. Maybe what they should have paid attention to was Jules herself—those early signals.

As a mom, you're always underreacting or overreacting. There seems to be no happy middle ground. Because Jules was born premature and those first months were so hard, Rose treated her like she was too fragile. In some ways she seemed to be: no child got more colds and ear infections in those first five years than Jules did. The grade school years were different. Jules became ultra-sporty in defiance of her parents' concerns and the dire warnings of one especially gloomy physician, who told them about preemies' higher asthma and heart problem rates.

Then came college. Jules attended nearby Northwestern—a compromise. She'd had her heart set on California, but Matt's faculty discount was too valuable to ignore. Although Jules's childhood home was less than fifteen minutes away, the university required students to live in dorms for their first two years—and thank goodness for that, Jules told her parents. She also insisted, freshman year, on minimizing contact with both Rose and Matt. *Can we please at least pretend I've actually "gone away" to college?*

The first semester went well. The holidays were normal. But then that February, Jules dropped out of contact. Rose assumed she was talking more to Matt and Ulyana. They assumed Jules was in close touch with Rose. Their daughter's geographical proximity made them all complacent. *Imagine how those other parents feel with their kid thousands of miles away!*

It was a professor-friend of Matt's who let them know Jules had stopped showing up for class. Not an R.A., not a roommate, not some campus counselor who recognized that their daughter was seriously depressed and a good candidate for medication—like her mother and grandmother before her. They'd almost missed it. Minutes away, their daughter had nearly gone under, and they had done nothing about it.

Rose should have learned. She should have swung into action, the moment she got a bad feeling on Jules's twenty-third birthday, three months ago when Jules didn't check in. They'd never been out of touch on any of Jules's earlier birthdays.

Rose had asked about setting up a video call. No answer.

2 P.M. *Let's talk sometime today. I've never missed seeing you on your birthday!*

4 P.M. *I'm sure you're busy working but just let me know if tonight's a possibility. I can stay up.*

5:30 P.M. *Even if it's tomorrow, just ding me quick. Let me know you're good. We can set up a time tomorrow.*

Rose remembers her alternating anxiety and melancholy. *Your birthday was a special day for me, too. Can you maybe give me two minutes?*

But she knew that wasn't something you should put on a child. An hour or so later, when she was curled up with Netflix and leftovers, the texts and the mild disappointment behind her, she suddenly felt the strangest sensation.

She checked the clock: 7 P.M. Perhaps Jules was having a special birthday dinner.

She felt a chill run down her spine. She heard, or thought she heard, one word: "Mama."

That was it. Nothing more.

Finally around 7:30 P.M. the texts all streamed in at once, and she laughed with embarrassment and then started crying with relief.

Dawn hot and noisy, birds singing. One big fat cockroach scuttled out from under my bed to greet me. Is that lucky?

Later: *Happy Birthday to me! Not an auspicious start.*

Another one: *Typing these not knowing when they'll actually send since Wi-Fi is on the fritz. I'd really like to call you but I can't.*

Later: *Can't complain. Mimosas with a view.*

Later: *I'm sorry I've been so out of touch.*

Later: *I love you Mom.*

Later: *I'm sorry.*

There were never any more texts.

There was no information at all, until Rose and Matt decided that five days was too long to go without contact—that it wasn't like Jules to drop out of touch so suddenly with no explanation.

It took two more days to launch a full search, thousands

of miles away from home. Six weeks later, that search ended, though according to the police, giving up on finding a body didn't equate to closing the official investigation. Still, it seems the same to Rose. No active search, no likeliness of getting significant leads. Whether they were hoping for a body to lovingly bury or only a sense of Jules's final moments, Rose will always feel like they gave up too soon.

Tired of wandering, aware that siesta is upon them and many of the shops have closed for the afternoon, Rose retraces her steps downhill, toward the waterfront, and stops at the pizzeria she spotted earlier.

She is shown to a small table in the back, where she orders bread sticks—the smallest item she can find—and a diet soda. She sends Matt and Ulyana a text confirming she has safely arrived. Then she pulls out her e-reader and college-lined notebook, arranging them around her place setting.

Travel was never Rose's forte, but organization always has been.

In the first weeks following Jules's disappearance, Rose divided a notebook into four parts: background on Guatemala, police and investigator findings, messages from Jules and facts about Eva Marshall (birth name: Patricia Eve Myron) and Casa Eva.

In the first part of the notebook, she summarized Guatemala items gleaned from the news. There was a story about a young Japanese tourist who was beaten and died of her injuries. There was an equally brutal story of an Alaskan tourist falsely suspected of baby stealing, beaten so badly by a mob that she was left in a coma. Then there was the bigger, longer-term view: Guatemala's recent civil war, the country's role as a narcotics corridor and the plight of migrants trying to escape the reach of gangs.

Rose's small reward for finishing her review of Guatemala background notes is to flip to the next section of the notebook, where she can review the findings from the police. Here's where they logged the cursory info on the arrested drug dealer named Francisco "Paco" Marroquín and, in more detail, the arrest and later whereabouts of the German backpacker. Matt had pledged to keep an eye on Luka Bauer, via an American colleague who worked in the boy's hometown of Stuttgart. *If he makes one wrong step, if he bothers any young woman, if he gets picked up for something as minor as riding the U-Bahn without a ticket, I'll find out about it.*

So, that was that. A local drug dealer, punished. A young man who spent at least a few hours with Jules, identified. As far as the police were concerned, the drugs and the stolen book weren't necessarily directly connected to Jules's death, only to Jules herself, helping with the timeline and a portrait of how she was spending her time—not always with the most savory characters. The nailed-down details made it possible to attach other smaller details, gratifying Matt, especially.

Rose turns the page, willing herself to see it as an objective observer, someone who might notice something new. She rereads the highlights of Eva's statement to police, including the overlap with the German backpacker's assertion of a key detail. Eva said she'd been forced to "let Juliet May go" when Jules insisted on her plan to go on the dawn volcano hike with Luka, "regardless of her work responsibilities mere hours later." Jules had left Eva's orbit twelve hours before the hike and a full day before she was seen swimming.

None of these investigatory details are as important to Rose as Jules's own words. This is where the essence of Rose's daughter still persists, her voice captured in the third section of the notebook: a patchwork of pasted emails, texts and Instagram captions written out longhand.

These are amazing women, Jules wrote in a rare, longer email just after getting the personal assistant position. *They've gone through so much and yet they are strong, honest, generous and resilient. I'm so honored to help organize their trip just a little, to give them some comfort and troubleshoot so they can focus and get the love and help they need so they can write and tell their truths.*

Knowing what some of them have gone through makes me feel I've led a sheltered life. I should feel lucky, but I don't. How lucky can I feel when I have nothing to say, no stories to share? I know you won't get that part. Moms are supposed to want their children to lead boring, safe lives. I get it.

But let me tell you about Eva! She is the most beautiful and badass of them all. If you still haven't read her first memoir, the one I've been telling you to read forever, you should.

Rose has Jules's copy of Eva's first memoir, the one taken from the German backpacker and returned to them—a treasure because it bears the marks of Jules's many rereadings over the years. She read it soon after Jules disappeared and has thumbed through it many times since, even though it's not her kind of book. It's her daughter's kind of book. That's what matters.

Last Gasp (or *The Mascot*, as the UK edition was called) is about Eva Marshall's years as a runaway teenager, daughter of wealthy absentee parents from Palo Alto who never once came looking for her. Eva lived as a groupie in the world of London punk rock, from its late heyday in 1978 through the death of Sid Vicious in early 1979 and just beyond. A young American innocent abroad, Eva contributed no skills as a musician, but she did often pose nude—flat-chested, raccoon-eyed, with a blond buzz cut—on liner notes and in flyers. Within limited circles, she became a symbol of that era.

No wonder Jules developed a crush on Eva when she was

only a high schooler. It wasn't just that Eva lived a more adventurous life, it's that she turned every sad or scary thing that ever happened to her into a globe-trotting career. Maybe even into art. It was a much better story than Rose's own: settle on a business degree because it seems practical, marry young and start a kitchen reno company.

Rose is more interested in the epilogue to Eva's adolescent story than the punk memoir itself. After moving from London to New York, Eva piqued the interest of a major imprint. This was the *Mommie Dearest* era, back when nearly all autobiographies were about celebrities. Eva Marshall, a nobody, published a memoir when she was only nineteen years old. No wonder so many readers took notice.

In her early twenties, Eva next tried acting and singing, but the New York stage didn't embrace her the same way publishing had. She lived off magazine freelancing for a couple of years, then turned to fiction, where she flourished commercially, if not always critically, for several decades. Some of Eva's novels were dismissed for being too domestic, "women's fiction," with much attention spent, as one reviewer quipped, "on babies, bodies and bonding," often of the female-friendship variety.

Rose flips to her cut-and-paste compilation of Eva's newspaper and magazine essays, which spawned an equal number of counter-essays by other writers who got a kick out of criticizing Eva for "oversharing."

In her fifties, Eva admitted that she was estranged from the daughter she'd had at age twenty. A web journalist gleefully accused her of deserving the rift, given how often she'd invaded that daughter's privacy, using her as fodder in personal essays. But even when Eva wrote only about herself, the critics excoriated her. Eva wrote candidly about her small breasts, grown saggy after childbirth and breastfeeding. A critic sniped, "Many of today's writers have an unfortunate tendency to navel gaze; Eva Marshall's attention doesn't even reach that far."

Reading that comment now, while sipping at the warm remains of her second diet soda, Rose feels a hollow and fading sort of satisfaction. Despite Matt's constant reminder that Eva answered their key requests—filing a police statement, bringing her house manager to do the same—Rose always felt that Eva was holding back. The most detailed thing Eva told police was that she "got the impression Jules frequently traveled alone and disregarded common-sense precautions." But Eva also said, "Following our brief interview I saw her so infrequently that I'm not the best person to make guesses about her risky habits or state of mind."

Eva's actions might not be suspicious, but they were, at the very least, unkind. Maybe Eva had spent only moments face-to-face with Jules, if Jules was just one staffer of many. But Jules had spent years with Eva as a devoted reader. Did that matter? Should it?

Only now, reading public criticisms of Eva with all the detachment she can muster, Rose feels an uncomfortable new insight taking shape. It's not just that "death is bad for business," as Matt said ad nauseum as justification for Eva's stonewalling. It's also that celebrities were criticized whether they engaged or hid away.

For over thirty years, Eva was treated harshly by critics, trolls and everyday Goodreads reviewers. Any smart woman would come to rely on publicists and lawyers who'd tell her, "Don't link your name to anything sordid. When in doubt, keep a low profile." Rose hates to admit it, but it makes sense.

Rose checks her watch—still an hour before the party begins. Tonight, she'll meet the woman herself. She opens her ebook and returns to reading Eva's second memoir.

Unlike the punk-era narrative that appealed so much to Jules, this one involves no gritty setting or provocative set-up, just a voice whispering in her ear. As if this woman, Eva Marshall, has simply pulled up a chair to tell Rose the truth. It's a truth that hurts almost more than Rose can bear.

There was one thing I wanted more than anything in the world: to hold a child, my very own flesh-and-blood child, again.

Rose is so caught up reading that she doesn't notice the passage of time until women's laughter floods up the narrow alleyway, breaking the spell. She looks up to see a group strolling past the low front wall of the pizzeria: Rose's fellow workshop participants, changed into evening wear—long skirts, pretty jeweled sandals, cardigan sweaters—heading toward Casa Eva. Rose never changed or freshened her makeup. Maybe she'll get points for looking more natural.

By the time she's settled her bill, she's been left behind. She speedwalks to the main plaza beyond the alleys, where this afternoon's line of red, green and yellow tuk-tuks has been reduced to only one. The other women are puttering up the road without Rose, crammed in groups of three and four into colorful, toy-like vehicles, another feature of these charming villages.

Charming, yet Eva and Company warned them, via the emailed instructions: *Do NOT walk the road alone. Do not walk, even in groups, after dark. Do not go more than a quarter mile beyond Casa Eva. On the way back to town take a boat or a tuk-tuk, always with a partner.*

Well, Rose has no partner for the five-minute ride up the mountain road.

"Hola," she says, crossing the narrow street and swinging into the back of the sole tuk-tuk. "Buenas noches. Un minuto, por favor."

She opens her bag, pawing through printouts of instructions, but there are so many she can't find the address for Casa Eva. When she looks up, Rose notices an old, dark-skinned man with bowl-cut hair and a thick, boxy shirt—homemade, handwoven—looking back at her from across the narrow road. He neither smiles nor frowns. He takes a step closer, into the street. One of his eyes is filmy blue.

The tuk-tuk driver shoos him away. "¡Vete!"

"What does he want?" Rose says, forgetting for a moment to use Spanish. "¿Qué quiere el hombre?"

Maybe the old man is a beggar. Maybe he's offering his services as a guide. Maybe he simply wants to share the ride.

The man steps closer, oblivious to an oncoming truck.

"¡Vete!" the driver shouts more forcefully. The old man steps back just in time to avoid being hit by the produce truck. But still, he doesn't stop staring at Rose.

"¿Dónde?" the driver asks Rose, sounding annoyed.

"Casa Eva," she says, hoping it's enough.

"Casa Eva, adelante. Bienvenida," he says, finally smiling into the rearview mirror. "Habla español muy bien."

She smiles back, but the good feeling evaporates as soon as he guns the motor. The roads are bad here. Even a short ride feels reckless, all the more so in a tiny, half-open vehicle like this one.

She hasn't been here one full day and she's already doing what Jules would have done. What she *did*, allegedly. Rose is ignoring local safety advice, wandering around town and well beyond it, alone. That old man almost got run over; the same thing could happen to her if she keeps wandering around with her head in the clouds.

Also, she's carrying too much cash. She feels for the bills in her pocket, the maximum quetzales she was able to withdraw.

She was supposed to leave it in her locked cabin room, not travel with it on her person. Stupid.

Rose imagines Jules's voice: *It's okay. Jeez. Really.*

But it doesn't feel okay.

The driver is watching her intently, instead of the road. He revs the engine faster.

After the first bend, the paving ends and the road disintegrates into a rutted track. Rose grabs hold of a silver pole attaching the seat to a sort of metal canopy. It looks like a vehicle from an amusement park. The tuk-tuk's wheels bite into gravel, throwing up clouds of gray dust. It's so thick she can no longer see the driver's eyes in the mirror.

There's a reason Rose never liked traveling to out-of-the-way places, and it's partly this: the feeling of having no control, of not even knowing when to be afraid. Before, she didn't want to imagine every specific risk Jules was taking when she traveled. Now she has no choice but to imagine them, to see around every corner the way someone could get hurt.

6

JULES

"I never had a mentor," Eva tells me after I've made the embarrassing little video, which she doesn't review. She seemed happy just to watch me make it—camera panning slowly across the book cover and the view, talking about what her book meant to me.

I'm all nerves, trying not to ask too many questions as I fumble with my phone and her laptop, getting the video transferred and posted as she observes, making use of autofill passwords and knowing I'll have to get my own Mac up and running with all these accounts ASAP, because Eva is already talking about what she'd like me to do today: catch up on the week of email, do a PayPal transfer but only after I talk to someone named Barbara, talk to the hotel in San Felipe but only after I've talked to someone named Hans, talk to some restaurant manager in Antigua.

"Oh, and with social, don't forget that you're not done once you post. It's the comments that take up the time. If we're not engaging, it's pointless having the content."

"Engaging?"

"Reply to people's comments—not everyone's, just the first, to reward readers who keep me in their notifications.

And don't just 'like' them. Four words or more, so you affect the algorithm. But you probably know all this, at your age."

I don't, actually. "So, you want me to reply to people as . . . myself?"

"You reply as *me*. That's the point. We're turning readers into fans, and fans into superfans."

Of course.

She warns me, furthermore, that the Wi-Fi is only strong in certain places around the house, but even so, the signal is variable, plus it can just plain flicker off for hours.

"Is there anything we can do about that?"

"You mean, like relocate to somewhere that's not Guatemala?" She lets loose a long, pleased honk of laughter.

"Never mind," I say, unable to resist smiling in response. "Right."

"And don't leave anyone hanging. Between the airport and the Antigua hotel and the launch and the cabins, women get nervous. That's why we send them all those instructions." She chuckles again. "If only they would read them!"

Those instructions. (Find them.) *Antigua hotel.* (Which one?) *Launch.* (She must mean the dock at Pana.) *Cabins.* (Must be the ones closest to the San Felipe dock.)

She's treating me as if I've already attended the workshop, as if I will intuitively grasp the schedule and all the possible problems on the horizon. Mundane details like shuttles, allergies and special requests seem to bore her, understandably. She'd much rather talk memoir, which is incredible. When I'm not staring at the hummingbirds and straining to memorize her every word and trying to pinpoint why the coffee is so good—is it cinnamon?—I'm pinching myself.

You did it, Jules. You walked right in and you did it.

Eva sets down her empty coffee glass. She runs a hand through her blond tresses. "But let's talk about your writing," she says, still refusing to sit. "And I'll want to read it of course! All that other stuff will get done, but you came to Lake Atitlán for the same reason everyone does, because it's inspirational."

She wants to read my writing.

I keep trying to keep my expectations in check, to not let my brain get stuck on the "M" word too soon. Because jobs are easy to get. Mentors are something else. And yet, Eva already used the word.

Eva paces, musing about the challenges of memoir and what she wishes someone would have told her when she was only seventeen, trying to figure it out on her own. "Never forget, you're both the author and the narrator of your story. The first is obvious. The second is more complicated."

"Yes," I say, so desperate for something to write on that I've opened to a blank page at the back of my Lonely Planet guidebook and started scribbling notes there.

"And as far as who 'you' the narrator are, which 'you' is that? Speaking from what distance to the event? With how much knowledge? In what voice? I know you've taken some writing classes. This may seem basic."

"Oh, not at all."

"You have a lot of choices as a narrator," she continues. "For example, when to insert reflection. When to show or tell. Most important: what to leave out."

"I can't leave out much," I say, making a weak joke. "I'm only twenty-two. Twenty-three in a week."

She cocks her head. "That book of mine you love. I published it at the age of nineteen. Do you really think I left nothing out?"

Of course I know that.

"We leave almost everything out. That's the secret. Here," she says, finally noticing that I've been writing inside a guidebook. "We give locally handmade journals to the participants on the first full day. Welcome and enjoy." From a stack of fabric-covered books on the bench behind her, she takes a blank journal and puts it in my hands.

"Write it down," she says.

I obey.

Leave almost everything out.

She's right, but I love Eva Marshall most for all the parts she leaves *in*: the things I never would have dared to say out loud, much less write—and not just about sex. She also writes about messy friendships, body insecurity, family problems, the audacity required to become a writer, and the hardest thing of all, how to imagine and construct a life. The one *you* want, not the one other people want to sell you. But I'm making her sound like a self-help author when she isn't that at all. She's a storyteller. And the stories she tells are the ones I need most.

Eva's cell phone rings. She mouths the words "Trish, Miami" and gestures for me to leave, whispering, "We're good for now. Go to the kitchen and introduce yourself to Hans, Barbara and Concha."

And Mauricio, who still doesn't have a clue that I've joined the staff.

I pull closed the French doors between the balcony and her combination bedroom-office, trying not to dawdle in awe. So much luck. So many lessons.

We write to be understood. To tell some form of truth. For the sake of art, we discard nearly everything—just as Eva says.

But then there is the other pile of discards: the things that simply refuse to fit, like what I hear Eva say next.

"Don't tell her you told me," she says to her Miami-based assistant, without lowering her voice. "Just avoid replying and see what she does with that. If she wasn't happy when she was here, she should have told someone on the first day. Anyway, she's stage four. She won't keep following up, trust me."

The comment freezes me in an awkward posture, hands still on the ornate bronze door levers. *Stage four.* As in, cancer. She's talking about some former workshop participant on her deathbed, a woman who wants a refund. But Eva won't give it.

I'm still crouching, absorbing. Maybe the unhappy workshopper was a mean, self-centered pain in the ass. Maybe she has been emailing day after day, driving the entire staff crazy. Just because a stranger has a terminal illness doesn't mean she has a valid complaint.

I look up, through the glass doors, terrified of Eva's reaction to my unintentional eavesdropping, but her relaxed expression makes it clear. She looks directly at me, wrinkling her nose and rolling her eyes. *Some of these people.*

Day one and I'm already an insider. I feel the moment in my body—this feeling of belonging in my blood and bones. I allow myself to imagine what being an insider *means.*

First, there are all the questions I can ask: about structure, about memory, about voice. About reflection and exposition and description and dialogue and revision and self-doubt and self-criticism and a million other things you wish you could ask a successful author you admire.

Next, there are the connections: People you might get a chance to meet. People who might someday be willing to take a look at your work. People who care about the things you care about, like truth, and story and at the very least, paying attention. Loving the world, and believing that it will love you back.

I've spent nearly a year since graduation wondering whether I'm inadequate or was just born into the wrong generation, and things just don't work the way they used to. Like you can't simply travel and observe and take risks and write your way into a career. But look at Eva. Decade after decade, she's done it all, seen it all, and even in her fifties, when people told her not to have a baby, she refused to listen, because she's still the rebel she was as a runaway teen. Her motto might as well be, "Never too early *and* never too late."

I'm vibrating as I leave her bedroom and find my way back downstairs to the kitchen, unable to contain my excitement, hands shaking so much it's hard to type the text to my mom, telling myself I won't get irritated if she doesn't share my excitement. I won't be disappointed when she starts asking about pay, schedules and all the other parts that don't matter, because I know she won't understand. She can't.

This may be just a gig. But it's a life-changing gig.

Mom, I just got the most amazing job with the most amazing person.

7

ROSE

_____

_____

___

It's a relief when the driver brakes just outside the Casa
Eva gate. He waves to a man raking leaves away from the
entrance. They seem to know each other. Everyone in these
lakeside villages must know each other.

The gardener points Rose to a yellow door in the gate,
painted with a green quetzal bird with a tail many times longer
than its body, like it's pulling long streamers behind it, taunting
any creature that might follow. It can't be evolutionarily smart
to have such a long tail. The jungle is full of predators. Beauty,
like truth, costs.

As the tuk-tuk motors away, Rose starts down a narrow
set of natural stone steps, flanked by thick tropical vegetation.
The descending path switchbacks into dark, jungle-like gloom.
She doesn't get far before catching up with the conga line of
women writers ahead of her. Many of them have dressed up in
heels or slippery-bottomed sandals, so they are going slowly,
chattering with nervous excitement. Ahead of them, someone
shrieks as an ankle turns. No one expected a hike.

"This is crazy, isn't it?" says the woman in front of Rose,
smiling over her shoulder. "I feel like we're a long line of sac-
rificial virgins on our way to a volcano."

A voice ahead shouts, "No virgins here!"

As the dozen or so women all inch forward, they murmur appreciatively about the landscaping: dense, flowering bushes and tiny statues—a small golden frog, an alabaster maiden—tucked into rocky niches.

"Hold on," says the woman ahead of Rose, reaching down to take off her shoes. "That's better."

Is there really no easier way in? There must be a separate gate, a driveway for deliveries.

Rose remembers Lindsay's comment, predicting that Eva will make a grand entrance. In fact, what Eva has done is arrange for the participants' own grand entrances: single file, one at a time, as they leave behind the rutted road and enter Eva's lush, magical realm. Even the smells here are different. Back at their cabins, along the road and the lakeshore, everything is dry and mostly scentless, except for a faint chalky smell along the beach. Town itself is clean—a bit of woodsmoke, but mostly nondescript, without the strong smell of overripe fruit and garbage Rose associates with touristy tropical towns. Only on this vegetated path does Rose realize what she's been missing: the smell of rich damp earth. Plants and flowers. Sensuous nectar.

Around a final switchback, the path spills out onto a jewel-green, close-cropped lawn.

And there she is: Eva. At last. Waiting at the bottom, gazing upward with a beatific smile, dressed in diaphanous, floaty layers of blue and green.

She's gorgeous, mom. Fifty-six years old but she looks forty.

Rose registers a mix of envy and admiration, opening herself to the undeniable fact of Eva's beauty. Even the best author photo hasn't caught the freshness of Eva's bronzed face and ash-blond hair, the way a single, longer wavy lock moves every time she turns. Photos certainly don't do justice to her smile.

It looks not just authentic, but reborn with intention each moment, as if Eva really is blessing them with wellness and creativity, making room for every one of them in her heart.

Eva greets each woman and whispers something in her ear. To some, a quick word. To others, something longer. Rose watches as Isobel gets a brief greeting. Scarlett, the young cyclist, bows her head and listens intently while Eva leans into her neck, murmuring. Watching Eva's lips at each woman's ear reminds Rose of how she felt reading Eva's memoir, as if it were just the two of them, author and reader, huddled together, sharing something urgent and intimate. The thought gives Rose a quick chill.

Before each woman moves on, Eva takes a shawl from the arms of an unsmiling Guatemalan girl next to her and drapes the wrap over the writer's shoulders. Scarlett receives an ivory shawl. Lindsay, about five women ahead of Rose, gets a red one.

They are being categorized somehow. Rose suppresses a nervous giggle, thinking of the sorting hat from *Harry Potter*.

Rose wants red, but she knows she isn't red—or innocent white, either. She isn't Lindsay, able to resist giving false praise. She isn't Scarlett, so pure of heart she believed she could bike across the country practically without money, depending on the kindness of strangers.

Rose's heart thrums within her tight chest. She feels queasy. It must be the altitude, all the travel, the anticipation. She's surprised by her own nerves.

Then it's her turn. She shuffles forward, preparing to greet Eva calmly and pleasantly. But Rose can't help it. She lets the bubble of excitement well up inside of her. Beginning to grin, she notices how odd her cheeks feel. She hasn't managed a wide, spontaneous smile for months.

"Welcome," Eva says. "And you are . . . ?"

Eva's eyes are green, the eyelids at the corners slightly heavy. Her forehead, close up, is finely lined. These minor imperfections only make her look more natural, more approachable.

"Rose. From Chicago."

Eva's smile vanishes, a lightning-quick shift that makes Rose hold her breath. Does Eva know who she is?

Rose banishes the thought. There's no way for Eva to know; since she refused to schedule a call, she's never heard Rose's voice. If Eva suspected, she wouldn't have let her register. Matt was right—Eva knows that death is bad for business. Eva helped the police, but they never had reason to step onto her property.

Eva's expression has softened, but she's still studying Rose. She leans forward, taking both of her hands, lips close to her ear. "You needed to be here, and we needed you."

Rose freezes, still feeling Eva's breath on her neck as she continues: "You have a long way to go. But that's all right. The journey starts today."

Rose closes her eyes.

You needed to be here.

We needed you.

The words are a rope lowered down a deep well.

Rose feels the warmth of the shawl being draped over her shoulders. Then Eva does something she hasn't done to anyone else in the line. She clasps Rose in a full embrace. When Rose opens her eyes again, Eva smiles and winks. "You need more hugs, honey. Now go grab a glass of wine."

Rose nods, dumbstruck, then steps forward, getting her bearings. The wide lawn is situated on a low bluff overlooking the lake, with a stone-walled two-story house to one side. The entire property is lit up like a wedding. Strings of fairy lights glimmer between the trees. Candles in hurricane lanterns flicker on linen-covered tables, next to vase after vase of birds-of-paradise and stalks of wild ginger.

At the back of the yard, Guatemalan cooks with wooden paddles tend artisanal pizzas baking in two enormous stone ovens. Young local women circle with large trays of appetizers, including prosciutto-wrapped melon and the biggest, reddest prawns that Rose has ever seen. They look like small lobsters.

Everything smells divine. Rose realizes that aside from a bite of breadstick, she hasn't eaten since breakfast. She hasn't wanted to eat for as long as she can remember. Suddenly, she's famished.

In the distance, the volcanoes are dim gray silhouettes against a royal blue sky. The black lake glimmers, reflecting the evening's first stars and the blaze of lights from Eva's lawn. Just over the bluff, a pier juts into the lake, nearly obscured by the bluff's shadow, with one lone rowboat tied alongside.

Rose heads toward the bar table, on the patio. "Cabernet. I mean, vino tinto. Whatever you've got. Gracias."

Still disoriented from her twenty seconds with Eva, she looks down to see what color shawl she was given. Green. It must mean something. She's an inexperienced writer. She's a jealous person. She's desperate for growth and renewal. All of it's true. From Rose's short writing sample or from something else—intuition—Eva knew.

Everything here seems to mean something. Every moment feels saturated, purposeful—the very opposite of the last three months, when life seemed random and cruel.

You needed to be here. We needed you.

This is a safe space—perhaps even a sacred space, given how many difficult stories women share here. No wonder Eva didn't want police crawling all over. The boundaries make sense only once you've seen Casa Eva firsthand.

Matt won't get it, Rose realizes. But that's okay. He doesn't have to get it. He always had his own way to deal with what happened. She was the one with nothing.

A woman standing next to Rose requests a sauvignon blanc. It's Pippa, the British woman who had no qualms sharing the details of her terminal brain cancer on the shuttle bus.

"She hugged me," Rose says to Pippa. "Eva, I mean. She didn't hug everyone."

"Darling, she knew you needed it. I could tell that just standing behind you. You were trembling."

"I got green. You got . . . ?"

"I got black."

Pippa laughs in response to Rose's look of shock. "It doesn't stain. That's the color I requested! On the form, remember? She asked our favorite colors."

"Oh. Right."

The logic drains the moment of its full import, but a sense of kismet lingers.

Rose gulps her wine, turns to the petite Guatemala bartender and asks for the glass to be topped up. Then she looks out at the sea of shawls on the lawn, searching for Eva. "I need to talk to her. I have some questions."

Pippa touches the scarf wrapped around her stubbly black hair. "Oh, dear. I think the serious writing talk starts tomorrow. And if it's a house tour you want, I already asked. Not tonight. But the bathrooms are all inside, so every time you have to go, you can take a little peek. I love her folk art collection."

Rose is still studying the crowd, trying to decide what to do next. She doesn't want to give away her identity. She doesn't want to trigger Eva's defenses or do anything to wreck this beautiful party. She just wants to absorb her presence—her strength and her clarity.

"I just want a few minutes of Eva's time."

"All these women want the same thing," Pippa says. "You

should try tomorrow morning, ahead of the workshop stragglers. But enough about Eva. Tell me the truth. How do I look?"

Pippa is wearing loose Thai pants printed with elephants. Underneath the shawl, a bright blue sequined top winks in the light. Large hoops dangle from stretched earlobes. Black stitches are visible above one of Pippa's ears, through the stubble half-covered by a scarf.

"You look spectacular. Definitely colorful, aside from the shawl."

Pippa laughs. "My children would hate this outfit. That's why I wore it tonight. Anyway, I've never been good at cocktail parties."

"Me neither."

"But it's different here, don't you think? There's no small talk. You walk up to a woman and she says, 'I was raped in the army.' You walk up to the next one: 'I lost every cent in the last financial crash and tried to kill myself.' It's kind of refreshing."

And kind of exhausting. Rose thinks of the stories she already heard on the bus and glimpsed in the writers' submitted pages. That was only a preview. But she can't keep trying to close her heart to others' tragedies. It's why they're all here.

"Except for you," Pippa adds. "You're not writing anything like that. You seem to have led a charmed life." They are halfway across the lawn, each carrying a skewer that was handed to them by a passing waitress. The comment stops Rose in her tracks. "You're a lucky woman, if the worst thing you could write about was the time your sister stopped talking to you."

Rose winces. She'd tried writing about her divorce, but it was just as bland. Not enough conflict. No scandal. Obviously, she wasn't going to write about the last three months—not for this workshop, not ever. Writing about Jules would be like stepping off a cliff. She isn't that brave.

"I'm not much of a writer," Rose says. "There's my confession."

Pippa takes a bite of shrimp and rolls her eyes with pleasure. "I think you have other confessions—"

"I'm really boring," Rose insists. "And lucky, like you said."

"I think you're just dipping your toe in the shallows, to make sure it's safe, first."

Rose doesn't know how to respond. But you don't have to tell people very much, she is discovering. Most people, even the kind ones, are lost in their own stories.

When dinner is served, Eva sits at the table farthest from Rose's. Stuffed on the first courses, Rose nonetheless manages to plunge her fork into a Guatemalan stewed chicken entrée with green sauce and pumpkin seeds, delivered in an individual, lidded ceramic dish, as well as rice and tortillas and a side salad, all produced in a flourish by the big bald chef named Hans and his half dozen assistants, most of them women in traditional huipil blouses and skirts.

More wine appears, not without a little finagling. Officially, the bar has closed, but new bottles are coaxed out of the kitchen by Isobel, badgering the staff, sliding them folded cash, making them giggle. Rose's bits of Spanish help, but it's Isobel's fluent, native Spanish that really opens the doors.

With the additional booze come more speeches. An alumna rises to talk about her memoir, recently accepted for publication by HarperCollins and optioned for a television series. Cheers, whistles, hoots. *You rock, sister! Hit it out of the park! Fucking awesome!*

Less predictable is the next speech from a different alum who has attended many times but never managed to publish her manuscript. The woman, whose name is Sam, explains that she started coming here five years ago, when she was a mess. She thought writing a memoir would heal her. It didn't. She thought her memoir would be published and praised. It wasn't.

"I wanted my book to prove that I had emerged unscathed. I wanted Eva and every woman in my group to see me as a heroine. But Eva finally showed me. I was broken. I still *am* broken."

Everyone stands stock-still on the lawn, clutching the stems of half-empty wineglasses.

"Eva loved me for who I am as soon as I got here," Sam says, "even before she read my pages. 'Sometimes it's easier when you come to Casa Eva with no pages at all!'"

A few women share a knowing laugh, quieting as Sam continues. "For years I couldn't write anything worth reading because I kept focusing on the perfect thing I wanted to be, or on the mess that I was, and I couldn't find a way to describe that other thing . . ."

Here, she trails off, and Rose is confused. Dizzy, also. Definitely drunk. *What other thing?*

Sam clears her throat and manages to finish, "A still-broken, beautiful thing. Cracks and all."

Eva wraps her arms around Sam, who seems more beloved even than the writer with a publishing contract, as if the fact of her failure—and her acceptance of that failure—makes her the biggest success of all. The two of them sway in a continuing embrace as Eva shouts, "Cracks and all!"

It seems to be an anthem, because the alumnae know to shout back, "Cracks and all!"

"One more time," Eva says, raising a glass. "Broken but beautiful."

Rose is confused. *But . . . still broken?* Complete healing is a lie, in a sense. That's what her gut tells her, too. She will never fill the hole left by Jules. She doesn't want to.

Maybe Eva means that you can heal and yet still be scarred, and you will fail at first but eventually succeed, or you will succeed because you have failed, or something that is just beyond Rose's ability to absorb. Maybe all of them will become the broken, beautiful things they were always meant to be if they only listen and pay good attention and . . . that's the problem. Rose is having a hard time paying attention. Her glass is empty. She wants more wine.

"I didn't hear you," Eva shouts.

All the women call back, "Cracks and all!"

Rose tears up, knowing that she would probably tear up no matter what they were saying. It's not the words so much as the energy of the group itself: women, united in a quest of self-knowledge and self-actualization (if people still use that word), embracing their flaws and espousing confidence in some hopeful, forward-moving effort.

Rose doesn't go to football games and she hasn't attended church in over twenty years, but she knows why other people do. There's something special about those places where defeats create cohesion as much as victories; where the bitter is accepted alongside the sweet.

She has felt superior, at times, for turning away from pop culture, religion and any kind of groupthink. But she stopped feeling superior as soon as Jules went missing. She recognized the emptiness of her superior attitude and the deep, unsolvable problem of her introverted nature. It's one thing to survive in the normal day-to-day world; another to survive when tragedy strikes. That's when you realize you have nothing. Your vague sense of intellectual superiority will not save you. Your refusal to believe in the tribe's big stories—*Who is God? Why are we here?*—will only condemn you to emotional paralysis and existential purgatory.

Once the speeches finish, the servers distribute desserts, but everyone is so full and tipsy that many small plates are left untouched. Rose retains an image of chocolate cake crumbs scattered across the tables and her own silver fork dropping into the dark, thick grass. She intends to pick it up, but instead she only stares at the sharp tines glinting beneath the fairy lights, too dizzy to bend over.

Sometime later, she finds herself talking to a tall, slim woman named K, the only one of them who has dared to wear jeans, paired with a sleeveless mock turtleneck that shows off her fit arms, honed by early years spent boxing and wrestling. She's the only Black person at the workshop, as she herself mentions, not surprised. "I knew there'd be a bunch of Liz Gilbert and Cheryl Strayed types here, but this is crazy. What is it about upper-middle-class blond women and memoirs?"

Rose doesn't bother to point out that Isobel is Mexican-American and a young woman named Noelani is Hawaiian and her own hair is shoe-polish brown, not blond, because she gets it. There is, indeed, a *type*.

In addition to being the daughter of a famous Chicago coach, K is a well-known stand-up comic, evidently. They have withdrawn to one side of the lawn, with the silvery-black lake sparkling below them, when Scarlett walks past. She does a double-take. "Is that really K-Tap?"

Rose has never heard of K-Tap.

Scarlett says, "You've *seriously* never heard of her? The new Chris Rock? But female and queer?"

"I'm sorry," Rose says. "I haven't been to a comedy club in fifteen years."

"Works for me," K says. "I don't need stalkers here."

After Scarlett walks away, Rose presses K to explain more.

That's when K confides that she is waiting to hear back about a Netflix special, hoping for it, worried it isn't going to happen, and her agent told her exactly why. Because she is good at making people laugh but she doesn't know how to make them cry, and that's what long-form stand-up needs now: a full arc, ups and downs and unexpected twists and turns, with a "dark night of the soul moment" around minute forty.

"I'm too 'one-note' my agent says. Drunk people in a club want to laugh till their stomachs hurt. People watching long-form comedy want laughs plus Greek tragedy and a Mozart sonata on top of it."

The same agent, a friend of Eva Marshall's agent, wants K to finish the damn memoir, the one she's already gotten an advance for.

"If Eva can help me find the sad, emotional pieces, I'll do anything for her."

"Anything?"

"Give her a kidney, at least," K says. "Naw, that's too common. Maybe a lobe of my liver. You know you can lose a piece and it grows back? I just read that in a science magazine. I wonder if Eva would accept my liver."

She goes quiet for a moment, smiling to herself, and Rose gets the idea this is how someone like K works. Think of something absurd and try to turn it into a story. Experiment, exaggerate, discard. But that's not how memoir works, right? Rose is still figuring that out. Memoir is about hard truths. Invent or inflate too much, and readers will know. It must be hard to be a comic and memoirist, simultaneously.

"Anyway," K continues, "that part about Netflix isn't for public consumption. I don't want to read that in a tweet two days from now."

"Lips are sealed. By the way, what does the K in K-Tap stand for?"

"Wouldn't you like to know."

Rose laughs. "Yes, but I don't *need* to know."

K nods. "I like you already."

They both seem to be enjoying standing comfortably just where they are, on the edge of the party, toes planted in the thick grass. Oh, it has been so very long for Rose. A party of strangers, without the feeling of being miserable, with no yearning to be back home, no sense of time at all.

Somehow, conversation turns to what they have in common, in addition to an agreement that Hannah Gadsby's "Nanette" is incredible and where to find the best pancakes in Chicago-land. Walker Brothers, obviously.

K faces her. "You're not from Chicago. Why do you keep telling everybody that?"

"North Side."

"Bullshit. Every place you talk about is Davis Street this and Green Bay Road that. Why don't you just say you live in Evanston." K grins. "Or is it worse? You're hoity-toity. You live in *Wilmette.* Or kill me: you live in Kenilworth. That's what you don't want anyone to know. Own up, Miss Richie Rich."

Rose feels her momentary sense of calm evaporate. She'd thought her plan to hide in the background was solid. Not only because she used her maiden name, but also because her face never appeared in the major newspaper coverage of Jules's disappearance. The *Chicago Tribune* reporter had misidentified Ulyana as Jules's mom in a prominent photo that spread to other papers before it could be corrected.

Yet it had taken K only minutes to figure out Rose is a North Shore suburbanite. If she could start over, she wouldn't mention Chicago either—too close. But then again, didn't the best liars embrace partial truths? A famous quote floats into Rose's head: *If you wish to preserve your secret, wrap it up in frankness.*

"Was the shrimp not fresh?" K asks.

"Sorry?"

"You look queasy all of a sudden."

"Tipsy more than queasy," Rose says, searching for a compromise between truth and fiction. "Let's just say I'm far from rich but I do live in Evanston. Don't tell, just like I won't say a word about Netflix. It matters, trust me. I'm not trying to pretend I'm someone else. I'm just . . . lying low."

With K, there is none of the hugging or hand clasping she has experienced with other women that night. K just turns and gives her a look.

"Lying low. That I understand."

8

ROSE

———————————
———————————
———

Rose sits upright, gasping in the dark, no idea where she is, only where she *was*: in the water. The deep, black water. She couldn't breathe. Couldn't touch bottom. Something was pulling her down. Glimmer of the moon receding, overhead. Body cold. Esophagus aching. Lungs filling until the pressure became unbearable, and yet she couldn't scream.

She grips the scratchy woven blanket. The mattress under her back is thin. She hears drumming and drunken, happy shouts somewhere far away. Outside the cabin, on the beach. Lake Atitlán. In Guatemala. She's actually here.

At home, she would turn on the bedside lamp, go to the kitchen, flood the entire house with lights. Wish the recurring nightmare away, as she has for the past three months.

But here, she's in a rustic cabin with a sleeping roommate. And there's another problem. Her tongue is dry and sticky. A yeasty smell emanates from her pores. She licks her parched lips and only feels woozier.

"Chicago," comes a woman's voice from across the dark room. "Water bottle is where you left it, next to your pants."

Rose reaches down, toward the floor next to her twin bed. In search of the plastic bottle, her fingers brush against damp cloth. *Wet.* Her capris are soaking wet. Next to them is the soft mound of her shawl, damp at the edges.

Oh shit. The party. Way too much wine. At some point, sparklers were handed out. Anyone who hadn't yet slipped off her shoes finally took them off.

The next hour evaporated. Then it was midnight. Ana Sofía, Chef Hans and a few other staff members herded the thirty-some party attendees down to the dock, where two water taxis had arrived to take them back to their cabins. The party had to shut down so they could all get up and meet for workshop in the morning, but not before a noisy argument erupted.

The spark came from Rose's disagreement not with Ana Sofía or Hans but a third member of the staff—a huge woman, tall and wide, arms folded over her chest, like a bar bouncer.

Barbara. That was her name.

It's too late for tuk-tuks, Barbara insisted, *and you're not walking back. Everyone's going by boat.*

Rose refused. The night sky was a threatening, spiky shimmer. An excess of stars. All those pinpricks of light, doubled in the mirrored surface of the lake, were messing with her head. She wanted nothing to do with boarding any boat. She wanted nothing to do with this horrible lake at night. Then something happened: a misstep, a wobble, and Rose fell off the pier and into the shallows. Only her bottom half got wet.

Now, Rose finds the bottle of water, sucks down as much as she can tolerate, remembering only light bulb flashes of what came next. Barbara, barking orders. Other women, the participants, trying to be helpful.

Another flash: Pippa tugging at her waistband, one foot lifted, trying to step out of her Thai pants with the adorable elephants. Rose's own pants were wet and she was going to be walking the road, whereas Pippa was only going for a five-minute boat ride, therefore Rose needed them more, according to Pippa. Drinkers' logic.

Rose remembers Pippa talking about her underwear, in her plummy English accent. *They're so pretty. But who sees them? My husband insists on keeping the lights off, such a waste.*

Until someone—Barbara again, bellowing—stopped Pippa from undressing.

Dear Pippa. Even when the search for Jules's body was at its most intense and Rose was at her most sleep-deprived, anxious worst, no friend had been that outrageously kind. No one had offered to pull off his or her pants on the spot and hand them to Rose, saying, *This might cheer you up for thirty seconds. Good for a laugh.*

"Chicago," the voice says again. "You going to be okay?"

"I've gotta go to the bathroom."

"Gonna be sick?"

"No, I just really have to pee."

"Flashlight's at the top of the ladder, where we left it."

From outside the cabin comes a relentless bongo rhythm.

"Did I wake you?" Rose says, remembering now who that voice belongs to. It's her third roommate, K.

"I was already up. Damn drumming."

"It's making my head pound," Rose agrees.

Her head would be pounding even without the drums, of course. The shame floods her now. Both what she did—drank too much, didn't keep track, didn't eat enough somehow even though she had been starving, didn't keep alternating with water no matter how often Pippa reminded her. Then the fuss she made, refusing the boat ride. Then: whatever came next.

The larger shame, the paralyzing shame, is that she can't remember. Bad enough when it was Ambien, and only days after Jules went missing—a justifiable loss of sanity. This time it was simple alcohol. At a party. She was actually enjoying herself, sort of. That realization leads to another, more complicated sort of shame.

Some part of her brain must have kept functioning, though, no matter how much she drank. Her shawl may be damp, but she didn't leave it behind. Rose can feel it now, the weight of it over her shoulders, trying not to weave as she turns away from the departing water taxi, one hand reaching for the staircase rail, the other patting herself—*does she have everything she came with?*

Her eyes widen in the dark, a spike of panic forcing her to sit upright. She reaches for the floor again. *Her bag.* The one she'd taken to the pizzeria, filled not only with her various writing supplies and retreat printouts, but also the notebook stuffed with culled information about Eva, her staff, Guatemalan crime, Jules's messages. She'd meant to leave all that back at the cabin, but she'd never come back to the cabin before proceeding to the party.

Stupid stupid stupid.

"K," she whisper-shouts, hoarsely. "Did you see my bag anywhere?"

"Like a purse?"

Rose can see it like a glowing X-ray: the pasted printout of Eva's police statement. What would a fellow workshopper think? What would Barbara, Chef Hans or Eva herself think?

"No, like a shoulder bag. Royal blue. Papers and notebooks and an e-reader inside. I think I left it at the party."

Maybe it's sitting in the grass, under a table, in the dark. She can get there before dawn. She can retrieve it somehow.

"Oh yeah," K laughs. "*That* bag. You were clutching it to your chest like a baby."

"Yes?"

"Yeah. It's downstairs."

Rose feels sick with relief. Bringing a shaking hand to her

forehead, she notices how clammy it is. If she moves too quickly, she'll get the spins.

"How did I get home?"

"It wasn't bad. No cars. Bats overhead. You wobbled. But we got here."

"You walked with me. Thank you."

"I *insisted*. I didn't like how that woman was talking to you."

"Eva?"

"She was in the house and missed the whole thing. It was the other woman. The big one."

Now she remembers K making her own fuss, saying to Barbara, *I live on Chicago's South Side. I'm not afraid of walking a mile on a road without traffic. Give me a fucking break. Don't tell a grown woman what she can't do. Stand aside, Frankenstein.*

So that wasn't just a mean, silent thought. K had called Barbara "Frankenstein."

"But it was Lindsay who got you all the way to your cabin," K says. "The last quarter mile through town, I had to pee so bad I took off."

Rose tries to dig up a memory of walking with K—then K running ahead to pee—and Lindsay sticking with her for the final drunken ramble. Her mind is a blank. A complete, blackout void, of the type she hasn't experienced since college.

"Oh, god," is all Rose can say, horrified by her amnesia.

"It's fine. I mean, you were crying, but it was fine."

Crying? It couldn't get any worse. She just hopes she wasn't talking.

Hours later, Rose still can't sleep. It's nearly dawn but the drums are still going.

Outside the cabin, pulling the door shut carefully so she

doesn't wake her downstairs roommates, Rose wishes she'd brought a jacket. She keeps forgetting that Lake Atitlán is high altitude—dry and often cool, not steamy hot.

Most of the stars are obscured by a high veil of thin clouds, but every now and again, the moon becomes visible, sending its light down to the lake, making it shimmer. Farther out, in the middle of the lake, there's one ribbon of water that's glassier than the rest. Maybe that's a current of warmer water, Rose thinks, breathing heavily as she barely catches herself from falling a second time.

She hops from the last of the big rocks to a flatter area of dry pebbles just a little larger than beans. Grubby black beans. A beautiful sand beach, this is not.

She postholes with effort, keeping her eyes fixed on the bonfire ahead, far down the beach. Shadows move. The bongo drums get louder, the flames brighter as she approaches. A loud pop, and sparks climb into the sky.

Now, she can smell pot. Voices rise above the drumming, blending at first, then breaking into the tinkle and squeal of a girl laughing and two boys talking over each other, in good spirits. One pushes the other and he staggers sideways, opening a gap in the bodies around the fire.

"Hey," a person says as Rose reaches the edge of the circle, hands in her sweatpants pockets.

"Hey."

Approaching from behind, she mistook him at first for an older woman, due to the thin, gray braid down his back. Rose studies the glowing orange faces, lit up by the fire. Except for this man, they all look to be in their twenties, light haired and light skinned. A scrawny white guy with dreadlocks is pounding the biggest bongo drum. He's got big, spiral-shaped horn earrings in his stretched-out earlobes.

Rose moves her chin with the rhythm, inventing a story

in her head. She can pretend she's a solo backpacker. Gray Braid here, he doesn't need sleep; why should she? She loves drumming, tribal tattoos and ear gauges. Loves mixing with strangers and inhaling their patchouli. God, has nothing changed since she was in college, with a roommate who bathed in the stuff?

"Have some?" Gray Braid passes her a joint.

"Okay. Sure."

He sways, bumping hips with her. Shit, he thinks she approached him on purpose. They're the only ones over forty here. His eyes are closed and he's whipping his thin braid, the end woven with a bead and a black feather. Several times, the bead strikes her lower back.

Mom, you're uptight.

Yes, I am, Jules. Just a little.

She's startled when one of the younger men opposite her lifts his arms, screeches and sprints for the water's edge.

Heads swivel. One of the drummers loses the rhythm, finds it again, repairing the beat.

Then a girl breaks the circle. She dashes to the edge of the lake, chatters like a monkey, flings her bikini top in the air and dives into the water. Others follow, shedding clothes as they race.

"Well, damn," Gray Braid says.

Rose, ever the mother and field trip volunteer, counts them as they go: one-two-three-four-five-six. With the first two, that makes eight in the water.

Which of these young people is smart enough to be traveling with a friend? Who will be missed in the morning, if they don't show up at breakfast? *Be safe. Come back to shore. Think of the people who will miss you.*

There, a flicker of white and another squeal before she sees gray outlines rising from the shallows, walking back to dry land. The water is cold. The moon is not yet full, its most enticing phase. Half of the group is returning but there will always be one who, in search of solitude or some kind of thrill, wants to see just how far she can go.

Back at the fire circle, a guy and a girl plop down on the pebbles and fall onto their backs, intertwining their closest legs. One young man lifts a can of beer to his lips and stares into the bonfire, eyes so big and round that Rose can see his dilated pupils even at this distance. He's clean cut, wearing a pale yellow oxford shirt, rolled at the elbows, jeans and the kind of white-bottomed deck shoes that Rose associates with sailing. He drops his empty can, steps closer to the fire, passing both palms over the leaping flame.

Rose keeps watching, wondering if he can feel the heat, wondering what drug he's on—wondering, also, how many of the people swimming in the dark are tipsy, stoned or just bad at swimming.

Accidents happen.

Especially in places like this: beaches. The dark. Drugs and alcohol. It's a simple story. Why must Rose make it needlessly complex?

The sky is beginning to lighten when Rose sits down on the gravelly beach next to Gray Braid, whose real name is Dennis. It doesn't take long to get his story. He lives in San Felipe nearly year-round.

"Retired?" she asks.

"More or less. Studio guitarist. You?"

"Writer," Rose says, trying the lie on for size.

"Fiction? Nonfiction?"

Rose panics, needing to choose. "Fiction. Nothing high-brow. Just your basic paperback thriller."

Dennis asks, "Would I know anything you wrote?"

"Probably not. I mean, you can't blame a midlist author

given this whole stupid blockbuster culture." Rose is channeling Jules, repeating one of her rants almost verbatim.

"Hey," Rose says, as if the segue makes sense and glad that it doesn't have to. Dennis is stoned. She's possibly still half-drunk. "Can I show you a photo?"

She swipes to a photo of Jules, from home. It shows her face in full, well-lit focus. "Do you recognize this girl?"

He pushes a long piece of hair out of his eyes. "Oh, yeah."

Adrenaline jolts Rose from her pre-dawn mental fog. "Yeah? You're sure?"

"She hung out at the beach parties. I saw her at least twice. Nice girl. We talked about hiking trails. Spoke Spanish, too."

"Did you see her go swimming with the other kids?"

"Nah," he said. "She kept her clothes on. Said she didn't like to swim."

"Did she . . . you know. Party?"

"Take drugs? I never saw that. She came, drank a beer with an arm hooked around the waist of her boyfriend the whole time."

Boyfriend.

"A young German guy named Luka?"

"Definitely not. A Guatemalan guy."

"Drug dealer? A little guy named Paco something?"

Here, at last, Dennis squints and shifts. "You're asking about Paco? The little guy missing all his bottom front teeth, with the big swallow tattoo on his neck? That guy?"

Rose has never seen a photo of Paco. She just knows what the police told Matt—that he was local scum, now rotting in some capital jail cell.

"Yeah, that guy," Rose says. "I think."

"Last time I saw little Paco Marroquín, he was leaving town on a really nice motorcycle, with a new jacket."

"I heard he was arrested."

Dennis scoffs. "Nicest 'arrest' I've ever seen. Going away party, I'd call it."

She resists the urge to ask why the police would do that—let someone leave. Possibly even give them money to do so.

"Maybe his family gave him the money, and the party."

Dennis laughs. "Only the gringos here have that kind of money to throw around."

Rose shakes her head. "But you mentioned this girl *did* have a boyfriend? So, you're sure he wasn't Paco. You're also sure he wasn't German?"

"Definitely Guatemalan. Nice kid, just like her. Clean, polite. Didn't swim. Didn't even take off his shirt. Drank one beer and then took off. Speaking of . . ."

He pulls a can of unopened beer from a woven shoulder bag and holds it up for Rose. She shakes her head.

"You're sure he took off with the girl."

"Yeah, the two of them. They didn't hang out for very long. The girl said she had an early morning job she had to get to. I remember that for sure, because most of these college students are here on vacation, and the ones who aren't tend to move in and refuse to leave, hanging around for months at a time, trying to get by on diets of brown rice, avocado and beer. But *that* girl—I never saw her again."

"You're sure." She leans closer, wanting to see eye to eye, even if his are bloodshot.

"I'm sure."

9

JULES

M auricio's face is stony as he unpacks loads of groceries transported from San Felipe and San Marcos, a neighboring village.

I whisper to him. "¿Qué pasa?¿Qué tienes?"

Cans of tomato sauce, onto the shelf. *Thunk, thunk.* Industrial-size can of pozole. *Thunk.*

I try again. "What's wrong?"

It's not about me working for Eva. We settled that yesterday, and quickly, when Mauricio found out I got the job and would be moving into a cottage with Gaby and Mercedes, just across the yard from the guest cottage he shares with Eduardo, the head gardener.

Mauricio's a practical guy. His surprise quickly mellowed to cautious acceptance. It's better for both of us if no one knows we are anything other than coworkers. In fact, secrecy adds spice. And yet today, he is cranky at the whole world.

"El orfanato," he mumbles, head still stuck in a cupboard.

So that's it. He's indignant about the three boxes of running shoes, collected from the last round of workshop participants, that he wanted to deliver to the orphanage before the other errands. Eva said there wasn't time before the guests' arrival. The priority is transporting food in, garbage out.

The shoes have been sitting around forever. The new group of writers will arrive and bring yet more shoes and clothes. What's the point, if they get pushed into a garden shed because the staff is too busy to deliver them? I know what Eva's answer will be: cash matters more. She keeps collecting clothing because it makes the workshop participants feel good, but handing over a few hundred dollars every few months would be much more efficient. With apologies to Mauricio, Eva's view makes practical sense.

While he continues slamming cans around, Chef Hans and Barbara are going over printouts of emails. During moments like these, I remember that Mauricio is three years younger than me, which is fun when you're out dancing or hanging out, and less fun when you're working side by side. I'm glad I haven't raved about him to anyone yet, least of all Mom, who would want to prove her open-mindedness by acting happy that I'm having *aventuras*, in both senses of the word. If I never see Mauricio again, post-Atitlán, there'll be no reason for anyone to hear about our fling.

Hans reads aloud while Barbara, Eva's accountant and house manager, makes notes on a steno pad: "Kosher, one; celiac, one; vegan, two; 'Shrimp give me hives,' one."

I chuckle. "So just don't eat them, right?"

Hans wipes his thick fingers on his apron. He looks at me, and I look down at his black Crocs, the biggest shoes I've ever seen on a human being. "Food allergies are serious."

"No, of course. You're right."

Hans ran kitchens in Ibiza (the raves must have been brutal) and opened his own restaurant in Los Angeles, but it went out of business. Then he spent some downtime in prison—"a ridiculous trumped-up charge," Eva assured me. That's where she met him, at a one-time prison workshop on the Power of Story as Liberation. Now Eva flies Hans into Guatemala four times a year for the workshop gig.

"Hey, Barbara," I say. "Eva wanted me to make a video of you for the socials. Congrats on your memoir coming out soon, by the way."

Barbara looks up from her steno pad. She has a square-shaped head, capped by thinning mouse-brown hair. Scowling puppet lines connect her nose to her chin.

"I mean . . . you must be really excited," I say. "What's it about?"

Barbara turns her steno pad around, so it's pressed against her chest. She sighs. "My husband was an asshole."

That can't be enough for a memoir. I keep waiting.

Barbara looks at Hans with a hangdog expression and then back at me, as if she has no choice to explain.

"When I came to Lake Atitlán with about thirty shitty pages, I said to myself, 'Barbara, you tell the truth about what this asshole did and if you can't finish, the lake's right there.' It's cold, it's deep, it'll do the job."

Hans snorts. I can't tell if they're both pulling my leg now. But then I look at Barbara's miserable face. She isn't joking.

"He took my money, my health and my dignity," Barbara continues in the same relentless monotone. "I'm a quadruple survivor. First, abusive infidelity. Then breast cancer. Then HIV. Then bankruptcy. All from him. Not the cancer, unless you assume the cancer came from the stress. But definitely the rest of it."

I should have been getting this story outside with the video running, because I doubt she'll be willing to repeat herself.

"I'm sorry. So, Eva taught you how to write about all that."

"Not at first. First, Eva taught me how to breathe. How to take a shower and remember to eat, to sleep. Then she gave me a job. Then when I was halfway sane again, she looked at my pages and said, 'This isn't it. Start over.'"

Hans is tapping his big Croc, waiting for our chat to wrap up so that he and Barbara can resume dietary planning.

"That must have been hard," I say.

"Someone telling me my pages were shit? Hard? No. At least she was reading what I'd written. That's more respect than I'd ever gotten before."

I offer a tentative smile. "That's quite a story. It would make a good Instagram Reel."

"No." Her expression hasn't changed once. She's not going to humor me. "You can find other people who will say the same about Eva, because that's the sort of person she is. She saves lives. Right, Hans?"

"Yep," he says. Also without a smile.

"Now get someone more photogenic than either of us to say it."

Barbara turns away to open a cupboard.

Okay.

My eyebrows are stuck high on my face, my eyes wide. For no particular reason I walk with soft steps as I depart the kitchen. I'd do a horrible job of explaining Barbara to internet strangers. Yes, she sucks all the air out of a room. But there's a certain appeal in someone who won't play the social media game and has given up on charisma, entirely. I think she might write honestly. I'd be willing to give her memoir a chance.

Unfortunately, I need to bother Eva again, because late work-shop payments are coming in and I'm not sure whether to reply to the folks who have paid or only the ones who haven't, or just turn to the backed-up emails in which people are asking once again about weather, crime and currency rates. (*Google is your friend, ladies.*) And then there's always the social media, which is like a baby who wakes up every two hours, needing to be fed and changed. The more you give it, the more it poops out.

Upstairs, on the balcony off her bedroom, Eva's talking on the phone to her husband, Jonah. She smiles and gestures that I should come and sit on her stone benches, amidst the tropical pillows, hummingbird feeders and magazines—including ones in which Eva has recently appeared, like the O magazine with a magnificent shot of Eva, Oprah and two golden retrievers strolling along the edge of a marshy pond. I try not to stare too long at the photo.

"Yeah, we've got a couple cancer survivors," Eva says to Jonah while pacing, pausing only to pinch the spent blossoms off a potted plant with large, trumpet-shaped flowers.

"Two incest," she continues. "One kidnapping. One 'life-saved-by-Jesus-plus-lots-of-cats.' I don't know how Trish let her in but now that she's coming, we'll deal with it. The usual."

She looks at me and points at the flower, silently mouthing: *Needs more water? Take care of it.*

Meanwhile, Jonah has just said something that makes Eva laugh. "No, honey, there is nothing new under the sun."

She sticks out her tongue playfully, as if to reassure me that none of this is private. I can stay and keep listening.

"How many?" she repeats back to Jonah while looking at me. "Nine?"

I mouth: *Twelve.*

Her brow furrows.

"Twelve writers, I guess. Well, they don't all stay. Maybe Jesus-and-cats will leave after the first day." She crosses her eyes, hamming it up even more, for my benefit. "No, no. The alums are here already as well, but they're not as needy. Only Wendy is signed up as a full workshop participant. Yes, *that* Wendy. No talent, but the lady doesn't quit."

Eva likes the repeat visitors—"alums"—who hang around the margins, like pretty peacocks strolling her lawn, as long as she doesn't need to feed or talk to them too often.

"Are you kidding?" Eva says to Jonah. "That, my beautiful boy, is not my problem."

When she hangs up, I ask, "What's not your problem?"

She falls back onto the bench, fluffing the pillows behind her, though we both know she won't stay seated long.

"Whether any of these memoirs get published."

"Don't you think some will?"

"Maybe one in . . . a hundred?"

"That doesn't sound like much."

"Look at Barbara. She worked on her memoir for nine years but it's finally coming out." Eva throws an arm over my shoulder. She smells like a subtle spice that isn't coriander or star anise, but something close. "Barbara will be ecstatic when her book is published, even if it is a small hybrid press."

"But most women don't get to see their stories in print. That's kind of sad."

"Listen, I don't promise anyone publication."

I think about all the social media posts I've seen, advertising the workshop. Maybe she doesn't promise, but she implies that anyone who does the work, who is honest and open, will ultimately succeed.

Eva says, "I learned a long time ago not to talk about the commerce side of things. That's why I have a different agent come for a Q and A at the end. This session it'll be Marcy. She gets the publishing questions, not me. Speaking of agents, I need to call Richard."

This, I tell myself, is the life anyone would desire, when you have to bounce between calls with your charming husband and your high-powered agent, neither of whom can wait to give you the latest good news.

"Come back in twenty minutes," Eva says. "You can start working on the essay you promised me yesterday. A thousand words? Email it to me tonight."

"Okay—"

"But wait, did you do a video with staff this afternoon?"

The interview I posted three hours ago, with the alum named Wendy, is old news. "Ten seconds of Concha looking wildly uncomfortable. Barbara . . . didn't seem eager to talk on camera."

"Nothing? But she needs to start promoting her book. And she loves to talk about how much she's grown here. Get it done before the day's over."

I reassure Eva that I can do little videos of more alums and staff. But none of it's a substitute. *She's* the one people want to see.

"You're right," she agrees surprisingly quickly. "Let's do a quickie right now. Then I'll call Richard."

Eva needs no time to prepare. She repositions her stool on the balcony, flips her hair, pats each cheekbone to rouse some color and lifts each breast a little higher in its cup.

"I thought I'd ask about how you first got published—"

"No," Eva says, gesturing toward my phone, to let me know I should start filming. "Let's talk about family conflict. *Go.*"

She already knows the questions that people always ask at readings. She launches into the story of how her sister didn't want her to write about their immediate family.

"The last time I spoke to my sister, she handed me my purse and opened the door and said, 'And now, you're probably going to go home and write about this.' And I said, 'Yes. I am. It's my story. It happened to me. You may have been present but so was I, and I own everything that's happened to me, and if you want to write about it also, you have that choice. And if that means you'll never talk to me again, then don't.' And she said, 'But you only have one sister.' And I said, 'That's true. But also, I only have one life.'"

Eva stops talking. She turns sideways, her profile to the camera, the volcanoes behind, so it looks like she's gazing off toward the tropical foliage that edges her yard, musing in a bittersweet way, measuring the cost and the benefit of what she did. Of course, from her essays I already know that Eva would never let anyone stop her from writing something. Not a sibling, parent, spouse or grown child. I also know that my love of her writing began well before people got their top book recs or writing tips from online videos, but sad as it is, the world changes. Ironic that it's a woman more than twice my age who is reminding me of that fact.

"Cut," Eva says. "Take out any pauses so we still get time for the gaze at the end. It's gotta be under thirty."

"That was great," I say, amazed to realize I spent thirty minutes on Wendy and Eva just did a self-interview in thirty-two seconds.

"Over the next two or three days, keep catching the alums when you can. Wendy was okay, but see if you can get anyone . . . less doddering."

"Old, you mean?"

"And don't film anyone who looks clearly unwell."

Most of the frequent alumnae are past retirement age, and quite a few are writing illness memoirs about cancer, strokes or chronic pain.

"We need more . . . *aspirational figures* in our social media feeds."

"But I keep telling you. *You're* the aspirational figure."

She tucks her chin into her neck, lips pursed, as if I've said something wrong. Then she laughs and spreads her arms wide: *ta-da!* "Juliet May, you are *too* much!"

In case I've misinterpreted, she sticks out her tongue again for good measure. Does Joyce Carol Oates ever stick her tongue out? Did Joan Didion ever crack a truly relaxed smile?

"I mean it," I stammer, sounding like an infatuated flunky.

"I know you do." She grows serious again. "You are an honest, authentic person. I knew that the first moment I met you. It's what I love about you."

That word—*love*—makes me feel uncomfortable. Then again, it's just a word. I can be overly literal. Plenty of room-mates and friends have told me so.

Eva's expression softens. She embraces me in a sideways squeeze, nodding toward my phone. "Blogs and photos and endless personal updates—my last memoir wouldn't have been published without all that."

"Really?"

Her voice sinks down into a gravelly, confessional tone. "It used to be enough to write a good memoir. Now you have to prove to the publisher you have readers clamoring before the book is even published. Not just 'liking' your social posts. But locked and loaded, on a private newsletter list, confirmed engagers with good click and conversion rates, prepared to take instructions."

My college writing classes covered none of this. My favorite professor, Rollo Wright, went so far as to say we should be protecting the sacred time in our lives when we could focus on the art of writing itself, rather than sullying our minds with the dirty details of sales and promotion. Only now does it occur to me that his viewpoint was condescending. Also, impractical. Did he think being ignorant would save us in the long run? In fifteen years, Mr. Wright has published only two novels, by the way.

"The point is, Jules, it's essential these days to convince readers to preorder books. From the right places, at the right time. Essential for the bestseller lists? I had fifteen thousand dedicated fans who were ready to preorder *In a Delicate State* before I'd written more than fifty pages."

"They were following your pregnancy as it unfolded," I guess, still trying to cover for my embarrassing lack of publishing knowledge.

"Honey, they saw every ultrasound. And they agonized over every attack of heartburn or hemorrhoids. They knew how I slept and whether I had doubts and . . ."

When she trails off, I worry I've pressured her to discuss something too sensitive.

"I'm sorry. That must have been—"

"It was intense. The immediate bond with readers, and the way that deepened the pain and the sharing of the pain, the grief and the gratitude. All of it. It was a lesson. Like everything. And maybe I burned out on being quite that connected with my readers for a few years. I've been a little more sluggish on the social media front. Jonah and Richard have both warned me I need to keep up."

"But so . . . this . . . feels right?" I'm still not sure why she's so happy with my videography, given that she's been posting and communicating with her public for so long.

"Yes, and it's about time. I spent years taking selfies and doing shaky videos. That seemed charming when it was all new. But at my age, the close-up selfie shot, ugh . . ."

I'm close enough to see the pale veins on her eyelids, the feathery wrinkles forming above her lip. But her green eyes dazzle and her skin glows. Anyone would be thrilled to look so good in her fifties.

"I'm happy to help."

"Only *happy*?" Eva says, crinkling up her eyes. I can't tell if Eva is teasing me for using bland language or testing me in some other way.

"Ecstatic? Flattered? Grateful?"

I'm watching her face, hoping she interrupts me before I get to a really hard letter.

"I love that. And I see you. Your gratitude is refreshing."

Eva leans in for another sideways hug and I try to relax into it. *Accept love. Show gratitude.* And I *am* grateful, of course. Who wouldn't be?

10

ROSE

When Rose wakes after barely two hours of sleep, she knows her first duty is to call Matt. Everything they assumed might be wrong. The drug dealer might have been a nobody paid off to satisfy the Americans that justice had been served, so that Matt wouldn't return for a second session of searching, giving the tourism industry a black eye with all of his "missing person" flyers and high-tech search and rescue gear. Luka, the German backpacker, really might have spent no more than an innocent few hours in Jules's company. Focusing on insignificant people could have given them tunnel vision—and maybe someone wanted it that way. There could be more leads out there.

Like the Guatemalan boyfriend. Jules never hinted she was dating someone. If her daughter could conceal something as important as a boyfriend, what else might she have been concealing?

From downstairs, Isobel calls up, "Coming with us to breakfast?"

"You all go. I need to make a call. Wi-Fi is better here than outside."

Rose descends the ladder in time to see Isobel applying

makeup in a mirror over the kitchen sink. Rose watches Lindsay strap on a pair of sandals, notice a blister at her heel, then take the sandals off and start fishing around in her luggage for a pair of canvas flats.

Go. *Please go. Can't you all get out of here and give a woman some privacy?*

The moment the last of her three roommates pulls the door shut behind her, Rose video calls Matt. And waits. And waits.

Finally, Matt picks up. Rose can see him standing at the granite-topped kitchen island, with one toddler sitting next to his side, pincering pieces of banana from a high chair. Matt's other twin isn't in the shot, but Rose can hear him fussing, resisting Ulyana's efforts to corral his squirming body into a pair of pants.

"We're almost in the car," Matt says. "Can this wait until this afternoon, after my last class?"

They're not almost in the car. Ryan—or is it Jacob?—is still eating. When Ulyana walks by, she's wearing a robe, even if her hair and makeup look perfect.

"No, it can't. I have new information about Jules. I talked to a person who saw her, Matt." Rose can't slow down. It's too important. "She had a boyfriend. Not the Luka guy."

Matt has leaned down so that she can only see the back of his close-cropped hair on the phone screen. She remembers that hairline, the perfect fade down his neck. Twice-monthly hair trims on the first and fifteenth. Never a hair out of place.

"Matt," she says, trying to get his attention.

He's telling one of the toddlers to stop throwing fruit. But if Matt keeps bending down to pick up the pieces, of course the kid is going to throw another one. It's a game. Has he really parented three children now without learning a thing?

"Matt!" she yells. "Leave the fruit! Please! God damn it!"

"Whoa whoa whoa," Ulyana's voice comes from offscreen. "This sounds like an adult call. Can you take it to another room, Matt?"

Yes, Rose concurs. *Take it to another room. Go. Now.*

Matt's face is back on the screen. He is holding his phone too close and walking around with it, the background spinning. "I've got to get the boys to day care. Then I've got an eight A.M. class that ends at eleven, then a lunch meeting with a new dean—"

"This can't wait," Rose says, incredulous. "Are you kidding me?"

"Not kidding," he says, sleepy. Matt has been sleepy for the last three and a half years. Rose has listened to endless stories about twins—how raising them is not twice as hard, it's ten times as hard. How they are picky eaters and never sleep, unlike Jules, who was easy. But Jules was only "easy" because Matt was never around to help.

"Can Ulyana take the kids to day care, so I can get a half hour with you? Please?"

Matt sighs. "She's got her own schedule to worry about."

Must be nice. To have a wife who is ten years younger than you. To have the wisdom, as a father now in his late forties, to know that time with your children matters. Every time Matt turns and the background blurs, Rose's stomach does another flip. Yes, it's from the alcohol, and from getting only a few hours of sleep. But Matt is the one making her dizzy from the effort of suppressing her exasperation.

"Let me get to my study," he says, voice still sleepy, "and then I can give you five minutes."

She hears Matt call to Ulyana again, asking for her permission. Her *permission*. As if Rose was calling to ask whether she should bring salad or dessert to their next potluck dinner, instead of calling to explain that the man with the swallow tattoo and no bottom teeth might have nothing to do with Jules's death at all.

"I'm waiting," Rose says, feeling hot tears fill her eyes.

I get along great with Jules's father.

Yes and no.

I even get along with his new wife. You could say we're friends.

Mostly yes. But also, sometimes, no.

Finally, there is quiet at the end of the line. She recognizes Matt's home office, with its dark brown bookcases, wall of diplomas and a folded US flag in a glass display frame.

"You've got intel," he says.

She rolls her eyes at the word *intel* but rewinds to the beginning, speaking quickly, her excitement building all over again, mixed up with her own frustration they didn't know this all before. Paco. Luka. Guatemalan boyfriend.

"Okay, wait," Matt says, sounding like he hasn't managed to drink a single cup of coffee even though she knows he would have had a full pot by now. "This beach dude—Dennis. He's sharp-eyed enough to see that 'Paco' motorcycled out of town with a new jacket, but not enough to see all the flyers with Jules's picture hanging all over town that same week?"

She pauses, flustered. Yes, Dennis recognized Jules. No, he said nothing about realizing she was the girl in locally posted flyers.

"I didn't ask him."

Matt smirks. "You didn't ask him." She can see the dimple in his right cheek. She used to like that dimple. Now she could punch it.

"Matt, he had everything else right. He knew Jules had a job to get to in the morning. He knew she spoke Spanish. He knew she didn't like to swim. He knew she was a nice girl."

"A nice girl!" Matt laughs. "That's pretty generic."

"And that she had a nice local boyfriend, supposedly."

Rose admits: she trusted Dennis's gut instinct when he called Jules "nice," but Rose didn't extend the benefit of the doubt to the newly discovered boyfriend.

Matt looks off to the side, like he's checking the time or pulling up an email or doing anything other than hanging on Rose's every word.

She summarizes more simply for him. "We should be looking for a Guatemalan guy. Forget about the German."

"The German had her book."

"But that's because Jules gave it to him!"

Matt turns his gaze to the camera again. "You told me Jules would never give away that book. You said she'd had it since high school. And when we got it back, we saw it was signed by the author. Jules wouldn't have given it away."

Rose growls with frustration. She knows Matt is going to end the call any minute. There's no point talking to him about Jules's writerly aspirations or the fact that she seemed depressed in her texts, like a person who might have given up on a dream—and yes, even given away a book, impulsively. He was never interested in those emotional details.

"Follow the money," Rose says suddenly, retrieving those words from the first and only journalism course she ever took, at Northwestern. It was where she and Matt met. "Remember how Professor Jenkins used to say that? *Follow the money*. If this Paco guy was paid to leave town, it means someone bribed him to do so. Someone who didn't want us hanging around San Felipe, asking questions. Like the police—"

"The police down there don't have a lot of money to hand out."

"Then someone else! But the police knew. They lied and said the drug dealer who sold something to Jules went to jail."

She's doing the math in her head. A new motorcycle, or even a shiny used one. Five thousand? Ten?

"And on top of that," Rose says, steam building up again, "do you like how they were so vague about the drug? We don't even know what it was. Just a *party drug*."

"That's political," Matt insists. "They want to name something that tourists might have brought down, whether that means ketamine or ecstasy or something else. They don't want to say cocaine or heroin, because those come from Guatemala."

"Heroin!" Rose shouts. Catching herself, she whispers, "I can't believe you're suggesting Jules did heroin."

"I'm not. I'm reminding you to flex a little intellectual muscle when it comes to culture and the government situation. Guatemala already has a bad reputation. It's a 'level three' country, meaning *reconsider travel*, as I told you before you decided to go there alone."

"As *we* told Jules," she says, feeling the pressure of tears behind her eyes again.

"And hey, before you forget, the cops down there went beyond the call. They let us park the rescue boat in their guarded lot. They gave us day-and-night access to their interview room. They called in anyone we wanted to talk to."

"Which made it so easy for everyone to meet and fill out statements in town. In a public place."

"Well, yes. Obviously."

"Instead of where Jules was, minutes or hours before she died. That row of expat houses down the lake from Eva's house—the spot where the Canadian retiree said he saw a girl swimming. You should have talked to him at *his* house, not at the police station. You could have walked the beaches and talked to people who weren't asked to come in. Maids, gardeners, whatever. People who didn't see the flyers."

She's never said any of this before—never even put it into one private, coherent thought—because it hurt too much to admit their compounding errors. But the truth matters more. It's what she owes Jules: *the truth*.

"Everyone saw the flyers," Matt says, sounding not just tired now, but disdainful, like what he's most tired of isn't feeling demolished by paternal heartbreak but *managing* Rose. "Except, evidently, your beach buddy, who is too nearsighted to see a flyer but not too nearsighted to spot a man's neck tattoo."

Rose feels stranded, no longer part of an evidence-sorting team. Was it always this way? Was she just too distressed to realize Matt didn't trust any of her intuitions?

"The white gloves," she tries, grasping at straws. "We should have narrowed it down: size, type. If they belonged to some boyfriend who . . . who . . ."

She can't say it: *who might have killed her*.

"We did, Rose," he says quietly. "They were women's, a very small size. Whoever wore those gloves probably couldn't have subdued another person, if that's what you're still worrying about."

"Did you tell me that?"

"I did. You even asked, about two months ago, if they were Jules's size. At the time, I told you that yes, they were, more or less, but it didn't matter."

"I'm sorry," Rose says, deflated now. "I don't remember that conversation."

"It's okay."

Rose hears the sound of Matt's office door opening. Ulyana calls from offscreen, saying she just put the kids in their car seats and the car is running. She'll wait for him outside.

"Yeah, I know," Rose says. "You've got to go."

"Okay." He half smiles. "Good work."

Fuck you, she thinks, but instead she says, "I'll call again if I find anything else."

After the video call closes down, Rose leans her head against the door, wishing away her headache, and that image of Matt with a toddler, the scene of domestic chaos but also domestic contentment.

I even get along with his new wife. You could say we're friends.

She'd said it to her therapist, as recently as last week. She's said it within Jules's earshot, many times, when anyone expressed surprise that they all still gathered for Thanksgiving and the Superbowl, year after year.

Now, Rose remembers Jules's reply, the thing she said a year ago, just before Jules's graduation, when they were having a minor civil disagreement about where the graduation party should be held. The choices were Rose's house, with the new patio furniture she'd bought just for the occasion. Or Matt's house, because the twins might need to nap and it would be easier for Ulyana.

"Mom. You don't have to pretend to agree with Dad about everything, even though you've had a so-called amicable divorce," Jules said.

"It wasn't 'so-called.' We took pride in handling that well."

"And you don't have to pretend to get along with Ulyana."

"I'm not pretending! She's great."

"She *is* great, I love her, too. And I like that you get along, most of the time. But."

"But what?"

"You're both moms."

"So?"

"Put two moms in the same room, anywhere, and they're going to compete."

"That's ridiculous. I don't compete with other moms."

"*All moms compete with other moms.*"

"Is that what you really think?"

"That's what I think. You're just too blocked to realize it."

"What does 'blocked' mean?"

"You shut out the bad stuff. You don't notice. You don't reflect. You'd know a lot more about yourself if you tried. Maybe keep a diary."

"A *diary*?"

At least she hadn't told Rose to write a memoir. Rose would have laughed her out of the room.

11

ROSE

Rose doesn't want to eat, but it's the only way to blunt her hangover. Twenty minutes after ordering, she is served breakfast on the guests' verandah, halfway between the cabins and the reception building. She's unable to eat more than two spoonfuls of yogurt, mango and granola, but she makes up for it by sucking down vast quantities of water and caffeine.

Other participants from the cabins puzzle over the breakfasts delivered to them. One woman's request for eggs somehow yields a delivery of French toast, while another woman's request for dry toast results in the production of a perfect omelet, topped with orange slices.

Isobel stands with hands stretched over her head, working out the kinks aggravated by her bad mattress. "Nothing can be as perfect as Casa Eva. We wouldn't be able to appreciate her standard of luxury if we got it here, in town."

"Contrast," Scarlett agrees. "That's what I love about travel. When you've been pedaling through rain all day and you're starving, that free grilled cheese a person gives you at a campground tastes like heaven."

Rose has interacted with Scarlett only briefly, in the cabin and at last night's party. Avoided her, in fact. But now she allows herself to look, long and hard.

There's no question. Scarlett is beautiful and fit. Though she started her cross-country cycling trip seventy pounds overweight, as her manuscript explained, she lost the extra pounds, leaving only curvy muscle. Today she's wearing close-fitting exercise tights and a high-necked T-shirt. Her hips are wide but her waist is tiny. All of her skin is covered, from ankles to collarbone, but her body is so naturally shapely that even the waiter can't help staring as he sets a plate of pancakes in front of her.

"I ordered chilaquiles?"

Scarlett doesn't seem to notice the waiter blushing.

"Did you really get free food from people?" asks Diane, a woman with chestnut-colored hair pulled back in a dressy ponytail, the top artfully backcombed in a poufy sixties style Rose would never dare attempt.

"All the time."

"Weren't you worried about depending on people's spontaneous charity?"

"Never."

"But what if you got to the end of the day and no one invited you to their campsite to share some soup or whatever?"

"Then I didn't eat. But that was okay. I started the trip a size twenty. I had a good safety margin."

Five women are seated at their table, with another four from their workshop at a second table across the veranda, looking at photos posted from last night's party on Eva's social media. K is the only one of them who hasn't signed the waivers. K browses, taking a surprisingly long time.

Does Ana Sofía really post that much? Does Eva really have that many different feeds? Instagram, Facebook, Twitter, TikTok, and maybe there were others. Jules never mentioned that, but why would she? Jules didn't care for social media very much. Even so, Rose thought she'd studied all the mainstream platforms in the weeks after Jules's disappearance. But she might have missed something.

The self-criticism stings, reminding her of the fight with Matt, who was willing to lob even sharper attacks. Rose resents the way he disregarded every new piece of information she gathered from Dennis. She still thinks it might be worth paying a visit to Chief Molina herself, but she has to figure out what to say. Accusing authorities of lying about a drug dealer's arrest will not make her any new friends.

But maybe Rose could mention to Molina that she now has a hunch Jules had a Guatemalan boyfriend. If she could just find an image of him, or of Jules with any man who looked Guatemalan, or anything else new that won't make the police defensive, then she'd have a good reason for stopping by. But how would she explain her presence at the workshop and her use of a false identity?

When Rose pulls out her phone, Isobel steps closer, pausing from her stretches to look over Rose's shoulder.

Isobel says, "You're not looking at the right Facebook Group."

"Eva has more than one?"

"Different one for every Atitlán session cohort." Isobel is breathing in Rose's ear. "You're still on the wrong page."

"Okay," Rose says, needing some room. Because now that she understands there are different groups, it isn't this session's opening party that interests her. She stays on the page from three months ago. But she sees no images of Jules.

Rose pauses her scrolling at a video titled "Last Gasp, Still Great." When she hits play, the video judders forward, but only for a second, stuck on an image of a paperback copy of Eva's first memoir, sitting atop a mosaic-inlaid table with blue water and volcanoes behind.

Rose's throat tightens. It looks like Jules's copy of the paperback—the same copy the backpacker somehow got hold of. The paperback Rose now has in her bag.

Then she catches herself. Every paperback looks the same. Even the crease on the cover means nothing.

The video starts and stops and freezes again, the audio failing, the camera still focused on the book cover, with only forty-six seconds left.

Maybe Rose did see this video before, way back when Jules first went missing. Her temples are pounding. The internet here is maddeningly slow. Never mind. She gives up trying to play videos with the slow Wi-Fi and pushes her phone back into her laptop bag.

The rest of the group is more interested in figuring out the schedule for the days ahead, including how the workshops will be organized. Evidently, there's a public session for each participant, but also a private one.

"I just hope we all get enough individual attention," says Diane from behind her big black lenses. "How many of us are there? Someone's still missing."

"Maybe the heroin addict with the vomit essay," Isobel says.

Rose remembers. Five pages, one long scene—an alcoholic, drug-addled, stomach-curdling fugue.

"She lost custody of her children . . ." Isobel drops her voice as a woman with stiff steel-gray curls slowly mounts the two stairs leading to the open-air verandah and pauses to rest, attracting the attention of the waiter.

"Her name is Rachel," someone whispers.

Rachel wrote about a binge the day after she nearly killed her children in a car accident. She lost custody of them both—a teenage son and daughter—before recovering her own sobriety. The woman in front of them has started talking to the waiter, but she seems to have a speech defect. She stammers. She keeps one arm tucked across her chest, like it's damaged. This woman looks anything but recovered.

"I'll give her my seat," Rose says, rising to leave, still gripping her coffee cup and hoping the final slugs will quell her headache. There's a patch of clean grass just past the verandah. "I'm going to spend my last bit of free time reading."

Rose is only pages away from finishing Eva's second memoir. She's riveted, but the last few chapters have been harder than the first ones. Rose has lived vicariously through Eva's many complications, both physical and emotional. When Eva decided to have a baby at midlife, she already had a grown child, Adarsha, the same daughter who doesn't talk to her now. One of their conflicts began with an essay Eva wrote for the *New York Times* column Modern Love, reliving a fight Eva had with her daughter when the thirty-something found out that her future sister would be named Adhika—*more* or *extra* in Hindi.

Adarsha thought the names were too similar. She resented being yoked to this "extra," afterthought child, a product of privilege and naivete. Adarsha thought Eva was being selfish, refusing to take genetic tests that would offer previews of any serious abnormalities. Eva's choice to hash the disagreement out in public was the last straw for Adarsha, a fact Eva candidly reports.

"Algo más?" asks the waiter standing over Rose's shoulder, gesturing to her coffee cup.

"No, thank you." Rose turns and smiles, handing him the empty cup. In Spanish she adds, "I'm reading a good book. I want to know how it ends."

"Con una muerte, o una boda," he answers. *With a death, or a wedding.*

Rose laughs. "You're right. I think that's the rule."

What would Jules have thought if Rose had decided to try for a baby in her late thirties or early forties? Rose was an inexperienced mother, made even more anxious by Jules's premature birth. Then she was blindsided by a profound case of baby blues, just as her own mother had been—proof of how little accumulated wisdom we manage to pass down, generation after generation.

Of course, Rose knows that a second baby could have been every bit as hard as the first, but somehow, she doubts it. Is it unreasonable, wanting to do it one more time? Is it just a pipe dream to long for that soft, fuzzy scalp cradled in your hand, that warm little body tucked into yours? She imagines Jules would have judged her for it, but maybe after Jules read this book and saw Eva's side, they could have had a mature discussion.

Rose feels it again: the question caught in her throat, the yearning ache in her chest for missed conversations. That, coincidentally, was what this memoir seemed to be about, too. The things we try to hold on to too tightly. The chances that slip away.

Rose has only two pages left when Lindsay crouches down next to her on the grass.

"You want to catch a boat with us, or are you going by tuk-tuk?"

"Tuk-tuk," Rose says, "the moment I finish this. Eva's second memoir. Did you read it?"

"Oh, yes. Horrible ending."

"Don't ruin it for me!"

Lindsay winks and leaves, fresh as ever in tight white jeans and a satin-blue blouse with a bow at the collar.

In the memoir, the baby, Adhika, is born—apparently healthy—to fifty-year-old Eva. The second-time mother, bold enough to venture into the world of online dating *while pregnant*, carpe diem, has gotten involved in a serious relationship with a handsome lawyer named Jonah. He is a prince, especially during those first blurry, blissful days home from the hospital. Eva writes a newspaper essay about how much she revels in this babymoon, in a way she simply couldn't with her firstborn, a difficult infant. (That essay, too—published in the following year, ahead of the finished memoir—will annoy Adarsha.)

Then, a week after coming home from the hospital, sometime after three in the morning, Eva dreams of a gray, misshapen stone falling out of the sky and plunging into a lake. Eva has always loved lakes, and swimming. Her dreams are often filled with water images. But the weight of this stone dropping leaves no doubt. It's a dark omen.

Eva checks the clock. Adhika hasn't woken to nurse. It's well past four. Eva goes to lift her out of her crib. Adhika is cool to the touch and strangely heavy. Eva lifts her, rocks her, lays her back down. The baby is gone—simple as that. Dead. Ten days old. Eva cups a hand around the baby's smooth, cold skull. Impossible.

The boyfriend, Jonah, has not moved in yet, though he will later. They will marry within two months. *Una muerte y una boda.*

Eva, stunned and alone, knows what will follow: if not a standard investigation, at least public recrimination. In her heart she already knows that an autopsy will find some genetic abnormality or disease casting the blame back on her, the middle-aged mother. It's just what the naysayers predicted: you can't have it all. Even if you are fifty, white and financially comfortable, with a great team of doctors. Many will say she shouldn't have dared to try.

Rose doesn't lift her head because she doesn't want any passerby to see the tears streaming down her face.

Only one page left now.

The baby is dead, stiffening, in the crib. Dawn is an hour away. Eva could call an ambulance. She could call her doctor directly. She could call Jonah. But there's no hurry now, is there? Nothing is going to change.

Instead, she makes a French press of coffee, extra strong. She brings the coffee, her favorite mug and a box of thin ginger cookies to her bedroom. She turns on her laptop. She begins the book that Rose is reading now, which Eva will write in a seven-week delirium. She writes the very first page, the very first line that tugged at Rose's heart.

There was one thing I wanted more than anything in the world: to hold a child, my very own flesh-and-blood child, again.

12

JULES

It's hard to wake up on my third day at Casa Eva, even when sweet Gaby comes to my bedside at dawn with a cup of coffee. For our roommate Mercedes, who has been granted the day off, Gaby brings a special sedative healing tea. It helps with her seizures, Gaby explains.

I shouldn't be envious when I see Mercedes snuggle back under the covers, but I am.

I jump up to dress, already anxious about the many tasks facing me today. Gaby watches me getting tangled in the overcomplicated straps of my sports bra.

"Tomorrow, I can bring you a bigger coffee," she says.

"Is it that obvious I need it?"

She doesn't ask why I left the cabin in the middle of the night. I have a feeling she knows where I was going, and why. I just hope I can trust her not to say anything to Eva. Mauricio told me about a time Eva went into a sulk just because a seventy-year-old workshopper gave Mauricio an innocent peck on the cheek. She'd blow her top to discover what Mauricio and I do when no one's looking.

Eva's protectiveness makes sense, though. When she first met him, after losing her baby and while she was recuperating at Lake Atitlán, Mauricio was staying in the orphanage. It's a local charity for children thirteen and under. Except that really, he was already fifteen. Like half the kids he grew up with, he doesn't have a birth certificate, never mind a passport.

Mauricio told me that he appreciates the employment and emotional support, the way Eva clearly took something sad—the loss of her own dream of becoming a mama again—and tried to turn it into something good. Royalties from *In a Delicate State* have bought Mauricio and other local kids lots of teddy bears and soccer balls over the years. But now that he's approaching the age of twenty-one, he has to decide when to tell her his real age. She's often talked about Mauricio coming to live in the US with her, and how that might be legally accomplished. It's all a bit . . . intense.

When I did finally sneak into bed last night, I couldn't sleep, worrying because I hadn't sent Eva the essay she requested, and at the same time, worrying that this was starting to feel like "homework" rather than a self-directed effort to create art, or at least truth. But maybe that preciousness was part of my writer's block since graduating. I'd always thought college was getting in the way of my creativity. Instead, the deadlines were helpful and now, without them, I'd been flailing. Eva was giving me yet another gift. I didn't have to write something perfect. I just had to *write*.

I pulled out my journal and flashlight and burrowed deep under the covers, intent on scratching out a few paragraphs. When I drilled some test wells into my subconscious, only a few topics sprang up. One was Mauricio—which wouldn't work, obviously. The other was Mom.

I remembered an argument we had just before I left, the one *after* the restaurant scene where I expressed disdain for her spendy food habits, the one *before* our final discussion about my plans to search for my own apartment soon.

The argument had been about clothes. She'd ordered me some travel pants and a long-sleeve matching shirt from a conservative retailer that sells ridiculously expensive outfits to women who evidently dream of going on safari.

"They . . . certainly have a lot of pockets," I said, lifting the pants and shirt from the gift-wrapped box. "And they are . . . rather large."

"But do you like them?" she asked.

"I think they might look good on *you*."

"They're quick-dry."

"So is skin. I mean, I just wear shorts and a T-shirt most of the time. Or less."

"What do you mean, 'less'?"

"Like, a bathing suit. Under shorts."

"But if you go somewhere nice, maybe in the evening . . ."

"Mom, I don't plan on going anywhere nice."

"Never mind about the clothes. Did you refill all your medications? It's a long trip. Are you sure you're bringing enough? And make sure to bring the prescriptions, in case you lose the pills or some border agent takes them away."

"Mom. I *know* how to pack. And no border guard is taking away my birth control pills."

"You never know. Catholic countries."

"*Mom.*"

But it wasn't my birth control she was really worried about. It was my other pills. The ones she has been terrified I'll stop taking ever since my freshman year, when I was prescribed them in the first place. I'm not ashamed to be on antidepressants. For my mom, it's like this big secret or this thing she wants to talk about and not talk about at the same time. She's on them, too. Nana wasn't willing to try them until she was already old, but she should have, obviously. What's the big deal?

"I just can't imagine what would happen if you were in a Third World country—"

"No one uses that term anymore—"

"—and suddenly decided you didn't need them."

"Mom. That won't happen." We both know how quickly things spiraled the first time. Admittedly, even *I* don't like talking about that part.

I knew how sad it made her to remember. It wasn't like I attempted suicide. I just became lost and strange and deeply disconnected, and the first time she saw me, six weeks after we'd last spoken, she started sobbing—which only made me feel more like a zombie. As if I had, in fact, died. Or worse, become something she could no longer recognize. It was as if I had rejected *her*—instead of just grown deeply, chemically estranged from myself.

"Okay, so you don't want the clothes? I'll return them." She grabbed the pants and the shirt from my hands before I could say anything more, her eyes filling.

Be nicer, I told myself after that argument. And that's been my plan: to think harder before I speak the next time I see Mom. To realize I don't have to spew every last thought in my head. To realize she loves me and does her best, even if it's not enough, sometimes.

And there I went again. Was my relationship with Mom really not enough? Wasn't it the kind of relationship anyone my age has, when she's made the mistake of living in the same town as her parents past the age of eighteen?

My late-night thoughts about Mom were uncomfortable but they were mostly resolved, which made for a boring essay. No journey, no discovery. To find something richer I had to dig harder, further back into the past. What I ended up with—just the first five hundred words—was the start of a short piece about my dad's marriage to Ulyana. Nearly as lame.

I had been given the gift of an audience and a deadline. I told myself that we all write "shitty first drafts." It didn't make me feel any better.

Laptop under my arm, I hurry from the cabin to self-serve breakfast and grab some cut-up fruit just before it's put away. Popping pineapple chunks in my mouth as I stroll, I find my way to Eva's balcony, where she's already talking to someone, as usual.

Phone pressed to her ear, she points to the stacks of paper-clipped pages I see on benches and the little bistro table, the same stacks that have cluttered this space since I first arrived at Casa Eva.

"Copy?" I guess.

She shakes her head.

"Recycle?"

She rolls her eyes.

Eva pulls the phone away from her ear and says, "Just wait."

Sorry! Okay. Waiting.

Barbara's face appears on the other side of the closed glass door. Eva flaps her hand, making a "go away" gesture. I raise my eyebrows and wrinkle my nose as if to say, *Sorry?* But I'm on this side of the door, and Barbara is on that side. I'm close enough to see her nostrils flare.

It's not like Barbara should be jealous. She lives here full-time and she knows everything about everything that makes the Casa Eva Universe go around. As Eva said yesterday, "The ideal assistant takes care of messes so that I don't have to see them." That's what Barbara—and Hans, and Trish in Miami—all know how to do. I can only learn.

"Juliet May." Eva has barely disconnected her call when she points to the paper-clipped stacks again. "Have you read all of the manuscripts yet?"

"I get to read them?"

"*Get* to? You *have* to."

She explains that she wants a five-minute summary for each, plus anything I think she should know in advance about the writer, based on cover emails plus online searches.

"Online searches?"

"Especially for the writers who might need extra hand-holding. This one, for example." She points to a pile of pages on top of the rest. "ZAHARA" is written on the footer.

Eva's eyes brighten again. "Is she still under contract with Glassnote?"

I've never heard of Glassnote.

"Trish read Zahara's cover email—something about a bad boyfriend and Las Vegas, but I didn't catch the rest. You get to sample her story first."

"Great," I say, scooping up the manuscript printouts. "Is this all of them?"

"We might get some emailed last minute. And remember: if you have only cover notes and no pages, focus on the writer."

Okay, I can't pretend to understand *that*. In college writing workshops, we were always told to focus on the pages.

"I wouldn't want anyone to think I'm stalking them online," I say.

Eva blinks and inhales, slowly.

"Sorry," I say. "Initiative. Right."

Eva's smile wilts. She puts her fingers to her temples, like she has a headache.

"Anything else you'd like to ask me today? You're here to help me, but you're here to help yourself, too, right?"

"Right," I repeat, as if it's that simple. Help her. Help myself. And also *help her feel good that she's helping me*.

"That's why I asked you for an essay when I hired you. If you're going to audit any part of the workshop, I need to see your writing. I want to help you, Juliet May. I always have time for that. Every woman needs a mentor."

I'm relieved that Eva hasn't forgotten she used that word before and that even though I haven't provided any proof of my abilities, she's still giving me the benefit of the doubt. I think back to what I wrote and feel panic. Even as a shitty first draft, it's still not good enough.

Her instructions were clear: I was supposed to have the essay finished this morning. And then again, she's asked if I have any questions. It's the oldest trick in the book, one that worked in high school *and* in college. Get the prof talking. He might forget about the quiz he had planned or the deadline he already assigned.

"Dialogue," I blurt. "Your books are amazing, with these long scenes that feel just like life. Everything your mother said when you came back from London, just for one example. Her voice, and the long speech she made about your teenage years. It's incredible."

Eva nods, looking bored. She rotates one finger in the air as if to say, *Keep going. Get to your point.*

"I mean . . . this is basic, but did you take notes right after that argument? Like, in a diary? Or did you try to remember when you started the book a year later?"

Yes, I'm trying to distract her, but at the same time, it's a question I've always wanted to ask. I've never understood how memoirists can make the past so cinematically vivid. Are the most important moments intrinsically sticky? Or do good writers have a way to access what's hidden but not yet lost? I have to assume it's something wrong with me—my poor memory, or laziness, or some trick I just haven't learned yet. I *want* to be good at dialogue. I *want* to be deserving of this opportunity. But Eva's expression tells me I should understand this all by now. It's Memoir 101.

Eva's phone rings again.

"Do you see?" she points at the offending phone. "This is why I can't write here. The workshop hasn't even started, and . . . *this*."

I see the name on the caller ID.

ADARSHA.

I thought Eva was no longer speaking to her.

"Do you know she wanted to be a writer, too?"

"Your daughter?"

"That's the one. But she wouldn't accept any help. No editing advice, no introductions or referrals, nothing. And so, she's a failure. Midthirties and she hasn't published a single book. Can you believe I'm related to someone that stubborn— and *stupid*?"

I shrug my shoulders—a quick, nervous twitch.

The name keeps flashing: *ADARSHA.*

Eva has forgotten my dialogue question altogether. Now she's wound up, energized by her rant.

"She doesn't like the story of how I got started in the business. You think agents were all clamoring to read a memoir by a teenager? Absolutely not. You think the New York parties I attended and the men I 'dated' the summer of 1980 didn't matter? I could tell you anecdotes that would make your hair curl. She refuses to benefit from what I went through."

ADARSHA.

"And none of that is to be shared, understand? Okay, so you'll get me that essay. I'm serious. This goes beyond our relationship. We are a community. Everyone here creates."

"Okay. I've got something halfway—"

Eva makes a flapping motion with her hand, like I should leave. I clutch the workshoppers' pages to my chest.

"Let's talk about it later today."

"Perfect!"

ADARSHA.

"I have to take this!" Eva barks.

I don't mean to mimic her volume, but I shout back, communicating my zest and my competence and my willingness to be a team player: "*Great!*"

13

ROSE

Rose catches her breath only once she is settled in the back of the tuk-tuk, motoring up the dusty road to Casa Eva, still thinking about the end of Eva's second memoir, both stimulated and bothered by it. Jules loved the book. Trust in Jules.

She looks down at her gray scoop-neck T-shirt from Old Navy and the white capris that seemed summery when she bought them but now just seem colorless. Is that how her daughter saw her? Colorless, conservative, boring. Not the type of person who would dare to get pregnant at fifty. Not the kind of woman who would have come to Guatemala alone, under normal circumstances. She sighs and gazes out at the landscape, trying to see it as Jules did—as an inspiring invitation to adventure.

On the steep hillsides to the left, patches of land are aflame. The smell of smoke is faint, not the intense choke and pall of massive wildfire. But she can see individual rising wisps and flashes of orange. The women were talking about it at breakfast. The farmers use some kind of slash-and-burn agriculture.

"Los incendios," Rose calls to the driver, asking him about the fires. "¿Todo bien?"

"Fuera de control, a veces."

Out of control, at times. But only "at times." The driver sounds relaxed.

Rose thinks of California fires, raging out of control, devastating entire towns. This isn't like that. It can't be. Don't underestimate Indigenous knowledge. She hopes the locals know what they're doing.

Maybe Rose worries too much. She's worrying even now about Eva's baby, dead and gone for more than five years. Rose hasn't nursed a child in over two decades but at this moment, imagining the pain of a lost infant, she feels a tingle in her chest, that familiar pinch and prickle before milk lets down. It's been years since she thought about nursing problems, including her endlessly soaked shirts, no matter how many pads she stuck between skin and bra. It was like her entire body was just listening for Jules's hunger, ready at any moment to open the spigots.

Maybe that's what's bothering her, too: the failure to explain the breastfeeding aspect, at the end of Eva's story. If Eva had slept later than usual, and the baby weren't alive to nurse, wouldn't Eva's milk be leaking into her shirt? Wouldn't Eva need to express milk and possibly change her clothing?

Rose imagines holding the dead baby for an hour or more until dawn breaks, milk letting down, shirt soaking through. Then: going to the shower, to let the water wash away the milk and the tears. Standing under the scalding spray with puffy eyes—as hot as one can bear—an experience Rose knows well from the last three months. Then dressing again and waiting for the authorities to arrive. That's how Rose would have done it. Instead, Eva wrote.

She spots three figures ahead, walking the road. Isobel, Diane and Rachel. They got ahead of her after breakfast.

"Stop," she tells the driver. "I want to offer them a ride."

Diane is the first to hop in. "Good! I wanted to be early." She smooths down her white slacks, gold bangles sliding up and down her narrow wrists as she rearranges herself. *Don't wear valuables around the village.* Few of them are being sufficiently careful.

When the noise of the tuk-tuk motor forces Diane to turn and shout over her shoulder, Rose can see what she overlooked at breakfast. Behind the dark glasses, Diane's left eye is surrounded by yellow and pale purple bruising. Yet she's in a fine mood. "We'll beat everyone coming by boat. We can get our names on the sign-up sheet."

"For being workshopped?" Rose asks.

"No, today's critiques are already scheduled." Diane pantomimes sticking her finger down her throat. "I got an email this morning, telling me I'm up first. I meant sign-ups for the other stuff, like private feedback meetings and massages."

Rose is confused. "So, to ask for a personal response from Eva, we have to schedule our own meeting?"

If it's up to them, Rose missed her chance to sign up early. But still, she'll get a one-on-one at some point, won't she?

"We were discussing it at breakfast—including the fact that we have to pay extra," Isobel says, lowering her chin to give Rose a meaningful look.

Diane glances at them both, then snaps her head back. "It's only another hundred dollars."

"But we already paid nearly six thousand dollars to come here," Rose says. "I thought getting personal feedback from Eva was the point."

"The extra goes to charity," Diane says, pushing her sunglasses higher up her nose.

"It's . . ." Rachel says, "a little—"

"Unexpected?" Rose fills in, trying to help.

"Strange," Rachel says, finishing her own sentence. In this

smaller group, she speaks more smoothly, as long as they don't rush her. "I've taken workshops before. You talk . . . in a group. Maybe you also get a private hour with the teacher. It's usually included."

"I don't think a hundred dollars is worth complaining about," Diane says.

Isobel says, "True."

Rose looks to Isobel, who is gazing off into the distance, frowning, like she has more to say but doesn't want to—which isn't like Isobel at all. It makes Rose wonder.

Isobel seems financially comfortable. She wouldn't worry about a hundred dollars. But maybe she's thinking of Scarlett. As they all heard at the opening night party, the young cyclist had to do a crowdfunding campaign just to come here. Last week, Scarlett was still a thousand dollars short. Before she could board a plane, she had to sell her *bike*.

Rose asks quietly, "Did Scarlett manage to pay the extra fee?"

Isobel murmurs, "I helped her."

"Oh good." Rose gently taps the back of Isobel's hand—a private, wordless gesture of appreciation.

Rose doesn't really resent Scarlett's youth, of course. It was just a feeling. The bigger feeling is that she wants Scarlett to have a good experience given how much she's sacrificed to come here.

"I don't even know why you're talking about it," Diane says loudly, wanting the last word. "It's absolutely worth more money to get Eva's expertise."

The tuk-tuk motors along, crunching the gravel and spewing dust. No one speaking.

To break the tension, Rose turns to Rachel, "So, you've taken workshops before?"

"Aspen, Bread Loaf," Rachel says, blinking and jerking

each time she speaks. "And in my MFA program, we work-shopped every semester."

The tuk-tuk takes a sharp curve. Rose clings to the metal pole on her left, feels the weight of the two other women sliding into her.

When they straighten out again, she asks, "Diane, you loved Eva's last memoir. What'd you think of the ending?"

"I cry every time. I can't listen to the end when I'm driving."

Rose tries to prioritize the questions in her head—the sorts of things she would carefully ask Jules, not wanting to offend.

Don't you think Eva should have called an ambulance and let someone try CPR on that baby, just maybe?

Isobel seems eager to make peace with Diane. "I *love* Eva's novels, and even with the ending, which was a little hard to read, I thought her memoir was exceptional."

Up ahead, they can see Eva's gate with its bright yellow door. The tuk-tuk brakes.

Rachel is trying to say something. "It's interesting to think . . . about the selection of details. The . . . the . . . the French press."

"Yes," Diane says, "and the cookies. The *ginger thins*."

But that's the second thing Rose wishes she could ask Jules. Would a woman who'd just lost a baby want to make coffee and eat cookies?

For Rose, eating was one of the hardest things to do. When Jules went missing, her stomach started doing flip-flops. When they found out Jules's most likely cause of death, Rose's entire GI tract, from aching throat to doleful belly, rebelled completely. She can't imagine sitting peacefully, munching ginger thins, next to a blue-gray infant corpse.

And then again: grief affects everyone differently. Some people retreat into paralysis. Some may disappear into work or a hobby. Rose thinks of her late mother, gardening with a vicious fervor the day of Rose's father's funeral, tearing at root balls, planting so haphazardly that half of the annuals died in a week.

The difference with Eva Marshall is that she didn't make a mess of that manuscript she started writing hours after her infant died. In interviews, she claimed—still claims—that *In a Delicate State* emerged fully formed, requiring less revision than any of her previous books.

They climb out, and Rose follows Rachel through the gate, hoping she'll say more. She doesn't. Maybe there's no more to be said. *The telling detail. The French press.*

Rose simply can't connect what she knows firsthand with Eva's behavior. It bothers her, perhaps more than it should, as if her own sense of grief—or even motherhood—feels threatened by this alternate possibility. And then again, maybe it has nothing to do with those things. Maybe it only has to do with art, which is something Rose knows nothing about. The real artist, it could be argued, channels her fiercest emotions into productivity. At least she thinks so. Jules must have thought about these same things. How could she not after reading *In a Delicate State*?

Stepping from one stone stair to the next, down the lushly vegetated path, Rose can only continue the discussion in her head, with Jules, the only person she'd trust to explain.

Is writing what you would have focused on, Jules, if you'd just lost your own child?

14

JULES

_____

_____

_____

At the water's edge, I'm all set up to read. The volcano is the color of an old brown fedora with the same crushed dent near the top. A light breeze etches delicate veins across the navy-blue water. The stories in my lap are far from perfect, but they are STORIES.

A woman named Beatrice just found her son hanging in the garage. (I red-flag it: This happened six months ago? A little early for critical workshopping, maybe? *Tell Eva.*)

Another found out her husband had not just one "other family" but two—one in the Philippines, one in Haiti. Men—the energy!

I pay extra attention to the manuscript by the indie singer, Zahara, who seems to be a hot mess. Reading her excerpt, about the kidnapping by the psychotic boyfriend, I should think, *I am so lucky.* Instead I note that she's only three years older than me. She already has a career, or rather, several of them. Her first side hustle, in the years before her music took off, was selling homemade purses covered in recycled computer keys. Her second side hustle is modeling.

It's one thing to know that Barbara, an older woman with a long resume of life tragedies, including divorce, breast cancer and bankruptcy, has a book about to come out. But Zahara is close to my age. What I lack most is experience, not only in writing, but in living. Mom thinks I'm reckless and antsy. Which is ironic, because little does she know how stupidly cautious I am.

All trip, I've tried to take chances, but each time I get a little dose of adrenaline, I panic. The scrapes on my knee: that was from my first tumble while rock climbing. I didn't do it again. Obviously, I didn't get up the nerve to try surfing in Costa Rica. Doggy paddlers don't belong in surf zones. So why did I even bother going to the coast?

But it's not just about physical risks. I know how my Instagram looks for those first weeks, before I basically stopped posting. Like I'm fearless. But the truth is I kept moving because it was the easier thing to do, not the harder thing. If I'd stayed longer in Panama or Nicaragua, if I'd gotten to know any community or even one person, I might have had something to write about. And yet, still not enough. The proof would have been in the pages. I don't have stories to tell. I don't have anything to say.

My reading slows, but I make it through the final manuscript pages. I sit on the end of the dock, letting the insignificance fill me, like gases in a bloating corpse, which isn't even a good metaphor, but I'm all metaphor-ed out. Do I wish I'd experienced rape, incest, kidnapping, drug addiction, deportation, war or extreme poverty at some point in my life? Of course not. Do I wish I'd started taking chances earlier, risked more, worked difficult jobs that helped me understand the heart of America, hacked through more jungles, cavorted with more lowlifes (only the interesting ones) and maybe had just one eensy brush with death that ended safely? Possibly.

I reach for my phone out of habit, knowing who'll try to

help me feel better. Mom. But I don't want to feel better. I knew before coming here that I had a long way to go before I'd be a writer. Before I'd *earn* that precious label. Now I'm starting to wonder if some of us just aren't meant to be read or heard. The world is so full of talent already: so many books, so many movies and songs. Barbara is stubborn, insistent on telling her story anyway. Many of these women are. But maybe the rest of us don't have what it takes.

I just wish people would be honest about the fact that we can't all get what we want. I think of Ulyana, the only woman who was willing to tell me about her fertility problems and warn me, "You probably can't wait as long as you think. It's the big lie that no one wants to admit."

There are lots of lies out there. You can't prioritize career and financial security and family all at once. You don't necessarily choose the ideal time to become a mom. You don't get to be a famous actress or painter or writer just because you want to, either.

And this is why I didn't finish my new round of grad school applications. I started them, just as I told Mom and Dad. I ordered undergrad transcripts and assembled the rec letters and the work samples, checking all the boxes in the online application portal, just as I told Mom and Dad. I just didn't pay the final fee or sign the final digital form. I didn't commit. When Mom asked if she could help out by driving the applications to the post office, I laughed at her—I laughed!—and told her she was so silly. The whole process was online now. *I finished those applications days ago!*

But I didn't.

Because I am a liar. And a cynic.

For months I'd been reading a private online forum for MFA wannabes, scrolling the endless laments, and I agreed with all of them. *"There are too many gatekeepers." "The writing matters, not the degree."* "*If you don't have connections, you'll get nowhere anyway.*"

And then one voice in the dark, a user named @brdtype23, said this: "*If you could find one successful writer willing to personally teach you, to guide you, to get you past those gatekeepers who block the other 99%, it would be worth more than a graduate degree.*"

And I thought: *You're right. And I no longer want to pay even a $50 application fee, much less $50,000 for tuition.*

I thought: *Let me travel first. Let me figure out what I want to write, what I want to say.*

I didn't think: *And I'll track down a famous writer!*

But of course I knew that Eva Marshall lived in Guatemala. Of course I left Guatemala for last—the final hope, the final test, the final plea for destiny to step in and relieve me of both my mediocrity and my confusion.

A cloud covers the sun. I'm wishing I brought my Roxy cover-up down to the dock, because my T-shirt isn't warm enough for these lakeside breezes. I'm still sleepy from staying up too late. Up at the house, people might be looking for me. I could use another coffee. Frankly, I could use a hug—or a face slap.

Wake up, Jules! You're fucking this whole thing up!

I linger for five more minutes, listening to the shush of water against the dock. I glance over at my closed laptop with the half-started essay Eva hasn't yet read. I don't even need to boot it up. I can remember the first line I typed last night—*When I first heard my father was remarrying . . .*

In comparison with the workshop pieces—bold and poignant, despite their imperfections—my essay is lifeless. No one will want to read it. I don't even want to read it.

I envision the delete key moving backward, one letter at a time, taking me back to the blank page and the blinking cursor, whose every pulse announces:

Imposter.

Imposter.

You are an imposter.

Marked-up manuscripts and summary notes for Eva in hand, I stroll up the garden path to the yellow door, where I catch the first hushed words of someone talking with Eduardo, the gardener. As I come closer, the questions become louder. Not just *Is Mauricio there?* But *Is he getting paid?* and *How often does Mauricio come to town?*

They stop talking when they spot me.

The guy is wearing a Hollister long-sleeve T-shirt, tight jogger pants and big white tennis shoes. His jet-black hair is short on the side, longer and gelled back on the top, the sharp lines of a comb still visible.

"Is Mauricio in the house?" the stranger asks me in English, as if he isn't happy enough with Eduardo's answers.

"No. Are you a friend?"

He turns back to Eduardo and says in rapid-fire Spanish that he'll come back this afternoon or tomorrow.

"¿Y quién es ella?" the guy asks Eduardo.

The gardener looks at me, expression blank. Eduardo has seen Mauricio and me holding hands—and maybe more than that.

"Una turista, nada más."

An hour later, when I see a water taxi advancing toward the dock, I run down the steps to greet it. It's Mauricio, returning from a trip to town to purchase shrimp and extra bags of ice.

When I describe the man who came looking for him, Mauricio says in Spanish, "That was my uncle. He doesn't look happy about it."

"Uncle? He looks so young."

"Only four years older than me. My mom's little brother."

"Why is he looking for you?"

"He wants me to move to Guate."

I'm not afraid of many cities, but I've heard enough about Guatemala City to steer clear. I also know Mauricio has extended family in the capital, but I guess I thought they were distant cousins or something. An uncle isn't distant.

"He wants me to work for him," Mauricio says.

I don't want to admit that his uncle looks shady, so I just ask, "What does he do?"

Guatemala has more gang members than any other Central American country. There are fifty different gangs in the capital alone.

Mauricio pulls me closer and nuzzles close to my ear. "Don't worry. I'm not going. Too many bad things happening there."

"Tell me."

"I don't like to think about it."

Not thinking seems to be Mauricio's defense of choice. Live in the moment. Put the worst of the past behind you and hope for the best. He doesn't understand Eva's memoirs or the workshops she leads. He's not illiterate. In fact, he loves poetry. But he thinks these women are lucky. Most of them have the option of leaving past tragedies behind.

Of course, he has shared some memories with me. One was of seeing corpses lined up for display in the town plaza. Mauricio's mother was murdered. Even since the Civil War ended, femicide has increased and many of his girl cousins continue to simply disappear. No one investigates. For Mauricio the search for meaning is a luxury. It's not a lesson Eva teaches.

"But if she's backed out, can't we try Charlize again? Don't lecture me about 'development hell,' Richard. This isn't my first rodeo. And no, she's not too young for the role. We look the same age."

I've just come running to the balcony, having been told by Gaby that Eva was looking everywhere for me—never mind I was never farther than a thousand feet from the house, doing exactly the work she'd asked me to do.

But I've arrived at a bad time. Eva is talking with her agent, Richard, again, and she isn't happy about the news. The movie deal for *In a Delicate State* has fallen through. I'm guessing it's because an A-list actress decided it wasn't a good career move to star in this particular story, with its dead baby at the end.

Eva is wearing a boatneck T-shirt, extremely low-cut. Her cleavage is rage-red. "You know I've got three mortgages, right?"

Ending the call, Eva holds up a finger—I'm not supposed to say a word—goes to her bathroom and comes out again, face and hair damp.

"I can come back," I say.

"No. We've got writers on the way. Have you checked email in the last hour?"

"I was on the dock, reading manuscripts." I catch myself, realizing that sounded salty, which isn't what I intended. "A few of them are really good, by the way!"

"I can't reach you on the dock. You should stay closer to the house where the Wi-Fi works best or no one will find you. I have ten women somewhere between their home airports and Guatemala City and Antigua, and you haven't checked email?"

Twelve women, I think, *not ten*. But it doesn't matter. "You told me that I should read the manuscripts and research the writers. I've made some notes—"

"Juliet May." She runs a hand through her hair, nervously scrunching the wavy strands. "Don't make excuses."

It stings. And it should. I do make too many excuses. She can see right through me, beyond the issue of emails and workshoppers, to the very core of my failings.

"Well?" Eva asks.

If I don't get a moment alone, I'm likely to break down in tears.

"Why don't I get us two fresh coffees?"

When I come back, smiling as brightly as I can manage, we go over the participant manuscripts. One of Eva's top concerns is deciding the schedule for who should be workshopped first, though evidently that's fluid, too, and she has a habit of changing it around.

"Here's the shorthand," she says. "We have the Avoiders. They want to write about anything but the most important thing that happened. We have the Agreeables. They'll follow my lead and it's actually better if they haven't started writing yet, since we'd just have to scrap their first efforts anyway. I'd rather get an email and we can talk about their idea. Win-win.

"Then we have the Forgettables," Eva says. "Followed by the Difficults. Forgettables can be socially pleasant. Sometimes they're repeat alumnae or older women who frankly don't have much to write or say, but they sure love our little lakeside retreat. I'll sometimes start with them as a way to control the energy level. Let the whole group wade in slowly. Calm the jitters. But the Difficults are something else. They're brittle, unpleasant people or they're writing difficult material beyond their capacity. Either way, they can ruin things for everyone."

I mention the woman whose son hanged himself. Never mind that the event was so recent, as the writer's cover note explained. It's also the writing itself: a series of horror-filled flashbulb images with barely any narrative stitching it all together.

"She hasn't started processing," I say, wincing. Eva hates therapeutic jargon. But I don't know how else to explain. "She could be a risk—to herself, I mean. Couldn't she?"

Eva, who has been pacing, stops. "Juliet May, do you want to know how long I waited, following a particularly traumatic event, until I started writing my last memoir?"

"You . . . didn't?"

"That's right. I didn't. Because I am . . ."

She waits, inviting me to fill in the blank.

"Different?"

"I am a writer. And you are, too. You said you finally got something started."

"It's not done."

"Nothing is ever done. Even books. You just give up and finally hand them over to someone else—same as you do with kids."

"Okay," I say, booting up my tiny, battered Mac, a process that takes about five years. "I know how busy you are. You really don't have to do this right now."

"Honey," she says. "I want to. Quit stalling."

Eva takes a seat on the bench next to me, pulls the computer onto her lap, and moves her face back and forth in a strange motion that reminds me of a hypnotized snake until I realize she's just having a hard time reading the screen.

I reach over and magnify the text.

"Okay," she says. "Let's see."

Watching someone else read your prose for the first time is difficult. Watching Eva Marshall read—chin tucked, brow furrowed, eyes squinting—is excruciating.

She searches for the scroll button, gets through page one and into page two—thank goodness there's little more—and then softly, quietly, almost tenderly closes the lid.

"Well," she says, turning to me.

We're seated so close that our thighs are touching. Her face is just inches from my own.

"Tell me about this essay," Eva says.

Not *your* essay, but *this* essay, as if it is a distasteful thing that can be held between pinched fingers.

"It's not my typical writing style," I say quickly. "I wrote it fast. Because you gave me that deadline. I'm not even done." I stop myself. "But those are excuses, and I don't want to be someone who makes excuses anymore."

"Relax," she says. "Now try again. Tell me about this essay."

"I thought I'd write about my father's second marriage to a woman who is only ten years older than me, and even though I like her—love her even—how uncomfortable the whole situation was at first . . ."

"Those aren't very high stakes."

"I was finding my way into it. I was trying to figure out my own feelings. You know how the word 'essay' comes from the French '*essai*,' to attempt? I was—"

Eva shivers with disgust, as if I've just blown my nose into a Kleenex and then pulled it open to show her the contents.

"Don't use foreign words or quote that kind of academic mumbo-jumbo to me. Know exactly what you're writing, before you write it."

I'm thinking of all the advice I've ever read from Anne Lamott, John Steinbeck and Stephen King about how it's okay to write fast and imperfectly, and revise later. But Eva nods her sharp chin, decision already made. "You can do better. You're going to send me a new essay tonight. I'll read it before bed. We'll talk about it tomorrow."

"But the women are coming tomorrow. The opening party—"

"The girls and the gardeners and Hans will be busy. I won't be."

I don't have a clue what to write about and I can't fall behind on my other tasks, but of course I say yes. Why?

Because I'm an Agreeable. It's better than the other choices. At least by agreeing, I've got to learn *something*.

I turn toward the French doors, about to leave.

"One more thing," Eva says. "Your name. Who calls you Jules?"

"My mom. Well, everyone. But she started it."

"Changing my name from Patricia to Eva was the best thing I ever did. Tell me the significance of your real name. The whole thing, 'Juliet May.'"

This story. I enjoyed telling it when I was a preteen. Not since.

"I was a preemie. They planned to call me Juliet, because of my due date, in July. They thought it was clever. But then I slipped out in May, and Dad wanted to name me after my *actual* birth month. Mom wouldn't budge on their original plan. She kept calling me Juliet, then Jules for short."

Eva was bored by my Dad essay, but I can tell from her expression that she is interested in this.

"My parents argued about a lot of silly things, back then. They're more reasonable now."

"No." Eva purses her lips. "That's not the story."

"Dad was stubborn. They laugh about it—"

"Forget 'Dad.' You already tried writing about him."

Okay.

"Mom's the one who won't adjust to reality. You were supposed to be born in July, but you weren't. Your premature birth was a failure of sorts—*her* failure. Her own body's failure. She expected one thing and life gave her something else. I'm sure that's defined your relationship more than once. Daughters are always turning into something other than we planned."

I can tell she's talking about me, but not only about me.

"Your mother will never completely *get* you," she continues.

"She's still one step behind. Juliet—or *Jules*. Not *May*. What else does she refuse to understand about you?"

I wait for her to tell me. When she doesn't, I say, "I'll think about that."

"Do," she says, granting me a wide, dazzling smile, the one I've been longing to see. Eva is never happier than when she's cracked someone's story code. "And honey," she says, "I think 'Juliet May' is too long."

Thank goodness. I've been feeling like a weird Southern belle every time she uses both names. "I agree."

"I think we should just call you May. In this case, your Dad was right."

"But he never did call me that. He wanted to, for maybe a week—but he didn't."

"All the better. Then it's still fresh. It isn't polluted with bad associations."

Part of me thinks, *Do I get a say in this?* But a bigger part of me thinks: *A new name. New possibilities.* Energy surges through me. Family arguments, crap writing, wasted months trying to decide about grad school: all of it can be left behind. Not just left, like all those program catalogs gathering dust under my bed. *Erased.*

"You're smiling," Eva says. "It's a different smile. You look different."

"I feel different."

"Even when I met you, I didn't think you were a Jules or a Julie, or even a Juliet May. I think you left that identity behind weeks ago—probably back in Mexico or Panama. Do you think?"

I shrug.

"When you walked in this door, you were already someone else. We just needed to find out who that person was." Eva keeps staring at me. "Do you know what I mean?"

"I'm not sure," I say, trying my hardest not to look away. *I see you, the real you.* That's one of her phrases, like *Cracks and all* and *Broken but beautiful* and *Story as liberation* and *Tell your story, reclaim your soul.*

I see you. It's a gift. A gift should be accepted. I suppose I'm accepting it now, by pretending to understand, when I don't.

I've always wondered if I'd look back on my life as a series of chapters, most of them exciting, hopefully. I thought a new chapter was starting the first time I stood on Eva's balcony, when she hired me. But I was wrong. That was just the last chapter winding down to a close. The real new chapter isn't about a mere job. It's about the chance she is giving me right now—I think—to live a bigger life.

Eva is still gazing intently, but then she nods once. We're done.

"Don't think too hard. Close the door behind you, May."

And so, I do.

PART
II

15

ROSE

———————————————

———————————

———

"Finally." Eva beams. "After much travel, after much sacrifice, you're all here."

They've gathered in the open-air classroom, to one side of the lawn. Last night's dinner party was only a hint of what's to come. It's here they'll truly get to know one another's stories. It's here that lives will change.

Eva glances from face to face, pausing to smile, scrunch her nose, raise an eyebrow, make a connection. When it comes to Rose's turn, she feels it, too: the kindness of that unhurried, attentive gaze, like they are continuing an unspoken conversation. It helps her let go of everything else: her exhaustion from the crazy night of broken sleep, meeting Dennis on the beach, reading Eva's second memoir, seeing the wildfires. What she must do—what she wants to do—is be here, now.

Direct questions have provided Rose with only one new possibility: that Jules may have had a Guatemalan boyfriend. That matters, but it's not everything, because if it was, Jules wouldn't have sent all those texts and emails about Eva and the women, about how she felt honored and excited to be helping them—until, suddenly, she wasn't. A fling can't be the whole story. Something happened.

The thatch-covered classroom or *aula* where they meet nestles against a vine-covered rock wall. The open side faces the lake. Across the blue water, the volcanoes form a permanent and bewitching backdrop, today made softer by haze. The scenery, fused with buttery light, could be a photograph, especially with the water so dreamy and still. The day is holding its breath.

A series of benches with pillows—casual seating for a half dozen—are on two closed sides. Most of the writers have already staked out their places in the other chairs, of which there are several kinds: director's chairs with canvas seats, slouchier camp chairs, a few stiff plastic chairs with attached desks. A whiteboard and stool are at the front of the class, where Eva stands, arms as busy as an orchestra conductor's.

"I hope you're comfortable," Eva says, gesturing to the open-air space with its mixed seating—a far cry from the typical boring college classroom. "Comfort is important. As is good food. You're going to be asked to do difficult things here, but in between those difficult moments, we hope to make you feel fabulous. That's why I encourage you to sign up for massages, to swim, to take breaks whenever you need them. I'll be working around the clock. You don't have to. My concern for your comfort is also why I gave you the shawls, since the winds pick up at midday, and here in the shade, it can be breezy. But it's a good breeze. You'll see here that even the weather knows what you need. It gives you quiet when you need quiet. It gets stirred up when you need stirring."

A few people laugh, but Eva isn't joking. She waits for complete silence before continuing.

"When I've had a problem, Lake Atitlán—this magical, ancient place between volcanoes—has solved it. I mean that, literally. Fight this place, and it will fight you back. Listen to it, learn from it, and you will not simply improve as writers. You will be transformed."

She takes another moment, closing her eyes to breathe deeply, prompting nearly everyone to copy her, until the whole *aula* is breathing as one.

"Good. That's right," she says, eyes opening again. "I don't use the word 'transformation' lightly. You might be surprised, but a few participants have changed their names after coming here. That's how much they feel like different people when they leave."

Rose shifts in her seat. She's always been resistant to motivational speaking, but this particular speech had been going mostly fine until that last part. *Changing your name after a writing workshop?* But then she remembers: Eva was once Patricia Myron. Rose has to admit: *Eva Marshall* has a better ring.

Eva scans the room again, reestablishing eye contact with each of them. "This place will touch your spirit. But the people here matter just as much. My staff and I are experienced. Trust us. We created Casa Eva for you."

When she stands and begins to pace, Rose notices her outfit. Eva is wearing a tight white tank that shows off a surprisingly perky bust—at least a size B or larger, not the pancake-flat chest described in her personal essay about breasts. Some surgeon did a good job. Her wide-legged linen pants have big clay-red buttons at the sides. She's wearing white sandals, her tan feet visible between the thin leather straps, with manicured, cornflower-blue toenails the same color as the cardigan she's thrown over the back of a chair.

Colorful, Rose thinks. *Creative. Confident. Like a woman who hasn't given up.* That's what Jules had wanted for her own mother.

Eva says, "Let's begin with a sampling from the manuscripts."

Pippa interrupts from the front, hands rustling through a folder in her lap. "Do we get out the notes we made—the comments we made on people's manuscripts?"

Eva takes a slow, yoga-style breath. "You don't need notes, Pippa. You don't need paper. We're not even workshopping yet."

Pippa calls out in her delightful British accent, "Soooo sorry!"

"Pippa," Eva says. "Everyone. Focus. I want you to listen— not speak. All right?"

The room is silent.

"All right?"

But they aren't supposed to speak. Except for now, possibly: just in this one instance.

A chorus belatedly kicks in. "All right!" "Yes!"

"Good. As I read aloud, I want you to pay attention to the language. Try to find the common element in everything I read to you. Just take it all in."

Holding a sheaf of printed-out pages in her hand, Eva begins to read single words and phrases. Some of the gathered participants close their eyes. One woman even reclines on a pillow-festooned bench. Rose can't do that. She sits at one of the schoolhouse-style chairs with an attached desk, pen gripped in her hand, notebook ready.

"Here goes," Eva begins.

"Depths of sorrow. Daddy issues. Damned if you do, damned if you don't."

Rose is tempted to scribble, to try to capture whatever pattern Eva is revealing. But she's supposed to listen. The common thread seems to be: Emotions? Unhealthy thoughts? Alliteration using the letter D?

Eva continues, "Inferiority complex. Normalized. Reframed."

Maybe the pattern is psychological labeling.

"Collateral damage. Mutually assured destruction."

Maybe the pattern is militaristic or aggressive labeling.

"Compartmentalization. Emotional roller coaster . . ."

Rose recognizes the last phrase from the writing sample she submitted, describing a summer with her older sister when their mother was away as an *emotional roller coaster*. And it was: extremes of happiness and melancholy, confusion and exhilaration. The roller-coaster image would have made sense even to her ten-year-old self, a young girl with little access to complex metaphors.

Well done, you.

In her surprise at being singled out, Rose has missed several words, but she refocuses.

"Benign neglect."

That was Rose's phrase as well, used to describe her parents' oblivious parenting. *Yes!* Determined not to sit up with too-obvious pride, Rose does the opposite, slumping in her seat, pretending not to notice she has been praised twice. *Twice!*

"There," Eva says, setting her sheaf of pages on the stool. She finger-combs her hair, scrunching the damp longer bits at the front. Giving them time to think. But not too long. "I'm not going to make you guess. I'm going to tell you."

Rose feels her face flush. So, this is how it feels to be in a writer's workshop, in your forties, having assumed you couldn't write, having told the world—your daughter, especially—that you had no interest in writing.

"Dead language," Eva says. "Every phrase I've read out loud—from *your* manuscripts—is an example of dead, abstract language. The kind of thing I don't want to read in this workshop ever again."

Tick—the sound of a dropped pen, hitting the floor. Then, silence.

Rose begins to sink, pulling her head low between her shoulders, until her shawl prickles her earlobes.

"But wait," says Lindsay, her finger in the air. "I mean, even 'compartmentalized?' I get that it's abstract—"

"Dead language," Eva says. "Overused. Therapy-speak. Dead. No value to any of us here."

A lock of Eva's hair has fallen in front of her face. She blows at it with pursed lips, then pushes it back over her ear with an exaggerated gesture. "Are we clear?"

It isn't easy to tell the truth. It can't be profitable. Surely, there must be other famous writing teachers who tell their students they all have artists within them. All they need to do is keep going. Shitty first drafts. *Bird by Bird*. Wasn't that one of those bestselling how-to-write books Jules was always referring to?

Eva would probably tell some of them that their birds are ugly, or worse. Dead in the shell.

Eva turns back to the stool and blinks as if she's lost her train of thought. "Does anyone know what time it is?"

Wrists turn; hands grab for phones. Voices clamor, longing to model cooperation: "Nine-oh-four!" "Nine-oh-five!" "Three minutes after nine!"

"Okay, okay," Eva says, clearly annoyed by the multiple answers. "That's our first craft talk. Now we'll discuss Diane's piece. You ready, Diane?"

Rose can see Diane's profile, her caramel-colored highlights, slightly upturned nose and expensive Jackie O sunglasses. But even the oversized shades can't hide the thin worry wrinkles crisscrossing her forehead.

"Is there any possibility of getting my piece printed out somewhere, first?" Diane asks. "I don't have a copy. I thought there'd be a printer."

Eva takes a deep breath. "We can only do printing for

you in our shared office in town. But don't worry. We're not going to be talking so much about the words you typed. We're going to be talking about story. We're going to be talking about *you*."

Everyone else is nodding, inspired by these bigger concepts—*story, yes*. The Holy Grail.

But Rose's hearing is getting fuzzy with white noise. There's an *office* in town? Eva told police that Jules worked *from* town, and Rose thought that meant running around to make arrangements at restaurants or checking on guests in their lodgings. But that couldn't keep an assistant fully occupied. It's part of why Rose kept imagining that Jules must have spent time at Casa Eva at least *sometimes*.

But if there's an entire office . . .

Rose remembers how Jules complained about the Wi-Fi. Sometimes Rose wondered if it was only her daughter's excuse for fewer texts and emails, but now that she's here on the shore of Lake Atitlán, she remembers what it's like to be traveling in a less-developed country. From Casa Eva, a working person can't get everything done.

Maybe Jules *did* spend all of her time in the village of San Felipe. Maybe Jules had hoped to audit a workshop or at least soak up some of the literary atmosphere, and never got to.

Maybe that explains everything about Jules's texts lamenting her inadequacy, her reason for giving up her favorite paperback to Luka. Maybe Jules felt too embarrassed to tell her mom that the entire Girl Friday job was a big fat disappointment from day one. That would make Eva a not-very-nice boss. But it would also make Eva completely honest. She always said that Jules worked in town, and Rose just couldn't get out of her mental rut, imagining something different.

At the front of the classroom, Eva says, "Okay. We're ready

to start. Diane, you stay quiet. I know it's hard. Just relax and let me guide us into this . . ."

Rose can't focus yet. She keeps hearing Matt's voice telling her she is wasting her time. She keeps hearing her therapist's reminders about grief and sleep deprivation. They both questioned Rose's judgment. They both warned her she wasn't ready to make this trip. She needs to get a break, but she doesn't want to walk out just when Diane and Eva are embroiled in a tense dialogue.

"In fact," Eva says to Diane, "your husband has battered you. And last night, you told me that you feared him."

The statement snaps Rose back to attention.

"Yes, that's true." Diane sounds grateful, not badgered. But she also sounds like she's in a hurry, wanting this preamble behind her, in order to get deeper into the writing itself, which never mentioned Diane's husband in the first place.

"I'm not here to tell anyone she should leave her husband," Eva says, leaning back against her stool. "But Diane, honey, and ladies, help me out here, please. Right?"

Pippa, who is Diane's roommate, pipes up first. "Yes, she has to leave him!"

Another half dozen women join the clamor.

"Oh yes, dear. Please."

"Take care of yourself first."

"Find a safe place."

Diane nods, trying to smile, one hand worrying the bangles at her wrist. "Is it okay if I talk now? I have a few more minutes, I think. If each session is an hour." She holds up her phone so Eva can see the numbers. "I'd like to ask about what I actually wrote. I know it wasn't good. But . . . what exactly could I do better? I mean, only if we have a little more time."

Eva walks toward the open side of the classroom, as if she's taking sustenance from the view. They all wait until she turns back.

"Diane has an amazing story," Eva says, finally. "By day, she manages hundreds of people. She has testified in front of Congress. She has attended parties with famous tech people. She has attended *orgies* with famous tech people. Sex, drugs, detoxifying smoothies—and a whole lot more."

Rose finds herself wondering, *Did Diane give Eva permission to share this with everyone?* These parts weren't in the manuscript pages any of them were given to read.

Eva continues, "As Diane told me last night, it's practically common knowledge: the decadence, the long weekends at retreats. Is that where you met your husband?"

"No," Diane says quietly. "He would have felt threatened in that atmosphere. As I said, I met my husband *after*."

"Don't get caught up in chronology," Eva corrects her. "Does anyone have the time now?"

"It's been one hour, exactly," Noelani says.

"Then we have to move on."

Diane raises a hand to get Eva's attention, which has wandered back to the printouts in her hand. "I just want to thank you, Eva. Not just for this, but for everything. Your books, especially the last one. Your strength and your honesty." Her voice cracks. A tear slides down her cheek. "That's why I came. Just to learn from that."

Pippa, sitting two seats away from Diane, hands her a tissue, then takes one for herself.

Rose feels tears welling behind her eyes, simply because crying is contagious. But she feels something else too—a scratchy lump in her throat, like she's swallowed a sharp bit of food. She doesn't understand why they never discussed Diane's writing. She doesn't know what to make of any of this—and at the same time, her attention is divided. Half of her is trying to understand how these workshops actually work. The other half needs to settle the issue of whether Jules ever spent significant time here in the first place. The best people to ask are the people their private investigator never bothered talking to.

"Isn't bravery contagious?" Eva says, looking pleased. "Thank you, everyone."

While the participants clap, Rose jumps up and trots out of the classroom with her head ducked low and a hand on her stomach—let them think she's having traveler's tummy troubles—across the lawn and into the house.

When she gets to the main-floor bathroom, it's already occupied. Rose waits her turn, looking at her phone and thinking about the scarcity of photos during Jules's entire Guatemala trip. She scrolls through a few volcano shots that could have been taken anywhere along this shoreline. But there's one photo that's more personal, even if it doesn't show Jules's face. A girl who is undoubtedly Rose's daughter poses with an apparently female acquaintance—their kneecaps side by side, their hands splayed as if they're doing a before-and-after manicure pose. Jules's hands are tan, her fingernails short and uncared for, matching her scabby right knee. The apparent friend has perfect pale fingers, French polished nails and slim, scratch-free legs.

Rose closes the phone in frustration. Why couldn't her daughter have taken more selfies—of her face, instead of her hands and knees? Why couldn't her daughter have used social media the way everyone else does: to show off and make one's life look perfect, instead of posting an ironic mystery shot?

After her turn in the bathroom, Rose pauses at the doorway of the kitchen, where Barbara stands with her arms over her chest, prohibiting entry.

"Are you lost?"

"I need to talk to the kitchen staff."

"About?"

"Food allergy."

"Didn't you put that on your registration form?"

"I forgot. It's really important."

Outside, on the patio near the kitchen's side doors, an alumna is having trouble with the coffee carafe. She pumps with vigor and spills extra on the table, leaving the sugar bowl open to a circling wasp.

"Oh, for heaven's sake, these people . . ." Barbara says, advancing toward the table, rag in her hand.

Rose grabs the opportunity to slip into the long, narrow kitchen, past Chef Hans, who turns and frowns at her. He's big and wide, with meaty forearms and massive feet tucked into enormous, ugly Crocs. His head is large too, a shiny bald pate, with a blue and red Buffalo Bills insignia tattoo on the bulgiest part of his skull, and below that, on his neck, a tattoo of a cleaver. His hands are hidden in oven mitts as he tends a glass pan of enchiladas. Rose smiles and keeps moving, as if she knows exactly where she is going.

"Eva wanted me to tell the women in the kitchen that the workshop session is running behind."

He rolls his eyes. "They won't understand you."

"I'll do my best."

"Fine. Concha's back there."

Rose focuses on the four Guatemalan women standing around the big butcher block table in the back, peeling scorched peppers and chopping ingredients for pico de gallo.

"Hola," Rose says, trying her best to sound casual. "Vamos a comer tarde. Según Eva."

They nod, looking only slightly relieved. Concha, nearest to Rose, has a sweat-speckled brow.

Rose pulls her phone out of her pocket. She only has a moment.

"Conoce a ella?" *Do you know her?*

Concha shakes her head without pausing the brutal rhythm of her knife. If she glances up at all, it's to send a warning glance in the direction of the three other cooks, who have slowed their chopping in order to squint in Rose's direction.

Rose angles the phone toward them, above the brimming bowls of tomatoes, onions and jalapeños. It's a picture from last summer of a hike in Utah. Jules in tank top and cargo shorts, mouth open, that one incisor slightly twisted.

Two of the women glance toward Concha, shake their heads in unison and resume chopping at full speed.

"No entienden," Concha says. *They don't understand.*

"¿No entienden?"

Or they don't want to understand, especially given Concha's warning glare? Rose recalls there are several Indigenous tongues used in the Atitlán villages alone. Kaqchikel? Tz'utujil? She's looked up the names of the languages several times, unable to memorize them and pronounce them, much less speak them. Point is, she's heard fluid, frequent Spanish from less than half the staff. She tucks away the thought and holds her ground, thrusting the phone closer to the women's faces, begging them to see.

Only one woman keeps looking. At the opening party, the lady bartender had frequently called out to her, asking for more bags of ice. Her name is Mercedes, Rose remembers. She has heavy-lidded eyes. She chops more slowly than the others, lips parted in concentration.

"La conoces a ella?" *Do you know her?*

Mercedes stares back.

Chef Hans calls from his post, near the ovens. "Ladies, I'm not seeing the calabaza soup out here. Concha, where are the tortillas?"

Rose thrusts out her phone. "La conocía a ella?" *Did* you know her?

Mercedes looks at Rose, back at Concha, then at Rose again. Her mouth is slightly open. Rose can see her tongue. Maybe she has Down syndrome. Maybe something else.

Concha drops her knife and hustles in response to the chef's request. Mercedes tracks the other women's progress across the room. She slices, waiting, until Concha is around the corner. Then Mercedes stops slicing, hand still on the black handle of her knife, squeezing it. She looks Rose in the eye. She dips her head just once: *Yes.*

16

JULES

It's great to feel needed this afternoon. The workshop participants are already in Antigua or en route, soon to rendezvous
for their dinner, and I'm busy bouncing between emails and
texts from anxious ladies, several with delayed flights.

I feel like a grown-up, an asset. Even when I have to check
in with Eva, she seems to realize that our social media feeds
can pause and breathe. There are real human beings en route.
The staff are excited, with the opening party just twenty-four
hours away. Mauricio doesn't mind being told to run into
town again for yet more wine, and even Hans chats with me,
if only to ask whether the salsa is too spicy.

In the evening, I'm shocked to find I have nothing to do at
eight o'clock. The Antigua dinner, hundreds of miles away, is
going well. No incoming participant has been involved in a
mugging, as happened one year, just outside the airport. No
one is canceling, freaking out and demanding a refund.

I'm about to head to my cabin and stop first in the kitchen,
refilling my water bottle from the big purified water *garrafón*,
when my phone starts dinging with texts. I'm relieved to see
they're personal, from Ulyana.

I don't like to interfere but your mom mentioned you haven't been texting as often. I told her it means you're having fun, but she keeps talking about mother's intuition. I thought she'd retired her psychic's hat once you graduated college. Text her?

I love Ulyana. She's part stepmom, part older sister. As usual, she's right, and yet her message pushes too many buttons all at once. First, there's guilt: I shouldn't worry Mom. It's my fault she's such a worrier, because at least once in my life, I gave her something to worry *about*.

Then I check in with another voice in my head. No, it insists. My mother worried about me before college, before kindergarten, even. She worried because I was born early—"slightly undercooked" as Dad likes to say. She probably worried about me before I was conceived. That long a history requires some serious retraining. How will I stop reinforcing her tendency to catastrophize if I keep answering every text? How will I convince her that I actually can have my own life for several weeks at a time, without it meaning something has gone wrong?

I'm just starting to respond to Ulyana's text message when Ulyana follows up. *Please don't tell your mom I texted you. Our secret.*

Secrets.

Ulyana and I have lots of them. I knew about her fertility problems a year before anyone else, and about Dad's financial problems due to the IVF. Thanks to Ulyana, I also knew what Mom told her, one boozy night when they were both trying their hardest to bond, about the bad case of baby blues she had when I was a newborn.

I don't know why Mom wants to hide the fact that she was depressed. Her generation has more mental health hang-ups than mine does—one reason of many I didn't want to tell her the first time I got severely depressed in college.

The fact is, she survived her postpartum depression, if that's what it was, and I'd be the last person to blame her for it. If there's anything worse than temporarily losing your marbles, it must be losing them while you're responsible for another living, breathing thing. When I was going through my freshman-year crisis, I wouldn't have been able to take care of a hamster.

She also got over divorcing Dad. Much as I love him, I don't think they were ever well-matched. In the end, I ended up with three great parents. Even when I've felt desperate for my own apartment and my own life, I've never wished Mom were a different person.

But I still have a deadline for Eva. I know my audience. Eva loves stories about secrets, difficult pregnancies and mother-daughter conflicts. It's time to apply what little I know about my mother's postpartum depression—with some embellishment, if necessary.

You are so creative. Even Mom said it.

Time to find out.

Three hours after emailing the essay in the middle of the night, I wake to the sound of roosters and the ding of my phone: a text from Eva.

Brava.

I stare at those five letters, feeling a warm flush of pride. Finally, I've done something right.

My thumb hovers over various emojis. None of them will do. I keep my response brief. *I'm glad you liked it.*

Her reply is swift.

Liked it. I loved it!

Another ding. *And sorry for yelling at you after my bad phone call with Richard.*

For a moment, Eva's apology feels great, like she gets it. And gets *me*.

That feeling, in turn, makes we want to apologize and

hastily explain: "I'm so glad you read and enjoyed my pages, but I may have exaggerated just a little." Or: "The essay doesn't quite capture how I feel about my mother, but revision will fix that. Thanks so much!"

And that would be stupid. You don't respond to praise with a confession that makes the person doing the praising seem less perceptive. You don't respond to possibility with reflexive self-sabotage. Right, Jules?

My thumbs hover. Last night, I felt boldly inventive. This morning I feel sheepish and fake. That impostor feeling? It never goes away, whether you are writing with all your heart or only with half of it.

Take the praise, I tell myself. If you're lucky, this isn't the only thing you'll write for Eva. They're just words on the page. A third ding. *Get ready. I'm taking you into town. Breakfast and mud facials.*

I squeal, loud enough to wake Gaby in the twin bed across the room.

Gaby mumbles, "La señora? Does she need something?"

"No, she wants to take me out."

"She never goes out the day of the big party."

"Today she is."

Mercedes, who rarely speaks more than a word at a time, sits up in bed. "*Imagínate*," she says.

Imagine that.

When Eva walks through the door, the spa receptionist claps her hands and presses them to her cheeks, giddy with joy.

"Paulina!" Eva calls. A tiny girl with long black braids bursts through a pink curtain and runs to Eva, burying her face in the side of Eva's leg.

"Oh, darling! How's my favorite little girl? And how's your brother?"

The girl keeps rubbing her face against Eva, too shy to answer.

"Now go up the street. You know what to get," orders the receptionist, who barely looks old enough to be the little girl's mother. Paulina breaks away, darting through the open door, just as I have my camera out, tempted to take a photo of the cuteness and slightly ashamed I'm already picturing exactly where I'd post it, which isn't like me—not the old me, anyway.

Eva flaps her hands in protest at whatever errand the barefoot little girl has been made to run, but she's clearly elated. "You don't have to do anything special. Our spa time is special enough!"

"No, no. Come. To the back. Hold on. Please wait, Miss Eva. I'm so sorry. Just a moment. You like the bigger room, with the volcano pictures."

"Don't make anyone leave before their time's up. Please!"

"And here, special for Mercedes," the receptionist says, ready with another gift. It's a repurposed cooking oil jug filled with a brown liquid, with small twigs and leaves floating inside.

"Perfect," Eva says.

The receptionist comes around to take my hands. "And then for you, Barbara, we are so happy to see you today! Miss Eva tells us we have a special celebration."

"I'm . . . not Barbara," I say. "But great!"

When we're alone again, waiting as the receptionist hurries other customers out of Eva's preferred spa room, Eva explains, "I can't stop them from rolling out the red carpet. If I protest, they just start making speeches, 'Everything you do for the orphanage, everything you do for the school.' It's easier if we just go along."

Behind us, the front door opens again and the girl enters, a carton of tropical juice in one hand. Precariously tucked under the other arm is a dusty bottle of white wine.

"Look at you! So strong!" Eva says, eyes twinkling. She whispers to Jules, "Bellinis on the house. Wine costs a lot in San Felipe and the locals don't drink much of it, so this is extra special. They insist." Under her breath she adds, "Beya's magic tea is much more valuable, but since they can make it from scratch, they don't think it's enough."

The grand gestures make me feel strange—both worried about the expense, and proud to be in the presence of someone so publicly adored.

As we wait to be shown into our special spa room, I whisper to Eva, "They were expecting Barbara?"

"Oh, don't worry about that." Eva waves her hand.

"But . . . a special celebration?"

"Her five-year anniversary, working for me. She thinks the spa is a waste of time and money, but I thought if she could just sit still long enough, she'd learn to like it."

I get a sinking feeling. "But then you asked me at the last minute, instead?"

"Honey! Don't worry about it. The house was *crazy busy* when we left. I don't know what I was thinking. I'll make a special appointment for Barbara another time. Pedicure, facial, the works."

I'm trying to wipe the worried look off my face. Even when I try to forcefully smooth out my brow, I can still feel the tension above my eyes.

"Did Barbara know she was supposed to celebrate with you, today?"

I'm hoping Eva will tell me it was a surprise—that Barbara never knew the plan, so she never had to know that Eva broke the plan. But Eva isn't answering. She's just staring at me with an impish grin. "Please, May. Let's make this special. Do it as a favor. For me."

"Friends' day out?" a different spa lady asks as Eva and I settle into a small stuffy room that smells of vanilla. Opposite our reclining white leather chairs, the wall is papered with a blown-up panoramic photo of the three lakeside volcanoes: Atitlán and Tolimán close together, with San Pedro further off to one side.

"We're family, actually," Eva says.

"Ahhh," the woman said, plunging a thin wooden stick into the volcanic mud mixture. "Sisters?"

Eva gives me a sideways glance, winking. "Do we look like sisters?"

The woman hesitates. I try to spare her the need to answer. "Almost!"

"May, take a quick video, okay?"

I take a second to process the request, still getting used to my new name. "Oh. Got it."

Having just settled into my chair, I pop up again and grab my phone from across the room, capturing Eva's face as it's spackled with volcanic mud. In two hours, I'll be posting this online with some bouncy graphics that emphasize the posh, rejuvenating extras available to Casa Eva participants. *Tell your story, reclaim your soul.*

"And take some candid stills, too," Eva says, eyes closed.

"Already did. You look great!"

"Doesn't it feel divine?"

"I'm sure it will." I scoot back into my seat and prepare to accept spackling from a second spa lady.

"Shut your eyes," the spa lady says.

"Sorry!"

Maybe I've just had too much coffee at breakfast, but my brain feels the need to stay on alert. A moment ago, entering the sweet-smelling room, I felt only bubbly excitement. But Eva manages to turn everything into a test. When I feel the woman's hand cup my chin, my eyes flash open again.

"You definitely could be sisters," the spa lady says. "Same coloring. Same skin."

"Exactly," Eva says, her voice sticky with pleasure. "But I was kidding. We're mother and daughter."

I freeze in my seat.

"Kidding!" Eva finally snorts. "We're just friends."

When the thick, sulfurous paste is added to the skin under my nose, I twitch.

"You don't like it?" the woman asks.

"No, it's fine." My sinuses fill with the ancient, flat scent of ash. It smells like death.

I hear the door open, then startle as someone new pulls my feet into their lap. I didn't ask for a foot massage, and I can't exactly relax and enjoy it. I'm on the job.

From her purse on a corner chair, Eva's phone dings repeatedly. "Looks like the house Wi-fi is working, at least." No one silences it. The buzzing and dinging is making me tense. "Beya, tell May here about what Lake Atitlán means, like you told me last time."

"'At the water,'" the voice from near our feet answers. "*Atl* is *water* in Nahuatl, the Aztec language. The local Mayan people call it Choi Lake. That also means *near the water*."

"But tell her the Nahuatl part. About purification? And a battle?"

"In the Aztec calendar, the day *atl* is about conflict. You purify by having conflict. No resting on the day for *atl*. It is a day for battle with yourself."

Eva's chair squeaks as she leans back into it, satisfied. "*Battle with yourself*. It sounds like writing memoir, doesn't it? May, that's the sort of thing you should write in your journal. You're still keeping a journal, aren't you?"

"Yes."

"May, what would you think if we organized future workshops according to the Aztec calendar?"

I take a deep breath while the traffic director in my head sorts through all kinds of thoughts. I didn't get a good look at her face when we came in, but Beya sounds Pakistani or Indian, not remotely Guatemalan or Mexican. Wasn't she actually wearing a red bindi dot between her eyes? I'm not sure if her knowledge of the Aztec calendar is even correct.

"I think it would require some help from a local shaman or an anthropologist to get it planned properly. And isn't the Mayan calendar a little different than the Aztec calendar?"

Eva isn't listening. She tells me about another property she has, a mile from Casa Eva. There are a few old yurts there, an old bus that's been turned into a tiny house, even if the roof leaks, and several adobe-walled huts.

"It was all part of some Mayan medicine ecolodge that went out of business before the main building was finished. The temazcal huts are great places to fast, sweat and cleanse. We could offer Beya's tea."

"I thought that tea was for Mercedes's seizures."

"It's good for much more than that. Think of all the writers who come to us—with anxiety, depression, migraines, chronic pain. Think of the creativity that could be unleashed if we could make them healthier and more serene, first."

Eva's phone dings for the hundredth time. "That must be Barbara. She's peeved I went out—"

My concern, exactly.

"—And she doesn't like when I try to expand my brand in too many directions."

"Well, she's probably right," I say, feigning disappointment.

"Still, I think people underestimate the power of natural rhythms. Cycles. The pulse of creation, both cosmological and personal." Eva brightens. "Beya, in the Aztec calendar, are there any good fertility days coming up?"

"Day of the rabbit," Beya says.

"And when's that?"

"May twelfth. Two weeks from now."

"Interesting. Don't you think, May? *Hello?*"

I hesitate, forgetting again—it's not just the month we're talking about. It's my new name. "Oh. Yes."

"And you were planning to leave when?"

I clear my throat. "On the seventh."

"Oh, that can't be right," Eva says, sounding playful. "So soon?"

On the tuk-tuk ride back to the house from the spa I'm not sure I've heard correctly. Eva's in the front, next to the driver. I'm in the back.

"Sir *what?*"

"Surrogacy," Eva shouts over the loud tuk-tuk motor and the crunch of wheels over gravel.

"You'd be perfect." She laughs. "*We'd* be perfect."

"Perfect for . . . ?"

"Making a baby. You didn't think I stopped wanting a baby, did you? I thought you were my closest reader."

"I thought you'd . . . given up."

The wind is whipping her ash blond hair into a cotton candy cloud around her head. She claws loose strands away from her mouth, then looks back at me. "Since when do I ever give up?"

I shake my head, confused.

"I'm asking a real question. You know everything about me, May. When do I give up?"

I shrug, and she scoffs and then mumbles something that's stolen by the wind, though her scowl can't be missed. I'm 'perfect,' but I disappoint her. We seem locked into that dance. Maybe we really are becoming like family.

"You seem surprised."

"Yes," I say, trying to buy time.

"Well then . . . ?"

I'm shocked and I'm not—the same way I felt when Rudy, my college newspaper faculty mentor, said he'd write me a grad school rec letter if we could go out to a bar and discuss the details, first.

Part of me thought, *Hey, he's just asking.*

The rest of me recognized I'd been demoted. From student and writer, a whole person, to a mere body. A physical, female body.

Rudy never did write that letter, by the way. He wasn't "just asking."

"Ten thousand dollars," Eva says. "Plus room and board for a year. I'd choose the father, obviously. You'd spend the year in Guatemala."

Her reasoning is that I have enough in common with her—coloring, smarts, interest in writing. Given that her eggs have proven to be too old, this is her best, last shot at making a baby that could pass as her own.

"You should be flattered," Eva says.

I nod. It's the best I can do. This is so sudden. So seemingly random. Eva isn't just sharing a daydream, she seems to want an immediate answer.

"You said you interned at a women's reproductive clinic," she continues. "I assume that means you're in support of a woman's right to choose."

"Absolutely."

"Well?"

"Wow," I say, waiting as I drop the bucket into the well of my flustered thoughts, waiting for the splash. "Is this why you hired me as a personal assistant?"

She turns, triceps soft against the top of her tuk-tuk seat, trying to face me. "No. I just thought of it this morning, after I read your essay. I said to myself, 'She's got some chops. She's a lot like me.' Which made me very happy."

Eva's natural joy is undeniable. I believe her. And she knows I believe her. She knows how much I need this—not just the money, but the validation. If this were all a big misunderstanding, it would be easier to laugh it off. But it's the opposite. It's an *understanding*, at least in part.

She adds, "Which isn't to say I haven't thought about surrogacy before. But everyone's always discouraged me, even when they know everything I've gone through, how much I've already sacrificed. I don't think that's fair. Do you?"

I think of my parents' attitudes about my dream of becoming a writer.

"No."

She points to her ear.

I think about the two MFA programs that rejected me.

"No."

She shakes her head, annoyed, still pointing to her ear, though I'm sure she can read my lips. I've managed to hear nearly everything she's said just fine.

"No!" I shout, over the wind and the tuk-tuk engine. "It isn't fair!"

She nods, satisfied. "Jonah doesn't necessarily want to be a father. He had a vasectomy years ago and has no plans to undo it. For him *what happened* might have been a relief in some ways. But Jonah's a good man. On the short side. With psoriasis. But a good man."

My mind is reeling, still trying to assimilate the (not very large) cash offer for surrogacy—a huge ask, a potentially life-changing transaction—plus the news that Jonah might have been relieved about Eva's baby's death, plus the fact that his lack of interest in children, like his stature and his skin flare-ups, did not prevent them from marrying. A mixed bag of the poignant and the trivial, which one might say is Eva's brand. Why hadn't I ever noticed that before?

"Barbara says, 'You're out of time. You'd be seventy-four when the kid's eighteen.' But then I think, 'Well, I would have been only seventy-two if you'd been more supportive of the idea two years ago.'"

I'm grateful that we're having this discussion in the tuk-tuk and that we'll be returning to a house in flux, the party only hours away. There won't be time for further discussion.

"Young writers leave MFA programs in debt," Eva says. "Depending on the school, what—thirty or forty thousand? One hundred and twenty thousand at a school like Columbia? Their own teachers can't make a good living from writing. It's a ponzi scheme! You know that, right?"

"Yes," I shout. I do know that. That's the problem. I wish everything about this were wrong. But it's only partly wrong, and it's the wrong part that has settled deep down into my gut, where I can't take it out and examine it properly. Details can be worked out. Payments and timelines can be negotiated. But *what I'm feeling* can't be negotiated, or silenced. It's a big, screaming air horn.

Eva bangs on the roof of the tuk-tuk with her hand. "Slow down, will you?"

When the driver ignores her, I say, "Más despacio, gracias."

"See? Good with languages. That's a plus." She puts a hand to her neck, sore with the effort of trying to look and shout over her shoulder. "If I were a young writer all over again—twenty-two, with no publishing record—I'd find a way to make a quick ten grand. Then I'd settle myself in a place just like this where I could live on less than one thousand a month. That would give me a year to write a book. You know how long it took me to write my second memoir?"

"Seven weeks."

"And they were good weeks." She looks wistful. "When it's the right story, and in you're in the right place, both geographically and emotionally, it's magic. And my most recent novel?" she quizzes me.

"Four months but really just three, because during one of those months you were on tour and that doesn't count."

I hear myself still trying to get the right answer, still trying to get the good grade and the recommendation letter and the someday-blurb, still trying to please her.

"Good girl. Anyway, I'd be covering your room and board. You wouldn't spend a thousand a month. You'd end the year with savings in the bank. Don't like Central America? Try year two in Thailand."

Her cost-of-living math is sound. And I've googled how much a woman can get by selling her eggs. That's how I know she's underpaying. If eggs are worth close to 10K, surely surrogacy should be worth five or ten times as much. It isn't like pregnancy is easy or risk-free. But it's not all about that. It's about much more. I want out of this tuk-tuk.

When we come around the final curve to Eva's house, I say, "I appreciate that you think I'd be a good candidate. But—"

"You're scared." Eva flutters her fingers toward me, wanting me to reach back and take her hand. Which I do. "Pregnancy is a beautiful thing. No one tells you this part: months two to six, you're a goddess. Big breasts, waist still not too thick if you start out thin and athletic like we are."

"It's not that. I'm just not interested in selling my body—"

Eva starts to open her mouth in protest. "It has nothing to do with selling."

"—or even renting it out."

Our hands separate. She faces forward. I lean back.

Just past the yellow door in Eva's gate, the tuk-tuk driver stomps on the brake. A cloud of dust rises and quickly settles again. It reminds me of a magician's flash powder, the perfect bit of stagecraft to signal the end of one trick, or the beginning of another.

"I see," Eva says, chin up, with a girlish grin.

I try to return her smile. "Sorry?"

"I don't have quetzales." She slides off the bench without looking back at me. "Pay him?"

I dig a hand into my pocket, glad I happen to have the right coins.

"And Jules. Think about it."

But I have. I've given her my answer.

"There's so much I need to tell you about my last pregnancy," she adds, turning back to give me an attempt at a smile, which really looks like a waxy grimace. The facial, instead of adding to her glamour, has left her with a shiny face and red eyes.

"I think—"

"It's about trust," she interrupts, her words smothering mine.

Her need is an uncomfortably warm, pulsing thing. She wants to confess something, and she also wants my body. She wants my youth and my health. I wrap my arms around my rib cage, feeling the need to protect myself. It's not logical. She can't talk me into something I don't want to do. There isn't any part of me that thinks she would try. And yet: something has changed now.

Eva adds, "We'll talk more when the workshops are all done. It's impossible to think clearly until then."

17

ROSE

If Rose hadn't gotten that nod from Mercedes, she would have walked out of this workshop and never turned back. But at least one person in the kitchen recognizes Jules. Her daughter might have worked in town, but she spent enough time at Casa Eva for a kitchen helper to recognize her.

The other women's reactions were just as telling. Concha barely looked at Rose's phone. The other women looked to Concha before making up their own minds. Mercedes's reaction was cautious. Rose can't be misreading all of their body language. They've been *told* to forget Jules.

Rose returns to the classroom, mulling over what she saw and glad that she can sit without being called on. If the next workshop is like the last one, they won't be asked many questions.

"This next one is extra hard," Eva says when everyone has finished their five-minute break. "It's Rachel's turn. And Rachel is not a weak writer. Strong syntax. Active verbs. No dead language."

Rose feels herself relax. She doesn't want to hear Rachel being interrogated about her present situation without any discussion of what she has written. To be honest, she struggled with Rachel's submission: the drugs and the vomit and the car crash in which Rachel nearly killed her own children. But now Rose has met Rachel. Rose wants to understand her story. She can imagine Jules here, wanting to listen and help—wanting also to *learn*. How is meaning extracted from grief?

"All right," Eva says. "The vomit scene. What did we think?"

Lindsay's hand goes up. Eva doesn't call on her.

"Too long," Eva says. "We're not willing to follow you as you vomit in the taxi, down the front hallway, in the bathroom and finally all over the bed. A few colors and textures: fine. Cramps, shivers, spasms, spins, spittle, dry heaves. But Rachel, really?" She's turned her head to one side, one eye shut, like she's looking through a peephole at Rachel. "You expect us to read all that? Five pages?"

"No," Rachel whispers, looking down.

Eva laughs. "Good! That part was easy. Now some more craft-specific stuff. I know you went to *graduate school* for writing."

Rose detects disdain in Eva's mention of schooling. Evidently, informal learning is good enough. That's what Jules had always said, too. *Mom, I don't need an MFA!*

Eva spends the next twenty minutes outlining three key points on the whiteboard.

One, scenes should be shorter. Condense.

"Two, no habitual actions reduced to boring summary. Not 'we *used* to get drunk every day by three P.M.' Not 'my husband and I *would always* fight to use the last of the heroin.' I want you to show me *one time*. A single occurrence, fully dramatized. In real-time.

"Example: Not, 'Every day, as my nameless husband and I both got more addicted and desperate, we'd compete for the last bit of some nameless drug that one of us had managed to score.'

"Instead: 'Joe pulled the needle away from me just before I was about to stick it between my toes. BEAT. He backed up against the wall, tightened the rubber ligature, and plunged the needle into his own arm. BEAT. Ten minutes later, he passed out, but I was still awake. I pulled on my wool coat, hands shaking so much I couldn't button it. I stumbled out the door, leaving it unlocked behind me. I had Tim's phone number. I knew I could find heroin, without Joe. BEAT.'"

Rachel's husband wasn't even named Joe, and no dealer named Tim had been mentioned, and for all Rose knew, Rachel didn't own a wool coat, but none of that was the point.

Someone behind Rose whispers, "Jesus. Wow."

Eva scans the room. "We all get that? One time that stands for many times she did the same thing. It can be seen. It could be filmed, should she be so lucky to have this memoir optioned. Basic stuff. Do you understand, Rachel?

"Okay, that's point two. Point number three, because we can't spend all day on this: dialogue. Hello? I want to hear your voices, and your husband's, and your kids', and of course, they all need names. Stop saying 'my daughter.' For god's sake, she's a person. Give her a name. Give her a voice, especially that moment when she comes in the door and sees you lying on the floor and thinks you're dying. Obviously, she said something. Don't make me slow down for every sensory impression of the vomit and then fly into fast-forward when there are other human beings in the room. I care about people. People break our hearts. And people speak, Rachel—goddammit. Let me see. Let me *hear*."

Rose can't tell how Rachel is taking all of these critical notes. Unlike Diane, with her bobbing head, Rachel is sitting erect, her head of tight gray curls motionless.

"But here's the problem," Eva says. "Like I told the class,

it's not the writing. No, the problem is Rachel herself. You ready for this, Rachel?"

Eva retreats back to her stool and leans against it. The rest of them are scrunched down into their chairs, cocooned in their shawls. Eva is the only active one, made warm by her ceaseless motion. Her bare shoulders glow.

Now, she pulls the stool closer to Rachel, closing the distance between them by half, then places her palms on the knees of her linen pants, anchoring herself for a hard truth.

"Rachel, you are a horrible person."

Next to Rose, Noelani is in the process of unwrapping the crinkly wrapper of a cough drop. Noelani stops, the lozenge still half-wrapped, her gaze meeting Rose's. Rose tries to give her a look that means, *Is this normal? Is this really okay?* Noelani's eyes flick away.

"I'm sorry," Eva says. "That's what the reader will think. *Selfish, addicted mother almost kills her own children.* Readers won't forgive that. It's unconscionable. I don't have time for it. Do any of you?"

Diane whispers, "I don't."

"Good!" Eva says. "And you? Noelani?"

Noelani drops the end of the long black braid she was nervously fingering. "Child abuse is pretty hard to take."

Eva locks eyes with Rose. "And you? As a mother, what do you think?"

Rose swallows hard. "I'm not a mother."

"Sorry?"

Rose clears her throat. "I said, I'm not a mother. I don't have children. So I can't really judge from that perspective."

Rose fixes her eyes on her notebook, head swimming with the words she's just uttered. *Not a mother.* She waits to feel something—either guilt or triumph for managing such a bald lie. She feels only sick.

Maybe that's why time is dilating. It feels like Eva pauses a peculiarly long time. No one else seems to notice.

Eva snaps her fingers, like she's just thought of something. "Simple question for you, Rachel. Have you seen your children since the court assigned custody to your husband?"

Rachel's mouth opens but nothing comes out. She seems to give up on speaking, shaking her head instead.

"Even though he was an addict, too. There's got to be a reason even the judge thinks you're a worse parent than he is."

Rose's chest aches from the tension, her own insecurities roused, hearing another person attacked for their parenting. Rachel may have been a bad parent, but worse than her husband? Why are women always the ones judged more harshly?

Eva shrugs, moving on. "Who in this room is ready to forgive Rachel?"

Rachel's face is frozen, her colorless lips pressed together, awaiting the verdict.

No one speaks. Perhaps that means no one is ready to forgive. Perhaps it means that some of them, Rose included, don't understand why they would be the ones to do the forgiving.

Lunch is brief and quiet. As they prepare to gather for the final workshops of the day, Rose passes Isobel, K-Tap and a red-haired woman named Hannah, whom Rose hasn't yet spoken to, lingering to one side of the patio.

Isobel whispers, "Do you think she approves of anyone?"

"I'm not sticking around to find out," K-Tap says. "This whole thing was a mistake."

"I'm such a fan of your stand-up. I really wanted to hear your workshop," Hannah says, gripping her phone tightly, like she's trying her hardest to resist asking for a photo.

"I've got to work a room in order to test out new material,"

K-Tap says. "I can already tell that Eva won't let me speak. She's a one-woman show."

Rose can't believe this is the same woman who was joking about wanting to donate a lobe of her liver to Eva.

"I hear you," Isobel says, fanning herself. Isobel hasn't had her workshop or her private session with Eva yet. But she did receive an email this morning that she read to her roommates. *What you submitted for discussion isn't memoir. It's history. It's too abstract. All that stuff about racism. No one wants to read that. You're going to have to start all over.*

Isobel, Rose observes, is taking the note. She's been rushing off with her laptop at every opportunity, trying to write some new pages to save Eva the trouble of publicly trashing the old ones.

Lindsay, fresh cup of coffee in hand, steps closer, voice hushed. "Maybe Eva approves more easily if you're young and pretty, like Noelani and Scarlett."

Even confident Lindsay is becoming defensive, Rose thinks. But she'll be okay.

Rose's mind wanders, returning to the thought that's been nagging at her since before the workshopping started. It's about the kitchen staff. Most of them speak Indigenous Mayan languages, not Spanish. The private investigator interviewed Eva and Barbara at the police station but he never came to the house. Even if he had, he only spoke Spanish. The staff are the ones who know something. Someone needs to speak to them. Someone needs to earn their trust.

Rose's phone vibrates with a text from Matt. It's about Jules's mail. They decided to finally go through all of it, even the junk mail. *I found something and followed up. It's not a big thing, nothing related to Guatemala, but it may upset you. Call me later.*

It's a perfect Matt text, enough to make her anxious and

sad, but not enough to give her any information. Rose pockets the phone, staring into space, trying her best not to think catastrophic thoughts.

The other writers probably think she's worrying about being workshopped. If only.

Isobel groans. "Guys. Look at me. I'm not even being workshopped today and I'm already sweating."

Under her arms, the green of Isobel's lime-colored blouse has turned a shade darker.

"You'll be fine," Rose says, trying her best to focus and be supportive. "And I *liked* your original pages. Aren't you allowed to talk about family history and racism in a memoir?"

"I thought so, before. But I've also heard it's practically impossible to get a memoir published." Isobel claps her hands, like it's her job to get the team excited again, ready to return to the classroom. "This wouldn't be a popular workshop if most people left feeling like they'd wasted their money or given up on their dreams. Right, ladies?"

Lindsay smirks. "I take it neither of you has ever been to Las Vegas?"

Rose can't find time alone to call Matt until after dinner, when she hurries back to the cabin ahead of her roommates who have stayed back, chatting.

"I knew you wouldn't want me to throw away anything, even junk mail with her name on it, so I didn't want to tell you at first," he says.

"Go on."

"All the same MFA program ads and packets keep arriving, and it made me realize: in all this mail, we never got Jules's acceptances. Or—you know—her rejections."

"True." For the first time since he answered the phone, Rose feels a touch of gratitude. He *is* still sifting for clues. Part of him knows this isn't over, either. Still, he's on the wrong track. "But she used online portals. That's how the programs would have responded to her applications."

"Oh, I didn't realize that." He sounds humbled. "I'm glad I didn't."

Rose hears laughter outside the cabin. Her roommates have gathered on the small patio outside the front door, still chatting.

"I called five programs," Matt says. "Three of them wouldn't talk to me, because I wasn't Jules, even when I described what happened and forwarded a screenshot of the *Chicago Trib* article."

"And the other two?"

He names the programs, both low-residency, one in Los Angeles, one in Vermont. Jules liked the multicultural emphasis of one, the woodsy flavor of the other. If she got into both, she'd have a hard time deciding, she told Rose.

"Jules never actually applied," Matt says.

Rose closes her eyes to screen out the voices on the patio.

"The admin people must be confused."

"At both programs?" He shifts into a lower register. "I don't think so, Rose."

"So you're saying Jules lied to us."

"Yes. Or she omitted some facts."

"Just like she omitted the boyfriend. Who you believe in, now."

Matt sighs. "Maybe."

"Maybe."

The silence extends long enough that Rose is about to pull the phone away from her ear, to see if the call was dropped.

Matt asks, "How are you doing, overall?"

He hasn't asked her that in ages. It doesn't matter that she can't articulate what's she's been through. She's glad to be asked, just the same.

"Good, considering."

He murmurs something—that vague sound of assent, half-military, half-professorial, that used to punctuate many of their phone calls, back when life was boring, safe and good enough.

"So, what do you make of this Eva character so far?"

How does she explain? "Bossy but bright? I think she knows what she's talking about, but I don't know. Mean? Impulsive? Sometimes weird, sometimes wrong, sometimes brilliant?"

Matt laughs—but it isn't a kind laugh. "Careful there, you sound a little like Jules. Those girl crushes are powerful things."

The gratitude she felt toward Matt moments ago vaporizes. "Of course I don't have a *girl crush*. Were you even listening?"

"Just—be careful. You're in an emotional place. And when emotions are running high, it's even more important to stick to the facts."

There's a noise at the door, as Lindsay, Isobel or K-Tap struggle with the sticky latch. Rose heads for the ladder, so she can be halfway up to the loft before they see her weepy red eyes. It would be easy to make up an unhappy conversation with someone back home. Her roomies love a good story about family conflict, one that can be nailed down in black and white. But she can't stand the questions. Correction. She can't stand the questions without *answers*.

"Rose, the main thing I believe, now, is that we didn't know Jules the way we thought we did."

"I don't believe that, Matt."

"You don't, or you can't?"

18

JULES

The opening party is scheduled to start before dusk, five hours after we've returned from our spa day, but those hours are busy with preparations—the stringing of fairy lights, the folding of freshly laundered napkins, the arrangement of flowers and lighting of candles. I might have succumbed to the enchantment if the surrogacy offer weren't still spinning in my brain. I'm grateful there's no time for Eva and me to share more than fleeting glances as the whole team dances around the kitchen and yard.

An hour before guests are expected, we're all dispatched to our cabins to change into clean clothes and "nap if we'd like." Even if I had more time, napping would be impossible. I'm too nerve-jangled.

When I enter the cabin, I see Mercedes already sitting inside, fully dressed in traditional huipil but tucked into bed, eating a cookie. When I ask her where she got it, she points toward my desk. The surface has fewer papers than I remember. I open a drawer. My passport isn't there. My journal isn't, either.

"Someone was in our cabin?" I ask her.

She lowers the half-eaten cookie, eyes wide.

"Did you see anyone take things from my desk?"

Her bottom lip begins to quiver.

Whoever invaded my privacy knows that Mercedes isn't a talker. Maybe the cookie was just to keep her occupied so she wouldn't run off to Concha before the snooper was finished.

Tears begin to flow. Mercedes raises her fist up to her face, hiding behind it.

"It's okay," I reassure her. "You didn't do anything wrong."

But the tears keep pouring.

"Never mind. We're going to have fun tonight. Let me change my clothes and then I'll braid your hair, okay?"

An hour later I'm still trying to believe my own promise. This will be fun. Eva's only comment: *Let's be sure everyone's having a good time.*

After the shawling and once everyone has a glass of wine, I spot a woman with stringy dyed-black hair that's shaved on one side. She's standing in the food line, talking with a woman four times her age.

"Well, your hair's okay," the older writer says. "But the tattoos and all that—it's just too much. I tell my granddaughter, 'If you want a good job at all . . .'"

"And what kind of work does your granddaughter do?" the much younger woman asks politely.

"Something with computers. And what do you do?"

"I'm a musician."

The old woman leans back to look at her again, as if to say, *I don't recognize you.*

But I do.

"I think your granddaughter will find her way," Zahara says. "I'm sure she was raised with a good work ethic. It'll turn out fine."

A nice person—though admittedly eccentric. In addition

to the grunge outfit, she's wearing white gloves that look like something British royalty would wear.

I'm getting my cabernet refilled when I hear the same pleasant, unhurried voice at my back. "*Perhaps one did not want to be loved so much as to be understood.*" She's reading the tiny, vertical typewriter font running down the back of my right triceps. "Wow. That's like the motto for why we're all here."

I turn and see two kohl-rimmed eyes looking up at me. She's a wisp of a girl, swimming in an oversized men's T-shirt and overalls. In photos, holding her guitar under bright stage lights, she looks bigger in every way.

"Hey," I say. "You're right."

"George Orwell. Your tattoo, I mean." She reaches a free hand out to shake, then drops it when she sees my hands are full. "My name's Zahara. I'm really coming across like a dork. And I guess it's dark enough to take these off." She peels off the gloves and stows them in her overall pockets. "Sorry, I'm a hand model. Yes, it's weird, but I need the money. Let's get that out of the way. It's fucking bizarre!"

I start laughing, not sure what to say next. "No one ever gets that my tattoo is from Orwell. Not even people who have read *1984*."

"I wrote a song called 'Clocks Striking Thirteen,'" she says, taking a glass of white wine from Gaby, who's bartending.

"Is *1984* your favorite?"

"No, *Homage to Catalonia*, actually."

"That's my favorite, too!"

"Oh, wow," Zahara says. "I've never met anyone under fifty who's read it."

And there it goes, from intimidation to platonic girl crush.

I have to resist the urge to commandeer her attention all evening. But Eva, seeing us chatting at the far end of the lawn, approves. I know she wants me to chaperone Zahara. On top of that, Eva's hoping to ask Zahara to perform a casual duet sometime this week.

Eva nods toward us both just before going to a microphone, where she welcomes everyone and launches into a speech about how everyone is broken but everyone is beautiful and if we listen, we all will succeed and all of our stories matter equally, et cetera.

A few days ago, I would have been shedding an inspired tear. Now I feel dry-eyed and somber.

A chant has started up—call and repeat, with applause between each round.

"Cracks?"

"Cracks and all!"

"It lets the light in. You are all standing in that light. You are broken but you're beautiful."

"Cracks and all!"

Zahara, standing next to me, raps her French-polished fingernails against the wineglass. She gives me a knowing, skeptical look and mouths the words: *Leonard Cohen?*

"That's it!" I shout back, but instead of catty pleasure, I just feel numb.

There is a crack in everything; that's how the light gets in. That isn't Eva's line. She "borrowed" it. Why am I not surprised?

The next morning around ten, I find Eva in the kitchen, hurrying to grab a bottle of sparkling water, face flushed with the pleasure of the morning's first workshop, which is now on coffee break. I have less than five minutes, which is more than enough. I've been tying myself in knots since going to bed last night, telling myself there's a simple explanation, while also aware I don't want to blame or panic anyone.

"Eva, I'm worried that someone stole my passport."

Her rebuke is swift. "You can't leave valuables out in the open."

"It wasn't out in the open. It was in a drawer. I trust my roommates."

"And I trust my staff. But people wander around. We get visitors. A shifty guy was seen up on the road, by the gate, just the other day."

The shifty guy. Mauricio's uncle.

"So you think someone took it?"

Her expression softens and her glance wanders, like she is remembering something, or else making up a story. I want her back on earth. It's my passport. Something I can't easily replace.

I stammer, "Be . . . because I—"

"Don't worry," she interrupts, laughing as she cracks the cap on the fizzy water, leaning back against one of the counters. "It's in my safe."

Dismay must be etched on my face, because she rolls her eyes, adding, "Hotels keep people's passports while they're checked in. It's more secure."

"I'm relieved, I guess," I say, though I'm not. Not at all. "But my journal is missing, too."

"Oh, *that*. I just wanted to take a look. You can run up to my office to get it. It's next to the printer, where Barbara works."

Heat flares through my body. I try to remember everything I've written about: my starry-eyed worship of Eva—she would like that part. But I also scribbled a bit about Barbara, Hans and of course, Mauricio. She won't be happy to know I've been canoodling with her darling orphan.

"You read it," I say, straining to control the tremor in my voice.

"Not every page. I don't have time for that." She winks. "And don't worry. I've heard you and Mauricio chatting in Spanish, like you think no one will understand. I've seen how he looks at you."

My blood is boiling with indignation and embarrassment. I don't believe for a minute that Eva understands much Spanish beyond "taco" and "guacamole," but it still unnerves me to think she's been spying on us.

"I'd like to get my passport back, too."

"Let me look into that," she says. "May! It's busy around here! Focus, please!"

Concha and Chef Hans enter. I'm in the way. Remembering Eva's "permission" for me to retrieve my own journal, I head through the house, up to her bedroom and into the office corner near the French doors. Barbara uses this spot, and I've sat here once or twice, making printouts.

My journal is easy to spot. Even as I grab it, I know I'll never write anything personal or authentic in it again.

Then I spot a box of recycled office paper under the desk. Blank paper isn't abundant in San Felipe. I grab about thirty pages, fold it in over into a makeshift booklet—never mind that each page is already printed with old spreadsheets on one side—and push it into my backpack. Journal number one will be the decoy. Journal number two will be this: sloppy but private.

Then I go downstairs and use my final ten minutes of freedom to freewrite about how violated I feel, and how strange.

The rest of the day, although the workshops are fully in progress now—the whole reason I was excited to be here, really—I'm only half-engaged. As I watch Eva interact with the participants—shutting them down when they simply want to explain or ask a question, probing sensitive areas the women clearly don't want to talk about and didn't write about in the first place—I can feel myself judging, deciding, emotionally retreating. Giving up on the idea of a mentor. Giving up, perhaps, on the idea of writing memoir altogether, at least at my age. Cutting my losses.

At midafternoon break, I find myself standing in a shady corner of the yard, next to Eva, who is doing her stretches.

"It's been a rough first day," I blurt and immediately wish I hadn't.

"What do you mean?"

"Beatrice and her son, hanging himself."

"That wasn't rough. We found her key scene. I gave it to her wrapped up with a bow. Now she just has to go write it."

Eva is wearing a transparent blue shirt with wide flowy sleeves over a tank top. She always wears elegant clothes, but often, there will be just one thing wrong. Yesterday, after swimming, she put on her shirt inside out. Today, she's misbuttoned the overshirt.

I point, finger an inch from her chest. "Your button."

She bats away my finger. "It's fine."

The rough physical contact startles me.

"Sorry," I whisper. "I thought you'd want to know."

"Not today, May. Not today."

I feel nervous. And when I ask myself why, the only answer I have is that Eva seems nervous. I think of one workshopper's essay about her experience living with an alcoholic mother and how she learned to read her mother's moods, tiptoe when she was angry, and never—never—say a critical word.

Eva is not an alcoholic. Eva is most certainly not my mother. I can't blame her for my own anxiety. Though I can—the thought comes to me now—start googling, the first free moment I have, the price of a one-way flight home.

Home.

There's always the moment on any journey when you start thinking of your own bed, familiar foods, liberation from the endless daily work of figuring things out—and that's for normal trips, not trips that have made you question your worth and your sanity.

When Barbara barks at me around three o'clock to transfer the latest PayPal payments, I'm only too glad. It means I'll miss the final workshopping session. The local Wi-Fi is too slow, so I have to go to town.

A half hour later, I'm at the share-space, a hot little eight-by-eight back room behind a travel agency, checking email messages from future workshop participants, sending a file that Eva asked me to rush to her agent and then taking a ten-minute break to continue my flight googling and check my bank balance. Predictably, a super-short-notice flight is wildly expensive. I have the money in my account, just barely, but that's not adding in a shuttle, meals, a likely overnight in Antigua, and several auto-debits that will be hitting my account in the next two weeks.

For a moment, I consider emailing my parents to ask for money. They'd give it, of course. They might not even ask many questions. *I'm* the one who asks questions, such as, *Your balance is so low you can't fly home—cutting it a little close, aren't we? And you're really willing to waste money when you could just wait a few more days and get a cheaper ticket?*

I'm rushing this. I can find a better flight. I can even leave Atitlán and kill some time somewhere else before I fly out, maybe somewhere less touristy than Antigua. This isn't an emergency.

I close my travel searches and get back to work, checking Eva's PayPal, as I've been directed to do. I usually do admin tasks without paying much attention to names or numbers, but because I'm procrastinating, not eager to be back at Casa Eva, I spend a few more minutes at the desk. I run my finger over the sticky soda-can rings on the desk while skimming: three hundred, one thousand, five thousand. I pause. A surprising amount of money is flowing through this account.

They are round numbers, not the amount we charge for either first deposit or full tuition and board. One of the biggest is from Wendy, the first alum I interviewed for a social media post. It's one of the few with a memo line: *Blessings for those beautiful children.*

Most of these have to be orphanage donations, in quantities larger than I ever imagined. How much did Astrid say the total was this month? *Three hundred dollars.*

God, it's hot in here. I feel a tickle on my hand and brush off an ant. I can see an entire line of them, crawling up the shaky table leg, attracted to the sticky soda rings.

It's one thing not to deliver the latest donated shoes and clothes, another to do this—and even I'm not quite sure what *this* is. It would be way too easy to divert money given by grateful women writers into personal accounts, to cover the costs of keeping up Eva's many houses.

Barbara is an actual accountant. She oversees all this. She knows better. Eva could get in trouble if someone doesn't clean this up and do right before it's too late.

Then I stop and realize. None of this is my problem, technically. I'm not a long-term employee, not an ally or a whistleblower. I'm just a girl who worked a handful of days and will be moving on, soon.

On top of all that, tomorrow is my birthday. It would be nice to spend just one day not thinking about Eva, her plans or problems or moods. I've got no way to celebrate it, but maybe something will come to mind.

I try to corral my thoughts in that one practical direction, leaving the hot little office behind me and forcing some bounce in my step as I head up the alley, into the heart of San Felipe. When I pass the pizzeria, I stop short. Mauricio's inside, at one of the front tables with an Indigenous man whose bowl-cut hair and woven shirt mark him as more traditional than most San Felipe men. My grin spreads from ear to ear.

When I get to the table, they're just getting up to leave. The man, who has the deepest wrinkles I've ever seen and one eye covered with a bluish-white film, smiles at me, but Mauricio doesn't introduce us. "Have a seat. He needs to catch a water taxi. Let me walk him to the dock, then I'll be back."

Giacomo brings me some breadsticks, on the house.

A few minutes later, Mauricio returns, alone.

"I'm sorry," he says, dropping into the booth next to me. "I just didn't expect to see you. My father and I were having a difficult discussion."

"Your *father*?" It seems like everyone I've met at Casa Eva has an odd relationship with the truth. "First, I find out you have an uncle. Then you have a father. So, you're not an orphan?"

"I never call myself that. Eva calls me that."

"But you lived in the orfanato."

"So did lots of kids whose parents were missing or just far away. A million people were kicked off their land during the civil war. Some fathers had to flee or be killed. Some mothers were left behind. When my mother was murdered, my father had too many enemies to stay. Then I had a cousin who got a tourism job in Pana. He brought me to the orphanage and left me there."

"You were born three years after the war ended, Mauricio."

"The death squads didn't go away. Some things are worse now than when I was born."

Mauricio focuses on the knots he's been tying in a straw,

looking down to evade my face, which I'm sure looks childishly furious. What the hell am I doing, needling him about his life in a war-torn country, something I know nothing about?

"I just want to know why you didn't tell me. I showed you photos of my parents. I read you my mom's texts. Meanwhile, your dad is walking around San Felipe and I think you're an orphan. So, he lives here, or not?"

"He lives in a village, six hours away by boat and bus. He only came because he heard through cousins that my uncle was bringing me to Guate. My father doesn't want that."

"*Is* bringing you to Guate? You said it would never happen."

"Jules," he says, resting his chin in his hands. "It's so easy for you."

"I want you to be safe."

"That's what Eva always says. But you know? I'm tired of being her project." He clears his throat. Another confession is coming, I can tell. "Eva wants her daughter to marry me so I can move to the US and get a green card."

"Isn't Adarsha, like, thirty now?"

"Thirty-six."

"Have you ever met her?"

"No."

"That seems like a problem. What does Adarsha think about all this?"

"She was considering, but I think Eva pushed too hard. Now they aren't talking again."

"Good," I say, not that it solves the problem. "I don't think you want to get that deeply involved with them."

"It's not that easy. I live at Casa Eva. It's a job."

"Well, you won't have a job for long if she keeps this up."

I dig into my pocket and unfold the paper with all of the donation figures. I'd told myself I didn't care about this. It's a mess and it's none of my business. But it *is* Mauricio's business.

"This is money flowing into Eva's accounts, I say, running a finger along the figures. Some of it seems earmarked for the orphanage. But it's a lot more than seems to actually be *going* to the orphanage."

When Mauricio doesn't reply, I play back my own words. Did my Spanish verb conjugations get muddled there? Is there a simpler way to say it? But his eyes don't reflect confusion—only exhaustion.

"Did you even hear me?"

"Baby, he says, everybody takes a cut here."

"Ten percent is a cut. This is not *a cut*." I lean back into the booth. "That's it? You're mad about the shoes and the clothes but you're not mad about this?"

"It's just the way things are."

"So, are you going to talk to Eva about it?"

"Me?" he scoffs. "Shit. No way."

"But you care about the orphanage, Mauricio."

"I do."

I'm trying not to share every thought that flits into my head. But I'm also disappointed.

"Can't you stand up to her? You have a close relationship. She treats you like a member of the family."

His head-shaking intensifies. "You don't get it. That makes it *worse*. She's sensitive about betrayal. Listen, it's not just about what I'd say. It's about the timing, too. With all the guests here, Eva gets really stressed."

"You sound like Barbara!"

"Barbara's right. When Eva's dealing with the workshops or when she's had a fight with Adarsha, she gets a little weird. When both are happening at the same time, I know to stay clear."

"Until?"

"Until she's normal again."

"Which takes . . . ?"

He's turned away, jaw stiff, eyes fixed on the tourists passing by the pizzeria. Maybe there's a pretty American out there, fresh off the water taxi, a girl who won't keep bothering him about accounting issues and ethics, one who will actually *listen* when Mauricio says, *Trust me, you don't want to work for Eva.*

"It takes what it takes. Last time it happened, Eva had to be alone in one of her meditation huts down the road for close to a week. She didn't eat."

His look of concern irritates me. "It's called a cleanse, Mauricio. It's what rich white ladies do. It doesn't mean she was having a nervous breakdown."

But then I stop myself. Maybe she was. And worse, maybe it wasn't just one breakdown. Maybe Eva's life is a series of breakdowns springing from some larger untreated disorder. It's good that Wi-Fi is so spotty everywhere or I'd probably start googling: personality disorders, narcissism, psychosis. I'm not trying to label or judge. I'm just trying to understand.

Mauricio expels a frustrated breath, back to tying more knots in a straw. Still not looking at me. "She was in a really bad place. When everything goes her way and she gets what she wants, she's happy. When she loses control, it's something else. You don't understand Eva."

"You're right. I don't. But it's not my job to make her happy. I'm leaving soon."

And then I remember, again. No, I can't leave yet. Not without my passport.

19

ROSE

———————————

———————————

———

"Write about the meanest thing you ever did to a friend," Eva instructs them on the second morning of the workshops as she hands out pretty gift journals with Guatemalan-style fabric covers. "Not in childhood. That's too easy. In the last decade. Make it count."

They open their journals. Workshopping is a slow-going process, Eva explains. It will be days before everyone's had a turn. Eva wants them to be more candid, to take more risks and have more energy.

"I'm giving you only five minutes for this prompt. Be brave!"

Rose gets stuck on the "friend" part, which bothers her tremendously, because it only underlined what Jules had told her—that she didn't have enough friends. Then she remembers a time when Ashley, her office manager, admitted she wanted to open her own kitchenwares boutique. Rose agreed to critique her business plan. Her notes for Ashley were all doom and gloom, predicting her business would fail. The facts were sound, but the motive was suspect. Rose wasn't protecting Ashley. She was protecting herself.

Rose has filled a page when Eva calls, "Time! Now pass

your journal to the left." They all look up, stunned. She didn't explain they'd be sharing these entries. If she had, maybe Rose would have written something different, less self-incriminating.

At the front of the room, Scarlett shares a loud, unconvincing laugh. "My handwriting's too messy for anyone else to read."

"Nonsense. Pass to your left. Hurry up. Pass, pass, pass."

They do, the wave of discomfort rolling around the circle as they hand over the textile-covered journals.

"Next prompt!" Eva shouts. "The most recent time you masturbated, including what you were thinking about."

Several women titter uncomfortably.

"If you'd be kind enough to explain," Pippa says in her droll British accent, tugging at her long earlobe. "Are we actually going to read each other's entries? I need more information."

Eva says, "Trust each other. With luck, the reader will trust you."

From the back of the room, someone whispers, "But *do* we read each other's entries? I just want to know."

"Quiet, please. We don't have all day for this. The answer to procrastination is time limits. Another five minutes. Go."

To Rose, the masturbation prompt seems more like a party-game challenge than serious provocation. They can feel daring without risking truly damning revelations.

Rose writes about the last man she dated, one year ago. His name was Boris. He wanted to watch her masturbate. It wasn't the performance she minded. It was his insistence on turning on every damn lamp. At her age, what she is willing or not willing to do with a man depends a lot on the lighting.

"Time," Eva calls. "Pass the journals. Ready. Next prompt: the first time you were forced into having sex without your consent. Ladies: *tell the truth*."

The room is so quiet they can make out the waves gently

shushing against the beach, just beyond the bluff. Out on the lake, a man stands in a small boat, casting a net on the silky waters. Hand over hand. Rose finds herself thinking of how deep the lake is beneath him, how black and bottomless. Yes, she has had sex without her consent. Alcohol, pressure, mixed signals—and times were different then. She doesn't particularly want to think about it. Did Jules do these exercises? Did she have to write in a gift journal and share her every private thought so openly? Did it help her feel like a *real writer*— whatever that means—or did it make her feel exposed and judged?

Eva says, "Two minutes left. Some of you aren't writing. I want those pens to keep moving. Pass the journals."

Someone sitting behind Rose clears her throat. "I need to go to the bathroom."

"Please wait until the hour is finished," Eva says. "This isn't comfortable, but writing never is. I want you to go to the deepest place within yourselves. It may be dark, it may be cold, it may be lonely. If you're not willing, you're free to leave."

Someone behind Rose whispers, "Leave this part? Or the whole workshop?"

But no gets up. No one refuses.

"Good," Eva says. "Next prompt: the time you wanted to kill yourself and chickened out. Go."

So many choices, Rose thinks glumly. She could write about the day they called off the lake search. She could write about several moments this week when she felt all hope of ever understanding her daughter's death slipping away.

But the worst time—the time about which she feels the most shame—was when Jules was ten weeks old.

It's not exactly a secret—everyone knows Rose went through a tough time after Jules was born. But no one knows how deeply she plunged. They all kept saying she was just tired. It was normal. But it didn't feel normal. Rose felt dissociated from herself—not just hating her wounded, bloated, postpartum body, but already hovering above it, as if ready to say goodbye.

And the baby. The baby, whose name they had fought over: Juliet? May? In the Guatemalan journal, Rose refers to her only as *her* and *the baby*. That's how she referred to her newborn daughter in real life, as well, conflicted over what name to use, but not only that.

Once they got home, the baby seemed alien to her. Just a mewling thing that made Rose wince. Not the girl they'd dreamed of. Not anything. But Rose wasn't anything either. She was an empty sack, or something hard and heavy, made of wood. Which is it? Words can't capture the feeling. And why would Rose even want those moments captured or exposed to the light, anyway?

Yes, Rose thought about how much easier it would be to disappear. For both of them to disappear. It wasn't logical. It was just a feeling, of nothing mattering, of wanting this whole mess done with. And maybe it was only chemicals out of whack, but it filled Rose with the deepest shame she'd ever known. She didn't love her own daughter. Her own baby.

There. She's written it. Enough. She didn't try hard with the first three prompts, but this time she has tried to be honest. To remember the pain. To try to find words—stupid words. And they *are* stupid. Because they fail to capture the fact that things changed. Six months later, everything was different. Six months later, she was madly in love with her daughter, and at home in her own body, again. Why go back?

And then again: If she'd ever been forced to journal this way a year or two after it happened, would the topic of depression have been easier to talk about? If she'd spoken earlier and more openly with Jules, could certain periods of suffering have been avoided?

This hurts too much. It isn't bringing Jules back. It's just making Rose realize how many mistakes she made, all along the way, and those moments can never be relived. There is no revision in life. There are only consequences.

"One minute left," Eva says. "Pens should still be moving."

Rose looks to her left and notices Rachel also looking up. Not writing.

Rose risks a glance toward the journal in Rachel's lap. The page is blank except for a single sentence, the handwriting blurred. Rachel's face is wet. The edge of her forearm is smeared with ink.

Rose whispers into Rachel's shoulder, "It's okay. You don't have to do this."

Eva, who has been flipping through some printed-out pages, snaps to attention. "I'm sorry? 'You don't have to do this?' Well, if you're not here to be part of our circle, our community of women, then you don't."

She glares at Rose, then softens her expression, pushes away from the stool, and approaches Rachel.

"Are you all right?"

Rachel looks down. "Yes."

Eva passes her a tissue. "I'm glad. Keep writing."

After a few more seconds, Eva shouts from the front of the room. "Better!" She's gathering up the journals, but she's looking directly at Rose. "See? That wasn't so hard."

Chef Hans and two Guatemalan women enter the open-air classroom with big wooden trays of freshly baked cookies and two glass pitchers of some kind of home-brewed Mayan tea. Rose looks around for Eva, who has swept out of the classroom, toward the house. Keeping her voice low, Rose asks Pippa, "What did you think about those prompts?"

Pippa brings her hands together in a gesture of prayer. "Two years working on this shitty memoir and I just revealed more in twenty minutes than I've dared to reveal in two hundred pages."

From the row of seats ahead of them, Scarlett says in a quiet voice, "I'd like my journal back."

"But which one is even yours?" Pippa asks. "We had to write in several of them."

Scarlett doesn't turn to face Pippa. "Eva didn't explain the rules before we started."

"Well," Pippa smiles. "Now you know the rules. Anything goes."

20

JULES

It's five o'clock, and the second day's workshops are finally over. There were tears of sadness and moments of stunned shock and brief upwellings of joy—or at least that pleasure that comes when the pain stops. The lady who was writing about Jesus-and-cats did end up stalking out, as Eva hoped she would. Two hours later, the woman whose son recently killed himself also left. Eva doesn't mind. They've already paid. It makes everything easier.

I noticed the little mood boost that happened each time one of these "Difficults" left. The people who stayed shifted their chairs into closer arrangements. At lunch, it was easier to fit everyone at two tables, instead of three plus overflow on the lawn.

I briefly thought it was my job to warn Eva if workshoppers were having a hard time. Now I know: Eva wants it to be hard. The tension brings down people's defenses. It opens them up to what she has to say. It knits the remaining group together.

But I don't want to talk about any of that now. I'm looking for Barbara. If Eva is as sensitive and controlling as Mauricio claims, maybe it's smarter just to talk to other staffers. One of them must know the code to the safe where my passport is being kept.

Reaching the edge of the bluff, I smell cigarette smoke.

"May," Eva calls out, smiling with slitted eyes through an expelled cloud. Her hair is damp from a post-workshop swim. "Did you ask Zahara about doing a duet with me at staff night tomorrow?"

I did ask. Zahara was absolutely clear.

"She wants to stay out of the limelight while she's here."

"Ask again. And have you thought about the other thing we discussed?"

I hoped Eva was ready to drop it. Part of me even fantasized she'd apologize for pressuring me too hard. But now I can see that she's expecting contrition from my side.

"No. When you offered me that . . . opportunity . . . I felt pretty sure right away." Long pause. My underarms prickle with nervous sweat.

"I'm going to interpret that as indecision. You are an indecisive girl, May."

"Actually, I'm not."

Eva says, "We'll talk about this again after the workshops are over."

When the workshops are over. Mauricio warned me. The workshops are stressful. She can't see past them. I have to stop treating Eva as if she's guided by logic.

"Okay. But have you seen Barbara? I just need to ask her something quick."

"She went to San Felipe for a couple of hours. Is it about the staff party? Because you'll have to get Gaby's help checking all the extension cords and the speakers. One has a buzz. Zahara can play my guitar."

"I'm really sure that Zahara doesn't want to."

"But we don't have enough content without her. The videos

you've posted weren't very good. You promised you'd be a fast learner, doing our socials."

"I'm sorry—"

"I mean, it isn't hard, is it? Telling a story? Here." She drops the cigarette on the stubby grass, grinding it with the toe of her sandal. "We need more content. Take out your phone."

"Another video, now?"

"The lighting is beautiful right now. This whole goddamn place is just *beautiful*," she flicks her chin toward the volcanoes across the water. "Toss me a question. You know I'm quick."

It's as if her good mood and the sunset and the serenity make her hungry rather than satisfied—for more attention, for a way to make this aesthetically perfect moment permanent and shareable.

"Fine," I say, holding my phone up to record. I can do this. I can perform. And then by tomorrow or the next day at the latest, all of this will be over. "*In a Delicate State*. Was it written here at the lake?"

"Oh no." She smiles for the camera. "I came down here after I finished the first draft. Atitlán feels like home to me now, but I was just getting to know it back then."

"So, you spent your final trimester where, exactly?"

Something happens to Eva's face. Her smile, which was a little lopsided but natural, becomes a stiff, unmoving line. She doesn't blink. I don't want to keep asking questions, because I'll have to edit them out of the video. It's better if she just keeps talking. But she isn't talking. She's frozen.

"Never mind," she says, finally. "Delete that one. It's probably too dark anyway."

"No, these phones are amazing. I could see you just fine."

She holds out a splayed hand, in front of her face.

"Delete. Delete delete *delete*."

I press stop with an exaggerated gesture and slide my phone into my back pocket. "Sorry. You're right. It was too dark."

Nod. Smile. Pretend that wasn't a weird moment.

But: Why doesn't she want anyone to know where she spent her third trimester?

Eva smooths her hair back. I wait until she's lit up a new cigarette. "Let's just focus on the staff party. I don't think you're cut out for social media."

"Possibly."

"Some of us learn faster than others. Anyway," Eva says, "Astrid will be our MC."

"Astrid," I say. "That reminds me . . ."

I feel in my pocket for the paper scribbled with PayPal figures. Maybe it's because Eva keeps bouncing between insulting me and giving me new trivial things to do, on top of pressuring me about the thing I am absolutely unwilling to do, as if I'll simply get flustered and give in to all of it. I promised myself—and Mauricio—I'd stay out of this, but it's just too tempting. I don't want to rattle her cage so hard she freaks out. I just want to poke.

I pull out the paper and hold it between us without unfolding it. "I'm sure Astrid plans to announce where you are with the orphanage donations. It looks like there might even be ten thousand? I know she's not expecting that. It will knock her socks off."

Eva looks startled. She takes a step backward, so close to the bluff, I reach out without thinking and grab her arm.

"Don't grab me, May."

I brush her forearm apologetically and keep going.

"I just think you should know that your accounts appear a little . . . problematic."

Eva hasn't taken the paper from my hand. It's obvious now that she doesn't even want to look at it.

"So, Barbara was right," Eva says, surprise replaced by a dark smirk. "She found confidential documents in your cabin. Stolen directly from my office."

"Stolen?"

The word—however ludicrous—makes my heart quicken, even though I've done nothing wrong. So much for poking *her*.

"Financials."

It clicks. Eva's talking about the paper I borrowed to use as a new journal once I realized that my Guatemalan "gift journal" wasn't actually private.

"If you mean paper from the recycling bin—"

"The shredding bin."

I know Eva's office is a mess, her standards low. But I've spent some time in nonprofit offices. A lot of them are disorganized. I know better. "I'm sorry, Eva. That was sloppy on my part. But I really wasn't thinking of that paper as confidential. I was just looking for something to write on. And besides, the paper I took to write on, from your bedroom office, wasn't how I found out about this."

I hold out the PayPal figures one more time. She cups her hand around mine, closing my fingers tighter around the folded paper.

She doesn't want to see, and clearly I am supposed to take this lack of curiosity as a blessing.

"Good," she says. "Relationships matter to me more than administrative details, which is why I have staff. The point is, I didn't want to think badly of you. You have to understand. We take theft *very* seriously here."

She looks over her shoulder as if someone might be listening. "Remember when I told you about Simone?"

"The last personal assistant?"

She lowers her voice. "Took off with about seven hundred dollars in petty change from the safe. Felt she was entitled to it. I was the stupid one who gave her the code." Eva makes a fist and raps on her temple. "Now, we have a new policy. Only one person knows the code."

"Barbara?"

"Nope," she says, flashing an enigmatic smile. But then she's serious again. "May, it was terrible. The worst part was that we accused three locals first. Concha, Eduardo, Eduardo's brother—he won't even work for us now. I felt *so bad*. I was the one who let Hans off his leash—not a good idea."

"Off his leash?" I ask. But she doesn't elaborate.

"Then we brought in the police, embarrassed everyone. Thank goodness Chief Molina is such a gentleman, and a real friend—and don't you know he'll get an extra Christmas gift from me, this year!"

I'm absorbing it all.

Chief Molina is her friend. She gives him gifts.

Mentioning the financial stuff was a mistake. I'd just wanted some sort of validation—proof that she knows that *I* know.

"*Terrible*," she whispers. "I hate thinking about how we badgered innocent people. It isn't easy running a business in a foreign country. The cultural differences, alone." She reaches forward to push a strand of hair out of my eyes, and the tender touch surprises me. It also *reminds* me—of how much I wanted her to like me not so long ago. Even *love* me.

Eva says, "That's why I get so attached when I have someone here I can *trust*."

She laughs, like she's just so glad we got all of this out in the open.

I'm ready to forget the paper in my pocket. Forget everything but making my travel arrangements and getting my passport and leaving this place, still in Eva's good graces—and Hans's—and Chief Molina's.

"I wish," she says dreamily, "that I didn't have to waste so much energy worrying about people. Who's got your back. Who's going to betray you. It's exhausting."

I dip a toe. "Maybe you just need some . . . time off? Mauricio says you've been stressed lately."

Eva screws up her face, trying to smile. "Aw! What a sweetheart he is."

I hear the waver in her voice. She looks away just as tears fill her green eyes, making them look even bigger and brighter. She doesn't want me to see, which must be a sign her emotion is genuine. The Mauricio comment really touched her.

There's a part of me that wants to start over, even now. A part of me that thinks of the author I idolized, Eva Marshall, and remembers the first time she used the word "mentor," and recognizes how much she really does try to inspire women and help them tell their stories.

Maybe my destiny here wasn't to get writing feedback, craft tips or an agent connection from Eva. Maybe my destiny here was simply to learn that *people are complicated*. Not all good or all bad. Not purely altruistic or purely self-serving. Eva is doing her best, walking across a cultural and political minefield, still grieving the baby she lost, still absorbing the fact that her fertile years are well behind her, trying to run a luxury retreat in a developing country, employing locals and depressives and ex-cons whenever she can, and it all leads to this: confusion, paranoia, boundary issues and some very bad accounting.

Eva wipes her face in her sleeve, then she nods, with an "I'm all better" smile.

"But back to the party tomorrow, and you and Zahara."

"Sure thing," I say, glad we're returning to practical matters.

"You're the best two in this batch. She's got a more compelling story and a big following, but you're a better writer."

There it is, the validation I always craved. I can't pretend it doesn't pluck at my heartstrings.

 Eva's bitterness is leaching out, her mood lightening. You both could stay as long as you like, give Barbara and the others some vacation time."

"That's really kind of you, Eva. But I can't stay. I need to get home."

Eva folds her arms and looks over her shoulder, back toward the house. This time, she doesn't bother to hide her face. This time, she just starts crying. She lowers herself to the ground as she sobs.

"Are you okay?"

She reaches for my hand and tugs me down to the grass. I keep expecting her to say something more, but she clamps her mouth with one hand, as if intent on stuffing the tears and the feelings all back inside.

Is this really all because I said "no" and she finally heard?

"I didn't mean to upset you," I say.

She can barely talk over her raggedy wailing. "Oh, May."

I say more loudly than intended: "*Jules.*"

"If you knew the truth, the whole damn mess of it. If you *knew*."

I don't think it's about the accounting anymore, but I have no idea what she's talking about.

She shakes her head and drags a tear-soaked sleeve across her runny nose. "I tell everyone they should put their stories out into the world. 'Your story, your truth.' But I can't tell, Jules. I can't let people find out. I'd lose everything. This, my houses, my career. If they knew. Richard and Jonah and Barbara all know. But not the others. Certainly not my fans. If they only *knew*."

Every new outburst makes me question why I keep giving Eva second and third chances. But the truth is, I still feel bad for her. This can't be an act. She's suffering.

"You should tell someone," I say, even though I don't know what there is to tell, because it seems like the right thing to say to someone who needs a therapist or a lawyer—knowing Eva, probably both.

Her voice is hoarse and high-pitched, unpleasantly childlike. "I can't."

"I really think you should try."

She looks over her shoulder again before turning back to me, pulling my hand into her lap, entwining our fingers. "I won't say it more than once, so you need to listen."

"Okay." I face forward, ignoring the discomfort in my hand as she squeezes.

"I lost Adhika before she came to term. At twenty-five weeks."

"What?" That's the single, dumb word that drops from my open mouth. I can't help it. I'm remembering the last chapters of her memoir. There was no mention of Adhika being born that early. "She was born premature?" I stop myself from asking: *And died months later?*

"No. She was stillborn."

"At . . . at home?"

"No, at the hospital."

I imagine Adhika as Eva described her on the page: healthy, chubby, normal, at least until she died unexpectedly, of sudden infant death syndrome.

"But in the book . . ."

Her voice drops. "Forget about the damn book for a minute."

"But," I say, unable to think of anything but the book, which made no mention of a stillbirth. "Adhika? What went wrong?"

"You remember the part when we go to the hospital, because I'm spotting?"

"Yeah."

"That part was mostly true."

But not the important part. Eva wasn't spotting. She was hemorrhaging. There was nothing to be done.

Things got more complicated a week later. By that point, Eva's Facebook, Instagram and Twitter were all blowing up with thousands of fans asking why Eva hadn't posted her daily updates. Was something wrong?

"Richard and Jonah told me to keep the blog and social media updates going. *Just be vague for now.* But a writer can't be vague. So I did the work. I wrote the scene."

"The scene of you coming home, after the bleeding stopped? When you and Jonah have breakfast in bed?"

"That one."

"It was one of my favorites."

"Thank you," she whispers. "It was just so . . . *comforting.* To write it the way it should have been. The yogurt with fresh berries, the orange juice—Jonah's with bourbon. The way he took the brown bag with my bloodied underwear out to the trash can. The way I talked to unborn Adhika and told her how she'd scared both of us, but him, especially. My new love, who until that moment hadn't fully realized how much he wanted to be a father."

I think about the details—which ones are probably true, which entirely false. The bloody underwear and the bourbon: true. The idea that Adhika was still alive: false. But the break-fast in bed and the idea that Jonah was now more committed to fatherhood—those parts were a load of crap.

"People ate it up," Eva says. "The fact that I'd been offline a week ramped up everyone's curiosity. It doubled my followers, who'd been worried about Jonah's ambivalence. This was a good moment for him as a new father, in their eyes."

She's smiling ruefully. I want to shout, *Not too good a*

moment for Jonah if it never happened! But I can't process this yet. I still don't completely understand.

"Richard had been telling me to keep my platform growing," Eva says. "He told me to keep doing what I was doing."

More blog posts and updates followed. She wrote about bed rest, about eating well for healing, about her ever-swelling breasts. She wrote about the true cost of middle-age fertility treatments for AARP's magazine. She wrote about fifty-something sexual desire for *Cosmopolitan*. She wrote about her love for Jonah—and the trickiness of third-semester sex—for Modern Love, an essay that was optioned for a television episode.

Now her fans thought she was eight months pregnant. In reality, she was one month past losing Adhika.

"I considered everything," says Eva, who has been squeezing my hand so hard it's gone numb. "I was staying up all night, researching adoption. I thought I'd get that arranged, then come clean about the death, but still manage to write about it all in one package—including my brief inability to tell the truth—but it would have a happy ending. My fans would understand. We hate a person, we decide she's beyond forgiving—and then we *do* forgive. Hate the sin. Love the sinner. We feel better about ourselves for being so generous. It's sunshine after a storm. Everyone feels clean again. My beautiful new adopted child would be the focus. It would be fine."

"But you didn't adopt."

"It's not so easy," she says, spitting out those words with a final burst of venom. "And Jonah didn't want to adopt. I would have gone ahead without him, but with the time pressure and everything else going on . . ."

That week, Richard sold the unfinished memoir at auction with six publishers bidding. He knew everything, but he wasn't concerned. *One thing at a time.* The recent articles and essays and Eva's solid follower numbers sealed the deal.

She kept blogging about the end of her pregnancy. And about the birth itself. And about the first days after the pregnancy.

She blogged about her decision not to post baby photos, much as she claimed she wanted to, because she had considered the matter in depth and taken inspiration from Uma Thurman and other Hollywood actors who keep their babies out of the media.

I'm losing track of it all, stuck in Eva's hall of mirrors.

She gets a dreamy look. "The responses! People loved that I was opening up."

"But you weren't opening up. You were inventing."

I can't reconcile this complicated deceit with the author who guided me through my adolescence. Those candid, heart-breaking stories had to be true. The idea that any place or event or even something simpler—a face in the crowd, an emotion, even a smell—was invented makes me feel not only distant from her but from my own younger self, the girl who felt trapped in suburbia and lost her virginity in a sandwich shop and would have given anything to be Eva Marshall, mascot of the punk era, living it up in her teens and then, decades later, still refusing to take shit when her dream was on the line. I couldn't bear to lose that version of Eva. I couldn't bear to lose that hopeful version of *myself.*

"But all this you're telling me now, it's all true?"

"Of course it's true! Why wouldn't it be true?"

Eva is pulling so hard on my right arm that it's impossible to sit up straight. I'm awkwardly hunched, my back aching, my expression frozen.

Even now, she talks about the death of her baby at home, as if it were real.

"So you didn't find her that way. You weren't at home. You didn't sit down and start writing the book with her next to you."

"But that's what I *would* have done. And even that tender portrait of a mother's grief was enough to make people write terrible things online. Imagine if they knew those last three months had never happened. Imagine if they knew where I was living when I . . . when I . . ."

Wait. "Where you were *living*?"

We're back to that question again.

I try to remember scenes from the later chapters of her book. I recall the vague outlines of a beautiful house, a brightly lit kitchen with oil lamps and a blue ceramic bowl filled with local organic pears. I picture evergreen trees visible out the window, light and fog. Was this her California house? Her other one in Maine? Or maybe it was Vermont.

Pears or pine cones in a decorative bowl. Cypresses or spotted cows visible through her kitchen windows. Such beautiful, concrete details in everything Eva writes. But the details don't matter. None of it happened.

Eva presses the heels of her hands against her cheekbones, blotting the tender, damp skin. "People are always asking me where I am, wanting to send me wine from their vineyards, or goddamn fruit baskets. And those cookies! When my biggest fans heard I was in the hospital, they deluged me. '*DM me your address. I won't share it with anyone else. I just have this wonderful thing to send you, to make you and Adhika and Jonah feel better.*' This was when I was at the hospital, spotting."

In real life she was bleeding heavily. In real life, Adhika was stillborn. In real life—I am putting it together, finally, including why her location mattered so much—hospital records might be traceable. Individual records are private, but what if someone could determine that in a certain small town or county, not a single infant died on a certain day, week or even month?

"That video you asked me to delete, when I asked about where you were, when you wrote *In a Delicate State*, and just before . . . ?"

"That's right." She sniffles. "It all got so complicated. It wasn't my fault!"

The lake is a shiny black mirror beyond the bluff. A band of bright stars is visible through a break in the cloud-streaked sky. We've been talking for over an hour.

I smell cigarette smoke. I know someone is nearby, but I'm focused on Eva. I have no idea what to say. I don't feel sympathy. I feel robbed.

"I wrote my first book without anyone watching," Eva says, straining to control the tremor in her voice. "No one cared. I was already at the end of the experience. I had time to figure out the story and tell it on my own terms. But now, in today's publishing climate, with today's technology, a book can get away from you. And then, what do you do? Return the advance? Pay back the royalties? Apologize to every reader personally?"

"But," I wade in carefully, "you got away with it. Right?"

"Got *away* with it?" Her shout veers alarmingly into a sobbing, animal-like grunt. "I still don't have a goddamn baby!"

Then she looks up. Eva smells the cigarette smoke, too. She must sense that someone's been listening because she finally stops talking and squints toward the house, then back at me, with a somber finality that fills me with dread. I've already received her confession. I can't do anything more for her. But she seems to think I can.

She whispers, "I can't imagine anyone else who would understand. You're a better version of myself, thirty years ago. We have so much in common, Jules. You'll do this for me. I know it."

That's the only reason she's managed to confess. Not because she cares whether I understand what she's done. Only because she needs me to understand what still has to happen next.

She wants a baby—*needs* a baby. And I'm the one, Eva thinks still, who can give it to her.

21

ROSE

———————————
———————
———

Later that day, on the way back to the classroom from a bathroom break, Rose follows Rachel to their seats. She wants to say something about the difficult workshop yesterday and the invasive writing exercises today. But Rachel speaks up first.

"I've decided to write some hard new scenes involving my children. This time, I'll use their names." Rachel laughs, but the mirth sounds forced. "Can I email pages to you?"

"Me?" Rose asks. She feels inadequate to the task—possibly the least experienced writer here. "Why me?"

"You seem like someone who thinks for herself."

The compliment catches her off-guard.

Rachel adds, "I mean, I understand you don't have children, so that part of my story may not interest you. And obviously, I led a messed-up life—"

"No," Rose interrupts. "We've all done things we regret. Of course I'll read your pages."

"And make a few notes? Eva doesn't really let us critique each other, but that's why I came."

"I'll do my best. With pleasure."

Rachel has turned back again, digging into her backpack

for a pen, when Rose adds, "Thank you for giving me something to do. I feel so . . . useless sometimes . . ."

She stops speaking. The emotion has balled up in her throat. Any moment now, she could easily break down into sobs, and no one would understand why.

Or maybe, even without any explanation, they would.

Rachel reaches for Rose's hand and squeezes it.

"Me, too."

The next two workshops—Pippa, Hannah—are followed by a late lunch. Then they regather for a final activity. Eva rings a bell at the front of the classroom to get their attention. "A little break from talking about writing."

Good, thinks Rose. Anything but another prompt requiring her to confess something sordid or sad.

"We have a special guest, or that was the plan, if that certain person will please *hurry up*."

A Swedish woman named Astrid, who is somehow associated with the local orphanage, asks, "Should I start?"

"Maybe just a few words."

Astrid is thirty-something and slender, with white hair tied back in a ponytail no thicker than Rose's thumb. A brightly colored woven belt cinches her slim jeans. On top, she wears an Indigenous-style shirt, embroidered with big flowers, tucked in.

"Guatemala, as you know, has spent many of the decades since its independence in 1821 struggling through various periods of conflict—"

"Let me just go see what's keeping him," Eva says. "Astrid . . . go ahead."

"Beginning with the United Fruit Company—" Astrid starts.

Eva interrupts, "Maybe skip to the civil war."

"Not the US-backed coup, first?"

Eva says, "I'm sure they all know about that."

Rose looks at the blank faces around her. No, they don't know about that. And they still won't, because Astrid has now jumped ahead.

"From 1960 to 1996, for thirty-six bloody years, the government clashed with leftist groups. Among the issues were land distribution and the inequality between mostly white, European-descended landowners and the Indigenous poor."

Rose wonders if she's the only one noticing that Astrid is European, that Eva is American, that everything they are hearing would suggest that white people, white companies and white governments haven't been such a good deal for Guatemala.

But that's where money comes in, right? This is a fundraising spiel, she realizes. Does donating offset the fact that they are enjoying this foreigner's home on a beautiful lakeshore that once belonged to the Mayan locals?

A figure emerges in the kitchen doorway, separated from the open-air classroom by three hundred feet of lawn. As soon as Eva sees him, she spreads her arms wide, like she's greeting someone at the airport.

"There he is," Eva interrupts.

Astrid stops her speech midsentence.

To all the women gathered, Eva says, "I mean, you get it, right? This country's been through hell. And the orphanage needs money. That's really all that Astrid came to say! Shoes are fine, clothes are fine, but the best thing is cash. They need cash." Eva puts her arm around Astrid's shoulders and squeezes. With mock exasperation she adds, "You'll understand better when you have a real human being to illustrate all the facts and figures Astrid has been telling you. Here he comes, *finally*."

The young man advancing slowly toward them has

walnut-dark skin and wavy hair. He's wearing expensive looking loafers and a Western shirt with button-snap pockets. Italian? Texan? No telling. But he's undeniably handsome, Rose thinks, admiring his full lips and long eyelashes.

Halfway to the classroom, he pushes back his shaggy forelock. The nervous gesture makes him look younger: twenty or even eighteen. A child.

Eva's entire body is wire tight and quivering, willing him to walk faster, but the young man refuses to hurry, like he's not eager to be trotted out for public inspection.

Rose notices Lindsay lifting an eyebrow. *Interesting. Eva's boy toy?*

"This innocent young man was orphaned by war," Eva explains.

Suddenly, the young man looks up and catches Rose's eye and he startles, inhaling audibly. Their gazes lock. He looks scared.

Rose feels her entire face and body flush: *Is anyone else seeing this?*

It takes less than a second for him to look away again—less than a second for her to distrust her own interpretation of that one intense moment. She's losing it. She really is. It's just like Matt and Ulyana tried to tell her. There was no reason to come here. She's too fragile.

The young man's gaze stays conspicuously diverted from Rose from that moment on. He climbs the step into the front of the classroom, approaching close enough for Eva to loop an arm around his shoulder and pull him in for an awkward hug before Eva spins him to face the women writers.

"Mauricio, meet my class. Class, meet my son."

After Mauricio has left the *aula* and Astrid has taken the names of five writers who are interested in pledging donations, Eva says, "And one more thing before our final activity. Dinner tonight is on your own, in town. Ana Sofía emailed you a list of preferred restaurants. Dress code: modest. The men here don't see much, do you understand?"

Pippa deadpans, "I'll put away the backless dress I planned to wear to the pizzeria."

"That isn't funny, and I'm not worried about you, Pippa." Eva turns to face Scarlett, frowning. "*You*, on the other hand. You remind me of my daughter. Do you have anything less . . . snug?"

Scarlett's wearing a T-shirt with a surf logo on it. The shirt is form-fitting but high-necked, as all surf shirts are. Above the white collar, her face turns a sort of papaya color, the flush visible despite a thick layer of foundation.

"You don't need the eye makeup either. You're already beautiful."

Scarlett says nothing.

"Good," Eva says. "That's settled."

"One last writing prompt for the day," Eva announces, "then we'll be done. I see a few of you squirming. If you need to use the ladies' room, go now and hurry back."

Isobel and Scarlett jump up. Rose, always eager for one more chance to peek around the house, or be anywhere but the classroom, follows.

Isobel is the first to reach the nearest bathroom, just off the kitchen. Rose stands behind Scarlett, who is staring with extreme focus at her phone, trying to avoid conversation, Rose feels certain.

Rose copies the gesture, flipping through her photos, but her real attention is riveted on a quiet discussion between Chef Hans and Barbara about thirty feet away, at the doorway to the pantry. They're talking about how the landscaping and maintenance has gone downhill over the last few months.

"That's Eduardo's fault," Barbara says. "You can't have a gardener who needs to be supervised every minute."

Hans mutters, "I caught him having a siesta in the maintenance shed an hour before the opening party when the rest of us were working our asses off. We had a little chat."

Barbara scoffs. "If *I* catch him, we'll do more than chat."

"And napping isn't the only thing," Hans adds. "I went looking for him earlier and couldn't find him anywhere. His truck was gone, too."

There's a pause before Barbara says, "Don't worry about it."

Rose closes her eyes to listen better, trying to understand why the mention of the truck seems to have killed Barbara's appetite for bullying gossip.

Hans continues, oblivious. "This morning, Eva was saying she needs someone to gas up the truck. A tank usually lasts two weeks. She must know Eduardo is using the truck too often if she realizes he's emptied the tank . . . unless they're going somewhere together."

Rose waits for Barbara's reply. It doesn't come.

Hans says, "You don't think that's weird?"

Rose wishes she could see their faces, to get a better sense of whether Barbara is simply ignoring Hans or actively shutting him down. *Eduardo the old gardener, and Eva.* It's hard to imagine they're having a tryst.

Barbara looks up and catches Rose staring.

Rose takes a step closer to Scarlett, pantomiming renewed interest in her eyebrow piercing.

"I just noticed. The area around your brow is swollen."

"Oh, yeah." Scarlett acknowledges Rose over her shoulder with a slight smile. "It gets that way."

"Is it new?"

Mom, what do you think about my piercing?

I'll get used to it.

"Two years. It gets infected when I travel or when it snags on something. I've caught my shawl on it three times this week, already."

Rose looks right and left. Hans has stepped deeper into a pantry. Barbara has stepped out to the patio and doesn't seem to be coming back. Conversation over.

Rose asks Scarlett, "Have you tried salt water? Quarter teaspoon to one cup warm water. It has to be non-iodized. The table salt has chemicals that will irritate the skin worse."

"I'll try that."

Rose misses giving advice, even if that advice was usually ignored. She misses, too, letting her daughter know how beautiful she was—though how many young women are ready to believe it?

Scarlett is gorgeous in that same effortless way—with hourglass curves on top of it all.

Rose remembers Eva's essay about deflated boobs, post-breastfeeding. But looking at Eva now, you'd never know it. She's no longer flat. She's no longer saggy. She wears close-fitting outfits. But evidently, a young woman like Scarlett shouldn't.

Rose had to bite her tongue around Jules, too, knowing that men can be predatory. When Jules was thirteen, Rose wished she wore less mascara. By the time Jules was sixteen, Rose realized that a little less mascara wasn't going to save her daughter from harm. Any thoughtful woman knows it, too.

It's one thing when Eva attacks writers about their manuscripts, but watching Eva pressure Scarlett about her appearance opens up a gap in the clouds that have hovered too persistently around Rose's head lately. Light, fresh air and common sense all come streaming in.

Eva attacks them all where they are weakest. Sometimes about the writing. Sometimes about the serious life mistakes they've made. But a woman as young and vibrant as Scarlett hasn't had time to make many mistakes.

Like Jules.

Even when Rose tries to care about someone else, even for a moment, it always comes back to her daughter. She can't help it.

"Can I ask you something?" Rose asks Scarlett. "It's just that I saw you looking at your Instagram."

"Oh," says Scarlett, snapping the app shut. "Bad habit. One I almost kicked before coming here. When my anxiety flares I go right back to it."

"I didn't mean you shouldn't be on Instagram. I was just wondering. I have this cousin about your age. She used to post lots of travel photos, and recently she's stopped. It made me worry. Like, she might be going through a rough patch I don't know about."

Scarlett, who until now was addressing Rose over her shoulder, turns around with a concerned look on her face. "Not necessarily."

"But if someone your age goes off social media, doesn't it . . . ?"

"Mean they took a mental health break? Maybe they realized that social media is a ploy to make us compare ourselves to each other and feel bad?"

Rose laughs. "I guess it could mean that."

"I'll be honest. I posted a ton of photos at the beginning of my cross-country bike trip. I loved the comments. *You're so adventurous. So brave. You can do it!* And then, a month into my trip: *OMG you've lost a ton. What??? You're f-ing gorgeous now!*"

"I can imagine," Rose says, smiling. But Scarlett doesn't smile back.

"I'd take a shot of my strong calves or do a selfie with a

bicep curl. Nope, not, *You're a beast!* Just: *You're so pretty now! You're skinny! Now we see what was hiding under there.* By the time I got halfway across the country, I refused to post anything with my body in it. It was all barns, bridges, and water towers. Even my best friends kept saying, *Show us what you look like now! Jelz!* Scarlett pauses to explain. "That means jealous."

"I guessed."

The bathroom door opens. Isobel steps out, wincing. "Sorry ladies. I should have let you go first. I think I was trying to avoid the final prompt."

"Understandable," Rose says with a conspiratorial wink.

But Scarlett doesn't hurry into the bathroom just yet. Her eyebrows knit together. She might even be tearing up. "Sometimes when you stop posting, it just means you finally got a fucking grip on what matters in life."

Rose hesitates, wanting to put her arms around Scarlett. She doesn't. "Thank you. That makes a lot of sense."

"But really," Scarlett says with her hand on the bathroom doorknob. "You could just ask your cousin directly. That's always the best thing."

Walking alone, back to the open-air classroom, Rose feels heavy. Poor Scarlett. *Smart* Scarlett. But still, poor Scarlett. To ride thousands of miles only to realize your friends are idiots and the only thing people are excited about is your weight loss.

And poor Jules. When she stopped posting lots of photos, why didn't Rose simply *ask*?

For the same reason she doesn't like memoirs. She reflexively turns away from things that are sad or uncomfortable. She doesn't like digging into the past, or focusing on the negative, or unleashing barely tamed inner demons.

You don't have to pretend to get along with Ulyana, Mom.

You shut out the bad stuff.

You'd know a lot more about yourself if you tried. Maybe keep a diary.

Three months ago, Rose might have replied to Jules's sassy criticisms by saying, *Look at your Instagram. You're a private person, too! Hiding your face all the time!*

Maybe Jules hadn't been hiding at all. Maybe she was hiding back in college, when she posted hundreds of falsely cheerful photos, even when things weren't going well. Maybe over the last year, Jules had decided to stop playing that game. Maybe, in the final months of her life, she was on the way to becoming her best, most authentic self.

And then again: Jules lied about the grad school applications.

No, Rose thinks, refusing to let the doubt infect her all over again. *No.*

Jules tried to tell her. A degree doesn't make you a writer. Rose was the one who wouldn't listen. Jules would have told her when the time was right.

She was trying to put her foot down. She was ready to decide her own future.

Jules may have been anxious, but she wasn't apathetic. Rose knew Jules. She knows her, still.

The view in front of Rose gets glassy. Never mind her daughter's Instagram. Rose has her own family photos, and the smiles in them are genuine. She brings her phone closer, flicking in search of a favorite image from their last family holiday, when a hand drops onto her shoulder.

She spins around, startled. It's the young man—Eva's son—from the orphanage talk.

He grabs her by the arms, his thumbs firm against Rose's biceps.

"It's you."

His voice is strange. He's standing too close.

Rose's heart bangs hard in her chest. She twists out of his grip.

He lets go of her arms and takes both her wrists, clasping hard enough to make her wince.

"I thought . . . thought . . ." he stammers.

His eyes seem to be fixating on something: maybe the silver bangle she's wearing.

He whispers, "Don't be afraid," but it comes out as a guttural sob, like he's overcome by emotion.

She follows his gaze to the spot above her left wrist-bone, where she has a tattoo no bigger than a dime half-hidden by the bangle: R and J in cursive, intertwined, with a rose next to it. Her daughter had the same one on her ankle. It was Jules's idea to get matching tattoos for her twenty-first birthday.

At that moment, Astrid comes walking toward them from the house.

He releases Rose's hands, their faces still close, switching to Spanish: "I have to talk to you. Do you understand me?"

She nods, her biceps and wrists still registering the pressure of his fingers.

Astrid smiles at them, sauntering past, "Hey guys. Workshop almost done?"

"Yes," Rose barely manages to say.

"You and Mauricio doing a little garden tour?"

Mauricio reaches down and snaps a blossom off a flowering bush at the base of the stairs.

"Pretend we're not talking about anything serious," he continues in Spanish, holding the pink blossom close to her face. "Smile. Am I talking too fast?"

If Astrid spends a lot of time in Guatemala, she must understand some Spanish, Rose thinks. But maybe not. Eva doesn't.

"You do a great job with the plants," Rose says in English,

feeling torn between wanting to hear what he has to tell her and needing to put some distance between them. She can't quell the alarms in her body. He grabbed her so roughly. She stammers, "What's this flower called?"

Astrid stops ten feet away from them. "Mauricio, is Eva still in the classroom?" She shades her eyes with a hand. "Never mind. They must be wrapping up. I see her coming."

"It's not what you think. Don't let anyone know we've talked. It's important, you understand?"

Mauricio pushes the flower closer to Rose's face, his hand crushing the petals as his eyes continue past her, tracking the progress of not only Eva but all the women pouring out of the classroom.

"We have to go somewhere private, so I can explain."

"So pretty." Rose nods. "And who are you, exactly?"

"Mauricio."

"That's not what I meant."

But she knows already. The boyfriend. He must be.

Rose leans closer, pretending to smell the crushed petals—and she *can* smell. Not the flower, but him: layers of scent. Cologne, hair gel, but also sweat. She can see a sheen on his forehead, the panic in his eyes. His trembling fingers touch her cheek. She can smell his fear.

In Spanish he whispers, "If I can't find you again in a few minutes, I'll meet you in town. I can't let her hear . . ."

Rose whispers back, in Spanish. "You know where I'm staying?"

He nods. "I'll find you. Please." His face is reddening, like he's about to shout, or cry. "You're her mother . . ."

That last phrase weakens Rose so suddenly she almost falls to the ground. *Su madre.* Yes, she is. Oh my god yes. He knows something.

He whispers, "Tengo miedo que—"

Afraid? Her mind is spinning. The words won't come fast enough. "¿Sobre qué? Dígame."

"No confíes en—"

Don't trust who? Which one?

"Please," Rose manages to say and then it's too late. Eva strides toward them, her voice a bright bell, ringing with adoration for Mauricio. "Honey! There you are. We need to meet with Astrid about the orphanage, all three of us."

She steps between Mauricio and Rose, physically parting them.

To Rose she says, "You missed the prompt!"

Eva might as well be talking gibberish. *Prompt.* Not on your life. Rose has found someone who wants to talk. Someone who *knows.*

Eva loops her arm around Mauricio's waist, pulling him away. Rose stays a moment longer, wondering if he'll look back, wondering how she'll find him again, watching as Eva guides him toward the house, hoping he'll be smart enough not to look back. But he does. He looks and he mouths something that she can't decipher completely. A three-syllable word.

Milagro. A miracle.

Or *peligro.* Danger.

But which one?

22

JULES

I stride through the dark back to my cabin, eager to shake off Eva's desperate pleas. Gaby and Mercedes are at dinner in the main house. No thanks. I can't deal with a group, and I've got my own granola bars.

My phone dings. A text from Eva. *I'll have your passport returned in the morning.*

See? It's all going to be fine.

I search flights. The first affordable one is an entire week away. I could head to Antigua on the way and kill a few days there.

To celebrate my near-freedom and shake off my anxiety about Eva's roller-coaster moods, I decide to go to bed early, then join a group pre-dawn volcano hike, organized by a woman who works for the hostel in San Felipe. It's my last chance to do anything adventurous around Atitlán.

I send Eva a text, saying I'll make sure to be back well before 8 A.M., in time for work. I can be reasonable. Maybe it will help her be reasonable in return.

She responds, *Not my preference, but do what you must.*

Good enough.

The hike is easy; the sunrise, partially obscured by clouds

and wildfire smoke, but still pretty. The backpackers *ooh* and *aah* at the volcanoes and the shimmering lake below, but the truth is, I've spent all week looking at similar views. I've started to associate the landscape less with magic, and more with illusion, even if it is a beautiful illusion.

Our hiking group splits into two: half want to walk slowly down, even if it means joining a different shuttle van for the ride back to San Felipe, and half want to move fast. I remove and distribute some heavy extras from my backpack—an unopened bottle of water to a Japanese hiker, a book I no longer feel the need to keep to a German guy who was complaining San Felipe has no bookstore. My heart feels lighter. I take off with the fast group, scrambling down the mountain.

When the shuttle van drops me back at Casa Eva, I'm groggy, but there's little point trying to nap. On the bed in my cabin, I find a note from Eva, inviting me to swim. It's the only message to greet me. I keep my notifications on, eager for the first burst of intermittently functioning Wi-Fi, when I might hear some birthday messages ping in.

I put on my suit under my loose Roxy cover-up and jean shorts. I bring two cups of coffee from the kitchen and take the steps from the bluff down to the rocky beach. The volcano ahead is navy blue and even darker—velvet purple—at its base. The sky is cantaloupe-colored, the rising sun hidden behind a low bank of clouds.

Even before I reach the end of the dock, I call out in the most pleasant voice I can muster that I have no intention of going into the water.

"Not my thing," I say, trying to hand her the mug. "But here."

"Not now." She ignores the coffee. "You're sure you won't swim?"

I pull off my baggy shirt. "No, I'll just get a little sun. Feels great." In truth I've got goosebumps on my arms. I lower myself to the edge of the dock, dangling my feet over the side.

Eva laughs with exasperation. "I can't even talk you into swimming. Juliet May, I don't believe I've ever talked you into *anything*."

When I don't reply, she asks, "You really haven't changed your mind about our important decision?"

I'm fascinated by the mess she's made of her life, and as someone who idolized her from a distance, I feel cheated. But I don't hate her and I don't want her to hate me, even now.

"I'm sorry," I tell her. "I will never, ever tell your secret. But I can't help you make a baby."

I wait as she lowers herself to join me. She's wearing only her bathing suit, and when she sits, her thighs are narrower than mine, the skin loose around her knees but the line of her hamstring defined all the same. She's fit and strong, a woman who has constructed a life that includes most of what she wants: daily swimming, multiple beautiful homes, a swarm of adoring, loyal people catering to her whims. I wish it could have been enough for her.

"I want to clear something up," she says. "I'd rather talk babies, but I guess we are really, truly not destined for that. You'll have to forgive me for being so obstinate. I'm like a dog with a bone."

"It's fine."

"Good. As long as that part isn't happening, let's just make sure your visit here hasn't created other problems. Barbara says I'm stupid sometimes." Eva swings her legs next to mine, playful again, like we're just friends or sisters, passing a summer morning together. "No one else has my back the way Barbara does. Not even Jonah. So I put my trust in her to keep it all straight. But I also talked to her about the donation question. Thank you for alerting me."

I turn toward her, surprised.

"She had a very good answer. Can you maintain confidentiality?" When I nod, she says, "Pedro, the local man who runs the orphanage, likes to skim off the top. Big donations make him greedy. We give a hundred, he takes ten. We can't possibly wire him ten thousand dollars. He'd jump in his truck and go on vacation and never come back. See what I mean?"

"You're trying to parcel the donations out over a long period of time."

"I knew you were a smart girl."

"Like all the shoes, stored in the gardening shed." When Mauricio told me about that, I looked in the little scratched window to see for myself. All those running and basketball shoes piled up, because Eva couldn't let her employees take the time to deliver them.

"That's different. The minute this workshop is done, we'll get Mauricio to drop those off. We just got busy."

My expression must betray me, because Eva grabs one of my hands, the same way she did last night. This time, though, her fingers are dry and cold.

"You are such a sweet girl. You know that we do amazing, life-changing things here. A few things fall between the cracks. But life is not the cracks, Jules."

"You said there was a crack in everything. Cracks let the light in. 'Cracks and all.' Wasn't that supposed to be a good thing?"

"Well, that's all true."

"But now you're telling me to ignore the cracks. Ignore the things your staff does that aren't right. But only when it's convenient for you." It feels good to say it—not hard at all. Like I'm just warming up.

She releases my hand forcefully. "Why do you have to make things—"

"So difficult? Because the differences matter. *Words matter*."

Eva has lifted one hand, like she's preparing to slap me. I stare at it, incredulous.

Then we both hear someone clear her throat, up on the bluff behind us. I see Eva's face rearrange itself into a semblance of normalcy. She turns and waves to a thin figure up on the bluff: Zahara, scheduled for a private meeting.

"I need to swim before my next appointment," Eva says. The offending hand returns to where it belongs. "You stay and think a bit. Cool down."

I close my eyes, trying to let the irritation pass.

"You were right about Barbara, by the way," Eva adds quietly. "She really is upset with you. She's worried you're trying to replace her, and she still thinks you might spill the beans about the orphanage money."

I remember Mauricio's lack of shock about the missing money. I remember, too, how Eva referred to her "good friend," Chief Molina. "Not that anyone would do anything about a little missing money, right?"

"Well, people will donate less if they have concerns. Most of all, it would be a distraction from the good work we do here."

The good work. She still believes, despite everything, that her moral ledger balances.

"I promise not to talk about the money stuff. And you can definitely let Barbara know that replacing her is the last thing on my mind."

"Even so, she feels threatened. When she gets like this, I can't talk her out of it. Anyway, I had your passport returned to your desk drawer. Nothing can stop you from going home, tomorrow. I've already let Hans, Concha and a few of the kitchen girls know. You can say goodbye tonight, at the staff party. One last fun evening?"

"Wow," I say, genuinely surprised. First, she wouldn't let me go. Now she can't wait for me to leave. "And today?"

"I want you to stay here. Hang around in case Zahara needs some company. She's already told me she doesn't want to go on the field trip, but I can't have her just hanging around. It's her day for workshopping. She might be a little . . . well, *you know*."

Fragile. Usually, Eva won't even admit it, which probably means that Zahara is even more of a mess than I realize.

If it was anyone other than Zahara, I'd resist. But not only do I like her, I feel protective. Everyone's tried to get a piece of Zahara, from her ex-boyfriend to the music producers and now Eva.

"I can do that," I say.

"Good!"

Eva dives into the water, an excellent racing dive, toes pointed.

I stay behind, thinking: *Damn. I just turned twenty-three and I've been fired from the first job I ever cared about.*

I pick up my phone and type a text that won't send until I'm closer to the house—if the Wi-Fi isn't stuttering. It might not send for hours. *Happy Birthday to me. Not an auspicious start.*

Zahara's private meeting goes well, it seems, because, at a quarter to eight, she and Eva come out of the house arm in arm, bouncing along like teenagers, headed toward the outdoor classroom.

I head into the house, toward the supply cabinet where we keep extra whiteboard markers. Closing the cabinet, I turn and almost walk into Barbara's chest.

"Looking for something?"

"Just these," I say, inching back. "Eva told me to bring a fresh set to the classroom by eight o'clock."

"You know," she says, blocking my path, "Eva has new favorites all the time. Like that new singer girl. So don't feel special."

"I don't."

"I've changed the passwords. You're not to check email, PayPal, anything. Eva doesn't need you."

"That's great."

"And you'll never write like her."

"*I'll* never write like her?" I laugh. "That's really . . . interesting, Barbara." I start walking out, nearly make it to the doorway before turning around. "Eva did remind me that the low cost of living here is fantastic for a writer. It's a magical place. Truly inspirational. Maybe I should stay."

Barbara's hand flies up to rake her thinning brown hair. It takes so little to hurt her. Threatening to remain anywhere near Eva's domain is enough.

I keep walking, glad for the fresh air. But I feel wrong. Jumpy and off-kilter. I shouldn't have said so much to Barbara. I shouldn't have taunted her.

I'm on kitchen duty until nine-fifteen, and I stay out of view, because I don't have energy for dealing with workshoppers this morning. Luckily, after Zahara's group workshop, they all head down to the beach to catch a water taxi. They'll spend the entire day shopping for woven handicrafts at a bigger village across the lake, giving the staff a huge break.

"Yo," says Zahara, at my shoulder when I wander out to the patio for a cup of coffee.

"So, you really didn't want to go on the field trip."

"I didn't go."

"You're very special, if Eva is letting you hang here all day."

"Very special," Zahara repeats.

"You all right?" She's dreamy, a complete change from the high-bouncing, fast-talking person I saw yesterday.

"Private meeting with Eva was weird. We only talked about my music. In the group workshop, on the other hand, we finally *did* talk about my writing, which was sort of . . . worse? I don't know . . ."

She trails off, face darkening.

"No offense, but did you take something? I wouldn't judge. It's stressful."

"Taking something. Good idea." She lifts the lid of a large cooler under the table. It's empty. No ice, even.

"No, I'm asking in the past tense. *Did* you take something?"

She tries a cardboard box next to the cooler. "Bingo."

She lifts a tequila bottle and holds it next to her face, pressing it into her cheek. The amber liquid winks in the sun. Her kohl-rimmed hazel eyes, a shade darker than the tequila, look *mostly* normal, the pupils only slightly enlarged.

"That's for the party. We'll have margaritas tonight, I promise."

"Margaritas are for kids."

"They really aren't."

"Play hooky with me."

"We don't have to play hooky. We're not at school." I *was* asked to help tidy up the garden paths. But I've also been asked to keep an eye on Zahara. Direct order, from Eva.

"I've got my bathing suit on," Zahara says. "Do you?"

"Under my clothes."

"Good. And I need something to take the edge off."

"I think the edge is already off."

She finds this hilarious. "Never mind." She pats her hoody pocket.

Whatever is in that pocket isn't our friend. If she continues to go the pill route, there's no way I'll be able to monitor her. I already nixed tequila, for now. The goal is to reduce risk. Eliminating it entirely is impossible.

"I've got something perfect. Stay right here and I promise to bring you a present." I dash into the kitchen and come out with a bottle of sparkling white wine, a carton of orange juice and two plastic cups.

"Jules, I love you!"

"And you'll still love me in the morning, let's hope."

It's just like babysitting, if one were allowed to administer small doses of sedative to the toddlers in one's care.

We sprawl on the deck, tanning and drinking mimosas that warm as the day passes. After a while Zahara decides to wade into the lake. She's wearing her white gloves, which is a good sign. She can't be too drunk if she's remembering to protect her hands.

I continue catching up in my journal, one loose page at a time, unwilling to toss those spreadsheets Eva was so worried about because this handful is all the paper I have. I tuck the finished ones into my backpack until I can store them safely later, with the others, in the cabin. When I have to pee, I hop off the base of the dock into shallow water, wade to my waist and let her flow. But no farther.

"If you'll come dry off, I'll find us a bag of tortilla chips," I tell Zahara.

"And another bottle of white wine. And a cup of ice? And while you're gone, can I borrow a piece of paper from you? My phone's dead. I need to write something down before I forget."

As we enjoy our second batch of mimosas, heavy on the wine and light on the OJ, she finally tells me what happened during the workshop.

"I'm not in denial. I've already written two songs—three if you count today—about what happened in that fucking hotel room. I don't need Eva to drag it out of me. With a song, you can get the emotion and the imagery without having to be all . . ."

"Anatomical?"

"Exactly. And my mom! What about someone like her? I don't want my mom having to read hundreds of pages about those five days in Las Vegas. If it's just a few pages I can slice them out with an X-Acto knife and send Mom that copy with a note, 'Cleaned it up for you.'"

"You'd do that?"

"Absolutely. And she'd understand. It would be like me picking one of those wicked long red chile peppers out of the chicken kung pao and telling Mom, 'I'm just pulling out the part that will hurt you.'"

"Aw, my mom used to do that for me, too—pick out the chile peppers!"

"That's what moms do."

"That's what moms do," I repeat, getting misty. Oh shit, babysitter down. All those mimosas are nothing for Zahara, but I'm getting wobbly.

Zahara pulls out her phone to show me pictures of her mom.

"Battery's dead," I remind her as she keeps pressing the button. "Oh fuck. I miss my family so much!"

I break down, then, and tell Zahara that it's my birthday, and I'm not even getting messages, and no one seems to know I'm here, and I just want to be home now.

"Oh, honey!"

I'm heading from self-pity to indignation. I'm tired of being the voice of reason. I'm craving abandon. And that's not good.

I fetch the tequila bottle and bring it back to the dock with a lime sliced in half. The light is getting soft. Shadows are creeping up the base of the volcano. The lake has turned from bright blue to a flatter, silkier navy.

Zahara wishes me a happy birthday every time we drink. She tells me more about her life as a musician. I tell her about my own career confusion.

"Look at you, writing all the time!" She gestures to the pages sticking out of my backpack.

"Doesn't mean—"

"That's the only thing that *means*. Trust me. If you write, you're a writer. If you make music, you're a musician. Identity comes first and it's yours once you claim it and start doing the work. Not when you're published, not when reviewers say you've done a good job, not when you get awards, not when you have a million followers. We're not going to see each other after this week—"

"We might!"

"Girl. Get real. We won't. But this is my gift to you."

She kisses me on the lips. Not sexually—I don't think. She hands me the tequila bottle again and I drink.

Several more shots later, Zahara gets a funny look. "If you're still missing your mom, try smoke signals." She extracts two cigarettes from her pocket and hands me one. One itty-bitty social cigarette on my twenty-third birthday can't hurt.

"Now do this," Zahara says, blowing perfect smoke rings that hover over the water, dissolving slowly in the soft light. "And now, when you blow out, think of your mother hard, put the thoughts into the smoke."

"That's the last thing my mom would want, me thinking about her while I ingest carcinogens."

"Just do it. She'll forgive you for the cancer part."

My head's getting lighter and lighter as I try to get at least one good ring to form, thinking of my mother the whole time, knowing I'll tell her the story later, even knowing what she'll say. *That's great, Jules. But maybe bubbles next time? Or a pretty floating lantern?*

"She's receiving your thoughts right now," Zahara says in all seriousness.

"How do you know?"

Zahara stubs out her cigarette under her sandal. "My mom received all the thoughts I sent her a year ago, from the hotel room in Vegas."

"No," I say under my breath.

"Yes. She knew something was wrong after just the first day. She had a racing heartbeat and an upset stomach. Day two, she started trying to contact Brad. That's the asshole's name. Day three, she was on the phone with my producers and two of my friends. My fuckhead ex-boyfriend said I'd gone on a silent retreat in Joshua Tree. My mom tried to believe it but she couldn't stop feeling sick. Meanwhile, Brad was ordering room service and refusing to let any maid change the sheets."

"That's awful."

"They're used to that shit in Vegas. If the toilet hadn't backed up, I think he would have kept me tied up for a month."

"I'm so sorry."

"Yeah, it happened. Anyway, this works, too." Zahara cups her mouth and starts howling out across the lake. "Mom! Mama!"

"I can't do that. It's too embarrassing!"

"Have you noticed how it's the same sound in so many languages? Spanish? Chinese? Everyone likes to say it. It's a sound that makes you feel good. A billion babies can't be wrong."

"Okay, fine." I try it, glad for a reprieve from her sad story, wanting to share a few moments of silly joy.

"Louder. Like this. Mama!"

"Mommy!" I double over with laughter.

"Mom. Mama. Mommy!"

It feels so good, so ridiculous and anxiety-purging.

Zahara switches into a wolf howl but I stick with the basics.
"Ma-ma! Ma-ma-ma-ma!"
"Ah-wooooo! Ha-ha-ah-wooooo!"
"Mom! I miss you. I really do. I love you, Mama."

My cathartic session with Zahara, howling for our mamas across the lake, doesn't go unheard. Mauricio comes down the bluff to wish me *feliz cumpleaños*—he remembered!—and check in with us, but I tell him that neither Zahara nor I are performing at the staff party tonight. I wish him the best of luck on the poem he's planning to read, by the Guate poet, Isabel de los Ángeles Ruano. It's about complicity—the ways in which we are all guilty. I like to imagine Eva listening to it, eyes narrowing as she wonders if there's a message in it for her. But that will never happen. First, because she doesn't understand Spanish. Second, because she's always so damned sure she hasn't done anything wrong.

When I look back from Mauricio to Zahara, she's just popped something small into her mouth and is closing her lips over two fingers, smiling like some naughty cherub.

"Be careful with that. We just had a lot of tequila." I squint at the bottle, only one-third full.

A few minutes after Mauricio leaves, I smell cigarette smoke coming from the bluff over our heads. I'm certain it's the person who's been eavesdropping on me and Eva.

Eyes closed, Zahara mumbles, "Can you go get me one of those?"

"Cigarettes are bad for your skin. Even the skin on your hands. Go back to sleep."

I feel dizzy from the drinks but I also feel like I've done my job. Zahara's napping. We've shared some personal shit but she hasn't gone overboard with anxiety or melodrama, and by tomorrow, this day will be behind her. Then she can decide if she wants to stay or cut her losses short. Of all the women here, Zahara is the one who needs Eva and her connections the least.

I spend ten more minutes journaling—about the tragic death of Rogelia Cruz, the subject of Isabel de los Ángeles Ruano's poem "The Closed Silence," about anything I can think of, and it feels good. I follow my thoughts as they wander, without forcing them. I *essai* and test out thoughts, leaning into the permission given by essayists like Montaigne or Phillip Lopate, the writer whose best-known anthology introduced me to Montaigne—all that old stuff that Eva dismisses. Nonfiction writing that doesn't fit into a box; memoirs that aren't about best-selling trauma topics. I enjoy personal writing for what it is: *personal*. Not designed for public consumption from the first draft, but a process, instead. A way to notice more. To turn outward, sometimes, not exclusively inward.

If you write, you're a writer. Zahara made it sound so simple. It's a better mantra, one I'm willing to take home with me.

I run the three bottles and empty juice carton back up to the kitchen. I come down again and make a few more notes.

Zahara rolls to her side, wiping drool from her cheek. "Sweaty. Need another swim."

"This late?"

It's cool now. The sun is only minutes from dipping below the horizon.

"Going in," she says, groggier now than she's been. "And Jules, you appreciate that mom of yours. I won't be seeing mine for a long time."

"Why?"

Zahara has waded up to her thighs and peeled off her white gloves. I don't see them on the dock or on the beach.

"She died. A week after I got out of the hotel. Aneurysm."

With that, Zahara plunges headfirst into the water.

23

ROSE

Rose loiters on the lawn long after most of the other women writers have left to catch a water taxi to town, replaying the conversation with Mauricio. Surely, he'll find a way to talk to her privately. Town is small. He'll find her. A better plan than talking here. Safe. Simple.

But if it's so simple, why does she feel at this moment like she dare not leave? Like there's a chance he knows something about Jules and she might never see him again?

She lurks near the steps, watching the house just in case Mauricio manages to sneak back out. But he doesn't, not even after Eva reappears, crossing the lawn toward the classroom again.

"Don't walk the road alone," Eva says as she passes Rose, without bothering to look up. "At the very least, pair up!"

Rose notices that both Diane and Lindsay have stayed back as well, each of them eager to get a few minutes of Eva's time.

Diane is bubbling over with enthusiasm for the orphanage talk. She's hung back to promise a donation. "Whatever you need. I can't imagine anything more important."

Eva asks, "What were you thinking of giving?"

Rose strains to hear Diane's answer, but Diane has lowered

her voice, murmuring with Eva, who seems much more interested in chatting with the workshop stragglers than she was just a minute ago, now that a donation is at stake.

"Go up to the house," Eva says to Lindsay. "I'll be there in a minute."

Lindsay follows the order, winking at Rose as she passes, stage whispering, "*My private session.*"

"Good luck," Rose says. "I'll wait for you."

Eva and Diane chat a moment longer before Eva returns to the house, leaving Diane standing alone, gazing off into the distance with a blissful smile on her face, as if everything has gone her way this week, when it hasn't. She never had her pages reviewed. She was told to leave her husband. Clearly, it doesn't matter. She got what she needed: attention. Maybe a new purpose.

Women's voices trickle down the steps toward Rose, confusing her for a moment, because after all, the workshop participants just left.

"Beautiful day," says a sixty-something woman with impressively inflated lips, painted the same shade of red as her stylishly oversized eyeglass frames.

"Yes," Rose answers, stepping out of the group's way. "Are you all here for private meetings with Eva?"

"No. We come here before dinner, just to write," a second woman says, gesturing to her laptop bag. "It's an alumni perk."

They've already stepped past her and are fanning out, with two heading toward the edge of the bluff, one to the open-air classroom and one to an Adirondack chair at the far side of the lawn.

That moment with Mauricio, unnerving as it was, has fired her up. She doesn't expect he'll have all the answers. But she realizes how many people might be out there, still holding back something they'd share, if they could only be approached the right way. Desperate not to lose her chance, Rose calls out, "Anyone here last May?"

Only the woman in red glasses turns back, curious.

Rose splutters, "I'm thinking of coming again next spring, but I want to know if the weather's good enough."

"Oh, it's always good," the woman says unhelpfully, before turning away again.

Diane, who has been watching Rose's pathetic failed attempt to chat with the alums, strides over. "Nice try. They're a bit cliquey, aren't they?"

"A little." Rose is still rattled, worried about whether Mauricio will return, and equally frustrated that she hasn't managed to extract any useful info from the regulars. "They seem to avoid the first-timers."

"I made a few inroads," Diane says with a self-satisfied smile. "They're more welcoming when they find out you're not a 'one-and-done' kind of person. So, how about you? D'you think you'll come back?"

"Why not?" Rose improvises. "I mean, if that's what it takes to finish."

Diane nods with approval. "Some of us understand what it takes."

She looks out over the lake, her face blissful again, adding, "I can imagine having my own cabana here. I suggested to Eva that she should build some guest structures so we don't have to stay at those dark little cabins in town. She owns a separate piece of land down the road. I'm thinking of little adobe casitas . . ."

Rose nods, unable to concentrate, her mind wandering the moment the information isn't essential.

"I'm sorry," Rose says, interrupting Diane in the middle of a tedious explanation of straw-bale architecture. "I wonder if any of the alums have their own organization, even an unofficial one."

Diane raises her palms to her cheeks. "That's brilliant! Think of the fundraising possibilities. I mean, I pledged five thousand before I came, and I just told Eva I'd gladly give another five."

"That's so generous," Rose says, swallowing her surprise. *Ten thousand dollars?*

Hadn't Jules told her that most of these visiting writers were incredibly well-off? For some of them, the workshop fees are nothing.

"Do you wire it to the orphanage?" Rose asks. "I hope they don't make it complicated."

"Not complicated at all. You just send it to Eva—the same way we sent our trip payments. PayPal. Two minutes."

"Oh good," Rose says, hoping her smile looks genuine. "And you know, that's really kind of you, Diane. I'm sure Eva will be grateful."

"Some women give more." Diane narrows her eyes in the direction of the alumni clique.

Rose follows her gaze and mirrors her expression. "Well then, I'm thinking of donating twenty. Thousand, I mean. The orphanage is such a deserving cause."

Diane's self-satisfied smile fades, like she's not happy being outbid. Maybe Rose should have pretended she was donating *fifty* thousand, just for fun.

"Shame, though," Rose adds. "It would be so fun to tell Astrid and Eva right away. But even if the PayPal part is easy, my financial advisor will have a fit if I don't do a little research first. Have you checked out the orphanage's nonprofit profile on Charity Navigator or any of the other charity sites?"

"Oh, no," Diane says with enthusiasm. "It's *completely*

different with a small foreign charity. They're not on any of those websites. They're probably not even an official non-profit."

How convenient, Rose thinks.

"Then Eva should form one for them! They'd get much bigger donations that way. You and I know how this works. Never mind bothering Eva first—she's too busy. Let's set up a little meeting with Astrid."

This is the most creative Rose has felt all trip, and her inspiration isn't yet spent. "And you know who else we need at that meeting? A few other alums who have donated in the past. Any ideas?"

Diane gestures to a bench on the edge of the bluff, where a white-haired woman is sitting with a walking stick across her knees. "Wendy tells me she gives a few thousand dollars every quarter to the orphanage. I was just talking to her."

The older woman has been taking part in the workshops, but always silently, from the farthest back seats. Rose never guessed she was an alum.

"Every quarter," Rose repeats. "Is that how frequently Wendy attends the workshops?"

"I doubt anyone comes that often," Diane says, but her expression has changed. "But maybe. I asked her the same question, and she was vague."

"But not vague about her donations."

"No. Completely proud of those!"

Rose remembers something Lindsay said about a "soft rule" that didn't allow alumni to come back two (or three?) times in a row. But maybe it was "soft" because it all depended on which alum you were and whether you reliably opened your purse every time you were asked.

"Maybe she's just embarrassed how long it's taking her to finish her memoir," Rose says, keeping her eye on Wendy, and equally focused on gluing herself to Diane, at least until she has figured out everything Diane might know about the money that is conveniently routed through Eva's organization to another one.

"The question," Diane says, "is really how much the orphanage needs."

"Well, I plan to find out. I have a site visit scheduled, first thing in the morning."

Where did Rose get the phrase *site visit*? Why did she say *morning*?

"I'll get us some info, and then we can assemble our little alumni development team and go from there."

Diane looks around to see if anyone is close enough to eavesdrop. "Good plan. But as much as I like the meeting idea, I don't think it should be with Astrid. She's only volunteered at the orphanage for four months, but Eva just told me she isn't doing a very good job and they plan to replace her soon."

Rose savors that morsel of gossip. Why would you let someone like Astrid go? It might be to stop her from mismanaging donations. But it might also be to stop her from realizing other people are mismanaging donations.

Follow the money. Her old journalism prof's dictum.

Don't trust . . .

Mauricio was trying to tell her.

And then there's the piece from Scarlett, an insight the sweet girl didn't even know she was offering. *Sometimes when you stop posting, it just means you finally got a fucking grip on what matters in life.*

It took Rose less than seventy-two hours to notice that Eva's orphanage donation scheme might be fishy. Jules may have been enamored with Eva, but Jules wasn't dumb. In fact, because of her summer internships, she knew more about nonprofits than Rose does.

And if Jules felt the way that Rose does now, that would have put Jules in a place that was . . . . *uncomfortable.* Which isn't the first word that came to Rose just now, much as her brain is trying to deny it.

The first word that came to her was: *unsafe.*

Diane jogs into the house as Lindsay, private session completed, makes her way toward Rose, face lit up with an enigmatic grin. The late afternoon sun is shining on Lindsay's sharp, bronzed cheekbones, catching the glitter in her makeup. Her hair is even more aggressively spiked. Less Emma Thompson today, more Billy Idol.

"Good session?" Rose asks, gesturing to the stairs so they can walk back to town together.

"Nope!"

It's only once they're through the gate and walking down the road that Lindsay turns and pauses, shoving her polished nails hard into the pockets of her pleated pants. "She said I should write a Modern Love essay."

"Not a good idea?" Rose asks. She's heard the newspaper column mentioned a dozen times since Antigua, as if it represents the highest goal any writer can hope to reach.

"It's what Eva tells everyone so she doesn't have to discuss their memoirs. In my case, I have a complicated story. And an agent. Modern Love only pays a few hundred bucks and they don't allow pseudonyms. Given my line of work, I *need* a pseudonym."

"I'm sorry, I know nothing about publishing," Rose says, "and to be honest, I don't read Modern Love."

"Me neither!" Lindsay hoots. "It's so weird how preoccupied Eva is with one column! But you knew this place was fucking weird or you wouldn't have come to see for yourself."

Rose stops walking. "What?"

"You said you didn't trust it. Casa Eva. San Felipe. After the opening-night party, you told me you thought there were secrets here."

"I did?"

Then it comes to Rose. She wraps her arms around her ribs as if to protect herself from the gut punch of shame. She was drunk. She spilled her guts to Lindsay two nights ago and she doesn't even know how much she said.

Lindsay smiles tenderly at Rose. "You don't remember."

"No."

"You were really upset. It's okay."

"I don't know what I told you."

"You needed to vent. I've got you, Rose."

Tears prick Rose's eyes, because she believes Lindsay, even though she barely knows her.

"Did I mention Jules?"

Without missing a beat, Lindsay says, "Jewels? As in diamonds and rubies? No. You just said that you had a reason to keep a low profile and you needed to be here. Believe me, I pushed. I'll push again, if you'd like."

"No," Rose says quickly. "There's something we need to talk about, first." There's no better person to ask how to catch a thief than another thief. "I need to visit the orphanage tomorrow. I think there are big donors who are handing over money every session at Casa Eva, and I think it's a really easy way for someone to skim money."

"Sure, I get that," Lindsay says with a quick nod.

"You're not surprised?"

"That someone like Eva or her staff would siphon money from an endless flow of rich visitors, half of them grieving or traumatized, to a charity that probably doesn't keep good records, in a country where no one pays attention? I think it's clever." Lindsay shrugs. "I target men, because they think with their dicks. I've never thought about conning women. And I'm not saying I would. But you have to admit, this is a pretty easy place to find targets."

"Okay," Rose says, glad to be on the right track. "*Follow the money.*"

"Yes, and . . ."

"And?"

"Don't forget, money is the whole story for a short con, but not for a long con."

"I don't understand."

"When it's a long con, or any kind of long-game involving human beings and their foibles, you can't let yourself get tunnel-focused on the money at the exclusion of everything else. You have to understand your protagonists first."

"Are we talking about creative writing again, or crime?"

"Both. You need to understand what your characters desire. What they believe. What their stories are. When it's a short con, you follow the money. When it's a long con, you follow the *story*, and ultimately you get to the money or whatever the person is trying to acquire or protect. It isn't always a *thing*."

A tuk-tuk comes up from behind them, spewing gravel and dust. It slows down, but Lindsay waves it off.

Then she takes Rose's hand. "You go to the orphanage, ask some questions, so you've got that angle nailed down and it won't keep worrying you. But keep your mind open. Frankly, a few thousand dollars—even ten or twenty K—is pretty small stakes."

"But do you think her staff is taking the money? Barbara, or Hans, or Astrid?"

"Astrid is a hippie do-gooder. Hans doesn't even wear a fancy watch. Barbara looks like she bought her wardrobe at Target ten years ago and hasn't replaced it. On the other hand, you never know when someone has an expensive addiction or too many alimony payments."

"And Eva?"

Lindsay's eyes narrow. "Good question. If I had to come up with a word for Eva, it wouldn't be 'greedy.' It would be 'sloppy.' She seems too distracted to be stealing systematically. Diane would have been just as happy to donate thousands of dollars to some kind of alumni scholarship fund, and it would have been nearly impossible to track those donations. Instead, Eva was thrilled Diane wanted to give to the orphanage."

"So, it's not Eva."

"She wouldn't be my first guess."

"And if you were someone working for Eva who knew this was happening and didn't like it?"

"Then I'd have to be careful," Lindsay says.

The first public buildings of San Felipe are coming into view: a minimart first, followed by a barber shop for locals. But still, it's quiet here, and they're alone. There might never be a better time.

"That person who should have been careful?" Rose asks, ready to tell Lindsay everything now. "That was my daughter."

24

JULES

I'm sitting here now, at dusk, watching Zahara sidestroke in circles. Occasionally she'll stand up and smack her hand against the water, where it's shimmering, like she's trying to smash a bug. I've called her back several times but she won't answer me. I like her but she's trouble, that girl.

All of our day's conversation, muddled by hours of mimosas and tequila and sun, is coming back to me in snatches. Her mom won't ever read her book. Can't. That's a lot to take in.

I'm glad I wrote some of it down, but maybe I got it wrong. Maybe we get almost everything wrong.

But one can hope a little truth and light gets through anyway. Through the cracks. Or despite them.

That's what I'm still thinking about, in my melancholy haze, eyes pleasantly closed, nodding off, when Barbara comes rushing down the stairs and out to where I'm sitting, shaking the dock with her heavy steps.

"She's drowning!" Barbara yells, her thick forearm flexing as she undoes the rope from the cleat. "I saw her from the bluff. She went under."

"What? Where?"

I'm too confused for the guilt to fully hit me—too confused even to think about whether we should get help or start looking for Zahara ourselves, before it's too late.

"That girl shouldn't have been allowed to swim so far," Barbara shouts. "You were supposed to be watching! Get in the boat!"

The last bit of orange has leaked out of the sky. It's so dark now. I don't remember it getting this dark.

My knees are shaking as I jump into the rowboat, careful as I step past an extra detached oar and a rock attached to a rope. "The bow seat," Barbara yells. "Hurry up, and Jesus, get lower or you're going to tip us."

"Sorry!"

With her back to me, hands on the oars, she barks, "Look for the splashes. If we hurry, we can still get to her."

The volcano ahead is a gray silhouette against a navy sky. The lake is black. When I look straight down into the water, I feel a spike of fear. I try looking toward the horizon instead. But I'm not seeing any trace of Zahara. None at all.

I'm hyperventilating now. It's all my fault. How many drinks did we have? How many pills did Zahara take? How long had Zahara been swimming when Barbara spotted her struggling? How long can a person last, under the water?

My eyes search so hard that they begin to see what isn't there. The glimmer of moon becomes Zahara's pale face floating, just below the surface. The bubbles released by some fish near the surface are her final bubbly breaths. But every time the boat lurches forward, the illusions disappear. The lake is a silky sheet that stretches all the way to the volcanoes. Moonlight is only moonlight.

Barbara hasn't spoken for ages. We're both silent. Because we're searching. We're in this together. I'm facing away from

Barbara, occasionally twisting to glance over my shoulder, scanning the lake both ahead of and behind us.

"I don't think she swam this far."

Barbara doesn't answer.

Panic subsides as I try to picture Zahara as I last saw her, splashing and paddling around. Time and fresh air are clearing my head.

"She's not that good a swimmer," I say with more confidence. "If she went under, she'll be in shallower water. We need to turn back."

So why doesn't Barbara turn back?

The wind stirs, raising gooseflesh on my damp arms. That's when I know: we're not in this together. We never were.

"Barbara," I say, keeping my voice level, "you're taking us out too far."

Eva's biggest worry was her massive memoir deception. Barbara is more practical. She knows that stealing charity money would look undeniably bad. The problem is, I know about all of it.

"I want to go back," I say.

I know. Barbara knows that I know.

As much as I hate to stop searching the lake's waters ahead, just in case Zahara is still out there, I turn sideways, hand reaching for the gunwale so I can steady myself as I change position. I'm about to speak again when I sense movement— Barbara has risen to a low crouch, and she's reaching for something at her feet. I look up in time to see something long and dark coming toward me. I push to a half-standing position, confused, eyes on the oar as she lifts it like a baseball bat. Then a blur. My legs buckle.

I scream, falling forward.

There's a second horrible crack.

Fireworks blast across my skull.

The taste of metal as blood fills my mouth.

I'm grabbing for something, anything; I'm trying to keep my mouth closed though every part of me wants to inhale. There's only water, greenish-black water, and necklaces of silver bubbles, and the dance of the moon on the surface over my head.

But you know the rest. Everyone does.

Somehow, I drowned that night, on Lake Atitlán.

Somehow, I was never found.

25

ROSE

————————————————
   ————————————————
     ————

That night, some of the women go to a local bar to eat chicken wings and play poker with lessons from Lindsay. The talk of the evening is about K-Tap, who already packed up and left in a shuttle bound for Antigua.

"Our first defector," Isobel whispers. "I think there will be others."

They all swap gossipy guesses about the comedian's true name. Scarlett thinks K stands for "Karen"—not the best name for a Black woman stand-up comic in the current era. "Unless it is," Scarlett laughs. "She could have built a funny routine around it."

Noelani says it has something to do with K's abusive father, a wrestling coach who forced her to compete and practiced even more brutally with her in private, forcing her to "tap out." Noelani thinks that was the harder story K needed to tell. "But she got cold feet."

"I just don't know why she had to keep it secret," Pippa says. "Maybe it's a drug reference. Speaking of drugs, anyone seen Rachel?"

No one has.

"I'll peek into a few windows on my walk back to the

cabin," Rose says, looking for a way to make a quick exit while the other women stay behind, playing cards.

Through the dark alleyways, she keeps her promise, peering briefly into the pizzeria, the fish taco place, an even dingier bar where Noelani thought she saw Rachel sitting alone yesterday evening, hand wrapped around a beer bottle. Rose is worried about Rachel, ruminating in some corner booth. But the person Rose needs to find the most is Mauricio.

He said he would come find her. Where can he be?

Back at the cabin, she sits at the little table near the door, listening for every crunching footfall along the gravel path just outside, every echo of voices from the nearest alley. Nothing.

With too much time to think, she lets herself imagine. What if Mauricio was Jules's boyfriend. What if they both knew about the mishandling of money. Eva couldn't get rid of Mauricio—he's her own adopted child. But Jules?

Mauricio doesn't show up that night. The next morning, while the others are eating breakfast, Rose takes a tuk-tuk to the orphanage, a mile down the road, opposite the direction of Casa Eva. She needs confirmation that something is amiss with the orphanage fundraising. Only then will she know how it connects with her murky feelings about Casa Eva.

When Rose arrives, she's shown into a dining hall where thirty children, ages six to fifteen, are eating breakfast. The director, a Guatemalan man named Pedro, recognizes her as a well-heeled American eager to give money. He shows her the dormitories, the kitchens with their enormous tin pots where several cooks are already heating up the next meal of beans, rice and shredded chicken. He points out the newest wing being added, which currently has window frames without installed glass.

"And how much would it take to finish all this?"

"Oh goodness. A lot."

A girl who looks about two years old raises her hands up to Pedro, wanting to be lifted.

"If someone were to give you all the money you needed for the whole year, how much would it be?"

Pedro hoists the girl up to his hip, where she begins to tug at his glasses, her not-entirely-clean fingers covering the lenses so he has to gently move her hand in order to reply to Rose. "To finish the construction? Maybe twenty-five thousand quetzales."

"So, in US funds, maybe three thousand dollars?"

"With that, we'd be all finished and we could house ten more children. It would be a miracle."

Milagro. Or *peligro.* Which word was Mauricio trying to say?

"Surely, you get close to that every month."

"Oh, no." He laughs. "The monthly donations are usually only hundreds of dollars in total, you understand." He catches himself, and Rose is almost certain he is blushing. "We are grateful, of course. Gracias a Dios."

"Do you thank donors publicly?" she asks.

"Of course!"

He brings her to a painted mural that's been designed to look like a lake, covered in fish of various sizes. She notices a cluster of tiny, silver fish covered with American names: Wendy, Beatrice, Jennifer.

"We appreciate all the fish," he says.

"These are the small donors," she says, pointing to the distinctly Anglo corner of the mural.

"There are no *small* donors," he says, smiling.

She has to trust her intuitions. He doesn't have a clue—and she has more clues than she requires.

One cup of coffee later, Rose is shaking hands goodbye when she thinks to ask Pedro, "Do you know Mauricio, the local boy who was adopted by the writer, Eva Marshall?"

Behind still-smudged glasses, Pedro's eyes widen. "Adopted? A Guatemalan child can't be adopted by a foreigner. It became illegal over ten years ago."

"Maybe I misunderstood," Rose says, remembering how giddy Eva was to introduce her "son."

"But I do know Mauricio. He delivers clothing donations from Casa Eva. Are you trying to reach him? I could give you his phone number."

"Oh! That would be perfect. I have . . . sort of an emergency question."

"I can call him for you from here," Pedro says, pointing toward his office.

They get no answer, only voicemail. Rose fumbles to leave a message in Spanish, with Pedro watching. "Soy Rose. ¿Necesitas hablar conmigo? Espero verte en San Felipe."

After she disconnects, Pedro says, "He'll get right back to you. This place has always meant a lot to him. Especially with your interest in donating, Mauricio will be grateful."

Rose pays the waiting tuk-tuk driver to take her back toward San Felipe. This has all gotten too big. There are still details she could uncover as long as Eva doesn't know her real name. *Follow the story*, Lindsay told her last night. But it wouldn't hurt to let the authorities know she's onto something.

The tuk-tuk stand runs along a small plaza, at the back of which sit two offices: the Tourism Bureau, with a bold blue sign written in English, and the Subestación de la PNC, or the Substation of the National Civil Police. Foreign police stations always make Rose nervous, more so in Latin America where there always seem to be three or four different types of police, not always on friendly terms with each other.

Rose stops under a shady tree, flipping through her notebook, trying to remember if the police station so helpful to

Matt was here, in San Felipe, or in a bigger town just up the shore. Are they all called substations? Is there a main station nearby? She already knows that the moment she presents herself, ready to make a report, she may have to register, using her real name, and she doesn't want to start showing identification or mention Molina's name in the wrong place.

Playing the dumb tourist, she darts into the tourism office first, where a young Mayan woman in a pale blue button-down blouse grabs for a map the moment Rose enters.

"Can I help?" the woman says eagerly, like she doesn't get many opportunities.

"I'm looking for the local police chief."

"The wrong door," the woman says, "but you are very close."

Her smile broadens, broad cheeks dimpling. Rose smiles back, a little puzzled by the enthusiasm. It's only when the young woman lifts a hand to wave that Rose understands she's been looking over her shoulder, past Rose, to someone else out in the plaza.

Rose glances behind her, then snaps her head back. It's Hans, from Casa Eva. He's holding two large takeout coffee cups. This is bad. For a moment she thinks Hans has come to deliver coffee to the tourism bureau employee.

But as Rose steps to the side, pretending to be fascinated in a carousel of volcano postcards, she notices he isn't coming in.

"You need any police, like to report a crime? Or the police chief?"

"The *jefe*," Rose says. "Molina, yes."

"Okay," the woman says, "I show you," bringing out an unnecessarily detailed, photocopied map of the plaza, showing an ATM, a jewelry shop, an ice cream stand, two separate entrances to the police station, the first only fifty feet from where they are now standing.

Rose feigns confusion to buy time, hoping Hans will have moved on. She can't exactly walk into the police station while he's watching.

When the tourism woman's face lights up again, Rose cringes. *Go away, Hans!*

The woman comes around the desk. "Never mind, I just walk you over—"

"No, you don't have to—"

"—because look, you don't even have to go far. There he is!"

Rose can't believe her eyes. The man being pointed out is surprisingly light skinned and light haired, with a ginger mustache that Rose remembers without question from one of Matt's photos. Chief Molina, in the flesh. She *has* seen him before.

And worst of all, he's the one lifting a hand to receive the coffee from Hans, both of them grinning and chatting, like old friends.

Rose runs, crouched over, holding the plaza map in front of her face for cover, toward the nearest tuk-tuk. First, because a tuk-tuk is the easiest place to hide. Second, because Casa Eva offers her the only remaining chance of running into Mauricio, as well as Wi-Fi, so she can keep calling him, on the hour. And third, because the police station is now completely off-limits.

When Rose creeps into the classroom twenty minutes later, smiling with her head down to signal that she's sorry for arriving late, Eva finishes writing "Show Don't Tell" on the whiteboard, then sets down her black marker.

"Come here."

Rose has just made it to a seat in the back of the *aula*. "Me?"

"Yes. Come to the front." Eva's pinched expression relaxes into a forgiving smile.

Rose whispers apologies as she moves to the front of the room, where Eva stands, waiting.

"Breathe," whispers Isobel as Rose passes.

When Rose is directly in front of Eva, Eva throws her arms around her shoulders, squeezing tight. Relieved sighs and tender exclamations fill the classroom.

"All right," Eva says when she nudges Rose gently away, still clasping both of her hands, so that they remain attached at center stage, with everyone staring. "When you didn't show up on time this morning, I was worried. I thought maybe those prompts yesterday morning overloaded you emotionally."

Rose looks around, notices that others have failed to show up as well. K-Tap, who has left town. Rachel, whom no one has seen lately. But Rose is the one Eva claims to be worried about.

"And yet," Eva says, "you did it, didn't you? You dug deep. You found a story. A *real* story. A story about motherhood. One that matters to you, more than your little essay about your sister."

Rose scrambles to remember what she wrote about. The man who wanted to watch her masturbate. That's not it. The one about . . . she flashes hot . . . the one about postpartum depression. Oh god.

But she never named Jules. She only said "the baby." She probably mentioned Matt, though—but there's no way for Eva to know who "Matt" is. And she might have mentioned Ulyana, toward the end when her defenses were down and the words were pouring out of her. *Ulyana.* Rose remembers how glad she was that her own photo didn't show in the major news items about Jules's disappearance, because it made her confident no one would recognize her, here. But Ulyana's face was in those photos, along with her highly recognizable name.

What was she thinking?

Eva winks at the other writers before locking eyes with Rose again. "Cracks and all."

From the front of the room someone whispers, "Cracks and all."

Eva hugs Rose again, rocking back and forth in a locked embrace that Rose can't break away from without offending Eva.

"Cracks and all!" another writer calls out, and then the wave spreads, as everyone joins in, chanting the anthem. "Broken but beautiful. Cracks and all!"

Once the anthem dies down, Rose duck-walks back to her seat, face burning. The craft talk continues, but Rose can't hear a single word. White noise is fizzing in her ears.

Rose thinks of Rachel's workshop two days ago, that strange moment when Eva locked eyes with Rose and asked, "As a mother, what do you think?"

Rose said she wasn't a mother. She actually said it twice, because Eva made her repeat it.

At the time, Rose wasn't worried about Eva's question—but she's worried about it now.

Eva knows, because of the prompt. Worse. *Eva knew.* From the very first morning of workshops, if not before.

Rose snaps to attention now, because Eva has called on her again. "Rose, can you go ask the kitchen staff what time they'd like to serve lunch? I know how much you like to interact with staff, and your Spanish is so good."

The compliment feels forced but Rose answers the only way she can. "Um, sure."

With her cheeks and chest still flushed with nervous heat, Rose gets up again, walking past Isobel, who is fluent in Spanish, and past Diane and Noelani, both of whom like to help. Rose has been given this task, why? Certainly not to make it easier to eavesdrop on Barbara, or Hans—who probably returned to Casa Eva ten or twenty minutes after her—or to walk around hoping to catch a glimpse of Mauricio.

It makes no sense, unless Eva is completely unaware that Rose is here to get information.

It makes no sense, unless Eva is *very much* aware, and wants nothing more than to watch Rose squirm.

Eva wouldn't take the risk of making Rose uncomfortable if she had something serious to hide. So that makes Eva . . . innocent? Unaware of some staffer's bad behavior? Unaware of what happened to Jules?

Rose is almost to the house now, feeling suddenly shaky, like a mouse who has to cross a vast field, aware of having no cover as a hawk circles overhead.

Concha comes into the kitchen just as Rose enters, stammering a single word. "¿Cuándo?"

Concha gestures to the steaming trays of tamales that are ready for transport to the patio. "Diez minutos."

Rose nods, unable to smile. She doesn't know if Concha is to be trusted. She has no choice but to try. She gets up her nerve to ask, "Ha visto a Mauricio?" *Have you seen Mauricio?*

Hans comes around the corner, big hands hidden in cooking mitts. "Mauricio was arrested last night."

"What?"

"He stole from Eva." Hans pulls off the mitts aggressively, like a defeated boxer yanking off his gloves. "Yeah, it blows. He's been taking money—cash he was supposed to be delivering to charities on Eva's behalf. Little shit. Won't be doing it anymore, now."

Rose feels like she was going down the stairs, in the dark, and just missed a step. Her stomach drops.

Eva's own "son," arrested, with her knowledge, and almost certainly, with her assistance.

Maybe he did steal. Maybe he knew he was about to be

caught. Maybe that's why Mauricio was acting so strangely yesterday, when he confronted Rose and pretended he wanted to talk to her.

But Rose doesn't think so.

"Go ahead," Hans says, turning back. "You're supposed to go tell the writers that lunch is in ten minutes?"

Noelani dashes in just as Rose is turning to go. "Second message from Eva—she says we are behind schedule, so serve the lunch in the classroom and we'll eat there."

Rose's sense of dread deepens. There won't be a full lunch break. No easy way to leave Casa Eva without being noticed. No easy way to huddle at the far end of the lawn, talking privately with Lindsay.

It's almost as if Eva wants to keep a close eye on Rose.

Rose has another possibility to consider. Eva is upset about Mauricio's arrest—one of her greatest success stories, undone. If she feels like her chosen family is crumbling, she'd want to surround herself with the women who adore her, yet another form of substitute family. Even if the police were going to show up any moment—and Rose knows they aren't—she can picture Eva workshopping to the very end, basking in the respect and gratitude of her favorite students. This was, after all, a woman who sat typing next to her dead baby. No problem is too large to distract her from writing and writers and anything else that makes her feel important and needed. It's what she's done her whole life, ever since her own parents failed to show up and prove to her that she was already loved.

Rose remembers Lindsay's advice. *When it's a short con, you follow the money. When it's a long con, you follow the story.*

Until just minutes ago, Rose would have said she didn't know what Eva's most important story is. But of course she does. Everyone does.

PART
III

26

She didn't mean to do it. She just gets that way sometimes, but I saw. I got there quickly. And you were a trouper. Sometimes we really do need to be thrown into the deep end to find out what we're made of.

Take the straw—I know it hurts, but you have to drink. The jaw won't heal if you use it too much, too soon.

Good girl. A little more. It's the perfect thing to flush out all the toxins. And then I'll get the bucket, and I'll let you have more tea. It doesn't do any good to cry. You're safe, now. It's all right.

27

JULES

33 DAYS AFTER THAT NIGHT

"You have to eat," comes the voice near my head. I roll away from it, burying my face in the mildewy travel pillow. Just wanting to sleep again—for days, if I can.

Something soft and salty is pushed into my mouth. Tamale dough. I manage to swallow the first time, but after the second mouthful, I gag. The choking splits my skull.

"Fine. That's enough."

When I sleep, the pain ebbs. The hot ache of my broken jaw mellows into a dull throb. The fire in my shattered shin settles down into a warm pulse.

But less physical pain means nightmares. They flow together, a parade of images and overheard conversations. I don't know what I'm remembering, what I'm imagining. And except for the most terrifying moments—like the hot blast of pain as something hard whacks my lower leg, followed by black water closing over my head—I don't care.

I am a six-year-old, playing with a red plastic View-Master my mother found at a garage sale. Press the plastic lever and the thin wheel advances to the next tiny slide. Woody

Woodpecker. Popeye. The Flintstones. I push the viewer so hard against my face that I'm left with a line across my forehead. My parents find it hilarious that in the age of computers, 3D movies and widescreen television, their daughter is fascinated with a retro toy.

But they don't understand. I don't need much to believe—just a tiny celluloid image glimpsed through a tiny hole.

Maybe the smaller view is better, actually. Easier to control.

Click. Another picture.

Click. Forward again.

In my fragmented sleep, I try the same thing, convincing myself that if I just roll over and find a cooler spot on the tiny pillow, if I squeeze my eyes shut, if I just purge the last picture in my brain and make room for a new one, then the next dream will be better. It has to be.

A woman is cooing sympathetically as she dabs my forehead with a washcloth and smooths my tangled hair. *Mom.*

But it isn't.

"Just put it there, Eduardo." I crack open one eye and see Eva pushing a *garrafón* jug into the small, round room.

She's been the one voice in my head for who knows how long. The one nursing me.

"Water," I croak, though the second syllable sends nails into my mandible.

"You've had enough," Eva says. "The tea is better. Take the straw."

I push my head away. The straw scrapes along my cheek. Eva holds the back of my head and forcibly turns me back, mashing my lips against the straw. Then she repositions her strong fingers at the nape of my neck and squeezes.

"Wakey wakey," Eva says as my eyelids flutter. "This is helping your bones knit. You can't heal without it."

So, I drink and drink. Ignoring the burn at the back of the

mouth and the resistance in the straw as twigs get sucked in, blocking the flow. Something in the tea must be irritating my chapped lips. The inside of my mouth stings.

"Eduardo," Eva says. "Help me with this."

Next, I am being lifted and held in position over a bucket, my eyelids again too heavy to open. When I was a child, I sometimes dreamed I was going to the toilet, only to wake up with the realization that I was still in my bed, about to wet myself. I have the same worry now. I don't want to make a mess if the bucket isn't real.

"I don't have all day," Eva says. "Stop holding it. There we go."

Even while I am trying to find the words, I hear the patter of urine into the bucket, like rain against a roof. Is that where I am, camping in some rustic cabin?

"You're in a healing hut," Eva says, as if I've asked—have I? I don't know.

To Eduardo, she says, "Add the deadlock to the second door."

I listen hard to what sounds like a broom whapping at a carpet, outside the hut, faster and faster. I can't get the image of a carpet out of my mind until the noise reaches its peak, right over the hut. Then I realize I've been hearing the rotors of a helicopter—approaching, circling once, then fading away.

I'm under again, the sound of the electric drill adding new colors to my next dream—a bright bolt of blue lightning every time the noise starts up. A relaxing moss-green when the drill stops.

Despite the soft comfort of the mental moss, my brain wants to find its way back to reality: it's a drill. Why is he using a drill? Why are there helicopters? Why can't I stay awake—and why do I care? It's so much easier to sleep.

"For now," I hear Eva's voice coming from farther away. She sounds annoyed, and maybe frightened. "I don't know. We're just taking it a day at a time."

28

JULES

———————————
————————
———

"How long?" I manage to say through clenched teeth. "How long until your jaw is better?"

"No." I close my lips, inhale through my nose, prepare for the hurt. "How long have I been sleeping?"

"Oh," Eva smiles, palm soft against my forehead. "Does it matter? Your job is to get well. That's all you need to worry about."

My wakeful periods have been extending and improving. I've gotten a better look at my lower leg. The entire shin is mottled purple and yellow, so swollen it's like a natural cast, which I know can be a good thing.

I remember the gruesome chapter I read from runner Deena Kastor's memoir, about her disastrous experience at the Beijing Olympics. How her foot broke suddenly in the first miles of her run, due to an extreme calcium deficiency she didn't even realize she had. I think of that terrible moment anytime I turn an ankle, hiking or trail running. Kastor heard a sound "like a Popsicle stick breaking." She watched as her foot ballooned, larger than her head. She stopped running but she didn't get care right away. The doctors credited the lack of immediate emergency attention to saving her from surgery later, because the natural swelling pushed the fractured bits into place better than inexpert local responders might have done. That's the takeaway I cling to: your body knows what it needs. Swelling isn't necessarily bad.

Thank god I read Kastor's book when it came out. Who says memoir can't save your life?

What worries me, whenever I get up the nerve to look at my throbbing, abraded leg again, is one red and black line of scab, about two inches long, encrusted with bits of yellow. The first time I dare to touch it, the pain is so bad my entire field of vision goes dark and I have to lie back down, sweat breaking out over my forehead and upper lip.

The next time I can ease myself to a sitting position, I force myself to touch the spot again. Even through the swelling, I can feel the sharp bulge of a bone poking up, piercing layers of muscle, with the thinnest bit of flesh and a weeping scab trying to heal over it. Just thinking about it pushes me to the edge of nausea.

Fibula? Tibia? The shinbone. I think it's the tibia.

I breathe, eyes closed, waiting for the urge to vomit to pass.

Deena Kastor's foot bone didn't break through the skin. Within a few days, she was receiving expert care and physical therapy back in the United States. Whereas, I am here.

I look around the round, dark, windowless, adobe-walled hut, trying to make sense of it. There's a hole over my head, covered by a rusty, thick screen. The ceiling is darkened, unevenly so. That must be the temazcal's smoke hole. Fires have been stoked in the middle of this room—but not lately. It's been transformed.

"A healing place," Eva says.

A holding tank.

"A retreat center."

A cage.

In the beginning, I heard voices often, but never for long. Time was scissored into fragile ribbons. My naps were invaded by enormous rainbow-colored lizards. When I opened my eyes, the walls of the hut shimmered and undulated, like terra-cotta-colored waves or curtains.

"Northern lights," I said once, "but red and brown."

"They're pretty, aren't they?" someone replied, possibly, unless it was only my own thought. I couldn't always tell.

At some point I realized that someone changed my clothes following my near drowning. My jean shorts are hung on a clothesline strung across the room. The baggy overshirt I was wearing isn't here; I only vaguely remember trying to pull it off, while I was thrashing and sinking. Later, I was stripped nude, dressed in soft yoga pants and a baggy T-shirt—admittedly, with care. I want to block it out, because the thoughts are such a mixture of gratitude and humiliation that I can't make sense of them. I feel both violated and lovingly tended at the same time.

Whenever I woke fully during those first days, it was because Eva was holding my head or pushing something toward my lips. But now I frequently wake alone. I am trusted to drink liquids, to eat mashed banana and tamale. I am trusted to use the bucket, even if I'm not the one to empty it. I can't, because I can't walk steadily or lift anything. I have a fever that comes and goes, further clouding my thoughts, like a dirty window that obscures my time-sense and the ability to make even the simplest decisions, like when to get up and pee and when to just hold it, as long as I can, so I don't have to put weight on my leg again. My jaw, at least, is healing faster, though eating or talking invariably results in a headache as powerful and obnoxious as a klaxon.

Maybe Eva is staying away because she is growing tired of my questions. Like the time I asked her, point-blank, why I wasn't being taken to a hospital, given the fact that my leg is so clearly broken, swollen and infected. She refused to answer, but she did bring me antibiotics and told me I'd need to stay on them for twelve weeks.

Twelve weeks?

The antibiotics have helped with the fever, but the leg swelling hasn't abated, the bruises haven't faded, the scab keeps weeping. But I can't just stay in bed.

On the first day that I'm able to stay awake and clear-headed for well over an hour, I spend my energy investigating the door system. I'm locked inside. There is a double entry—like an arctic entry, except we are far from the arctic—with a sheltered area between the doors. It's a small chamber with built-in wooden benches. In the temazcal's days as a space for steaming, that must have been the place where people who needed a break from the heat could sit, still protected from the sun or bugs outside.

I've heard the outer lock turn and the outer door open, then boxes pushed or stacked outside the inner door, followed by a quick knock, followed by the rasp of another sliding mechanism. I figure out that this unlocking is meant to allow me to retrieve the new supplies that are left in the in-between space. But at some point, the inner door gets locked again.

It's a solid structure—the doors heavy, the adobe walls thick, no windows. I run through all the most obvious ways of getting out. None of them will work.

One day, from my bed, I hear a double rap of knuckles.

I call out, "Eduardo?"

He raps on the door again, like he's trying to send a reassuring code. Then I hear quick steps away and the closing of the outer door, followed by the slide of the lock and a final knock to tell me he's done and gone.

I limp to the door, wincing, and I pull the inner door open.

There's a wooden crate with some overripe papaya chunks in a paper bag, a single ripe avocado, tortillas wrapped in a warm napkin and more tamales. On top of it is a yellow notepad and two pencils—gifts from Eva, no doubt, to help me pass the time. Also, inside the tortilla napkin, is a tiny wooden cross not much bigger than two hand-whittled toothpicks. Someone working in the kitchen is feeling sorry for me. Someone besides Eva and Eduardo knows, or has guessed; someone who understands that unspoken communication is sometimes the safest kind. Mercedes?

I'm too tired to walk back to bed, so I sit, like a monkey pressed up against the glass in a zoo, and eat some papaya, trying to puzzle over my situation. It's surprising what the mind refuses to concede. It's like the thought of being dressed by someone when I was unconscious, too mixed up with overwhelming feelings of vulnerability. My jaw tightens painfully just thinking about it—a mixture of fear and fever sending me crawling back to bed, where I hide my head under the smelly pillow.

I keep seeing the image of Barbara, facing me in the rowboat with an oar in her hands. I keep hearing Eva's voice in my head, whispering that I'm safe now. Safe from Barbara? Who still wants to kill me? I'm a worse problem for Barbara than I was at the beginning of this mess.

I can open the shutter of my mind only briefly. One flash of truth at a time.

If Barbara were the only problem, Eva would have called her friend Chief Molina and had Barbara arrested.

But maybe Eva doesn't want her to be arrested. Maybe Barbara would tell the world about Eva—her financial shenanigans, her literary duplicity, and Eva's dream life would collapse.

I try to put myself in Eva's shoes, the same way I'd put myself into the mind of a fictional character. I think about how knotty problems are constructed. We want two things, and we can't have them both, and neither of them are so good, anyway, so we get ourselves stuck—on the horns of the dilemma, as Professor Wright used to say.

I can't be dead. That would make Barbara a murderer.

I can't be alive. A victim set free longs to speak.

I think of Eva's lie about Adhika in her memoir, and how when Eva couldn't find a way out, she simply prolonged the fiction, hoping the problem would go away—and it did. Fans believed in Eva's story. When *In a Delicate State* was published, Eva didn't just become a bestselling memoirist again. She became an icon. Her refusal to come clean—her strategy of just waiting it out—worked to her advantage. She got everything: money, fame, even better reviews.

Not everything, I think. She didn't have a baby.

She's waiting it out now, the way she did before.

I can wait it out, too. *Twelve weeks.*

Maybe if the antibiotics work and the leg heals and I no longer look like an attempted-murder victim, Eva will be able to let me out.

She'll need to be reassured that I won't press charges. I can do that. I can help her believe in the fiction she's creating yet again—the imaginary world in which there are no consequences for her actions or anyone else's.

The next day when Eva visits, I have a monologue ready. I'm prepared to tell her that I don't blame Barbara, we both were responsible for our angry tussle, it was all just a big misunderstanding, and I'm grateful that Eva showed up in her kayak just when I was on the verge of drowning.

"And so, I think we should agree that when I'm feeling stronger—"

Eva won't let me get the words out. She pushes the straw into my mouth.

"Three more big sips," she says. "No cheating."

I choke and sputter, swallowing as much as I can. The luke-warm, acidic tea stings my throat.

When I try to speak again, she gently sets the tips of her fingers against my chapped lips.

"Shhhhhh," she says. "Your jaw. Remember?"

Her eyes are wide, the eyeliner around them blurred, giving her a sleep-deprived, manic look.

"Eva," I try to say, but she presses harder.

"Shhhhhhhhhhh."

She claps her entire hand over my mouth, one finger pushed too close to my nostrils, so it's hard to breathe. I try to pull away, but it only makes her press harder.

She sounds scared, and the fear is infectious. I struggle to inhale, breath hitching, the shallow incomplete gasps making me lightheaded, the desperate hunger for air taking me back to those moments in the cold black water, twisting, lungs burning, panic rising.

From behind her fingers, I mumble and beg, sputtering, but she doesn't give an inch.

"Stop," she says. "No, I mean it. *Stop now.*"

So I do.

I force myself to be still, to not pull away or shake my head. I need her to see I'm calm now. I won't speak. I won't do anything to set her off.

She slowly lifts her hand away so that I can breathe more clearly. Her expression hasn't changed: eyes still wide, eyebrows arched. She looks deranged.

It's what I feared. She's not just stressed, not just unpredictable, not just taking the briefest of breaks from reality. This is the real Eva Marshall, not the meticulous construction she created on the page.

"Eva?" I ask after a few minutes have passed. I don't want her to cover my mouth again, but I have to try.

Using the whispery, about-to-cry voice she used the night she told me about her *In a Delicate State* fiasco: "Yes?"

"We're friends, aren't we?"

She nods, slowly.

"More than friends. I know you care about me."

She nods—again, slowly. She smooths her hair back and looks to the door. "Things are . . . things are getting busy again. I won't be able to come here every day."

She hasn't been visiting every day, already. "I understand."

"But you have things to occupy you, don't you?"

She looks around the nearly empty hut, reminding me of all the things I *don't* have: books to pass the time, my antidepressants, medications beyond antibiotics and the medicinal tea, even the most basic toiletries, like tampons, which I'll need soon. I can tell, because my belly feels heavy and crampy.

That tells me something about how long I've been in this hut—about a month. Maybe more, maybe less, because I've always been irregular under stress, never mind the fact that I suddenly and unintentionally went off birth control. I've been taking the antibiotics for about two weeks. A calendar is forming in my mind: how long I've been here. How long until my leg infection might be under control, if the antibiotics work.

Eva seems to shake herself, as if from a dream. "You should be writing!"

"I appreciate the blank notepad you gave me," I say quickly, ingratiatingly.

"Yes! And you should be writing."

For the first time she smiles, and her wide, anxious eyes return to almost normal.

"I should be writing," I repeat back. "That's exactly what I'll do."

After she leaves, I think about the last time Eva was truly

pleased with me, when I wrote about my mother's postpartum depression. That was the essay that earned her "brava" and a visit to the spa. Eva loved the story because it was about a secret, and because it was written by a bitter young woman seeking distance from her mother.

Lying on my side with the yellow pad on the mattress, trying to find a position for writing longhand that doesn't hurt any part of my battered body, I think back to that earlier essayist persona. I write about an accident, keeping the details vague. I emphasize all the ways in which the accident and my injuries were my own fault. For added interest, I write about my anger at my real mother and how, even in my current state, she's not the person I'd most like to see, because she always judges me. I describe my situation, healing slowly within the safe confines of a temazcal, enduring physical pain and sunless isolation—Eva won't believe this essay if everything sounds rosy—but I act as if it's normal, preferable to being out in the real world, an epiphany that could elevate this little think-piece into something inspirational you'd forward to a friend. *Everyone needs time alone to become grounded, to strip away the falsities, to embark on a new transformation.* I wince as I use the metaphor of a chrysalis and the butterfly. The writing is so bad that I have to push away the notepad for a while, chuckling quietly, but only until my jaw throbs. Such dreck!

And yet, how easily it flows out of me. Two pages of fiction, all to try to win over a woman who has the power to decide how long I spend here, "healing."

29

JULES

One day runs into the next, my mind even more restless now that I've finished the dishonest essay. Eva visits only briefly, avoiding conversation, not bothering to answer when I tell her I'm growing stronger, I could use more solid food, more protein. I don't mention that the last drop-off of unwrapped tamales had been crawling with ants. I ate the tamales anyway. I don't tell her I spend entire nights awake, having napped too much in the daytime, replaying old conversations, old mistakes, crying quietly in the dark.

A week has passed since Eva took my finished essay away, not commenting on it, when I'm wakened by a truck engine, followed by voices outside the hut.

"I don't know why," Eva says, her tone strident. "I just *did*. Haven't I accepted your actions? You weren't exactly making good choices, either."

The second voice is muffled.

"Well, now we're stuck," Eva says. "At least Eduardo can follow directions."

A truck door slams, but the two are still talking.

"It isn't the easiest time to move a body in any condition," Eva says. "Sometimes, you just have to put things on hold.

They won't look forever. And maybe when she's better, at least in terms of moving her . . ."

I hold my breath, trying to catch the ending of that sentence, but it slips away from me. The frustration brings tears to my eyes.

"So you made a mistake and I made a mistake and now we're even. But that doesn't mean I agree with you."

But Eva didn't make a mistake, at least not at first. She *saved* me. I'll be better soon, with a healed leg as proof that it wasn't a big deal, if that's how she wants to play it—and as I myself have played it, in the pages I wrote specifically to reassure her.

None of it matters, I realize now. Eva's indignation brings the volume up one last time. "I'm telling you, I don't know! It'll be done soon, one way or another. And don't worry. There's no better time to dump a body than *after* everyone has decided there's no body to be found."

I am already halfway back to the bed, hobbling. Adrenaline rockets through me, my brain refusing to believe what I've just heard.

There's no better time . . .

She wouldn't say that. No one would say that.

There's no better time to dump a body . . .

I'm hearing things, just as I've been seeing things. Lizards aren't rainbow colored. Walls don't move like ocean waves.

The last time Eva visited, she seemed addled, but she didn't seem angry. What changed? Has someone, aside from silent Mercedes and compliant Eduardo, figured out I'm being kept here?

Mauricio. He would have wondered why I disappeared without saying goodbye. He might have thought I was just being feckless at first, but what if he kept texting? What if he refused to believe that I'd skip town and proceed to ghost him for over a month?

And yet, that can't be the whole picture. Eva would find ways to deceive Mauricio, just like she finds ways to control the rest of her local staff. If she's feeling pressured to do something crazy, it must be something else.

I think about Eva and her moods. She's been getting busier. There must be a lull after the end of every workshop—a month or so when Eva recuperates. But halfway to the next one, things start amping up again, with people registering and making travel plans. That must be happening now. Visitors will be here soon. Even if I'm well in six weeks, she can't exactly let me out while Casa Eva and San Felipe are swarming with writers.

I haven't been thinking clearly. Why the hell can't I think more clearly?

But I know one reason, aside from the pain.

My eye follows the curve of the temazcal wall, where the big blue five-gallon *garrafón* jugs of medicinal tea have been lined up. There is one full, five empties, with tiny twigs, leaves and reddish-brown sediment still stuck in the bottoms. I figured out long ago that this is the tea made by Beya for Mercedes, the sedative tea that Eva wanted more of her anxious writers to try if she ever expanded into the healing-workshop business.

I believed Eva when she said it would help knit my bones. Maybe it did. I wasn't suspicious of its sedative qualities—I wanted to lose myself in the depths of a dreamless sleep whenever possible.

But I need to be alert now. I need to think *harder*.

She wants to get rid of me.

When I hear the outer latch being drawn, I grab the smaller plastic bottle of tea on the floor, next to my bed, and guzzle. I can't risk appearing uncooperative.

Think.

I'm sitting up, tea on my lips and bottle almost empty, when the inner door opens.

Eva startles at the sight of me, sitting upright. She covers up her surprise with a wide-eyed, manic grin. "Look at you! Someone's feeling better!"

"Except . . ." I start to say.

Think! But it's hard to think with the burning in my mouth and the nausea building. I'm inches from needing to vomit.

The solution comes to me.

I throw myself onto my stomach, head aiming for the bucket, and I begin to purposefully retch.

The first line from Eva's second memoir: *There was one thing I wanted more than anything in the world: to hold a child . . . again.*

I force myself to gag.

There's no better time to dump a body than after everyone has decided there's no body to be found.

The dry retch isn't convincing. I tense my stomach and open my mouth, arching my back.

There was one thing I wanted more than anything . . .

It's coming.

There's no better time to dump a body . . .

I manage to vomit up a thin stream of papaya-bright liquid.

The whole time, Eva has been watching with her hands on her hips, head cocked.

"Poor sweetie," she says, her expression inscrutable. "Has this been happening for long?"

"When was your last period?" Eva asks the next time she comes to the hut, a day after I convinced her I had morning sickness.

"Gosh, I'm not sure. I've lost track."

"Oh dear," Eva says, but she's smiling. "That's no good. It's been more than a month since your stay here began."

My stay. As if I checked out on that last day—luggage

packed, best wishes imparted—instead of stepping into a rowboat with a murderous woman.

"Is that right?" I ask, shaking my head. Portrait of a confused and subservient girl, the one who showed up at Casa Eva only wanting a short-term job, desperate to please Eva and earn her favor, the one who does not see the gears turning in Eva's head. "I just think I'm late because I've lost weight. I can't be pregnant. I mean . . . I *can*."

"You can?" she asks, still smiling.

It takes no effort at all to make my eyes water. All I need to do is close them and think of home, of my mother wondering where on earth I am.

"Oh, honey, it's all right! Mistakes happen. And sometimes they aren't even mistakes. Life is like that."

Tears flowing down my cheeks, I nod again, trying to communicate gratitude for Eva's wisdom.

The hard part is not saying too much. Letting Eva steer the plot. After a sideways embrace, she pulls back and looks me squarely in the eye. "Is it Mauricio's?"

I hold back from what I want to say: *Does he know where I am? Has he come looking for me? Has anyone come?*

"Yes," I finally say. Deep exhale.

Mauricio of the broad shoulders. Mauricio of the lovely smile and resilient demeanor. Watching Eva, I feel like I can see into her widening pupils, imagining how adorable our baby would be, mine and his. Jules for the writing ability and fair hair. Mauricio for the gorgeous complexion and better temperament—and the dark eyelashes. Our baby should have his eyelashes.

See how easy it is to play this game?

"The important thing is to eat and drink carefully now," Eva says, a deep furrow appearing between her eyes.

"I feel good," I say, almost too quickly. "Except for the morning sickness, I mean."

It won't help if she thinks this fetus has some defects from the powerful herbs she's been forcing into my stomach, day after day.

"That's good."

"Even the tea, it was natural, right? I'm sure it's fine. But I can't keep it down now, even if it *is* fine."

This is more talking than I've done in weeks, and I already feel the throb coming on.

"The tea was strong," Eva concedes. "We'd better not risk it."

"Right, right," I say, glancing at my poker hand, trying to decide how much to risk. "I don't know what I'd do without you, Eva."

Eva says nothing. I feel my heart pounding. Do I fold and wait for a better hand? Do I go all in?

"My mom . . ." I say, knowing the word itself is dangerous, because it reminds Eva. I am not alone in this world. Someone knows I'm missing. "My mom would talk me into an abortion."

"No," Eva says, eyes flashing.

"Yes. She was the one who wanted me to do the internship at Planned Parenthood."

Eva's lips thin, her glance goes to the far edge of the room. She's further elaborating the story I've already given to her in pieces.

"I mean, I'm pro-choice. I know you are, too. But a *baby*, when it's my own. I just couldn't . . ."

"And yet you're too young to keep it," Eva says, her tone flat again. Still testing.

"Oh god. Yes. Way too young."

Eva stands up suddenly, light on her feet, a wide grin transforming her face.

Now that I'm not drugged, I have time. Too much time. Little did I realize how being unconscious was saving me from the burrowing, itching anxiety of being in this tiny, dark, squalid hut that smells of tamales, bark, sweat, urine and feces.

I notice the cockroaches now—shuffling into the crate in the corner, disappearing under my bed. One afternoon I wake from a nap with a big, reddish-brown cockroach tangled in my hair, and I start screaming and flailing until I'm able to pluck it out and hurl it across the room. I sit in the bed, shivering, knowing that during those drugged weeks there were probably dozens of roaches crawling over me.

At times, I smell smoke and at first, it alarms me. But then I remember the slash-and-burn agriculture I saw all around Lake Atitlán, back when I was free. Small fires are common, but I wonder how often they get out of control.

I wonder what would happen if a major wildfire erupted. I find myself almost hoping for it, because it might mean the arrival of more people wandering up and down the hillsides. If a firefighting brigade passed within earshot, I could shout for help. But then again, if the fire blasted through, without people on its trail, trying to manage it, I'd be in big trouble. Roasted inside the hut. Cooked inside a clay pot.

I think of castaway movies, of Tom Hanks talking to his volleyball, of *Swiss Family Robinson* and *Robinson Crusoe*. I try not to think about more murderous plots involving girls chained up to satisfy their captors who are nearly always male. I am something in between: not a stoic character sidetracked by natural forces, not a psycho killer's inevitable prey. I am simply a problem. It is my life's goal, then, to demonstrate that I am *not* a problem—not to Eva, not to Barbara, not to anyone.

My unborn baby—*hello baby, how are we today?*—makes me an asset. But only until I'm past the first trimester and Eva notices that I am not showing.

My period finally arrives, late.

It's not a heavy flow, but there's no doubt, either.

I don't have laundry detergent. I don't have a way to hide the stained underwear. I scrub the stain as best I can in a pail filled with a squirt of drinking water, and put the wet, still-stained underpants on to dry, terrified that someone will catch a glimpse, somehow. Eva can't know I'm bleeding.

The irony strikes me. I'm hiding my bleeding. Eva hid her bleeding. She didn't want anyone to know she'd lost a baby, months before Adhika was due. I don't want the world to know I *don't* have a baby. I never meant to inhabit Eva's upside-down, mirror-filled world.

And then I realize a second thing: this isn't the first lie I've decided to tell. I started lying the moment I walked into Casa Eva. I kept lying when I wrote the first essay, wanting to impress her. Maybe my lies aren't as big as hers, but I'm not famous, either. It's a slippery slope. Even *before* I came to Guatemala, I lied to my parents about applying, the second time, for grad school. How would they feel if they found out?

One particularly endless night as I lie awake in the dark, swollen leg throbbing and hot to the touch, roaches skittering near my bed, I think about all things I did just before flying to Central America. I argued with my mother at a fancy restaurant, loud enough for everyone around us to hear. I judged Mom for being friendless. I made fun of her clothes! I made sure to let her know I thought she was brutally, unacceptably boring. I made sure both Mom and Dad knew I didn't want to live with them anymore. I whined about having no future. I wouldn't stop talking about travel as if it were the only thing in life that mattered.

What could they have thought, when I suddenly disappeared? Now, it seems obvious.

They didn't think I had an accident or was kidnapped. They thought I was somewhere even farther off the beaten trail, living the dream I'd had since I was a kid—the bohemian wanderer, old identity cast off like a worn shirt. George Orwell in *Down and Out in Paris and London*. Eva Marshall in *Last Gasp*.

I can imagine Mom crying, blaming herself, because we're alike that way. *We shouldn't have had so many arguments right before she flew out.*

I can imagine my Dad's voice. *She'll come back on her own time. Nothing we can do about it.*

No wonder no one has found me.

With effort, I eat every bit of tamale that's provided to me, even down to the dry, salty crumbling bits. I must fatten up. One, to look at least a little pregnant. Two, to gain strength.

Every day, I test putting more weight on my left leg. Once, I get too ambitious and plant my left foot flat, then raise my right leg off the ground, but it's too much. I scream out in pain, feverish heat flashing through me.

So, not full weight. But even with a palpable bump beneath the skin where the fractured bone is poking, the flesh around my shin is healing. If I'm careful, if I eat well, if I can just get through a few more weeks and then, if I get the right opportunity. Maybe I can hobble—not far, but somewhere. Timing is everything. Get out too soon, and I'll move too slowly and be caught immediately. Wait too long, and my ploy will be revealed.

One day Eva steps into the cabin, smiling, with a box in her hand.

"Pregnancy test!" she calls out cheerfully.

My entire body erupts in hot panic.

"Not really necessary." I try to laugh, hand on my belly.

Eva isn't smiling this time. "It'll reassure us both."

"Okay," I stammer. "Yeah."

"Do it now? I only have a few minutes before I have to get back to the house."

My mind races. "Oh, I just peed."

She looks flustered. "This is a very busy week. I can't just be running out here all the time. The next few days are completely booked. I have things to do, you know!"

"I'm sorry," I say, wishing her eyes didn't look so big and wild. "But I don't really think we need a test at all."

She purses her lips, studying me for a long, agonizing moment. "Pee again."

Eva opens the box, unwraps a urine test stick, and hands it to me, gesturing with her chin toward the plastic toilet bucket across the room.

I ease off the bed, hobble over to it, and squat with most of my weight on my good leg. Meanwhile, I keep a firm grip on the crotch of my underwear, pushing it out of the way in case I do accidentally dribble, but also hiding the stained patch that Eva absolutely must not see.

"Oh," she says, sympathetically. "That looks tricky. I didn't think about how hard that must be, with your bad leg."

"Yes," I say, shin on fire, heart pounding, holding back tears. I don't see a way out of this. I can't think.

I manage the squat a full minute, holding back the pee while I squeeze my eyes and furrow my brow, as if I'm pushing with all my might.

"Darn," Eva says. "Maybe you're dehydrated. Can I bring your water bottle to you?"

The tears are running down my face now. "I really need to get off this leg." And it's true.

"Okay," she says, disappointed. "But drink up, use the stick, and I'll be back to take a look tonight."

"Yes, Eva."

When I interned at Planned Parenthood, my favorite part was contributing to the blog. In our communications meetings, we brainstormed topics, like basic facts about sex, contraception, sexual and gender identity. The fun posts were the surprising ones. Can you get STDs from sharing razors? Yes, possibly.

Equally fun: dispelling myths.

These, however, were tricky territory. Telling people about an urban myth didn't necessarily go the right way. Tell people that it's not a good idea to make home pregnancy tests using household ingredients (shampoo, vinegar, sugar, bleach), and they just might try. But I found those kinds of posts, popular all across the internet, fascinating. I never thought they'd save my life.

One day at lunch, sitting next to my internship bestie, Cassandra, we laughed about all the ways people try to fake pregnancy tests, whether to create a false positive or false negative. Most of the efforts were questionable, if not impossible.

As the sun drops and the hut darkens and I listen for the sound of Eva's truck returning, I am willing to try. But I have no Coke. Or apple juice. Or any of the other questionable liquids described in extremely questionable online discussion forums. I have nothing.

When I can't bear the tension any longer, I decide to pee on the stick.

I know what it will say in a few minutes. Negative. *No shit.*

I'm crying again, left aching even worse than earlier today, right leg cramping from the difficulty of a one-leg awkward squat. I hobble back to the bed, pee stick in my sweaty hand, cursing with pain at every step, wracking my brain for excuses.

Come on, Jules. *You know more reproductive trivia than any woman your age. Figure this the fuck out!*

It's the broken tibia that's making this all harder. My leg is still swollen. The surface skin, stretched for an extended period, looks like mottled parchment. It's ghastly. My entire body is probably being poisoned by this fracture. If it gets any worse, I could die from blood poisoning.

I can't stop crying now, silently but steadily, drips wetting my T-shirt. Fists against my cheekbones, trying to hold it all in. I look over at the pregnancy test, on the floor next to my mattress, and see the single line where I need a double. *Think, Jules!*

I can't give up. There has to be a solution.

The pain is the problem.

The pain is the problem. I look up, blinking. That's it. Or *part of it.*

Moments later, I hear the truck.

When Eva walks in, I shout before she's even fully in the room.

"I wasted the test! I forgot you have to do it in the morning when the HCG is higher and your urine is more concentrated."

Eva sighs, smiling. "Oh, shoot. You're right."

I'm right. I'm *right.*

She pulls the box out of her yoga wrap pocket, shaking it. "But we have two tests!"

Of course we do.

"Now don't waste this one," she says, heading back to the door, looking agitated about something beyond my stupid pregnancy test. "I have to go to Antigua. I won't be back for three days. But the morning I come back, do your test, and do it right." She puts on a forgiving smile. "No more excuses!"

Three days.

What I remembered, as my leg throbbed after that last bucket squat, was to think about the *unintended* ways you get a false positive. Nothing as stupid as dipping a stick into a can of soda. But other things can do it: medications, like certain anti-anxiety meds. And also raging infections, especially the chronic kind.

I look at my leg. "Sorry about this."

I mash up a handful of antibiotic pills, in case anyone thinks to count later this week, and dispose of them in the pee bucket, where they dissolve. There's no going back.

It takes a day for the bump on my leg to turn purply-red again, and another day for the fever to come on. The fever, and the nightmares it brings back—Barbara, black water, drowning—almost make we want to give in and take another pill, but I resist.

The wound at the spot where the bone is almost poking through keeps changing shape, the tender skin over the bump crusting over, partially healing, then reddening again, with yellow pus along the blackened, scabby edges. It looks very, very bad. I've succeeded in ramping up the infection. I just hope I don't regret it like I've regretted so many other things I've done.

The morning that Eva is due back I faint on the way to the pee bucket. When I come to, I reach a hand down to touch my leg and feel the damp spot where the sore has broken open again. Bile stings my throat. I swallow hard, crawl to the bucket, and manage to piss on the stick.

I'm so exhausted when I get back to the bed with the stick clutched in my urine-splashed hand that I close my eyes and fall into a restless sleep.

When I wake up, I remember to roll over and look.

And there they are: two lines.

I sob with gratitude.

30

JULES

"Can I touch?" Eva says one day when she stops by briefly—no new delivery of groceries, she was just so curious, and things are getting busier back at Casa Eva, and she didn't know when she'd be coming next. "I mean, unless it's too private."

I want to burst out into crazed laughter. *Private?*

I force a shy smile onto my face, slide to the edge of the bed, and push my belly out.

Eva lifts my shirt and places her palm just above my navel.

I hold my breath, and push a little harder, arching my back. She pulls her hand away as if shocked.

I startle in response, watching her hands go to her mouth. I feel sick with terror. She noticed what I was doing. She knows I'm faking.

I stare at Eva, my eyes wide. She stares back.

Then she starts to giggle.

My relief is so strong that I start giggling, too.

"Did you feel it?" I ask.

"Wait—did she kick?"

I note the pronoun. *She.*

"I think she did. Or is it too soon? Maybe it was just a gas bubble."

Eva giggles again, and then her eyes are overflowing. "It usually happens at twenty weeks."

I smile, eyes crinkling. "And this is . . . ?"

"Let's see," she counts on her fingers. "Closer to twelve."

I stow the information for safekeeping. "Maybe she's precocious."

Eva's face lights up. "Of course she is. Oh, Jules. This is beautiful."

I throw my arms around her. She squeezes back. While I'm clasping with all my heart, my mind is racing.

I can restart the antibiotics, with only about two more weeks left in the prescription. My leg will heal. Maybe now that she believes me, I can get out of this hut. If she lets me stay at Casa Eva, I can escape.

"Please," I say. "I'm just so lonely. I mean . . . happy to have a baby. But it's so hard, here, living by myself . . ."

She jerks back. A button pops loose from her flowy green blouse. She looks at me, and then down, sighing. "There goes. That was my shirt for the opening party."

"The opening party—for a new workshop session? Already?"

Part of me is excited. I've lost all sense of time. People are coming, already! The more people visiting, the better chance someone will realize Eva is acting strangely, or Eva herself will slip up.

But the bigger part of me knows this isn't good. There's no way Eva will let me come stay at her house. Plus, the workshoppers will stress her out.

She may reverse course. She may decide a baby that isn't biologically hers isn't worth it, after all.

Eva is still looking down, oblivious to my flustered expression. "It's okay. I'll pick something else."

"No. That's your best shirt. I love that shirt. You look like a beautiful forest fairy in that color green."

Eva tugs her shirt shut, but it won't stay that way. The top of her bra shows above the topmost remaining button.

"Here," I say, grasping my eyebrow bar and sliding the piercing out of the tender skin.

She looks at it with an expression that is half disgust, half curiosity.

"It's just jewelry," I say. "Like a tie tack, or a pin. To hold your shirt." I reach forward and push it through the fabric, replacing the missing button.

"I don't know," she says, but her hands remain at her side, letting me fix her shirt.

"Promise me you'll wear it," I say. "It makes me feel like we're together, even when we're not."

She starts to laugh. "You're making this sound like you're a fraternity guy, pinning his girlfriend."

"Or a daughter pinning her mother." I watch her face for signs I've gone too far. "Or the person she wishes were her mother."

She looks down at her shirt, clasping the ball end of the post I've affixed and removing the piece of jewelry, which she slides into her pocket.

"It didn't look right," she says. "But I *will* treasure your gift, Jules. I promise."

PART
IV

31

ROSE

———————————
———————————
———

"You're sitting way in the back, Scarlett," Eva says after the hurried lunch break in the classroom, when it's the cyclist's turn for her workshop. "I can barely see you. Take a seat up front."

Rose exchanges looks with Lindsay and Isobel from the back row, just behind Scarlett. Rose wasn't the only one who noticed Eva's changing mood today, her apparently frantic need to move things along, to reprimand writers for speaking up when they haven't been called on. They're all being watched, but Rose feels like the central target of that anxious sweeping beam of attention. There's a feeling, in the *aula*, of a tightening noose, as if everyone, and not only Rose, is being corralled more tightly together.

Rose wishes she weren't here, but since the incident in the plaza, seeing Hans and Chief Molina, nowhere feels entirely safe. Rose has redialed Mauricio's number covertly, hand manipulating the phone from within her bag. If he picks up, she'll pretend it's an emergency call from home. She'll duck out and run to the edge of the bluff, where no one can hear. She has that right. Eva can tap her foot or stand with her hands on her hips, the way she's standing now, still waiting for Scarlett to move to the front. So what?

Scarlett, with shawl, laptop and several notebooks finally tucked under her arm, trades one last dread-filled look with the other women in her row. Rising, she drops a pen.

Rose scoops it off the ground, and at the same moment, notices something small and silver glinting on the rock-paved floor, next to a leg of the chair, easy to miss. She picks it up, recognizing it as the kind of small metal bar used in an eyebrow piercing.

"Did you lose this?" Rose asks.

"What? Oh." Scarlett touches two fingers to her eyebrow, confused. "No, it's not mine."

"That's odd," Rose says.

She studies the metal piece—a steel bar, with a tiny ball at each end—so much like jewelry she remembers Jules wearing. She can even picture herself a year ago, dabbing at Jules's brow, where the piercing got infected. If Jules had pulled the jewelry out, perhaps because it got infected once again and she decided to let the piercing close, she might have dropped the bar from a pocket or purse. But would no one have noticed it for three months?

Now that Rose is staring, she sees all sorts of things trapped in the floor's cracks: twigs and gravel and bits of grass, a paper clip, and across the room, an elastic hair tie. She'd never looked down before. People rarely did.

At the front of the room, Eva taps her foot. "I'm waiting."

Scarlett hurries forward, dragging all of her belongings. When she's finally resituated, face flushed, Eva says, "You remind me of my daughter. The last time I saw her, I told her the same thing I'm going to tell you. You have a beautiful face. You have a beautiful body. You don't need to wear all that makeup. You certainly don't need to wear skintight clothing."

Heads crane to check what Scarlett's wearing to have merited this second lecture. She has big, dark lashes, but she's not wearing more makeup than anyone else. Scarlett has a big chest, but she is wearing a loose sweatshirt. Eva's the only one with a bit of cleavage visible above the line of her white tank.

"Has anyone ever told you that?" Eva asks.

"Yes," Scarlett says, keeping her voice level. "Since the seventh grade. Not about the makeup. About my body."

"Was it your mother?"

"No, it was Mr. Hanshew. My teacher."

"And how did it make you feel?"

"Like I'd done something wrong."

"So what did you do?"

"I ate more."

"You didn't reconsider how you were dressing?"

"I wasn't dressing any differently than the other girls," Scarlett says, her voice struggling to hold firm. "Just like I'm not dressing wrong today."

Lindsay speaks up from the back. "Hear, hear. If Scarlett wore a garbage bag, she'd still look like Marilyn Monroe."

Scarlett looks around. "It's okay, everyone. You don't have to defend me. We can talk about this. The fat part of my past—that matters. It's the 'me before' of my bike trip, so I'm fine with it. But the rest—how I dress, whether I wear mascara—I don't think that's part of my story."

"Interesting," Eva says. She paces a few times before settling back on her stool. "Actually, we're not going to talk about the bike trip today."

Rose feels her brow furrowing. *Not this again.* Scarlett *sold her bike* in order to come to Lake Atitlán and learn how to write about her bike trip. How is it possible that Eva isn't going to talk about her bike trip?

Across the room, Diane takes off her sunglasses, folds them

and closes her eyes, as if preparing for something stressful. A few women mimic her—eyes closing, breaths deepening. But not everyone. In the back, someone starts to make noise, packing her bag.

"I didn't say we were finished," Eva says.

The shuffling stops.

"Scarlett needs some help finding her story. I think we all know what that story is."

Another minute.

Rose reminds herself that breathing is healthy. She should do as the others are doing. Breathe. Meditate. Learn to be comfortable with silence, and with this, whatever it is. Just another version of what they've been through before, as long as Scarlett goes along.

Eva says, "Mr. Hanshew touched you."

Rose expects another full minute of silence, is already beginning to count, when Scarlett speaks up.

"Yes."

"That's why you felt wrong. Because he talked to you about your body. He made you aware that you were developing ahead of the others. That he saw you in a different way. And he touched your body. You blame yourself for that."

Scarlett doesn't answer.

Rose tries to open her mind to the possibility that Scarlett *does* want to talk about this. And maybe all kinds of therapy work this way: resistance, challenge, negotiation.

Eva says, "A scene requires a place and a time."

No answer.

Eva asks, "You don't remember? Of course you do. Let me guess: a classroom."

Silence.

"Or a car?"

Rose risks a peek over at Scarlett, who is staring at her knees.

"No," Scarlett says, finally. "His house."

Eva's voice brightens. "Better, Scarlett. Now, tell me about the room."

Scarlett has her hands on her thighs, palms up. Rose can feel her trying—feel her refusing to shut down, if this is what it takes.

"Just a living room."

"There is no *just a living room*. Describe, please. Concrete. Specific."

The air feels thick. Out on the lake, the standing fisherman is long gone. Time drags as Eva extracts the details from her.

Loveseat, harvest gold corduroy cushions, the nineteen-inch television left on, the sound of the dog scrabbling behind the closed kitchen door.

"Not habitual actions, Scarlett," Eva says. "One time. No montage. No fast-forwarding."

They're supposed to know this already. They're supposed to follow the rules for good writing.

"Are you seated now, in this moment?"

"No."

"Standing? Reclining?"

Scarlett whispers something that Rose misses. Eva looks pleased.

"If you're on your knees, that's important. There's a rug underneath you? Is it bothering the skin of your knees? You're wearing shorts? No—a skirt. Are you uncomfortable? We need to see it. We need to feel it."

Rose recognizes the shift in Scarlett's resigned voice, the recognition that sometimes the only way out is through. But wasn't that also why she let Mr. Hanshew do what he did? Because it was easier and quicker to give in than to resist?

Everything matters, Eva tells them, repeating the mantra until Scarlett supplies more satisfactory details. The hair on the back of his knuckles. The way his elbow, red and calloused and hard, dug into the top of Scarlett's shoulder. The tink-tink-tink of his belt buckle, still threaded through the pants down around his ankles.

"Better, Scarlett," Eva says. She pushes a lock of hair behind her ear and then flexes her fingers, like she's a midwife poised to catch a slippery baby. "But I want you to go back. You're doing this too fast, and that last comment was from Scarlett *today*. I only want to hear about Scarlett *then*. The moment you go into summary or reflection mode, we're out of the scene. And this has to be a scene. So let's rewind again. I have to know exactly what happens next."

Rose tells herself Scarlett must be fine. She has to be fine.

Was Jules fine? Are any of these young women—the fragile ones, the inexperienced ones, the ones with big hearts and big ambitions and desperate desires to please an authority figure like Eva—really going to be fine?

Rose looks over to Lindsay, who is sitting with lips pressed tight, fingernails tapping out an annoyed rhythm on her desk.

It's almost over. Later, they'll all try to pick Scarlett up and put her back together again.

Please be fine, Scarlett.

Because if she's not, isn't it their fault too—all of them, just sitting here listening as Scarlett is dragged back into a slow-motion nightmare?

The story Eva likes to tell about herself is that she was and still is a great mother. Self-sacrificing. Wise. Caring. Fiercely attached. But for whatever reason, she can't seem to stop mothering—perhaps the better word is *smothering*—vulnerable young women.

It's painful to watch Eva repeating her toxic formula—but satisfying in one small sense. If Eva ever seemed like a mystery, she isn't one now. And yet . . . Rose is still missing something.

Maybe Eva tried to mother Jules, to control her somehow. And at the same time, Jules got wise to Eva's invasive teaching and problematic fundraising. But if that all came to a head, then what?

Eva claims she fired Jules. Makes sense. Jules seemed upset on her birthday, just before disappearing. Makes sense.

Then what, Rose asks herself. *Then what?*

The rest of the group thins out as most head down the stairs to the beach to catch a water taxi.

Rose assumes she'll be making the walk alone, but then she spots a woman with silver-blond hair and a walking stick, heading for the steps that lead up the road. *Wanda?*

"Wendy," the woman introduces herself as they begin to climb.

Wendy.

The alum that Diane pointed out, the one who donates to the orphanage every quarter. Rose planned to speak to her, to collect more evidence. But after the orphanage visit, Rose had all the evidence she needed to convince herself that Eva or her staff weren't forwarding all that money after all—and yet she also decided it wasn't safe to tell Chief Molina. What was the point in more anecdotes if there was no one to tell?

Still, Wendy was a longtimer. *The* longtimer. She might know if Eva is the ringleader of the money scheme, an apathetic colluder or even a completely unwitting accomplice.

"You're walking to town?" Rose asks Wendy.

"I was supposed to have my private session with Eva, but I think she forgot, because she told me just now that she had to run an errand."

"She doesn't have other people to do that for her?"

Wendy ignores the question. "I asked her if she could give me a lift to town, but she said she was going the other way."

"What's the other way?"

"Not much," Wendy says, squinting at Rose. "Maybe her other properties."

"And you don't mind that she's skipping your private session?"

"Well," Wendy looks around, as if someone might hear. "Eva's been that way lately. Distracted."

Distracted, Rose notes. So maybe Eva doesn't know the money is going astray. Maybe someone else—Barbara or Hans—is benefitting from Eva's obliviousness.

"It's hard work, doing everything she's doing," Rose says, watching Wendy's body language, the way she started pulling back when Rose sounded too critical. "I imagine it gets tiring after a while. I heard you've been studying with her a long time?"

"Seven years," Wendy says.

Rose steps closer. "That is *amazing*."

"Some people would say it's too long."

Rose touches Wendy's shoulder. "Absolutely not. What should you be doing instead, playing golf?" Rose laughs, waiting for Wendy to join. "Why do people think it's okay to spend time and money on things that don't matter—*cars, fancy clothes*—and when we try to improve ourselves—to *learn something*—they judge?"

When Wendy surrenders a smile, Rose asks, "So, you come every year?"

"More often than that. Sometimes a few sessions per year. Sometimes four!"

"Four sessions." Rose nods, reminding herself to keep nodding, look thoughtful, not desperate. "That's great."

Wendy was here.

Rose adds, "I have so many questions about memoir and this whole workshopping *thing*. You could teach me a ton.

I'm just sorry I didn't introduce myself to you sooner. I hope I didn't come across as unfriendly."

"No, no, I'm to blame," Wendy says. "I socialized more the first few years, but once you've been here a lot, it changes. And I move slowly. I usually don't try to hike out, but I needed this today. If you want to go ahead . . ."

"No, no. The slow pace feels good. I find it hard to breathe sometimes."

"Precisely."

Rose can feel Wendy wanting to say more, but if Rose hurries her, she'll balk. She won't want to say anything bad about Eva, or Casa Eva's staff, or anything she's experienced in this place that has become practically a second home.

"This spring," Wendy says after a moment, "I really thought I was about done with my book. Even my critique group back home loved it. But Eva said I should come back. She tells me, 'Don't rush it.' I remind her, 'Rush it any less and I'll be dead before this damn book is finished!'"

"Eva is so patient. I love that about her," Rose says.

"But this may be my last time."

"Oh?"

Wendy lifts her walking stick to point at a small pink flower growing in a crack between two flat stone steps.

"Pretty," Rose says, waiting for Wendy to continue.

"It helps with the writing, attending as often as I have." Wendy shakes her head. "But the stories you have to hear. Like Scarlett's. I had a hard time with that one. Aren't these gorgeous plants. Everything so green."

Rose murmurs agreement.

"I worry for Scarlett," Wendy says. "She's a sensitive girl."

Rose chooses her next words carefully. "Our whole group's a little—*fragile*, I guess you'd say? But I bet some groups are more problematic than others. You would know."

Rose sees Wendy's shoulders rise and her chin drop down into her chest.

Rose presses on. "Eva said something about 'learning from her mistakes,' after something that happened during the last session. And after seeing some of these workshops—Rachel, and especially Scarlett—I can imagine. But what *exactly* happened in May?"

"May?" Wendy asks, eyes flitting to the shadows along the trail. "I didn't say I was here last May."

"Weren't you?"

Wendy grunts as she ascends the next stone step.

Rose puts a hand on Wendy's elbow, like she's just trying to help her with the climb. But the touch isn't casual. This is one woman talking to another woman, where no one else can hear.

Rose tries again. "You were here in May. I know you were."

Wendy allows herself to be helped up the next step. "Eva asked alums not to mention it to new folks. We're sort of her cheering squad, you know?"

"But Eva admitted it herself, that something went wrong. So, it's not a secret, right?"

They both know it is.

Rose looks directly at Wendy's face, but the elderly woman is looking up the remaining stretch of trail, avoiding Rose's gaze.

"Every time you get at least one unhappy person," Wendy says. "It's challenging."

"And how did you know this person was unhappy?"

"Well, she was looking bad, the morning of her workshop. Thousand-yard stare, and then she did a vanishing act."

"Vanishing act?"

Now, Rose really *is* finding it harder to breathe.

Jules would have wanted to audit the workshops. It would have been the only thing that kept her here, even as she started to see past Eva's façade.

"Not in the morning, when she was workshopped," Wendy explains. "But that night, I guess. She went missing a little while and then they found her passed out on the beach. I heard she'd been swimming. That spooked Eva a bit, realizing the girl could have drowned. That was the scuttlebutt."

"She passed out, but she didn't drown?"

Wendy leans on her walking stick. "No, of course not."

Rose has to fight the urge to pinch the arm she is steadying. "What was her name?"

"'Sarah,' I think. Or, like the desert. *Sahara?*"

"What did she look like?"

"Skinny as a twig. Pale. Blackish sort of ratty hair. A rock musician. That explains the look, I guess."

Rose's breaths are coming more quickly now. For a second, her vision darkens.

"Are you all right?"

"It's the altitude."

But it's not just her lungs protesting. It's her heart. She feels sick and angry. At herself. For hoping, even if it was only for thirty seconds. For falling for that foolish hope that any parent of a missing child falls for. As if it were all just a misunderstanding, somehow; as if her own daughter didn't really drown, and even now, Wendy is confused. Black hair/blond hair; musician/writer. And what: Jules was going by a fake name? Sahara? And then after nearly drowning, she ran away? As if she would have let her family go through hell, thinking she was dead, and all for what? Ridiculous.

Rose always told herself she simply wanted the truth, but what Rose *really* wanted, still *wants*, is her daughter back. She remembers the time, on Jules's birthday, when she thought she could hear a voice calling out *Mama!* She thinks of the times she has felt like there is a thin cord reaching out into the dark universe, still connecting them somehow.

She remembers all the times she has seen young women who looked like Jules, and how—for just a fraction of a second—she wanted to believe and to trust her mother's intuition over every expert, including Matt.

"Halfway there," Wendy says, pulling away from Rose's grip on her elbow. "At the top, maybe we can flag a tuk-tuk down."

"Please. Tell me about this Sahara girl."

"She had a bad workshop. Like what we saw with Scarlett. And then the girl fell apart. But she was a basket case to begin with, of course. Did I mention her ratty hair?"

"You did."

"She had another friend helping her, at least. We never saw what happened because we left on the textiles field trip, but the assistant girl—"

"Which assistant?"

"I couldn't possibly—"

"American? Blond hair? *Jules*?"

For the first time, Wendy looks directly at Rose. Her wrinkled mouth loosens its troubled pucker, making way for a pensive smile. "Yes, *Julie May*, I think."

Rose says gently as she can manage, "Her name was Jules."

"Anyway, they were together."

"But when you came back from the field trip—what happened, exactly?"

"We didn't come back to Casa Eva until the next day. Sahara had already left by then. It was only gossip at that point—that she'd spent the day drinking, on drugs, whatever. That she'd nearly drowned. But she didn't."

Rose lets it all flood her with a strange mix of horror and calm.

"I understand that Sahara didn't drown," Rose repeats. "But what happened to Jules?"

"She left. I don't know if it was that night, or later."

"Did you see her the next day? Or ever again, at the workshops?"

They've arrived at the gate. "Let's see," Wendy says, stepping through it, holding it for Rose, then latching it behind them both with agonizing slowness, her arthritic fingers fumbling. "I guess I didn't."

"But surely you heard about Jules having gone missing? The search?"

"Oh, that was days later. After we'd all left workshop. After we'd flown home."

"It was days later that the search started," Rose says sharply. "Not days later that she went missing."

A cloud of dust rises from the road. "We're in luck," Wendy says, squinting toward an approaching tuk-tuk.

Rose grabs her hand. "The point is, a second young woman went missing. What did you *think*?"

Wendy looks stunned. "That the assistant had been fired—I don't recall the reason, and I don't really care. Then she went into town, and a few days later, she drowned. Casualty of some beach party, most likely."

"You didn't think that was strange?"

"Not at all."

"You didn't consider that maybe both girls went swimming together, at the same time? Or that Jules swam after the first girl, because she was drunk and high like you said, and a basket case like you said, to try to help her, and that's when Jules possibly drowned?"

"No."

"But why not?"

"I told you. Because that's *not what Eva said*, when she told us about Sahara, before we went home. No one said anything like that. *No one*."

Wendy pulls her hand from Rose's grasp.

The tuk-tuk brakes in front of them. Wendy hobbles toward it, waving her walking stick.

Rose remembers the Instagram photo of two girls' slim knees and hands, side by side on a dock. She always knew the scabby knees belonged to Jules. The unblemished knees and perfect hands with perfect nails belonged to this other girl: Sahara.

Check.

This is the first clean-fitting puzzle piece in a dilapidated set of torn and bent pieces. It's the first one that makes sense rather than upending everything she thought she knew about her daughter. Now, Rose can imagine the last hours, the moments she'd never understood from Jules's birthday texts. *Can't complain. Mimosas with a view.* Jules had befriended this girl. Jules was sitting with her, consoling her and protecting her from further harm. It's what her daughter would have done.

That *sorry* at the very end of the last texts Jules ever sent wasn't a suicidal sorry.

I'm sorry I've been so out of touch.

I love you Mom.

I'm sorry.

It was just a sorry that they weren't together—a sorry that there were moments when things between a mother and daughter weren't easy, but they didn't have to be easy. Love doesn't always have to be easy.

The word "closure" doesn't capture this feeling, as Rose reimagines those final moments. It's not "closing" anything. It's getting back a piece of her daughter Rose had lost. And it explains why Eva was elusive. Her workshop with Sahara created this situation. Her "brand" could be called into question. She wasn't willing to face it, not willing to accept even the smallest bit of responsibility, not willing to change a single damn thing.

"Wait," Rose calls out to Wendy.

"No *thank you*."

Wendy starts to climb into the back of the tuk-tuk without inviting Rose to follow. "The bad workshop with the musician made Eva sad. I'm sure the accident with the assistant girl made Eva even more sad. But that all happened later. And none of it was her fault. Things just happen. And please," Wendy's voice is warbling with emotion now, "don't tell Eva I talked to you. I didn't spend seven years cultivating her good graces for you to come along and make her think badly of me."

"Why do you even care?" Rose calls back.

She covers her mouth and nose with her hand, coughing on the dust cloud that Wendy and her tuk-tuk leave behind.

32

JULES

The new session is underway. I can tell from the changes in Eva's habits, the way she is always in a rush, more preoccupied than ever. The workshops have started. She can't manage *that* and *this* at the same time. Something has to give.

I'm mentally prepared for yet longer stretches when no one comes to visit me at all. So, when I hear footsteps outside the hut, I'm surprised.

"Eduardo?" I call out, as soon as I hear the first lock turning.

Outer door open, the footsteps continue to the second door, but these steps are heavy, slow and shuffling.

Barbara?

"Hello?" I say, listening. I try to sound cheerful. "Everything's fine here. Thanks for coming!"

Only an idiot would believe I am okay with being held captive. Barbara is not an idiot.

Eva wants a baby, and even so, her delusion—that I could give birth to a baby and give it to her, then go on and lead my life without somehow implicating her or anyone else—is fragile. But Barbara? She has no reason to delude herself.

As the dead bolt slides, I hold my breath.

Barbara is about to step through that door and try to kill me.
No.

Barbara is about to step through that door and try to kill me *again*.

At least I'm more prepared this time. I lean back, reaching for the clothesline I took down and stored under my pillow as an improvised garotte.

The door opens.

It's her and it's not her. Barbara's hair has changed from fluffy pale brown to mostly white. Her clothes hang off her, like she's lost at least thirty pounds. Her jowls and eyelids droop.

She looks terrible. Sick—and weak. And even so, I'm afraid.

"I didn't mean for any of this . . ." she starts to say, then sticks a hand out to prop herself against a wall, as if she's been struck by a dizzy spell.

"Are you all right?"

She scoffs. "You're asking *me* if I'm all right?"

Her weariness doesn't assuage my fears. It's the fatigue of someone who has worn herself down with a job but won't stop until she's finished. Until *I'm* finished.

"Barbara," I say. Aren't you supposed to repeat people's names, if you want to win them over? "You don't look well."

"This whole thing has been killing me."

"It doesn't have to."

Head tipped down, jowls sagging, she gives me a long, pitying look, like she can't believe I don't see the obvious.

I shift forward, toward the edge of the bed, and that's enough to startle her. Barbara hurries out the door and closes it, latching it behind her. The crate of food and new *garrafón* she was dropping off remain in the in-between space.

I listen for the fading footsteps, the second door and the

second latching lock. But I don't hear it. I hear the groan of wood as Barbara leans against the inner door, lingering.

"Barbara?"

Through the door she says, "Your mother is here, at the workshops."

I assume I've heard her wrong.

My mother. Here.

I move so quickly, trying to get off the bed, that I fall to the floor and collapse on my weak leg, cradling my shin, seeing stars. I crawl the rest of the way, on my knees, until I reach the closed door.

"My mother?"

"She registered under a different last name."

"She's looking for me?"

"Not looking, exactly. Trying to figure out what happened to you. I doubt she'd be sitting through a day of workshops if she thought you were anything but dead and gone."

I'm stunned speechless.

Dead and gone.

"Does Eva know my mother's here?"

"She didn't tell me at first. I think she's trying to find her own way out of this fucking mess she's made."

That you also made, I want to say. But Barbara's version was simpler. She wanted me dead, at the bottom of Lake Atitlán. It was Eva who wanted more than that. It's always Eva who wants more, time after time, constructing her fragile houses of cards that can be toppled with the lightest puff—like someone arriving to ask questions, finally.

I set my forehead against the door. I want to wail. Bad enough, my mother thinks I'm dead. Worse, she's here, with no idea what she's walked into.

"Barbara," I say. "Help me. And warn my mother. I'll make sure no one presses charges."

When she doesn't answer, I pound my fist against the door. It makes no sense to appeal to a violent and impulsive woman, but I have no other choice. Barbara's adoration of Eva seems to have faded. I know the feeling. Why would she have come at all, why would she have told me, unless she wanted to help?

"Barbara, at the very least, don't tell Eva you told me. She'll feel cornered."

When Barbara doesn't answer, it occurs to me that maybe Barbara *wants* Eva to feel cornered. Maybe Barbara wants Eva to take care of her own dirty work, for once. I'm all too afraid that Eva will.

"Please, Barbara!"

But then I hear the steps, the second door, the second latch. Somehow I know, Barbara is never coming back.

I'm woken by the sound of the door, a flashlight swinging in my face. No one has ever come at night, and although I am momentarily blinded, this arrival gives me hope. It could be anyone—Mauricio, a remorseful Barbara, the police. My mom.

A voice from behind the white light says, "You're not feeling well?"

Then the light clicks off and she's at my side. Only Eva.

My gut clenches. She never comes this late. It can't be a good thing.

I tell her that I've started vomiting. I can't keep anything down. It feels like morning sickness again.

"Well, you're still at the right time for that—three months, give or take."

"But I'm getting dehydrated. It's really bad." My brain goes searching for likely details. "My mother was like this during her pregnancy with me. She actually had to be hospitalized or she would have lost me."

I wait for Eva to suggest something, but she doesn't.

"A doctor, maybe?"

"No. Absolutely not."

The mattress shifts as she stands. My audience is almost over.

"Tea," I say. "Not the Mayan medicinal kind. When I was a kid and couldn't stop vomiting, I always had special ginger tea."

"Okay," Eva says, sounding tired. "Hans makes something like that."

"Thank you."

"And Jules, I brought you a fresh journal."

Maybe I went too far in the last pages I wrote. Maybe I didn't go far enough.

"Thank you," I say, without asking for any explanation.

"This way, you can start fresh and write about Aadhya."

"Is that our baby's name?"

"Do you like it? It means first power, or the beginning."

Eva's living daughter is named Adarsha. The one that died was Adhika. This baby is "the beginning"—but whose beginning, and whose ending?

"Do you like it?" Eva asks again.

"It's perfect."

33

ROSE

‾‾‾‾‾‾‾‾‾‾‾‾‾‾‾‾‾‾‾‾‾‾

S he didn't have the nightmare.

That's the first thing Rose thinks, opening her eyes to the dim light filtered through the cabin's curtain-covered window. After her melancholic final evening on the beach, thinking about Jules, she thought the nightmares would plague her all night. But they didn't. She didn't dream at all.

Maybe after so many nights of interrupted sleep, she was simply too tired. Or maybe this is the part of her brain that knows she is going home and it's time to start dealing with the past in a new way, inviting some sort of peace into her heart.

Because Rose is going home. First, she needs to ask Modesto at the front desk how to arrange an earlier shuttle back to the capital. Later today, she'll call Matt to tell him what she's learned. He'll be surprised she's coming back early. But less so when she tells him what she has discovered. With his preference for facts and figures, he'll help her figure out how to report the fundraising corruption—to someone *not* based in San Felipe, necessarily, but someone who cares, in the US if not in Guatemala. He can also help track down the musician, Sahara, just to confirm those final details about Jules's last day.

And then, at home, they will find some other way to honor the end of Jules's story.

Home. Can it really be home at all, once you've lost the person who mattered most to you? But you have to live somewhere. You have to work, eat, sleep and find routines that will take you from this time in your life toward whatever will come next. She thinks of the few times she enjoyed herself during this trip—the opening party, moments talking with Lindsay, Isobel and K—and she issues herself a stern reminder. You can't feel shame for small moments of joy. Jules never would have wanted that. Jules would have wanted her to make new friends, to have new experiences, to learn and to travel. Rose has done all those things here, much as she still resents Lake Atitlán and hopes never to return.

Rose is standing at the reception desk, waiting for someone to notice her, when she hears a maid and the manager in the back office, talking about someone who was found just two hours earlier, outside her room, on the sidewalk, passed out. Briefly, they thought she was dead. The maid panicked. But then the woman regained consciousness. She refused help. She wasn't willing to wait for the sun to rise. She only wanted a taxi—and to leave Atitlán as soon as possible.

Rose's first thought is: *Scarlett*. But she's wrong. It isn't Scarlett. Or Noelani, who comes to mind only because Rose heard her walking outside the cabins last night: swearing, stumbling, giggling, drunk.

It isn't Diane, either, even though they all heard Diane's plan to sever ties with her family and quit her job, even though it was the one thing that Diane seemed to like about her old life.

"Did you hear?" Lindsay asks when Rose comes down to breakfast. "Rachel left."

"That's who it was?" Rose grabs her phone from her bag, opening email, in case Rachel sent her anything that would explain, but instead she sees only an email from Eva. "I feel terrible. Wait—let me see if Eva has sent us all details on what happened."

Lindsay shakes her head. "This isn't right."

Because it's bad enough that Rachel has fallen off the wagon, so distraught by the last forty-eight hours here in Atitlán that she'd be willing to throw away years of progress. What's even more disturbing is the fact that they weren't sure it was Rachel. It could have been any of them, given how the last several days have gone.

"Someone should talk to Eva and set that lady straight," Lindsay says.

Rose skims the email from Eva. "She says she'd like to hear from anyone who knows how Rachel was feeling the last few days, ASAP. Maybe Eva feels the need to get some cover, in case people start talking."

"I think we *all* can guess how Rachel was feeling. Like *shit*."

Rose seizes on an idea.

Eva has avoided her all week. Rose's group workshop was last on the schedule, only a little later than Rose's one-on-one. She's never even managed to get seated next to Eva at lunch.

But now, finally, Rose has something Eva wants: insight about Rachel, if only to spin the story of her breakdown more favorably.

"Rachel was asking me to read her new pages. Maybe Eva will think I've read them and know what made her break down."

Rose starts typing a reply even before Lindsay chimes in with encouragement.

"Meet Eva for dinner, maybe," Lindsay says.

"I don't want to wait that long."

Rose presses send and keeps the window open, watching her inbox.

"If she'll meet with me, I'll start gently."

"About Rachel's workshop?"

"About more than that." Rose feels nervous, but excited, too. "Maybe Eva feels just as insecure as the rest of us and she'd prefer real feedback, for once. The people who question her tactics are usually the first to leave. How can she figure it out if people don't stick around and tell her?"

"Oh, Rose."

"What?"

"You're a sweeter and more optimistic person than I am."

And there it is: the reply email in bold. Rose clicks. *Meet now. Time to talk and swim.*

Eva seems spacy when Rose gets to the dock, almost as if she's forgotten that she just emailed Rose.

"You wanted information about Rachel," Rose prompts her. "I thought I could help."

"Right," Eva says, dropping the towel she's carried to the dock from the house. "So, tell me. How did Rachel seem to you, day before yesterday?"

"Motivated. I think the workshop was challenging. At first, she had good things to say about it—"

"I'm glad to hear it," Eva says. Then sploosh! She's in the water, headfirst, swimming confidently away from shore. After a half dozen strokes, she turns around. "Water's fine!"

"Couldn't we talk a little more up here, on the dock?"

"A cleansing dip first. Clear the brain, open the heart. Nothing better than water to do that."

Rose lowers herself to a squat, reaching toward the water with her fingertips.

Eva blows a raspberry. "Don't dither. Just dive in!"

Growing up along the shore of Lake Michigan, Rose never liked swimming. Pools, sometimes, but even then, she preferred to walk down the steps into the children's shallow end first. On vacation, she was happier with hot tubs. It was her fault Jules was equally timid around oceans and lakes. When Jules was eight years old, they made her suffer through a month of park district swimming lessons but once Jules could doggy paddle for two solid pool lengths, Rose and Matt let her quit.

Eva disappears and comes back up again, smoothing her hair back. "Faster is better, always. Lake swimming and writing have a lot in common."

Of course, Rose has a special hatred for this particular lake. But it's time to stop giving the lake—and Eva—so much power. The lake isn't dangerous, it's just deep. Eva doesn't mean to damage women, she's just misguided. Every session, another dozen women have witnessed her tactics. But how many have confronted Eva, letting her know that for every writer she's helping, another woman has been damaged?

Rose jumps. She resurfaces, sputtering, and breaststrokes toward Eva, who waits for her with a know-it-all smile.

"I figured you'd be a slow starter."

"Yes," Rose says, "I'm not so good with cold water," still getting her breath, ignoring the warning voice in her head, focusing instead on that other internal message. *Confront her. Tell her that what she did to Rachel and Scarlett was wrong.* And when that's been covered, tell her that she already knows what happened to Jules. It isn't about asking questions anymore, because Eva is an unreliable narrator even when she's trying to tell the truth.

"You'll warm up," Eva says. Her tone seems friendlier. "We haven't had our private session. This is good. But first: Rachel."

Eva floats on her back, kicking away from shore. Rose follows, wondering how far Eva will go. Why not stroke parallel to land instead of away from it?

It's less glassy out here, away from the protection of the points curving out from either side of Eva's property. On the dock they were surrounded by tropical birds, roosting in the bluff's bushes, a morning chorus. When Rose starts to sink, ears just below water level but mouth still above, straining for air, that music ceases. In its place she hears her own shallow breath and something else, faint but high-pitched. Ticking, clicking. Buzzing. Shrimp? Fish? Distant motors?

Eva says, "Somebody saw Rachel drinking the night before last, at the pizzeria. She heard the siren call of her old vices."

"She needed a crutch. She was doing something hard." Rose has to speak in short sentences, struggling for air between them. "Writing hard scenes involving her children."

"No, that's not it."

"She said she was writing—"

"No," Eva interrupts. "The writing didn't make her drink. The addiction made her want to drink, and the lack of self-control made her give in. Don't blame art. Everyone blames art. Weakness preceded any attempt to make art of weakness."

"You don't think being at this workshop . . . pushed her over the edge?"

"I think it pulled her back from the edge, long before she got here. She registered months ago. We gave her a point on the horizon. Rachel was living on borrowed time."

"I don't agree," Rose says, but Eva has slipped under the water, unable to hear.

It makes Rose nervous, waiting for Eva's head to emerge, even knowing that she's such a good swimmer. *One one-thousand. Two one-thousand. Three one-thousand.* It couldn't have helped Rachel, being told she was a horrible person and pushed into writing what she wasn't ready to write.

Rose tries to keep her cupped hands moving smoothly, until

water slips into her mouth and she starts to sputter and cough. Her rhythmic strokes degrade into frantic paddling.

"Eva?"

Eva pops up like a cork, farther away. "This is heaven! Swim harder."

"I'm not comfortable."

"Don't doggy-paddle. You'll tire yourself out."

Rose switches back to breaststroke, pausing every few strokes to roll over on her back and calm her breathing. She's closed the distance between them by half, but Eva keeps kicking, moving away.

"Does it happen often?" Rose calls between strokes.

"What?"

"Do people fall apart? Like Rachel did?"

"I can't hear you."

Rose knows that she can.

"I'm thinking of Scarlett, too," Rose begins to say, the name *Sahara* further back on her list, saving the most important name of all—Jules—for the moment when Eva has exhausted all of her excuses. "The way you led that workshop wasn't good for her." Another breath, so she can say the rest before Eva submerges again. "I know you mean well, but you're not a therapist."

This isn't an easy place for any kind of conversation, at least not for Rose. But it's worth letting Eva be in her element if it will make her listen. She puts her head down in the water, trying to swim instead of thrash. Without intending to, she opens her eyes. She sees her white hands flashing beneath the green water. She sees the curtains of bubbles released by her flailing feet. It brings it right back: the old panic, the old nightmare.

Rose manages to lift her head again in time to hear Eva shouting, "Still waiting!"

When Rose finally catches up to her, she hears the smile in Eva's voice. "You're not a very good swimmer."

"I . . . told you that."

"You can tell a lot about a person when they're at the edge of their comfort zone. Or out of it."

Rose opens her eyes to blue sky. When she tips her head back, she can make out the profile of the volcano.

"I don't coddle people," Eva says.

"No. You *hurt* people." She kicks and tries to lift her head higher, gathering her breath and her courage. "And it's not only this session. It's a pattern. Don't you see it?"

If only Eva will take responsibility. *The road to hell is paved with good intentions.* Rose's late mother loved that proverb, but until now, Rose has never seen it lived out so clearly.

Eva hasn't replied to Rose's direct question. Patience is called for. Another of Rose's mother's sayings: *People don't change overnight.*

Rose's head, low in the water, picks up that buzzy sound again. She was about to ask about Sahara. Only then would she talk about Jules. But Eva starts crawl-stroking hard for shore, leaving Rose behind. The gap between them grows ever larger. Eva doesn't slow down or look back.

The dock is too low in the water to be seen from a distance. Higher up on the shore, Casa Eva looks like a dollhouse. She shouldn't have come out this far, and she's wasting energy trying to talk.

Rose calls out, "You didn't answer—"

But then a small wave curls over her head and she startles, inhaling water. For the first time, she's down deeper, fully submerged. No blue sky, no volcano, no birdcalls. She opens her eyes fully underwater and sees only dark green, her pale hands, bubbles.

She's losing energy with every flailing attempt to stay afloat.

She inhales water again, chest burning. She's panicking—as Jules surely panicked. For a moment, her head clears the surface, but she's swallowed too much. She can't stop coughing.

When she sinks again, her mouth is still open. Eyes squeezed shut, hands grabbing at nothing. For one dark second she can't tell which way is up.

Then a sudden pressure against her back, an arm reaching around her neck. Rose yanks her head around to see, wet hair plastered against her own face, her vision obscured, the pressure at her throat too tight. She kicks back to defend herself but her feet don't make contact.

She fights with both hands, twisting away from the arm at her throat, captured again.

They emerge into the air together with Eva screaming at her, "Stop flailing! I'm trying to help you!"

But she isn't.

Deep green below, the water's surface over her head, silver dimples and streaks. A kick in the stomach makes Rose fold. She's clutching her knees to her chest, a heavy weight, sinking. A foot tangled in her hair. If Eva is trying to help her, why is she pushing her down so hard?

Eva is trying to drown her.

The underwater sounds of ticking and clicking are overtaken by a louder, persistent whine. Mechanical.

Rose feels a sharp pain at her scalp as she is yanked upwards, followed by the pressure of being choked again. But there is also light. She's on the surface, floating on her back as she is rhythmically yanked and lifted, yanked and lifted. Eva's toes, kicking hard, brush against her own. Opening one eye, she sees the water taxi, twenty feet away, all the faces gathered along one edge of the boat, watching. Voices erupt. People clap.

"Stop fighting!" Eva shouts again.

A moment later, hands grab her by the arms while Eva jams her shoulder under Rose's thighs, pushing upward. Rose feels a sharp pain as the head of a screw on the rail of the boat slices into her leg. Four people work together, trying to wrestle her over the side, like some big, dying fish. She is scratched and bruised. But she is alive.

"Keep coughing," a new voice says. "Get the water out of your lungs." It's Pippa. Gentle Pippa.

"She tried—" Rose tries to say, but the coughing won't allow her to speak.

"She saved your life," Pippa says. "We saw it all. It was bloody brilliant!"

34

JULES

For an entire day, no one visits. I'm wracked with anxiety about my mother, hardly able to sleep, wondering when Eva will return. When she comes the next morning, she brings the new kind of tea. I taste it. She's complied with my request and I'm no closer to my goal.

"It's not right," I say, because I can't let go of the only idea I have so far—that I need medical help, and maybe Eva will allow it if my supposed nausea doesn't abate. "Something is missing."

"Oh, lord. You've got to be kidding, because Hans went ahead and made gallons of the stuff."

"I'm sorry."

Eva starts rambling about all the needy women and their stories. I can smell something familiar on her—maybe it's just the smell of the lake, like she's just finished a swim. I try to picture everything she must be doing today: the workshops, the individual meetings, the bizarre writing prompts.

"But there are always a few good ones," I say, trying to sound chipper while really my mind is racing in search of solutions, a way to send a coded message. The eyebrow piercing didn't work, but now that I know who I'm trying to reach, I can figure out something better, something only Mom would understand.

"Yes, there are two girls with possibilities," Eva says, brow furrowing. "I don't know. Sometimes I'm just tired of the whole three-ring circus."

I'm not only valued for my healthy uterus. I'm also a good listener, as I prove now, encouraging her with my silence, so that she can pour out her complaints about the ungrateful participants and staff.

"And the grocery prices! Hans operates like he's running an Ibiza restaurant instead of a lunch for ten writers."

Twelve, at least, I think.

"We overbought avocados, more than anyone can possibly eat, and so now we have buckets of black guacamole on our hands. And now we'll have gallons of your special tea, which you don't want to drink. The workshoppers can have it instead."

"Pepper," I say as a new hope dawns on me. "Black pepper is the missing ingredient. And fennel. Do you have fennel?"

Eva sighs. "I think we do."

"That's what settles the stomach. The ginger, the pepper *and* the fennel."

"Sounds yummy," she says, standing to leave.

"It is. Good for fussy travel stomachs too. Let everyone taste. Hans will thank me."

I feel sick with anticipation, hoping that Eva won't forget, hoping that Mom will understand, hoping that my desperation hasn't landed us both in deeper water.

It's midmorning when she comes again, bringing the improved tea. I taste it with eyes closed, noticing the bite of the ginger and pepper, and the faint licorice aroma of fennel.

I am five years old, sitting up in bed with a tummy ache.

A tear slides down my nose and lands on my lip.

Eva asks, "Is it that good?"

I nod, unable to speak. This is my madeleine moment. But whether it will be the same for anyone else, I have no way of knowing.

I finish the tea and say, "I don't think I want to see my mother ever again."

"And why are you mentioning her?"

My throat tightens. *Careful, Jules. Only the right words.*

"No reason—except to say that I want to move on. I need to live my own life."

Eva says nothing, though her hand goes to her cheek, rubbing a spot that looks raw and red. I didn't notice it when she first came in.

I ask, "Did you get hurt?"

"A little. Just a swimming accident. But thank you for asking."

"You don't have to thank me, Eva. I care about you. Just like you care about me."

I notice her eyes getting glassy.

With little to lose, I say, "Remember you once tried to convince me I should just live in Guatemala a year—or Thailand—and write a book? Maybe fiction. I've had so much time to think lately. Maybe it's being pregnant. I'm fertile with ideas."

She tilts her head, wearing the expression of the writing teacher or the therapist, listening to her patient find her way through a maze of half-formed ideas, toward some truth.

I tell her, "I feel like I could just start over, in another country, with another name."

I worry that she can see the desperation on my face. Her non-replies thicken the air.

"Do you know what I mean, Eva?" I ask, my voice high and loud.

"Yes," she says, smiling. "I understand the feeling. I did that as a teenager in England, remember?"

"Yes," I say, grabbing for the end of the rope she's tossed. Ticklish optimism bubbles in my chest, competing with the nausea in my gut.

"My mother never came looking for me, either," she says. "At the time, I thought I was lucky. But looking back, I think I wanted her to come. In any case, I finally tired of England and went back to New York, as you know."

"But you remained estranged from your parents," I say hopefully.

"Yes, and no. I saw them several times after my daughter was born. The truth is, Jules, until your parents pass on, you will never be truly free."

Panic seizes me. "Not true. My dad has a new family. He basically doesn't think about me."

"But moms are different," she says, reaching out to slide her hand down my arm, her gaze resting on my abdomen, flat beneath my oversized T-shirt. "Even when there's conflict, moms can't ever fully let go."

I wrap my arms around myself, a chill entering my spine. I've made a wrong move. I shouldn't have steered Eva to contemplate how much easier it would be if my mother were simply dead.

My mother could be in danger. And even if she stays safe and leaves Atitlán at the end of the workshop, in another few weeks it will become clear. I'm not getting bigger. No pregnancy test will help me, then.

"In writing, a plot is the outcome of a character confronting a problem," Eva says, her expression wistful and more distant now. "No, that isn't quite right. It's the outcome of a character confronting an *impossible* problem."

Something has changed. She brought me the tea; she believes

I'm pregnant; she doesn't want me to lose "our baby." But something has changed.

I whisper, "We don't have a problem."

"But you're wrong, Jules. I'm sorry, but you're wrong."

35

ROSE

Lindsay bandages Rose's scrapes and makes her lie down in Eva's unmade bed, the last place she wants to be. She can smell the spicy scent of Eva's perfume. She can see the dents in the pillows, where Eva's blond head recently rested. She doesn't want to recuperate in the twisted sheets of the woman who just tried to kill her.

No one believes Rose—not even Lindsay, though she won't say it so plainly.

"I can't stay here, in her room."

"Eva isn't even here," Lindsay says, trying to press a hot mug into Rose's hands. But Rose won't take it. Her throat feels too raw. She gagged up lots of lake water, but she still feels like she might retch again.

"Where is she?"

"She left and said she'll be back in an hour. Cancelled the rest of the morning workshops completely. Ana Sofía got everyone right back on the same water taxi they arrived on. They're on a field trip across the lake."

"The one that was scheduled for tomorrow. You don't think that's odd?"

Lindsay makes no effort to hide her eye roll. "Eva has been blowing us off since the moment we all got here! It has nothing to do with what just happened to you."

"She made me swim out too far," Rose tries one more time. "She knew I would end up in trouble."

"Rose, I know it was scary. And I know she does bad things. But I don't believe she would plan to drown you."

"I think she knows who I am. She figured it out the first time we did those journal exercises, or maybe before then."

"But weren't you playing with her, too?"

Now Rose is the one scoffing. "I couldn't just come out and say I was the mother of the personal assistant who drowned during the same week she was working for Eva, and that I've started to think Eva knew about it and possibly even covered it up."

"You couldn't?"

"Not if I wanted a conversation that would last longer than two minutes."

"And how long did your swimming conversation last?"

"Longer than that," Rose answers, sulkily.

Lindsay laughs, but Rose doesn't think it's funny. "I wish I'd fought. I managed to claw her face once, but that's it."

The women arriving by water taxi saw what looked like a heroic rescue, which makes Rose's side of the story even more outrageous. They only saw the above-water Eva, champion lake swimmer. Only Rose can feel the hard kick in the stomach, the feet pressing against her head.

Lindsay will believe once she has the whole picture, Rose thinks, pausing to cough and reach for a nearly empty water bottle. When she's emptied it, she tells Lindsay everything she found out from Wendy about the girl named Sahara. But Lindsay looks unimpressed.

"A rock star almost drowned here?"

"And I think my daughter swam after her."

"You know the second part, *how*?"

"That's what Jules would have done."

"What she *would have* done. But nobody saw it, right?"

It's unravelling now—the sense that Rose had just yesterday, of everything finally fitting.

"Please don't start talking about how dumb people are—"

"My marks were rarely dumb."

"Or about people's fantasies," Rose says. "This isn't a fantasy. I'm not trying to protect anything."

"And good thing, or you'd make an easy target."

Rose can see what Lindsay is trying to say: She *is* an easy target. Someone could try to fool her even now, with the evidence to back up this latest story, or by claiming that they know *something*—even something as simple as where Jules's body can be found. Rose would pay dearly for it.

Lindsay takes both of Rose's hands. "I believe you just had a frightening experience, and you've had a lot to think about. Give it time. Let me get you more fluids."

"And then what?"

"If it were me, I'd still demand an audience with Eva. On land this time, with other people around, maybe even a lawyer or a well-armed bodyguard. Whichever you prefer. You think Eva covered up some facts about the week of Jules's drowning—the when, how and why. Am I understanding that right? I mean, you don't think she murdered your daughter."

The question makes Rose pause, and in that space, images spread like blood in water. Possibilities Rose has suppressed for so long overwhelm her, the expanding clouds blotting out the present, taking her back to that moment that is no longer a mere nightmare. Jules plunging into dark water, clawing, kicking, and someone at the surface, ready to strike and push

Jules back under if she manages to surface. The moon, bright. The wind, calm. But none of that matters, because Jules isn't simply trying to swim back to shore. She is being drowned on purpose.

Rose's throat has started to close. She takes a moment to gather herself, swallowing with effort. She rubs hard at the tears on her cheek.

"I wouldn't have believed if I hadn't been out in the water with Eva kicking me and dragging me under. But now, yes. I think it's possible."

Lindsay doesn't reply.

She thinks I'm the crazy one.

Rose says, "I know it's hard to believe anyone could kill another person. You have to see it for yourself in their eyes. You have to feel it in your own body." Rose shudders, feeling the spot across her ribs that's starting to bruise, the burn in her scalp where Eva yanked her hair.

"This is so much worse than I thought," Rose says, starting to cough again.

When the coughing spell doesn't let up, Lindsay hands her the mug of tea. The ginger hits Rose first. Then the rest of it: Pepper. And fennel. It's not just familiar. It's unmistakable.

She has to push the mug back into Lindsay's hands before she drops it. She can barely talk over the lump in her throat. "I don't understand this!"

"You almost drowned, and that triggered—"

"No. This too. This!" She points at the tea. "Where did you get this?"

"It was in a big pot downstairs. Hans made it. We've all had it before."

"Not like this. He added spices to it. It's the way I used to make it, the way Jules liked it. I can't even explain or you'll think I've lost my mind. You *already* think so!"

"Trauma—" Lindsay starts to say.

"Don't talk to me about trauma, *please*. I have to do something, and not later. *Now*."

"What could you possibly do now?"

That's the problem. Rose doesn't know.

36

JULES

I can't tolerate sitting here, waiting for my fate to be decided by others. Eva, flitting in and out of her fantasy desire to mother both me and "my baby." Barbara, struggling to find the resolve to finish what she started.

I stand up, next to my bed, and put my left foot on the floor. My leg can bear some weight. But how does that help, when I can't get out the door?

A lizard skitters across the screen that covers the roof hole above my head, shifting the leaves that obscure the light.

Sun. I need sun.

Is the screen attached? Could I at least prod it enough to clear the leaves and let more sunshine in?

There's not much in this room, aside from two buckets, the clothesline I already took down, a broom left only recently—a sign I'm supposed to be doing more to keep this place clean.

Standing on the bed, I can barely reach the roof hole with the end of the broom. I just manage to nudge the screen, which isn't fastened. A few more stretches, and I've managed to knock the screen off. I hear it sliding down the curved outside of the roof. Sun floods the center of the temazcal. For the first time, this dim, spooky hut actually looks like the hopeful, healing, glowing chamber it was always meant to be.

I sit back down on the bed, cross-legged, and bask in it, eyes closed, swaying side to side. Three months without sun. Can it really have been that long? Can one even heal properly without vitamins? I look down at my skinny arms. I pinch the sagging flesh around my knees. My legs are the color of a banana—mostly white, with a slight tinge of yellow.

The sound of someone opening the outer door startles me into vigilance. I listen, straining, trying to distinguish Eduardo's light steps from Barbara's heavy ones. A quick hard knock on the inner door makes me jump.

"Jules," comes the whisper of a familiar male voice. "Jules, it's me."

I crawl out of bed, tiptoeing toward the door, and press a hand against it. "Mauricio?"

"I was so worried about you!"

"Oh my god. Mauricio!"

I hear the familiar scraping sound of the second latch being withdrawn.

"It's a little stuck, but I'm coming."

I put my hand over my mouth, stifling a sob. If he'd known where I was, he would have come earlier, I'm sure of it.

"Wait, I hear something," he says, quieter. "Let me go see."

"Don't go."

"It might be a car. I have to check."

"Be careful."

I look down at my bare, emaciated legs and suddenly feel self-conscious. Besides, I'll be outside in a minute. I need clothes if I'm going to get out of here. I grab the only pair of pants in the room and begin to slide them on when I hear an alarming grunt, followed by the boom of something slamming onto the ground, just outside the hut. Then a noise I can't understand, like the sound of a shovel tamping down earth, followed by three higher-pitched grunts, the last one rising to a shriek.

"Mauricio?"

The door opens. Eva stands, backlit, shovel in her hand. Seeing me, she seems to wake from a dream, and pushes into the hut, shutting the inner door behind her.

"Where is he?" I ask.

The moan from outside has grown louder. Eva's eyes track across me. My abdomen is still flat. My breasts, the same B cup they've always been. "Any nausea today?"

I can't stop hearing the moan.

"Eva, what happened to Mauricio?"

"Come. Let's sit on the bed. Come."

She takes my hand and guides me to the edge of the bed. She starts to finger-comb my hair while I sit—rigid, listening.

To cover the sound outside the door, she starts to hum, and the humming makes me feel so agitated I can't sit still. Without thinking, I shake off her caressing hand. There's no time for caution anymore.

"Eva, I want to go see my mother. I know she came here."

Eva laughs, anxiously. It comes out in choking spurts.

"I've figured it out," I say. "Instead of just disappearing, I'll tell her that this was my choice. I'll get a chance to make a clean break of things. I can start my new life."

I measure the distance to the door. I note the tremble in my legs—I can walk, even if I can't run. The doors aren't locked. Mauricio is out there, injured or worse.

"It's too late," Eva says, her face collapsing.

I recoil, shocked by her words.

"It can't be," I say, desperately searching her devastated expression for clues. I can't let myself believe she's already done something to my mother. Unless I know for sure, I can't give up. "It's never too late. Right, Eva? Talk to me."

Her gaze goes to the door. "He's hurt. Enough to get me in trouble."

"We're smart women," I say. "We can find a way out of this."

"But only if they don't find him."

I have to expel my next breath slowly, silently. I give it a moment. Then I ask, "How hurt?"

"Very hurt."

She lowers her voice, nodding, like she's thinking it through. "But if he doesn't show up anywhere, it might be okay. They hardly investigate disappearances in Guatemala. There are just too many."

"Yes," I say, grasping at anything. "It will be okay, Eva. Definitely."

"The day before yesterday, after Mauricio and I had an argument, I told Astrid and Hans that he stole money from us, just to put people off track." She corrects herself. "And really, he did steal something from me. Just a few days ago, I had a son. Now that person is gone. He doesn't exist."

I can feel her spiraling into self-pity. I don't care about her metaphorical take on things. I need *facts*.

"The police didn't come and arrest him?"

"He took off before they could. Now they're looking for him."

She's still nodding, puzzling over her actions, so I mirror. I nod. I purse my lips—stoic and determined. It's the most sensible thing in the world. Of course, she would falsely accuse him, her own quasi–foster child. Given her relationship with Molina and the local police, Mauricio would have to run far. And he would have, except that he was looking for me. "You've done the best you could, Eva. Mauricio was a problem."

"Before he left, he confronted me, Jules. He must have been watching Eduardo, or me, wondering why we kept driving this way. He doesn't understand what we're trying to accomplish here. He just wanted to *ruin* everything." Eva stands up suddenly, like she just remembered something. "I need to get back to the house. I have to meet someone."

"We'll go together."

"No," she jabs a hand against my chest, pushing me back on the bed. I'm surprised, as always, by her physical strength. And even more surprised at my weakness.

Only when I'm sure she's gone do I empty the wash bucket onto the floor and turn it upside down on the bed, then clamber on top, favoring my strong leg as I reach for the roof hole. It's about as round as one of those manhole covers you see on a city street. The problem won't be squeezing through— only reaching it.

But I'm barely on top of the bucket when it topples over, dented. I roll to one side, stifling a shriek, the pain in my shin so bad I nearly black out. I need to be more careful. I can't get so hurt in the process that I won't be able to manage the walk down the hillside and along the road to Casa Eva.

The sounds of moaning coming from outside have stopped. The silence is even worse.

I push the dent out of the bucket. I remove the thin mattress from the wooden platform bed—something I should have done in the first place, to make a more stable foundation. I try again: no luck. I remember the tumble I took while rock climbing in Costa Rica—and how I gave up after that one try. I think of all the times my mom told friends how active I was, believing my stories, the occasional photo of me on some ridgeline: an easy illusion, masking the fact that I don't like heights, just as I don't like water or any kind of pain.

I consider the chair in the corner. Could I stand on it, inside?

But the roof is too high up—at least two feet higher than my highest reach, even standing on the tippy chair.

The whole time, the room grows warmer, and the smell of smoke wafts through the hole and fills my lungs, making them itch. The fires are closer than they've ever been. Even if that brings potential rescuers closer, it still can't be good.

I study the roof hole again. There must be a trick to this. Brains, not brawn.

I whack the broom against the back of the chair until it splinters. Now I have two pieces of stick, each jagged on one end. I retrieve the clothesline from where I've been keeping it under my pillow. I tie one end around the shorter broken stick, just a little longer than the length of my lower arm, from elbow to fingertips.

I aim the short stick like a javelin through the roof hole. Over and over, I use the attached clothesline to pull it back. Over and over, the entire stick-and-line contraption comes clattering toward me. Once it even knocks me in the head.

I try to pretend this is only a game—or like fishing, a pastime I always hated. I think of my father, taking me out once, on Lake Michigan. I think of my mom, the next weekend, taking me for a bike ride along the lake. *It's okay. Not all of us have to like boats. The water is pretty enough—at a distance. That's just how you and I are. We're not lake people.*

The lake. Barbara.

The terrifying image of her coming at me makes me clutch the stick harder, ignoring the splinters that have become embedded in my hand. I channel my frustration and send the short javelin toward the open circle of sky again.

Another javelin toss. Another chin-grazing clatter as the stick and line falls back in my face.

Then finally, on what must be the twentieth try, the stick rotates just right and it catches, horizontally, on the outer edge of the roof hole. I hold my breath. I give the clothesline a light tug. Then a harder one. The broomstick isn't budging. I look around the room one last time. It isn't easy to climb a slippery clothesline, but I only need to pull myself up a few more feet.

I try and fail, my arms too weak, the clothesline too slippery.

I make a final adjustment. I tie the bottom of the clothesline in a noose-like circle, even with my chest. I grab high, I kick, I place the foot of my good leg in that loop, I use it as a step, I push with all my might until I feel the breeze on my face—I'm through the hole, I'm on the roof and looking down.

I slide down the side of the temazcal roof and make the final awkward leap to the ground, rolling onto my right side as I land, hip absorbing the impact. Wind knocked out of me, it takes a moment to orient myself and catch my breath. I'm not quite ready to try standing.

Mauricio is seated, legs out and eyes closed, head lolled to one side, next to the closed door of an old hippie school bus, the visual centerpiece at the middle of a half dozen abandoned temazcal huts and a few yurts.

"Mauricio!"

I crawl forward and press two fingers to his neck. He coughs and lifts his head before I can get a pulse. His hair is black, matted with blood. One eye remains closed even as he struggles to squint at me with the other.

I'm afraid to touch him, to hurt him. "I'll get help. I thought you were . . ."

But now I can see the track, from the front of the hut to the door of the school bus. The ground has been swept by his agonizing crawl. There are dark marks, too, left by his bloody handprints.

"I'm going to get help," I reassure him, looking around for a broken stick I can lean on. Because of the strong winds, there are many. "We need to find you some shelter."

He needs protection from dangerous people, from sun, from the fire if it advances. I can't see any flames, only thick brown smoke severing the nearby mountaintops. I can't tell if the wind is blowing the fire toward us or away, only that the hot, acrid gusts are growing stronger.

I try to lift Mauricio, but I can't do it alone.

Then he says something about my mother.

"At the house," he whispers. "She isn't safe."

"But you . . . I'd feel better if I—"

"Go."

"Okay," I say finally. "I'll get help. I promise."

Limping, I reach the rough road, which clings to the lake. I squint toward the dim outlines of the volcanoes, orienting myself. Eva's place is to the right. I hobble, dragging my left leg behind me, lungs full of smoky air, thinking: *You're not getting away with this.*

I think of my mother standing at the top of the bluff. Walking down the dock. Clambering into a boat. She doesn't know what Eva can do, what Barbara has already done. My mother has to get away from them. I just don't know how to help her in time.

Then again, I've never walked far in this area without a truck pulling over to ask me if I need a ride. In these woods and down this road there are people who can help. That thought, instead of reassuring me, makes my heart race, my anger and indignation replaced by pure animal fear.

The paranoia cultivated for months almost convinces me to dash back over to the shoulder and hide in the brush, arms wrapped around myself, eyes closed. I have to fight it. Not every stranger is out to get me. I have to remember who I am—who I *was*. The person who traveled across Central America, who befriended locals, who was afraid of the occasional wave or tumble, perhaps, but never of people.

I take another step toward the center of the road, ignoring the pain, and when I see the first glint of metal as a truck comes around the curve, I thrust up my hands, waving for them to stop.

37

ROSE

Weird enough to be lying in your retreat leader's bed. Weirder still to step into her shower, choosing between her three shampoos, moving aside her pink razor to reach for the soap. Rose waits for the water to heat up and then moves under the hot falling spray, letting it pound her skin, the way she's done ever since Jules died. The way she had imagined Eva would have—or should have—after her baby died.

Lindsay has promised to wait for her, so she isn't alone here, even though she knows the house is full of other people: Concha, Gaby and several more of the other Guatemalan staff. Rose must leave before Eva gets back. She'll deal with a confrontation when she has someone tough and trustworthy standing alongside her, just as Lindsay advised.

Rose is almost done showering when a knock comes at the door. It's Lindsay, and she sounds tense: "There's something going on."

Rose isn't sure she heard right. She turns off the shower even though she's still soapy, to hear better. "Did you say fires?"

"Hurry up."

The entire time they've been here, there have been fires. Smoke in the air. Wisps and orange blazes on every hillside.

Gorgeous bronze sunsets. And always: *Don't worry. Slash-and-burn. They know what they're doing.*

But now Lindsay sounds concerned. "They want us to leave. The fires are too close."

"Coming," Rose calls back, rinsing as fast as she can.

A few minutes later, she runs out of the house and down to the dock, where Astrid and Lindsay are standing.

"The fire jumped the road." Astrid points to flickers of orange above the distant trees.

"What do we do?"

"Stay near the water. Maybe . . . get in the rowboats and row out, away from shore, to be safe. Everyone's coming. They're grabbing essentials, in case the whole house goes up in flames."

The dock populates with the staff: Concha and her kitchen staffers first. Gaby is carrying a pile of Eva's first edition books. Mercedes is carrying the Bible. As they all wait at the end of the dock, Mercedes steps up to Rose and tries to hand her the Bible, as if she is foisting the very word of God upon her.

When Rose refuses to take it, Mercedes looks around, then opens the big book, extracts a sheaf of loose pages and presses them into Rose's hands instead. Rose looks at the topmost sheet, recognizes the handwriting in a flash. She sees words: "Eva," "confused," "Mom," "frustrated," "help."

Every word, in that familiar handwriting, is precious.

And every word is galling. Her eyes skim. Here is the record of what Jules went through—what Rose couldn't save her daughter from going through. She knew there had to be more somewhere. Both her logic and intuition told her so.

"I didn't understand. Oh, Mercedes—thank you. Lo siento."

She almost missed this, but she now has a piece of Jules that once seemed irretrievable. She takes the Bible. She closes the loose pages, about thirty in all, between the faux-leather covers and presses the big heavy book to her chest.

Mercedes sighs, relieved of this burden she's been carrying for so long.

Rose feels the wood planks beneath her feet vibrate. It's Barbara, shuffling with heavy steps through the dim and smoky evening light, to the end of the dock.

"We've got two boats. Let's get the first group out to safety. Then we'll take care of everyone else."

Barbara starts shouting, calling for staff to come forward. Rose sees Eduardo, Gaby and another young girl, the daughter of Concha, the only one wearing a life preserver.

The smoke has thickened. They're all coughing. Unreality has set in. They've been looking at distant flames all week, smelling smoke, but now it's close, and real.

"One more," Barbara says. Concha's daughter steps forward.

Lindsay, already in the boat, says, "Rose, you need to come, *now*."

Concha's daughter steps back like she's been reprimanded.

"No, you go," Rose says, squatting down to look the girl in the eye. "Sí, *tú*. Te toca a ti. Todo estará bien."

Eduardo pushes off and begins rowing, then he pauses only a hundred feet from shore, watching.

Barbara shouts, "Don't wait! It's safer closer to San Felipe."

After they've disappeared around the nearest point, Rose asks, "Are there more staff in the house?"

"No."

"Didn't you say we could fit 'everyone else' into the second boat?"

The fire has advanced so close they can now see glimmers of flame at the back of the well-tended yard. They can hear cracking and popping. Rose's heart is beating fast and her eyes are bleary from the smoke. Every part of her body is telling her to run—but where? Only the water is safe.

Barbara unties a rope around the cleat of the smaller second boat and gestures.

It hits Rose now. Only the two of them are left.

"I'm not going into that boat with you."

"No. Of course not."

Barbara brings her hand to her forehead and there it sits as she slowly begins to rock, heel-to-toe and toe-to-heel, like she is soothing herself.

Finally, Barbara drops her hand and looks at Rose. "It's not what you think."

"I don't know what to think. I'm finished trusting anyone here—Eva, you, Hans. Anyone."

"I know what that's like," Barbara says, looking so tired now she can barely keep her eyes open. Her wrinkle-creased face is like a pillow that's lost half of its stuffing. Her shirt and her pants are both too big for her, like she's recently lost weight. Rose found her so intimidating before that she didn't notice she looked unwell. Cancer? Grief? *Guilt?*

"The hardest part is when you put all your faith in one person," Barbara says. "I took care of her. I moved things around to keep her out of trouble. All the houses, all the mortgages, all the things she likes to have—the clothes and the trips. Taxes, delayed advances. She's not a numbers person."

Rose feels the brief pleasure of long-delayed confirmation. "So, you were skimming money meant for the orphanage."

"Not really."

"Not really?"

"Not forever. It was just a way to make accounts balance for the time being."

"And Eva knew."

"She didn't want to know." Barbara sighs. "But I did that for her, always. I helped her keep her mind clear and focused, for the important things."

"And she relied on you for that."

Somehow that was the wrong thing to say. Barbara's words become garbled, lost between choking sobs. "She used to. We were a team. Without me, she couldn't write her next books."

"But Eva *hasn't* published new books since *In a Delicate State*."

Not the point, Barbara's frantic headshaking seems to say. Or *it is the point*, but it's not Barbara's fault. Or something has happened since that book came out that can't be talked about, and for some reason, it's hardly about Eva at all. It's about Barbara. She's the victim, supposedly.

"I've been betrayed so many times," Barbara says. "But this time—this . . . this . . ." She can't get the words out, and now tears are flowing down her cheeks and dripping off her chin. "I don't have the energy anymore."

Barbara lowers herself to her knees, one hand reaching out to anchor herself on the ground, the other still holding the rope, crying through her incomprehensible mutterings until she has to stop talking altogether.

Everything has turned upside down. Meanwhile, even the landward side of the dock has been consumed by the ever-advancing smoke.

Still clutching the Bible with Jules's journal pages inside, Rose decides.

"I'm not leaving you here."

"Eva . . ." Barbara tries to say before she is wracked with silent sobs that turn into coughs.

"Eva *is* in the house?"

Barbara shakes her head.

"Then don't worry. Eva's fine. I'm sure she's with everyone else, in San Felipe."

Barbara shakes her head again. Rose doesn't understand

and she doesn't have time to keep yanking the words out of Barbara.

"You're a survivor, Barbara. Right?"

That word seems to have unlocked something within Barbara, because she eases herself into the rowboat, moving like a zombie.

"Good, so am I," says Rose, clambering in behind her. "We're going to get through this." Their only hope is to get out into the middle of the lake, away from the fires and the smoke. "I'm not very good at rowing, but I'll try."

They are several hundred feet offshore when Rose feels the wind turning their boat around. She keeps trying to angle toward San Felipe, but they're making little progress. But at least, for the moment, the steady gust is pushing the smoke away, creating a pocket of fresher air.

Barbara makes a sound like a half grunt, half laugh. "It's harder, rowing against the Xocomil." It sounds like 'sho-ko-meel.' "That's the wind that starts up late morning, 'the wind that blows the sin away.'"

Rose will tolerate Barbara's sudden nervous breakdown, but she won't tolerate yet another lie.

"Nothing blows sin away."

38

ROSE

Rose has been rowing inexpertly for what feels like half an hour when Barbara dips a hand into the lake, cupping water that she splashes onto her red face. "We're not getting anywhere. Let me take a turn."

Rose and Barbara change seats, each of them squatting low, eyeing the other with suspicion.

After a quiet spell, Barbara says, "Jules isn't at the bottom of this lake."

The mere mention of her daughter's name makes Rose tense with dread, the horrible images returning. Barbara must know where Jules's body washed up. Eva and Barbara must have hidden it somewhere.

"Don't lie to me, Barbara."

"I'm not," she says, choking on the last word.

There's a small wooden club, stained with what could be blood, near Rose's feet. She's spent the last minute staring at it, hoping that the glittering scales stuck to its surface mean the club was used only to whack small fish. Rose grabs for it now, club raised shoulder-heigh.

"Then take me to her."

When Rose feels Barbara turning the boat, angling toward

the shore, she steels herself. The truth is coming, one way or another.

They pull up to a rocky beach between two houses. They clamber silently up a trail, to the road. And then, up another trail: higher yet, up the smoky hillside into a less developed area, a mix of forest and grassy, cleared patches.

When they arrive at the empty temazcal hut, and Barbara unlocks both doors to get to the squalid interior, it feels like the meanest trick of all. Because there, strewn across the room, are a young woman's clothes: underwear, a pair of jean shorts. As if Jules was recently here.

Barbara's mouth opens and closes once before she finds her words. "I saw her. I talked to her just yesterday."

The assertion takes Rose's breath away. "You're still lying to me. Why are you doing this?" Lindsay had warned her that other people would take advantage, and maybe that's what Barbara is doing now. Feeding her some elaborate story that will conclude in an outrageous request.

Barbara stammers, "Eva went somewhere early this morning, before she met with you. She kept running off, even more than usual. I knew she was planning to do something. Your daughter was just *here*."

Barbara pushes her stubby fingers through her thinning hair, eyes searching the room as if Jules will jump out from the shadows.

She says, "When I heard that Jules was still alive, it seemed like the first time in my life I could undo something. I thought I could persuade Eva, over time. But this morning, she was acting differently. She had blood on her cheek."

No, Rose thinks. There are too many details. These are the false elaborations of a practiced liar. Barbara is spinning a tale, trying to pull her into a spell of believing. *Why?*

"It wasn't from Jules," Barbara stammers. "Eva told me

she'd done something to Mauricio. She wanted me to be the one to do it—*again*. She confessed to me that Mauricio was still alive. She expected me to do it all for her. Finish off Mauricio; get rid of Jules, even though Jules had something Eva wanted. But Eva changed her mind. It wasn't worth the risk. Jules couldn't keep secrets. Eva wanted me to come here and clean up her messes."

Rose can't make sense of Barbara's ramblings. It makes little difference. Rose doesn't believe her version of events, anyway. They leave the temazcal hut just at the moment two local men come over the hill, dragging Eva behind them. Her face is smudged. She's trying to twist out of one man's grip.

"Barbara!" Eva shouts. "Tell them to let me go. Tell them you'll go to the police! They can't treat me this way!"

In Spanish, one of the men shouts, "This woman was trying to light more fires."

Rose doubts her own comprehension. Why would anyone . . . ?

But then she sees a third local man lumbering behind, supporting the weight of Mauricio, limping. His hair is matted. His face is stained.

Rose hears one of the men say, "She was trying to kill him! When we found her, she was trying to burn him alive!"

It's too horrible to imagine.

Incredible.

But not as incredible as what Rose sees next: the thin, frail figure shuffling behind all of them, hurrying to catch up, reaching for Mauricio's other arm as if she has any hope of supporting him, when this waif of a girl looks just as broken.

Rose's heart skips a beat. She's been wrong before. She lifts a hand to her mouth, trying to stop herself before she's wrong again. But she can't stop it. The name slips out, and not just the name, but the vain hope.

"Jules."

Jules looks up. Her face crumples. One moment, she's only halfway recognizable—too pale and wasted away to be the daughter Rose knows. And the next moment, she is both the little girl and the young woman Rose has always loved.

"Mom," Jules says. She starts to cry and can't stop crying as Rose rushes forward and embraces her thin, trembling body. "*Mama*."

JULES

Eighteen months later, I'm standing outside a bookstore called Women and Children First in Chicago, too nervous to enter. I had dinner with Mom at one of our favorite restaurants on North Ashland, but when she offered to come to the reading with me, I said no. I needed to do this myself.

"You're sure? We can sit in the far back. She won't see you."

"I want her to see me," I said. "That's the point."

"And you don't need your trekking poles?"

"*Mom.* The doctor wants me to walk without them now."

"Right," she says with a strained smile. "But I'll be parked nearby, reading in the car. Just in case."

I know Mom has her own need to deal with all we went through, even beyond the way she has opened up with Dad and Ulyana, given interviews to newspapers, consulted with lawyers and phoned her new friends from the Atitlán workshop, who now understand all that she was concealing.

My list of needs is different. And tonight, I decided, I need to do this one thing, alone.

Now, as I stare at the chalkboard on the sidewalk—*Eva Marshall reads from her new bestselling memoir,* We—I am second-guessing my immature need for this trivial gesture of independence.

But that's how the last year and a half have been. One small step and gesture at a time. First, three surgeries, which I was told weren't many, given what I experienced. It turns out the infection at the site of my broken tibia developed into osteomyelitis. Trapped for so long with a festering leg, I was lucky to have avoided either the chronic form of the disease or a much swifter and more fatal case of sepsis.

Next, remembering that before I went to Lake Atitlán, I was preparing to move out and be on my own. And I will, soon. I didn't expect to be hobbling quite this long.

"Are you going in?" a woman asks as I linger too close to the door.

"Yes," I say. "Sorry."

I take a seat in the back—just as Mom suggested—pulse thrumming in my throat as I listen to the moderator read through a bloated introduction of Eva and how she's become even more popular in the last year.

When the news came out that I had been found, the media swarmed. A publisher even offered me the chance to tell my own story in a book. For five minutes, I was tempted. Then I realized that writing a memoir about Eva and me was not how I wanted to start my career as a published writer.

By now, the publisher is probably grateful, given how muddy the story became. My parents and I consulted lawyers about pressing charges and finally decided it wasn't worth it. Barbara was in a foreign jail, and Guatemala showed no interest in extraditing her, even after an American journalist on Eva's trail started looking into Barbara's past and the suspicious nature of her husband's death. Whatever Barbara may have done to *him*—in addition to some shady financial actions on both sides of the border—eclipsed my brief role in her troubled life. If I'd had any idea, I wouldn't have been as sympathetic to her woe-filled memoir. She never admitted to hurting me in the rowboat, anyway, except to say it was a two-person tussle, both of us acting out of petty rage. I had no witnesses to prove otherwise. I only had my story.

In Eva's version of events, she was indeed helping me heal from the attack, and she had my own words on her side. After all, I'd written an essay expressing my gratitude for what she was doing: butterfly from the temazcal chrysalis, et cetera. Not many people seemed inclined to believe I wrote those pages as manipulative fiction.

As for Mauricio, I knew he didn't have many legal options for getting back at Eva. He called on his scary uncle for help. The upshot is that Eva no longer felt safe in Guatemala. She moved her entire operation to Nicaragua, and now it's even more upscale. Guests fly in by helicopter. The cost of attendance has tripled. Meanwhile, Eva's confession that she did in fact invent parts of her last memoir—but only due to deep grief—have only revitalized interest in that book. A film project is finally in the works. An A-list actress signed on, eager to portray Eva and her deceptions in all their psychological complexity.

I am wincing, thinking of what that movie will look like and whether I'll have the discipline not to see it, when thundering applause in the bookstore forces me to focus.

The moderator has stepped away from the podium. He's pointing to stage left, where I can just make out Eva's blond hair—longer now—from behind a scrum of people. She's trying to hand over something to another woman, who is facing away from me, blocking my view. Finally, I see what's holding things up. Eva's swaddled baby is fussing, even as the helper or nanny tries to grab hold of her.

"She has twins," a woman next to me whispers, the

admiration in her voice plain. "Adopted from Nicaragua. Isn't that incredible?"

"Yes," I say. "If she doesn't get tired of them."

"*Tired* of them?" The woman turns in her seat, trying to make eye contact. "Why on earth would she?"

"Because they won't be cute forever. They won't always do what she says. They won't always be grateful."

It's the sort of thought I should have saved for Zahara. We still trade WhatsApp voice messages every week or so.

The woman scoffs. When I take a peek, she's staring at me wide-eyed, like I'm a monster. Am I?

"Excuse me," I say, rising to stand. Irritated glances shoot my way, because I'm interrupting the flow just as Eva is reaching the podium. I bump knees and force someone's jacket to slide off the back of another seat. "Sorry. Sorry. There we go. Sorry again."

When I finally extract myself from the row of seats, I turn back and look at Eva. She's staring at me, flustered.

This is the moment I was waiting for. I had all sorts of long public pronouncements planned—castigating Eva for daring to write about me, Zahara, Diane, Rachel and Scarlett, and only in ways that framed Eva in the best possible light. For furthering Barbara's lies, and suggesting that she and I got into a brawl. For using my desperately written words to prove I was never held captive.

But above all, for daring to open her memoir with lines from the poem by the Guatemalan poet, Isabel de los Ángeles Ruano. The one about complicity, suggesting that "we" were all guilty for any unhappy or unfortunate events at Casa Eva.

"You," I say, standing just aside from the hundred or so seated bookstore guests. "You're the guilty one."

Everyone is staring at me, confused, and probably wishing

I would say more. But I won't. I only want her to know that I know. That I'll be keeping an eye on her. That I'll never forget.

"Not *We*. You."

Eva's mouth is opening and closing again like a fish, with no sound coming out. I thought it would feel good when I accused her. I only now realize that it wasn't a public exchange of words I wanted—not hers and not mine.

I just wanted this: her unable to speak, for once. Eva, silenced, if only briefly.

In that silence, I feel like I can breathe. In that silence, I feel like I can imagine, finally, finishing one episode of my life and starting another. I can imagine telling this story—as long as no one else will get to steal or warp it or tell me what it means. Maybe even as fiction.

ACKNOWLEDGMENTS

Juliet Grames, for whom Jules is named, threw down the gauntlet during a book fair lunch in Michigan, challenging me to write this book after I pitched its premise and inspiration. She is more than an editor and associate publisher, she is an amazing mentor and friend to authors, keeping many of us from drowning in the deep, cold and unforgiving waters of publishing. Alexa Wejko made the editing process a dream. I've never chuckled so many times during revisions, and her thoroughness, imagination and receptivity greatly improved every draft. I already knew that writing a suspense novel is fun; Alexa gets the credit for convincing me that editing suspense fiction can be just as enjoyable. And we didn't even need tequila shots to get through it!

Thanks now and always to Bronwen Hruska, Rachel Kowal, Janine Agro, Paul Oliver, Rudy Martinez, Johnny Nguyen and Steven Tran. Can I mention Rachel "never hits the wall" Kowal a second time, for all of the attentive editing at the twentieth mile/final hour? The longer I've worked with all of you, the more I realize how incredibly lucky I am to have the Soho team behind me, and the more I marvel at all of the great books you launch and all of the voices and creative visions you support. Thanks also to Mia Manns, Liza Voznessenskaia and Chelsea McGuckin for your talents.

My agent, Michelle Brower, was instrumental in shaping this book in its many iterations, with help from agents Danya Kukafka and Natalie Edwards. Thanks to all of you for your openness to the many ways in which this story could be told and the time you invested in improving this book.

Early readers were, as always, vital both to this book and to my general well-being. For essential comments on this project and others, thank you to Karen Ferguson, Kate Maruyama, Christina Lynch, Ellen Bielawski, Honoree Cress, Rachael Warecki, Deborah Williams, Allison K. Williams, Sky Burr-Drysdale, Shana Wilson, Shannon Kelley, Stephanie Dardenne, Gayle Brandeis and Caitlin Wahrer. An additional thanks to Karen Ferguson and to Chris Fletcher and friends (including Hans) for supporting me in my Ironman triathlon fundraiser by purchasing the opportunity to name two characters in the book. To Kaylene, Marianne, Matt, Lindsay, Nikki and Eliza, thanks for your interest during the earliest stages, as well as general friendship and support; I can't wait for you to see a finished copy!

It must be strange to read your mother's creepy novel about a daughter's disappearance, but my own daughter, Tziporah Lax, is both an avid reader and suspense writer, so she gets it. Thanks to Tziporah and my husband, Brian, for reading more drafts than any of us could count. To Aryeh, your creativity and discipline continue to be an inspiration.

To the many independent booksellers who have championed my novels in the past; you are needed more than ever. My gratitude to you.

To new writer friends with whom I enjoyed (and survived!) my trip to Guatemala, including SS and K, and to the rest of the Atitlán gang, wherever you are now, I wish you safe travels, creativity and health.

To KR, an Atitlán friend who passed away before this book was published, I can only say that in some other dimension we are still drinking margaritas, eating tortilla chips and talking snarkily about our manuscripts-in-progress. It still makes me sad that your book wasn't finished and published because you had an amazing story to tell. I leave this note in honor of you, but also so that anyone else reading these acknowledgments will have their own carpe diem thoughts and get that manuscript finished. Unlike the character Eva Marshall in this book, I do believe that most people have a story worth telling and I don't think it needs to be told formulaically or workshopped brutally. Quiet the self-censor, embrace imperfection and get it done!